# The Killing Collective

## A Stanford Carter Murder Mystery Thriller

### Gary Starta with Robin Firestone

*"Pygmalion had seen them living a life of crime, and having been affected by their wickedness....he sculpted white ivory happily with wondrous art and wondrous skill, and gave it form with which no woman is able to be born, and he fell in love with his own work."*

*- Ovid*

# Contents

# Chapter One

In a pitch-black auditorium known only to those invited, hundreds of people sat in a blanket of silence alive with the electricity of anticipation. They held a collective breath as a giant movie screen slowly lowered itself from the ceiling to center stage. Suddenly, it blinked to life, revealing the 40-foot image of a handsome, charismatic gentleman of an indeterminate age, head bowed. Slowly, he lifted his face until his intensely blue eyes met those of every living soul in the audience. His silent stare struck a match, their own fascination flames he could feel and control. Dramatically, he raised his arms, and in a grandiose gesture of welcome, announced himself.

**"Good evening. I am…the *Silver Man!*"**

The audience leaped out of their chairs and went wild. Stoically, patiently, he waited at least five full minutes before continuing.

"Welcome, all of you, to the *Collective*, a simple community of people who want a better, brighter future for themselves. Tonight's discussion will begin with the exploration of the many reasons we, the 99%, have been thrown into a pit of quicksand to drown in poverty while the 1% continues to grow richer and fatter. Once you all understand why and how you've been targeted as the fall guys with no other choice than to die quietly and alone, you will be taught exactly how to reverse it, not for future generations to come, but *right now* and for *yourselves*, so that you may enjoy the fruits of your own labor without ever having to fight for them again!

"In a country once known for moving boldly forward, a new breed of Capitol Hill robber baron is busy trying to put us back in sweat shops. A college education is suddenly out of reach for everyone except the elite. Those lucky enough to have jobs and keep them for any length of time must still find two or more just to stay alive. Where there used to be hope, there is despair.

1

"Your government has deducted a lot of money from every paycheck you ever brought home to pay for Social Security. Did they pay it back with interest? Will your monthly payout be adjusted each year to meet cost of living? No! Do you still believe that huge tax breaks to large corporations guarantee the smallest degree of corporate responsibility? Will their savings be used to give you a raise or to purchase your healthcare insurance? Does it gall you to know this nation is rapidly becoming a third world country where nothing is made, nothing is sold, and most services are outsourced? Because it *should*!

"But we keep on *buying*, oh *yes*, we keep buying. And we borrow. S*ure*! Just whip out another credit card at 26% interest and worry about it next month. But hey, don't *worry*! *Bad* credit? *No* credit? *No problem*! And it begins all over again.

"And we make garbage, oh yeah, we make a *lot* of garbage. Why? Because the man behind the curtain, folks, is 'built-in obsolescence'! It is what has driven our economy since the industrial revolution, and it's all about convenience, disposability, and next year's model. I have a news flash for you, America, now *you and I* are disposable, and next year's model has already been fully automated.

"Face it; you've been robbed, spied on, lied to, hacked, and forgotten. There are satellites in space *right now* that can tell Big Brother the color of the pants you're wearing as you relax in your living room watching television! The web, security cameras, web cams, interactive multimedia and virtual reality…all originally researched, funded and sanctioned by the government for military use and rolled out to *you* as an opiate and entertainment while you're robbed of actual human contact, your full cognitive abilities and most of the muscle mass in your arms and legs. We're a fat, sedentary, sickly, indoor race now, and we've given a huge silent nod to our own job loss by way of robotics and A.I.s. But we've dreamed of it and begged for it ever since we saw our first episode of *Star Trek*, haven't we? *We asked for this, didn't we?*

"Let's take a moment to talk about the dumbing down of America. We wanted everything faster and easier, and boy did we get it. Have you begun to notice that many of you have lost the desire and patience to read, write and solve problems? And the rest of you never learned to read or write in the first place! *Isn't that right, millennials?*

2

Did you really think the answer to everything was *'reboot'*? What happens when the electricity goes out? I'll tell you! We close shop and go the hell *home*! That, and far, far more, is unacceptable if we are to compete, on any level, in the world theater.

The *Silver Man* paused briefly for dramatic effect.

"Most of you have roots going back generations enough to understand this; the American dream has never been anything more than a hateful nightmare. Your president and his friends would like the world to think they stand for truth, freedom, and justice, but all they believe in are alternative facts, economic slavery, and justice for those who can afford it.

"These, and many other factors have combined to create one giant and unstoppable chain reaction. We need to stop pretending and face the fact that the whole damn house of cards is coming down, and it's coming down on *us*! There is no possible way to fix a system gone horribly wrong, and there will be no rescuing you from its effects if you don't do something about it on your own and right now, so I won't bother telling you otherwise. Every one of us here tonight knows that we are on our own. Some of us have already reached the end of the road and many more are close behind."

Alison Whiteway turned to the man seated on her right and whispered, "Wow! He's incredible! Why is he called the *Silver Man*?"

"Because he has to hide his identity. That's why he broadcasts from a secret location. Washington says he's an anarchist and a mad man. I suppose he is, in some ways, but he's also right. *Shhh*! I want to hear this."

The *Silver Man* delivered a stunning blow causing many to gasp out loud. "Within one year, the domino effect will ensure that only those that already have money, and a lot of it, will survive. The rest of you will not. It's as simple as that."

"Holy *shit*!" Alison was unaware she'd spoken.

"*Shhh*!!"

"Right about now, some of you are thinking that I'm flat out wrong or even crazy. Some of you are thinking that if you're lucky, you might still scrape by. The rest of you are thinking that you'll just have to hang on as long as you can. And when that is no longer possible, you'll do the unthinkable and go out quietly, like lambs.

"So, if everything I have told you so far is the truth, why am I

3

here instead of drinking myself to death?" The *Silver Man* lowered his voice to a near whisper. "Because this government can be dismantled, brick by brick, *quietly and quickly…* and reassembled to function better for everyone. With the right plan, a new and better America can be yours and mine. Yes! And *right now*!

"All you have to do is act. Is that a shocking notion? Unthinkable, even? *Why*? Because this is *AMERICA*? Because we've grown *up* and moved *past* war and revolution? You know that as long as there are hungry people with no hope, there will be wars and revolutions. And why *shouldn't* there be?! For *what reasons* would you fight and die if not for the chance to live a decent life in a decent home? For whom *would* you fight if not for yourself and your family? *Tell me*!

"Look around your home towns, your cities, your *states*! Who are the people you pass on the streets and chat with in stores? Do you know what they think and how they feel about these issues? Because if you don't, you *should*! How might their thoughts and feelings affect *you*? If you've never thought about this before, think about it, now. Where do you draw the line between relationships—casual or not—and politics? Is the 'friend' who looks away when you are marginalized and criminalized really your friend? Does the neighbor who voted for those Washington fat cats care about you at *all*? Would you knowingly maintain a friendship with a Neo-Nazi or a Fascist? The answer is *NO, NO, AND NO*!

"You are here, tonight, my friends, because you are already aware of the need to do anything you can to take back your nation. All right then, I will teach you! TOGETHER, W*E WILL FIGHT BIG BROTHER AND WIN*!"

The audience exploded in cheers. The *Silver Man* waited once more.

"But, who do we fight? Will marching on City Hall change the system? Sadly, the answer is 'no'. Our plan is to focus on the enemy's weakest links—the movers and shakers you never see on the news. They will bring down the building for us, and they'll do it from the *inside*!"

Applause shook the auditorium almost off its foundation. The *Silver Man* was quite pleased with himself. He'd successfully kindled the beginnings of insurrection.

*Not bad for a few hours of work.*

His goal for this evening had been to upset his audience while appearing brilliant, strong and fatherly. In the end, they had to be willing to follow him into the jaws of hell if he asked them to.

*It hasn't occurred to them that every form of government has been and still is unfair to its subjects at one time or another. Marxism. Fascism. Communism. Socialism. Capitalism. Whatever "ism" you choose, there will always be poor, uneducated, underfed and discontented people. And that is why my arguments are irrefutable.*

"You and I are *not* the world, the country, or even the government; we are simply people— *individuals*—trying to live decently and in peace. Make no mistake, ladies and gentlemen, there is a war going on all around you, and there always has been. It's a war meant to demoralize, decrease, and destroy *us* so that there is more to go around for *them*. When we are at war, we have a right to defend ourselves and survive any way we can.

**"I ask you now; are you prepared to go out like lambs, without so much as a whimper? Or will you fight to the death if you have to?"**

An explosion of voices flew straight up to the heavens in one massive blast, while stamping feet rolled like thunder. Alison had never seen anything like it. She sat perfectly still, rapt and silent, trying to decide whether she wanted to cheer or sob. The only thing she knew for sure was that this man was speaking directly to her.

The *Silver Man* pierced their ears with the seeds of insurgency and anarchy, urging them towards anger, blame and hatred. And he was just getting started. He shouted passionately, "If you, your family and your community—*this* community—must be protected and defended, is it right to fight? *I SAY IT'S MORE THAN RIGHT; I SAY IT'S A NECESSITY!* Men and women go to war every day knowing that they will be called upon to kill and die. They go willingly because it's their duty to defend their country. For most of us now, that means defending our community, home, and family. We will do what we have to because there is divine altruism in fighting and even killing to save, protect and defend one's ideals and way of life. And that is what every one of you must do if you plan to survive *and* thrive when the house of cards comes down!!"

The cheers, chants, whistles and screams that fed the *Silver Man's* enormous ego could be heard blocks away.

The *Silver Man* was pleased. As he paused again to dry his brow with a white linen handkerchief, he couldn't help smiling to himself like a cat that stole the cream.

*Give them a reason for their suffering—one they're willing to believe. Make sure they think it's the fault of a definite group of people they can blame and justify hating. Then, turn them loose to play judge, jury and executioner.*

Some of the attendees, first-timers who listened in horror, got up and left, their movements monitored by the *Silver Man's* staff from that moment on. Those who chose to stay would also be monitored. And just as closely.

\*\*\*

Alison had found religion and a messiah to worship all in one shot. The *Silver Man* produced a longing in her so great she already knew she'd do anything he asked.

*I'll dedicate myself to this man and this community if they'll have me. I swear I'll tear down what can't be fixed and build a better America for myself, according to his plan.*

Astonished and enlightened, she listened to every word he said—every awful syllable—allowing his words to flood her consciousness with new ideas.

"We think of certain thoughts and actions as either bad or wrong, but under the right circumstances, those same thoughts and actions are considered good and righteous and by the church as well as the state! Peaceful protest is always the first line of defense, but in a war meant to annihilate you, defense is good and offense is better! When your home, work, and daily bread are at stake, all bets are *off*! Violence is justified, even *required,* when war is declared on social and economic equality and your rights and freedoms. The church has fought wars and killed and died to spread its various forms of Christianity to people who never wanted it! Your country sent you to fight wars against other countries with whom you had no quarrel. Fight a war you believe in and want to win, instead! Fight dirty politics, crimes against humanity, treason, and all attempts to destroy democracy before they can take root in our society and grow too strong to fight."

The lights went on at the same time the screen went blank. Someone stepped up to the microphone and announced a ten minute break, after which the *Silver Man* was going to talk about something called "*Social Protectionism*". Alison hoped it would address her growing need to know what she could do to save herself and this community. She stayed glued to the spot until the room was cloaked in darkness again and he returned to deliver the second half of his speech.

"Periods of upheaval and turmoil—even complete *destruction*—are sometimes required in order to bring down evil empires and build true democracies in their place. Tonight, you will begin to learn about *Social Protectionism* and how to use its tools to route the enemies of the *Collective* and make America *great* again!"

"Who exactly are our enemies, you ask? Those who desire or steal everything you have and hope to achieve. Together, we will decide who they are and how we will fight them. And then...then we will toss them out with yesterday's *garbage!* Ladies and gentlemen, the power of solvency and the realization of your dreams for a better life begins NOW!"

The *Silver Man* had them right where he wanted them—perilously close to the breaking point.

\*\*\*

To Alison's left sat Jeannie, a casual acquaintance who could barely tolerate her. Jeannie had only stayed this long because she was Alison's ride home. She listened with a florid face, clamped lips, and squinty eyes. She'd driven Alison all the way to New York City from Sayreville, New Jersey for this, and she was good and mad about it. Was she the only one in the auditorium who thought he sounded like a raving lunatic? On the other hand, Adolph Hitler and Charlie Manson were raving lunatics, and people had listened to *them*. She shuddered because she knew it didn't matter whether or not the *Silver Man* really believed anything he said. All that mattered was that the people around her believed every word.

\*\*\*

7

"We will meet again regularly to share our thoughts and ideas and continue the process of transformation. As a new member of this close-knit community, I promise you will experience an intensity of friendship and camaraderie you've never known before.

*"WELCOME...TO THE EVER-GROWING FOLD...OF THE COLLECTIVE!!"*

A blizzard of silver glitter fell from somewhere above as if it was New Year's Eve. The audience leaped to their feet, some laughing and others crying. Strangers hugged each other in a perverse show of fraternity. Once more, the *Silver Man*, like an over-indulgent father, waited patiently for the crowd to quiet down. "Each of you will receive a personalized invitation by email to our meetings, which will never be held in the same place twice—for your protection and mine."

Softly and deadly serious, he delivered a parting blow as a warning to those he knew would attempt to turn him in. "The information we share here is secret. Before our work is done, some of you will try to betray me. Those that break my covenant shall be considered an enemy of the *Collective* and will be dealt with accordingly."

He paused to let that last bit sink in as well as to change his tone to one more conciliatory and hospitable. "The social element of our meetings is important because the exchange and discussion of new ideas reinforces the ideals of the *Collective*. It is equally important because we want you to understand that within the warmth and security of our own community, you are no longer alone. I invite you all to get up now and move forward to the open area on stage where you will spend the next hour getting to know each other amid soft music, wonderful finger food and the very finest champagne. Thank you all for being here. Until we meet again, I bid you good night."

The chimera reared one last time, roaring its approval and shouting for more. The *Silver Man* lowered his head once more, this time humbly as if in prayer, and held that pose. At the very height of the deafening applause, the screen blinked off and he was gone.

\*\*\*

Jeannie and Alison milled around, met some of the others and sampled the hors d'oeuvres. Delicious-looking drinks were being passed around by waiters dressed in bright red jackets with gold braiding. Smooth jazz floated in the air above them and the lights were dimmed just enough to create an atmosphere of friendly intimacy.

As soon as they had a moment alone, Jeannie let loose. "What a load of horseshit, Allie! Can you believe that nut job? And what's up with the incognito act?" She flailed her arms in the air and mimicked his voice. "I have a plan that will make you solvent! All you have to do is eliminate the competition! Embrace the community!"

"I think he discussed a lot of very interesting ideas."

"Oh, come on!"

"I liked what he had to say, Jeannie. Don't you think it's about time we stood up for ourselves and focused on the actual people keeping us behind the eight ball instead of blaming it on an unchangeable system? A very few ruthless, uncaring people have everything, Jeannie, and it's not fair! Why not take the chance to build something better if we can? Why not let people know they're done eating our slice of the American pie?"

"Oh, Allie, get real! You can't change people who don't want to listen. You can't just tear down society and rebuild it the way you want it because it doesn't suit you, either! They put people in jail for that, Allie, and throw away the key."

A staff member approached. "Good Evening, ladies. You are Alison Whiteway, I believe? I am Peter, one of the *Silver Man's* assistants. His executive staff would like to take a few moments to introduce themselves to you and get to know you a little better. Would you follow me please?"

She couldn't believe her luck tonight. "What about my friend?"

"Unfortunately, there's not enough time to meet all the new members personally. The *Silver Man* can see the audience on the monitors from his broadcast location. He noticed your enthusiasm while he was speaking and specifically asked that we hear more about what brought you here tonight. It'll only take a few moments of your time."

Alison looked at Jeannie. "Sorry, Jeannie, but I can't pass up this opportunity. It may never come again. Don't leave. Remember, you're taking me home."

\*\*\*

9

A scant fifteen minutes later Alison was back and bursting with excitement. She picked up another glass of champagne. "That was wild! Everyone was so nice to me! They wanted to know all about me and how I felt about the speech. The private office was beautiful, all decked out in red and gold. I think the border detail was real gold leaf! We talked about the *Silver Man's* dreams and plans while we drank champagne. There were petit fours and cappuccino, and…it was the single greatest experience of my life, Jeannie."

Jeannie rolled her eyes. "I know you didn't meet the silver-haired, blue-eyed mystery man back there, so who did you talk to?"

"His executive assistant. Everyone who becomes part of the executive community is in danger, so she wears a disguise."

"Really. What kind of disguise?"

"She wore the mask of a woman, a beautiful woman with a white face like you'd see in a museum—you know, like a statue or something. She was dressed in a floor-length black Chanel gown with a back that plunged all the way down to *there*! The funny thing is, she didn't talk at all; maybe she had a cold or something. Someone else asked the questions and answered mine in return, but she sat across from me and listened to everything. I felt so important!"

"Uh huh."

*You want to murder him. You can't wait to murder him.*

Alison looked around. "Who said that?"

"Who said what?"

"Didn't you hear that?"

"Alison, give me that glass; you've had enough to drink. Let's get outta here. This place gives me the creeps." She walked away to find their coats, muttering to herself about revolution, silver-haired men and masked women with no voices.

Suddenly, the room seemed to get smaller. The music faded away, and the voice she heard a moment ago spoke again, only it didn't belong to a person; it was inside her own head. For some reason, though, she wasn't very concerned about it. She was used to talking to herself and figured she'd just had too much champagne.

*He's a threat to the community. Kill him to protect us!*

Alison felt a little faint. A choir was singing somewhere, and she strained to hear the words. It was beautiful—the most beautiful song she ever heard. A second later, her brain flooded with something that made her feel very good and very mean all at once. Fragments of thought traveled at breakneck speed and leaped across synapses in the attempt to keep up with far too many neurons firing simultaneously. The song seemed very important to Alison, so she paid very careful attention to the words that would become the actions contained in the last chapter of her life.

*You are with the community. You have promised to protect it. You know a man who wants to prevent you from finding friendship and acceptance. He wants you to die in poverty so that he might prosper. David Florio will kill you unless you kill him, first. You hate him, Alison, and you want to murder him with your bare hands! We will come to you in your dreams tonight so you may know exactly how to commit this sublime act of allegiance.*

*You will contact this man by tomorrow afternoon and make a date for the same evening at his apartment. You will come straight home when your job is completed, and you will not remember anything. You will not remember anything. You will not remember...*

Jeannie snapped her fingers. "Alison? Alison! Anybody home? Come on, snap out of it, *stupid*!"

Alison blinked her eyes. "I thought you were getting the coats."

Jeannie looked up toward heaven. "Allie, I told you a thousand times all that drinking and drugging was gonna rot your brain—if you ever had one to begin with. Let's go; we've wasted enough time here."

\*\*\*

During the drive back to Jersey, Alison stared silently out the window at the night. She was very hurt by the low regard Jeannie had for her.

*No one likes me. And I try so hard! I'm not giving up on the community now that I found it. I don't care what she thinks.*

Jeannie snorted derisively. "You look like I just shot your dog or something, Allie. *Jesus H. Christ*! The man's trying to start a God damn revolution! How can you possibly take him seriously? He's deranged!

"Seriously, I worry about you. This is just the kind of thing you'd go for. Don't you realize how needy you are? It's sad, Allie, really, really sad. You drive people away with all your whining and begging and pleading for their approval. You agree with anything anyone says. You have no mind of your own! I'm telling you right now, do not allow yourself to be led by that *Silver Man* and his bunch of red-coated goons. Didn't you notice how many people left during his rant? Didn't you see the disgust on their faces? Honestly, if you hadn't been hanging on his every word and looking like you'd had an epiphany, I would have left, too."

Alison kept her head turned toward the window. She didn't answer; there was nothing to say.

*Why do I let her bully me? She walks all over me, and I just let her do it. The people at the meeting tonight liked me. I know they did. She's wrong. There are people who like me; I just never met them until tonight.*

It felt, to her, as though she'd slipped through a tiny crack in a wall and discovered all the secrets of the universe on the other side. The old Alison Whiteway disappeared, and in her place was a woman seduced by acceptance and baptized in venom.

She turned her head toward the woman who was quickly passing out of her heart. "I am absolutely not going to argue with you about this, Jeannie. The concept is far too big and your mind is way too small. We have a chance to make our country a better place and to live better lives. The *Silver Man* has a concrete plan for how we can do it. I'm standing on the brink of change, Jeannie, and with or without you, I'm jumping."

# Chapter Two
*Six months earlier…*

Stanford Carter whisked a hand across his thigh to smooth out the creases in his chocolate brown trousers. His wife, Jill, said that clothes made the man, and the former captain of the Boston P.D. agreed, as long they were all dark gray or black. A brown suit was uncharted territory. But, as discretion is often the better part of valor, he kept his mouth mercifully shut. Today, fashion ruled, no matter what he thought.

Carter was a devoted student of Zen Buddhism. It helped give him peace of mind and an understanding of the universe so that he could operate within it. For a lifetime cop, this was no small undertaking. So far, he'd found neither understanding nor a satisfactory way to operate, but he kept trying, believing the answers were there if he looked hard enough. What he hadn't yet learned was that an attractive philosophy didn't necessarily promise answers. Or peace. But Carter was stubborn, and he threw himself into a life-long journey wearing blinders and not much else. Staunchly refusing to analyze thoughts he wasn't prepared to face, he stumbled through his days and nights spectacularly ill equipped to face the past, present or future.

Carter sat outside Deputy Director William Fischetti's office, waiting. Fischetti had personally invited Carter and his wife, Jill Seacrest, to join the Bureau, hoping they could solve a string of murders that changed all the rules of the game. Carter was offered the rank of a seasoned agent and would also act as team leader.

Seacrest, a scientist at the very top of her profession, was to work directly under the supervision of the director of forensic sciences. They'd both heard the deputy director was notoriously capricious in nature, so Carter was determined to meet Fischetti on high ground and keep it, which is why he was more than a little surprised to be greeted by a middle-aged, balding man, about six inches shorter than himself and twenty inches wider around the middle. He greeted Carter with clipped speech and a curt manner while scribbling on a piece of paper. It was rude to multitask during a meeting, especially with a new hire. Carter was starting to have second thoughts when Fischetti finally looked up and spoke to him.

"Come in, Agent Carter. Have a seat. Welcome to the fold."

"Already in and sitting, sir. Thank you."

"I've wanted you both here with me for some time now. Your dossier is very impressive. Let's see; you've been with the Boston P.D. for your entire career; you became a cop because your cousin was the victim of a particularly heinous crime; your nose has always been clean; apparently, it is not possible to make you lose your temper; and you're a spiritualist, yet you chose a career that is frequently violent and requires you to understand how criminals think, capture them, and enforce the law rather than judge or change it. So, tell me, why did you finally decide to join us here in New York?"

"Expanding my horizons, sir. At least that's what my wife says."

Carter leaned back in his chair. Fischetti was toying with him, so he broke the tension by invoking the name of his wife, a woman with a temper even more fearsome than her I.Q. "We both needed more room to grow. She thinks New York is my next logical career move, and I think her talent and dedication deserves a post that will showcase her skills and prove her value in forensics, so here we are."

Both were so much a part of the other that, at times, their relationship blurred the line of distinction. But lately, they'd been going through a rough patch. She wanted to talk things out and he didn't, but he grudgingly admitted to himself that if he didn't switch gears soon, he might lose her.

"Let's get down to cases, shall we? In the last several months, we've had a rash of murders committed by perpetrators whose sole motive seems to be the sick thrill of killing. Can you beat that? Did you ever encounter anything like *that* in Boston, Agent Carter?" The deputy director leaned forward with his fingers tightly woven. "I need someone who can tell the trees from the forest. I'm hoping you're the man for the job."

"I appreciate your confidence, sir, but there must have been a host of capable candidates. Why me?"

Fischetti showed a glimmer of admiration for Carter. "So there's more to you than meets the eye. O.K., let me be frank. You're a seasoned career cop and an ex-captain. I'm well aware of your conviction rate in Boston, but I'm more impressed with how you handled multiple serials, even when it meant taking down some of your corrupt brothers in blue. Special Agent Blumenthal trained some of my finest people over the past decade, but he recently retired, and I have an outstanding rookie who needs to be taken under someone's wing until we can get the program running smoothly again."

Carter was suddenly very uncomfortable.

*Is he hinting at something? Am I here because he doesn't trust his own people? It sounds to me like he doesn't believe they're thrill kills. He mentioned multiple serials, but the odds of them all being related to each other is astronomical....*

Fischetti pretended not to notice the look on Carter's face. He kept fishing. "How'd you ferret out the bad apples?"

"I don't have an exact science or game plan, sir. I rely more on gut feeling and instinct than on what I'm told in the briefing room or read in the files. I'm perfectly at ease with my own ability to know the individual from the team. Like you said, it's all about being able to tell the trees from the forest."

*Let him think about that one.*

Fischetti wedged his chin in between the forefinger and thumb of his right hand for a moment. "Good. That's what I wanted to hear. Agent Carter, I'm going to have to trust you, because we don't have the time to see if that trust is warranted. I hope you can do the same. I believe in the integrity and values of the Bureau. That's a big chunk of the reason you and Agent Seacrest were asked here."

Carter nodded his thanks.

*He wants us here because he believes in the integrity and values of the Bureau. That more than implies there are those here who don't.*

"What's next on the agenda, sir?"

"You and Agent Seacrest both have to complete training at Quantico."

Carter sighed. "I've spent the last few years behind a captain's desk..."

15

Fischetti was amused and sympathetic. "You'll have to keep up with criminals and a rookie half your age, Carter. Her name is Shania Deeprose, out of Alabama and just back from Iraq. She'll have you back on the fast-track in no time and keep you there. Her enthusiasm knows no bounds, Agent. She could charm the clouds out of the sky, but be prepared for the accent. It's slightly nauseating."

Carter remembered Seacrest's intensity early on in her career, especially the times he heard her talking to herself in the lab. She may have seemed a little screwy to everyone else, but not to him. Anyway, he was pleased to have a partner who still saw the glass half full, because it wouldn't be long before reality set in, and a bad disposition was nearly always a sign that a rookie wouldn't last long. It took all his strength and every last drop of optimism to combat his own burnout. Meditation was essential to Carter's ability to last, even with the enduring and indefatigable support Seacrest gave him.

Fischetti stuck out his right hand. "Enjoy Quantico. It won't be a cake-walk, but getting back to basics is the best way to start over."

They walked out of the office and into the common area where a pair of elevator doors opened on an out-of-breath Seacrest, whose hand immediately shot out in introduction. "Sorry! I was parking the damn car. Boy, it's murder out there!" She smiled exuberantly. The men turned to glance at one another.

Fischetti murmured to no one in particular, "Interesting choice of words."

\*\*\*

*One week later…*

Carter held his gun with both hands around the grip. It was cocked skyward.

He mouthed silently, "On three…"

Flanking Carter to his left was hopeful Adam Royals, and just behind him was Seacrest. He barely mouthed "two" when Royals charged. Carter made a desperate grab for Royals' shirt, but he couldn't stop him. Earlier, the squad experienced a major telecommunications failure, leaving them at odds with the demands of the bank robbers inside the building Royals was already charging.

16

They had very little hope of getting assistance from a S.W.A.T. team now.

Royals' shadow fell across the sidewalk as he skirted around the corner of a brick building.

Seacrest stated the obvious. "He's going to get himself killed."

"We'll have to change the plan to compensate." Carter rose, but his breath rate did not. He sprinted with a fluid grace with which most men nearing forty can only dream. Seacrest tagged behind him darting to the left and right, each pivot carrying her forward on a horizontal plane in case there was a sniper aiming at them from the top of the building. It was a beautiful dance, a rhythm born of their long, hard years of partnership, and it was a breathtaking sight to see.

Ahead, Royals was bearing down on the bank's front door, gun drawn. Carter willed him to succeed.

*You've already committed yourself, so move with purpose; move as if you are an army of one…*

The young man, glory-bound and out to make his mark, instantly abandoned every protocol taught to him in the classroom. He'd made a wild card of himself, but Carter thought he could work around it. It made life a little more interesting even if it was also a little more dangerous. The outcome was not likely to be a good one, though. Royals had been counting on the element of surprise. Unfortunately, he was the one surprised.

*You'll make your mark, all right—a big, red one all over the pavement.*

With the advantage lost, the enemy's strength was in numbers. An armed man standing guard just behind the door's small window was not the first hostile to see Royals. A coded message transmitted by a high-tech hand-held communication device on the roof across the street already warned him to cut the head off the snake.

The guard was prepared to kill Royals, but before he could fire his weapon, the blinding light of a Personal Halting and Stimulation Response rifle, or PHaSR, threw Royals to his knees. The laser light bounced off the bank's windows blinding both of them. It was a one-for-one chess move well played by Seacrest, but whoever had been behind the guard now had direct aim on both her and Carter.

It was two against God-only-knew how many holed up in the bank, mainly because their infrared imaging scan could not distinguish enemies from innocents. Carter was going to have to rely on good old human ingenuity, instead. If he failed, the hostages would be killed.

He grabbed the rifle out of Seacrest's hands and threw it at the bank window, another wild-card play meant to throw off the enemy. Shots rang out from the inside, shattering glass and causing Carter and Seacrest to jump this way and that. Now they were forced to separate to maximize the odds that one would survive to save the innocents.

Carter was on one knee to the left of the entrance. Negotiation was out of the question. He and Seacrest were the only ones left on the Bureau's defensive team. Because their attempt to radio for help had gone unanswered, Carter couldn't blame Royals for his early charge. Nevertheless, they had no time to wait for help that might not come. The squad had to become offensive fast; every moment the enemies held the hostages at gunpoint increased the likelihood that lives would be lost.

Carter shouted, "I surrender! We'll meet your demands!" Seacrest watched in horror at the sacrifice, but no one was more surprised than Carter when the shooting actually ceased.

He held his arms above him like a pair of eagle's wings. "We're ready to give you a helicopter in exchange for the hostages, but our radio is jammed. We need to find another way to signal for one."

He didn't have much hope of buying time. The enemy knew by now they were only up against a handful of agents, but if he could keep them focused on what he was saying, there was a chance he could keep them from noticing anything else. It was worth a try, anyway. He waited to see what their next move would be. The silence was awful.

Seacrest heard the hostages screaming inside. Carter was still down, but she had an idea; she darted around the corner of the building, side-arm blazing, and headed toward the back. She was looking for an employee entrance. Fire resumed on both sides.

Carter rolled onto his side and remained on the ground to avoid being hit by a barrage of enemy fire blasting out the remains of the front door and windows. Royals, still blinded, flipped around on the sidewalk like a fish out of water.

Seacrest fired relentlessly at the unguarded back door, threw down her gun when the bullets were spent and grabbed another from her holster. Meanwhile, Carter had to make the enemy think he was out of cards to play, so he threw down his weapon and for the second time in fifteen minutes, stood up slowly with his arms over his head. Then, he waited for the enemies to show themselves.

***

When speech was no longer possible, Carter and Seacrest often resorted to communicating through an instinct born of their years spent together in the field, so she already knew what he wanted her to do. She raced through the employee entrance in back and pulled the fire alarm at the same time Carter charged the front entrance in a Hail Mary play. The alarm was supposed to send the enemy running out the front entrance thinking they'd been raided from behind.

It worked. She found the hostages bound together, huddled behind a desk.

*Please God, If Carter doesn't take them all out in one move, I'll die back here along with every single hostage.*

Less than a moment later, the S.W.A.T. team showed up in response to the alarm she pulled. They successfully took out the hostiles and saved all but one of the hostages, who'd taken a stray bullet in the head, but they were too late to save Carter. Despite his Kevlar vest, several bullets grazed the arteries in his neck and legs. Even if they could've staunched the blood, no surgeon could repair the damage.

Seacrest dropped down to the ground next to him and sobbed, even though they'd been able to pull off a victory in a no-win-scenario bank robbery staged on Quantico's academy grounds.

*There is no victory in death.*

# Chapter Three

An ancient suit of armor cast its long, lean shadow across the marble floor of the *Cloisters*. It was too prestigious, too powerful, and too damned awesome to be stuffed in a corner, and yet, there it was, with Michael Santiago standing inside of it. Inside the metal skin, he wondered how many deaths its wearers had claimed on bloody battlefields a thousand years ago when a thought struck him; all patrons were asked to be as generous as possible with their contributions, and Michael hadn't made one. He sincerely regretted not supporting the arts.

The *Cloisters*, a museum on New York's Upper West Side, was devoted to medieval art but also represented European architectural pride. It contained four installed cloisters from French monasteries and abbeys that depicted hybrid creations of man and beast in pink marble relief.

Michael Santiago, not surprisingly, failed to notice the beauty of the artist in the architecture. All he saw was fortress-like pointed Gothic arches and thick-walled exteriors, menacing reminders of simpler and more brutal times. Michael, who would have been dull and treacherous in any era, was here today to kill for profit, or so he thought. His plan was simple and direct because it never occurred to him that he could be caught. The thought had occurred, however, to the *Silver Man*.

The victim-to-be was the museum's curator and, at the moment, the only other person inside the museum. A security guard had been bribed to leave the heavy abbey door ajar shortly after closing time. The amount of money was impressive, but he was still a liability, and Michael knew he'd have to get rid of him, too.

The *Silver Man* warned him to keep the blood to a minimum, so

20

Michael was given chloroform to use on the security guard, who was to be eliminated first. He was told to use it on the curator as well, but when a sword arrived at his apartment in a plain brown wrapper, he forgot all about his promise. The *Silver Man* had known Michael would not be able to resist using the ancient sword.

Slinking through the door, he handed the man a heavy bag. The guard glanced at it, his first and last mistake. Michael slapped a handkerchief over his mouth and held it there. The guard dropped the bag of money and reached for his gun, but by then the chloroform had done its job. The security guard collapsed on the floor, out cold.

Michael buried him alive in a park off Margaret Corbin Drive. The hole was so deep he'd never be able to claw his way to the surface before suffocating to death. A few hours later, a stray dog wandering past perked up his ears at a faint sound that reached up to him from underneath his big paws. They were the security guard's final screams for help.

Other than the chloroform, all Michael needed to bring was his arming sword. It had been delivered to him by the *Silver Man's* assistant, a long, lean spectre who wore the strange mask of a woman with very white, chiseled features, and who declined to speak in his presence. The mask gave Michael the willies, and he was hard to spook.

The wealth amassed by the *Silver Man* was incalculable by Michael's standards, and as a short-order cook, he needed the payoff desperately. Yet, he found he was unable to resist the voices in his head demanding he bury the bag of money alongside the security guard. It made perfect sense to him at the time, but now that he was back inside the museum to finish off the curator, he began to wonder why he agreed to terms that left him with nothing for his pains. The voices returned and promised to keep him company if he'd leave the thinking to them. That also sounded reasonable, so he redoubled his efforts and squashed all thought.

Their echoes bounced off the inside of his body armor and dragged him down into an abyss of fury. The rush of adrenaline was becoming overpowering. He could have resisted the voices if he'd wanted to, but he didn't. He gave in to the euphoria of invincibility, domination, and the will to kill.

*This is your quest, Michael, as master protector of our community. It is what you were born for. Here, the curator moves freely among the most priceless art in existence, but he is a thief! He is stealing priceless national treasures and selling them to the highest bidder. He must be stopped, Michael; he is guilty. Guilty as charged! Kill the curator to protect the Collective. This is your duty, and you will not fail. You will not fail. You will not fail...*

Catapulted from the present to a distant echo of the past, Michael dreamed he was a great knight on a mission of great importance. He was to stop the enemy from stealing the king's treasure. As defender of the realm, he was unafraid to perform his duty and was unflinchingly committed to the success of the mission. With a heart made of stone, he waited for his victim to arrive.

*This fortress has hidden a million secrets since it was first built. Now it will hide mine, too.*

A mere arm's length away from him, the ring of a cell phone stopped the curator from inspecting the old armor, and the sound jolted Michael back to the present. Sweat dripped down his face, but he was unable to wipe it away without moving. It was worse than having an itch he couldn't scratch, but nothing mattered now except his mission.

He forced himself to loosen his grip on the sword in his gloved hand as he listened to the end of the call. "Yes, dear, I'll be home early enough to light the fireplace for our guests. Yes, of course I promise! Now I have to go, or I'll never get there. Good-bye, dear."

The sword plunged deep into the curator's back so forcefully that it almost came through the other side. He looked like a broken wind-up toy. When Michael ripped the sword free, buckets of blood spurted from the wound, splattering the ceiling, walls, and floor, leaving a pattern even a common murder mystery reader could decipher. He hadn't thought about that possibility before, but it was a dream, so he decided he didn't have to worry about it.

The fatally injured man staggered to his knees, unaware he'd been stabbed. In confusion, he looked at the blooming cabbage rose on the front of his shirt. Blood gurgled up from his throat in a pink, foamy mess. Michael was mesmerized by the look of surprise on his face as he began to drown in it. A long, agonizing moment later, Michael nudged the curator with an iron foot, and the old man fell forward onto his face, dead.

The voices were firm with Michael. There was no more time. His mission was complete, and his orders were to go straight home to bed and forget what he'd done. It took some time and a lot of noise to get himself out of the suit of armor. There was one final command from the voices as they faded away.

*Leave the sword here as a sign of your strength.*

He opened his hand and dropped it. It clattered to the floor, eager to find a new home in the outstretched arms of the empty iron suit before returning to a glorious, forgotten past. Michael went home, leaving behind him a trail of ruby sneaker prints that led to a nearby subway station.

\*\*\*

*Three Days Earlier…*

It was a couple of hours before the swearing-in ceremony. Stanford Carter and Jill Seacrest were going to pledge fidelity to their country after training in the fields and classrooms of Quantico, and they were celebrating quietly in a Virginia bar. At least that's what Carter thought they were doing.

"It's not too late to back out, you know." Seacrest took him by surprise, which was not easily done.

"Why should I back out now, after everything we went through to be here? What's wrong, Jill?"

"Nothing. Just pre-commitment jitters, I guess."

"You? Pre-commitment jitters?" Carter was teasing her. Jill was always fully committed to any decision she made. This was a rare opportunity he couldn't pass up.

"I had the jitters before our wedding, Carter. Did you?"

"No. I loved you then, and I love you more, now."

She looked away so Carter wouldn't see her eyes glistening. "Good."

"Don't you think I'm *meant* to be an F.B.I. agent?"

"That's neither here nor there, Carter. Do you *want* to be one?"

"It was meant to be, that's all. Do you honestly think I could fight fate, cheat destiny, and scoff at the will of the universe?"

"Be serious, Carter. This is your last chance to change your mind. I'll be in the lab most of the time, so I won't be in any real danger, but what's in it for you if you go back into the field?"

Carter nodded. "It's a little late to ask that question, Jill. Anyway, you know I don't dwell on what's in it for me. I never did."

"We've talked about Atlas shrugging a thousand times, Carter. You don't have to take this job. You don't owe the world."

"I thought we were ready for a change of scenery."

"Don't be flippant, Carter. You've put off this discussion over and over again, and we have to have it. It's now or never."

*Oh help me, Buddha. If you really do see everything, take me now! It would be far less painful than having this conversation.*

He waited for an answer from the great beyond, but a rescue was extremely unlikely, so he just sat there, mute.

*Brace yourself...*

"Look, change is a normal way to grow..."

*You idiot! You had to mention change! Just keep your head down. Maybe you can still avoid discussing... feelings. Anything but that!*

"... but you've done your bit for God and country. Now you have choices. I just want to know if you really left Boston to go back in the field or because turning in those cops on the take made it impossible for you to stay. Carter, what do you want out of this experience?"

"Isn't it enough to let the universe decide that for me?"

"Carter!"

His lighthearted tone vanished, and he spoke to her seriously, knowing that he could no longer avoid it. "I'm not kidding now, Jill. Let's not over think it. The decision just felt right. Can't we leave it there?" That old line never worked before, and he knew it wouldn't now, but he was grasping at straws.

"No, we cannot."

They stared each other down, but Seacrest couldn't keep a straight face for long. They burst into laughter and kept laughing until she wrapped her arms around his neck. "Carter, I want to say something to you, and you need to hear it. Honey, you always say that there's a reason we exist, that the universe has a plan for every individual. But, Carter, it's up to you to discover your reason and purpose. Maybe the plan the universe has for you is for *you* to decide what roads you want to take and when you want to stop and rest for a while."

"O.K., honey, I'll think about it, but you know I prefer to take trips without a road map. It's more fun that way."

"And you could do with a little more fun, too, Carter. No one will lose respect for you if you loosen up once in a while. Try living your life instead of pondering it so much. That's where the answers are. Dig deep and tell me what you want for *now*."

"For now, I think we should stay right where we are. There's a new rookie in town, and she needs some seasoning. I'll provide the salt. You bring the pepper. O.K.?"

"O.K., Carter."

"What would I do without you, Jill?"

"You'll never know. As luck would have it, I decided not to die. Made that decision just last week."

They clinked their beer glasses and drank.

\*\*\*

Carter had lost more than his share of friends and colleagues over the years, but he didn't discuss it, even with Seacrest. She was increasingly aware of this and was afraid he was starting to lose all sense of proportion in his life. If she talked about something unrelated to a case, he smiled and nodded, but she knew he was somewhere else, storing away memories and thoughts into neatly labeled boxes in the back of his mind. This latest box was labeled "fun".

For several years now, Carter had been closing cases at a higher rate than any other cop in Boston, P.D. history. Asked about himself, Carter would only say he measured himself against the highest standards of duty, integrity, honor, and service to his country. And that was true, because even if he lived to be a hundred years old, he'd never understand people—the non-criminal variety.

It wasn't that he never tried. He did. But unless he was in an interrogation room, where he knew all the tricks of the trade, Carter was at a complete loss. Many hearts were broken by his seeming indifference, but not Seacrest's. She knew as soon as she met him that he was uncomfortable with people and was just as unsurprised to discover he was terrified of women. It took a sledge hammer to get his attention, but once she had it, she hung on. Seacrest knew that she had to appear tough and resilient at all times for Carter's sake, so she

25

learned to appear that way, but she would much rather have been able to tell him how she really felt. It seemed like Carter hardly knew what she was like deep down inside, but that wasn't all his fault. For all her courage in the field, she was scared to death to admit her wants and needs at home because she was sure Carter could not meet them. In the end, she always decided it was better to go on as they had than to open that can of worms once and for all.

*'Carter, I can't breathe until I see you walk through the front door every night.' I wish I could say it—just like that, but the day I finally get up the nerve, you'll just stare at me and wonder if I've finally gone mad.*

*I think men and women really are each other's Yin and Yang. We're so vastly different and unable to understand each other! One of us is always guarding the boundary line while trying not to let the other one know it. I don't want us to live like that, anymore.*

"Carter?"

"Yes, sweetheart?"

"I'm glad we're on the same team."

"Me too, honey." Carter smiled.

# Chapter Four
*Two Days Earlier…*

After two tours of duty in Iraq and an honorable discharge from the armed forces, Shania Deeprose headed home to Alabama for the summer and then straight to F.B.I. headquarters in New York City. Carter imagined her as *Supergirl*, but with a mean right hook and an AK-47 in her rucksack.

Deeprose had a restless spirit. Whatever she'd been looking for, it wasn't just marriage. Petite and strong, she was still in shape, thirsty for life and optimistic enough to want a big swig of it. The neighbors were sorry to see her go away again so soon. Deeprose laughed a lot and the sound was good to hear.

Today, she wore her hair down. It was long and blue-black and framed a face with almond-shaped eyes and naturally terracotta-colored lips. Carter wondered how she was adjusting to the Big Apple. It wasn't an easy place to make your mark. Here, you either outclassed the posers or got the cold shoulder.

Deeprose interrupted his thoughts as she sailed into his office, all smiles. Pumping his hand as if water might flow from it, she introduced herself with the heaviest, most atrocious back-woods accent he had ever heard. Reclaiming his arm, Carter invited her to have a seat.

"How is New York treating you so far, Agent Deeprose? Don't let your accent worry you. It'll fade pretty quickly."

Deeprose answered with a straight face. "What accent is that, sir? Y'know, mah pappy used to tell me that the big city'd beat the tarnation outta anyone who ventured past Four Corners, but y'all seem pretty friendly to me! Now, ain't that a kick in the pants?"

Carter sat back in his chair unable to think of a thing to say in reply. She looked longingly over at his cappuccino machine, back at him, smiled real big and then…winked.

*Did she just wink at me? Was that a wink?*

"Oh, Ah apologize sir, Ah must have somethin' in mah eye."

Deeprose exploded in giggles. "How about we start over and, this time, make friends?"

Carter was impressed. "Touché, Agent Deeprose, and well done. I guess you've probably been insulted about a hundred times today. On behalf of myself and the City of New York, I apologize for your less-than-stellar welcome aboard and all the insensitive, stereotypical remarks I'm sure you've had to suffer. How about a cup of coffee?"

He crossed the room to fix her a cup, using the time to think. This woman would be responsible for watching his back. He couldn't help remembering Royals flailing around on the ground during the mock bank robbery at Quantico. Was she the hero type? Her file indicated a lack of commendations. Maybe she violated protocol.

Carter handed her a double espresso—no sugar.

*Now that I know she's clever and likes to have a bit of fun, let's see how tough she is.*

Deeprose knocked back her double espresso without batting an eyelash. "Ah imagine my profile produced some very dry readin', not much like the kind y'all find in those spy thriller novels. Ah do, however, have a talent for nosin' around until Ah find what Ah'm lookin' for, and Ah always have your back, sir."

Carter smiled. "You are the very portrait of humility, Agent Deeprose. Are you always this charming and disarming?"

"Yes, sir, Ah am." They were getting on famously. The banter was well under way, and Carter was noticeably relaxing. Anyone this clever, who could put on and take off a mask as easily as she did her lipstick could be invaluable to the team.

"Ah hear you've written the book on solvin' multiple-killer cases while stoppin' department corruption in a single bound."

*Supergirl. I knew it.*

"I wouldn't go that far, Agent, but I appreciate you doing your homework. I will share one pearl of wisdom, however. Know the enemy as much as you know yourself but without taking on too much of his malevolence. If you can do that, you'll make out just fine."

"Your record speaks for itself, sir. Ah'm ready to learn everything Ah can from you."

"I understand you're just back from Iraq, Agent."

"Yes, sir."

*Interesting. No quips this time.*

Carter wondered why she really joined the F.B.I.—in New York, of all places—but he certainly wasn't going to try to find out now. There would be plenty of time for questions. "I never thought I'd give up Boston for the Big Apple. My wife believes the cultural experience will broaden my horizons."

"Ah'm countin' on it, sir. Ah want to do everything, go everywhere, an' meet as many people as Ah can."

"Good. Then *you* can show *me* around, because I'm still in shock. If you have the time right now, Agent Deeprose, this would be a good time to get our feet wet. We have a murder to solve. The case has gone a bit cold with no one here to do the footwork before we arrived, but there's still a lot to be understood from the crime scene. How about taking a ride over there now? It's uptown at a museum called the *Cloisters*. Would you like more espresso before we go?"

"Are you tryin' to test me or kill me, sir?"

Carter couldn't stifle a guffaw. She was smart.

The ride was classic. They marveled at the fall colors, even in such a crowded city. Bright reds, rich yellows, and burnt oranges dazzled them under a still blue early autumn sky. Carter and Deeprose were both thinking the same thing; maybe moving to New York wasn't such a bad idea after all.

***

The *Cloisters* had improved their security since the murder. Other than that, it was empty at this hour, except for the acting curator who roamed its halls making sure every exhibit and piece of art was in its proper place before leaving for the night.

It seemed like all work on the case had come to a halt until now. Carter wondered what the motive for the murder could have been.

*Hm. Nothing missing. Nothing. In fact, some things have been added—a sword, a discarded set of armor, and a pair of bloody shoe prints leading out the door and toward the park.*

Arthur Moreland, the acting curator, came into the roped off room to greet them. "I never met the man in person. I'm terribly sorry I can't be of any help to you, but you see, I'm just a temporary replacement until a new curator is appointed."

29

"That's quite all right, Mr. Moreland. We're just here to revisit the scene. If we need anything, we'll let you know."

"Very well. If you'll excuse me, I must continue my rounds."

Deeprose looked suspiciously at the man who dismissed himself from the investigation so hastily. "Shouldn't we have asked him where he was the day of the murders, Agent Carter?"

"I don't think so, Agent, although I imagine they all travel in the same circles. He was hired after the curator was killed, and he told us he didn't know him. Besides, the museum's publicist verified earlier today that Mr. Moreland was in Cambridge giving a lecture at Harvard at the time the crime was committed. We can remove him from the suspect list." Carter turned away so she wouldn't see him smiling. Lesson One: Do Your Homework.

Deeprose held her phone downward at a 45-degree angle as if it were a divining rod. "Why don't we head down here, sir? My map tells me we're in close proximity to the crime scene."

Carter nodded but didn't need her map to find it. He was sensitive to negative and positive energy fluctuations and could still feel the killer's presence.

Deeprose came to a sudden halt and planted each foot in an opposite direction. Despite the empty corridor, she was poised for danger. Was it the realization that the crime happened right where she stood or instinct? Carter was willing to bet a ticket to Fenway it was instinct.

"You feel it, don't you?"

"Ah feel *him*. It was the same on the battlefield in Iraq. The enemy didn't even have to be in view."

Carter moved closer to the wall, where the suit of armor had stood. He muttered to himself, "What can we learn from this? What was the motive? Did the killer have a grudge against the curator? Money's a consideration, yet $75,000 was found in the makeshift grave made for Gino Cafferelli, the deceased security guard. Whether or not he was an accomplice or just a liability, why bury him with the money? If he was in on it, why didn't he disconnect the surveillance camera? It caught an image of a dark-haired man in his early 20's entering and leaving the museum. It's as if the killer is begging to be caught. I don't get it."

Carter still faced the wall, continuing his train of thought. "The image from the camera is horribly grainy, but I think the lab will be able to clean it up and enhance it enough to make out a face. I just hope the face has a record."

Deeprose continued. "If the lab can identify him and he comes back for the cash, we'll spot him. Should we put a couple of men on it, sir?"

"If he hasn't come back for it already, he's not going to. He must have read about the dog digging up the body by now."

"Of course. Sir, this is no ordinary hit. It's not well-planned. A professional would never have left bloody shoe prints or forgotten to check for cameras. It coulda been an angry amateur or even someone hired by an angry amateur. It coulda been his *wife*, sir. That's the first place to look, isn't it?"

"Yes, it is. Most murders are committed by someone the victim knew. But we can't rule out anything yet, and we're here now, so let's see what else we can learn before we visit Mrs. Dalton Wells."

Deeprose asked herself a rhetorical question. "Who might the curator's enemies be?" She ticked off the possibilities on her fingers. "His wife, any colleagues past or present, or...wait! The curator may have planned to steal the art himself but was double-crossed by the man wearin' the armor." She arched an eyebrow.

"Look around, Agent. Nothing is missing. A museum inventory report confirms it. Try looking at the additions, instead. What do you see?"

"The addition of the ancient armin' sword. Who would have access to that kind of weapon? And where could somethin' like that be bought? We also have bloody shoe prints and a photo we might or might not be able to use."

"We'll start by putting together a list of people to question. Our first stop will be the wife of the deceased."

"Who will we see about the forensic evidence, sir?"

"Jill Seacrest, my wife, is the lead forensic scientist on our team. She may be able to tell us where the sword came from and a host of other things, but the bloody shoe prints will have to be analyzed at the D.C. Bureau, where they have the *Solemate* database. We also want to know if there are any particulates in the print itself that will give us more information."

"What can the database do that we can't, sir?"

31

It can compare the pattern of blood picked up from the bottom of the shoes with the soles of the brands and models of shoes in the database. If we get a hit, we can begin looking for local stores that carry them, and, hopefully, who bought them. Seacrest may have a D.N.A. match by now from the blood taken from the floor, the armor, and Mr. Wells' body. We have to consider thrill killers and copycats as perps, too, so both the shoes and the killers may have come from anywhere and could be anywhere, by now."

Deputy Director Fischetti's words rang in Carter's head.

"If this is a 'thrill kill', sir, as y'all call it, gettin' our killer might be like findin' a needle in a haystack. Unless he strikes again and in the same manner."

"First we consider every possibility. Then, we eliminate everything impossible."

"And whatever remains, no matter how improbable, must be the truth. I read Sherlock Holmes, too, sir. But there is another way."

"And what is that, Agent Deeprose?"

"The only way to find a needle in a haystack is to use a magnet."

"You mean draw him out?"

"Not necessarily, sir. A magnet works both ways. Imagine he's our magnet and we're the needle. If we can profile him to the point where we can figure out what area he lives in or where he usually spends his time, and if we can get a good look at the face in that picture, we'll see him walkin' the streets. He's gotta go out sometime, sir. He thinks he pulled this off. It's a long shot, but that's what magnets are for, aren't they?"

***

Carter pulled up a photo of the curator's wife on his cell phone. "Cynthia Wells is a woman with her own personal wealth. She didn't need Dalton Wells' money and would certainly not profit from his death. If you look at it from that angle, the curator had more of a motive for killing her than she did for killing him."

He knocked on the apartment door, and left the condolences to Deeprose, who introduced herself and Carter after flashing her identification. "Ah'm so sorry for your loss, ma'am. May we come in for a few moments to talk to you?"

Each wall in Wells' Morningside Heights condominium sported a theme: Renaissance Art, Impressionist Art, Modern Art and so on. Carter roamed around taking it all in. He was looking for anything missing that might explain the sword left at the crime scene, yet this collection was comprised only of paintings and sculpture. None of it was from the medieval period, and nothing seemed to be missing or out of place.

"I am *very* distraught," Wells began with a shaky voice. "I don't see how I can possibly help you."

"We understand how you must feel, Mrs. Wells. We won't take up much time. Ah promise."

Carter added, "We wondered if your husband had any altercations before he died. Did he have any enemies or seem unduly worried about anything? Was he having any financial or professional difficulties that you knew of? Anything you can recall might be helpful."

"I thought the crime was art-related. I told Dalton *a hundred times* to demand increased security in that dirty, drafty, Godforsaken place."

Deeprose nodded. "Ma'am, did he ever speak with a raised voice on the phone or maybe here or at work? Perhaps he went out at times not usual to his schedule?"

"No. I don't recall anything like that. Are you telling me you have no idea who did this to my Dalton?"

Carter intervened. "Not at all, Mrs. Wells. Our role in this investigation is to examine all the possibilities and gather as much evidence as we can, and that's all. When there's something concrete to tell you, you'll be contacted. Mrs. Wells, would you allow us access to your phone and financial records? It could bring the case to a fairly quick close…"

Wells' bottom lip quivered, and she raised a hand to her forehead. "It sounds like you're utterly *clueless*. Are you asking for permission to investigate me, *Agent Whoever-You-Are?* Because I don't appreciate the implication. No one would want my husband dead. I had all the money! Look around you! Everything you see was bought and paid for by myself. By myself and for myself. Go ahead and look *that* up!"

Shaking and pale, she grabbed the back of a Louis XIV gilt-edged chair for support and shrieked, "The only way I could receive a *penny* of his life insurance was if Dalton died in an accident. Does a fatal stab in the back look like an accident to either of you?!"

Deeprose turned to Carter in some anxiety, but he used his eyes to direct her attention back to Mrs. Wells.

*Let her talk until she runs out of gas.*

Deeprose folded her hands on her lap. "Ma'am, what Ah'm about to say may sound harsh, but those records we just asked y'all for could solve this murder. Don'tcha want us to catch him, ma'am?"

Wells glared at her. "No!" Then she sighed. "I mean, yes, of course I do. What I mean to say is that it doesn't matter to me one way or the other who committed it. When he's caught, whoever he is, he'll be punished. All I want is closure. Don't you understand? This is too much to bear. I want it to be over with and done, that's all."

Carter leaned forward in his chair, his arms pressing on his thighs. This was getting very interesting. "When you speak of closure, what exactly do you mean? If finding out who the killer is won't give you that, what will, Mrs. Wells?"

Wells lowered her head, and shook it from side to side. "Knowing why. I want a reason. One that makes some kind of sense to me."

*She could find closure if there was a "reason" why someone murdered her husband? One that makes sense? Can murder ever make sense? Either she's a little nuts, she's too upset to know what she's saying, or she's one hell of an actress.*

"Mrs. Wells, you say all you want to know is why, but how can knowing why a sick individual killed your husband give you any peace? Please, help me to understand."

"I can't. If you can't understand how I feel, respect the fact that I don't wish to be involved any further. I don't want updates. I simply want to be told it's over, and then I want to know why it happened. Now, if you'll excuse me, I'm very upset, and I'd like to lie down."

She walked them to the door, turned and started to walk away. Then she stopped, sighed deeply, and turned back. "All right, Agents, I'll sign off on my phone and financial records and anything else you want. My lawyer will contact your office."

\*\*\*

34

Carter praised Deeprose once they were back in the car. "Interviewing the spouse is like walking a tightrope. You have to inquire without insinuating, and you have to be sympathetic without losing focus and objectivity. Well done."

"Is that what Ah did? Ah'll have to tell my daddy I acquitted myself well today. He was a colonel, you know. A career man. Kind of hard to live up to, if ya know what Ah mean."

"Yes, I do."

*No, I don't. Neither of my folks were hard-liners. It's none of my business, but something put a wedge between Deeprose and her father that made her risk her life twice in Iraq and now again for the F.B.I. She still needs his approval pretty badly. I wonder why?*

# Chapter Five

Alison was dreaming. She was pretending to be someone else, someone else named Deborah. She had to make this man, whom she had never met before, believe she was trolling the web for sex. His name was David Florio, and he was a very, *very* bad man. She didn't know why, she only knew that it was so. She was trying to get him to invite her over for dinner, and once there, she was going to kill him.

Alison set up a fake profile for a sexy bombshell called Deborah on *Dare to Dream*, a new online dating service. She invented Deborah to catch him for her. The site promised her that all her desires could be fulfilled if she was willing to take a chance. She was.

The bait was irresistible; she made damn sure of that. Deborah was a cute, athletic blonde who enjoyed hiking and exploring her wild side. And he only lived one town away, in East Brunswick. "I hope I'm not calling too soon. I mean," Deborah purred, "you did give me your number and all..."

"Nnn... No!" David stuttered. "I'm glad you did. I wanted you to call. The sooner, the better."

*Good. He's anxious, eager.*

"So," David gulped, "your profile said you like to explore your wild side. How exactly do you go about doing that, Deborah?"

"I think spontaneity and surprise are the real keys to exploring one's wild side. Don't you agree, David?"

"Absolutely, Deborah. May I call you Debbie, or do you have another nickname you prefer?"

*Why am I so unbelievably angry with him? Who is he? Oh, well, anything can happen in a dream, Allie, just go with it.*

Deborah found herself aroused by the phone conversation, but she was also confused by it. Was it lust or murder that turned her on?

36

She had never actually committed murder, but as the voice said, it was a dream.

*Why not go ahead and do it just to see what it feels like? It's not real; there won't be a price to pay. What was it that the Silver Man promised? Oh yes, he said that killing a thief, rapist, or murderer was a public service. David must be one of the three. It is my duty to protect and defend the Collective.*

"Uh, Deborah, are you still there? Hello..."

Deborah cleared her throat. "I was just thinking about what kind of mischief we might get into."

"I can't wait to see you. Would you like to come over for a quiet dinner at my place tomorrow night? I'm quite a gourmet."

"You're a fast worker, too, aren't you? I just hope you don't do everything as fast..." Deborah was delighted with her own power.

Alison heard Deborah's breathy voice fondling David over the phone. She could taste Deborah's peppermint-flavored lipstick and smell her trashy perfume.

*I don't want to do this. He never hurt me; why should I hurt him?*

The voices sang to her, rising up inside her and filling her up until she heard nothing but their song.

*I have no heart and no conscience. This man wants to hurt me; I will finish what they have told me to do.*

"Email me your address and the time you want me—for dinner that is. Or shall we say, dessert?" She let him hear a throaty growl. Then she hung up, leaving him panting on the other end of the line.

Alison didn't have a car, but hey, it was a dream. She'd make Jeannie drive her there.

*** 

### Twenty-Four Hours Later

Alison's consciousness blotted out the next day and fast-forwarded her straight to evening. While dressing, the voices commanded Alison to remember her mother, curled up in a protective ball, afraid for her life and begging her father to stop hitting her. She could still hear him shouting, "You're only good for one thing and even that's no damn good!"

It was then that Alison admitted to herself she hated men and that they frightened her. When she dreamed she was Deborah, though, she felt sure of herself and as strong as any one of them. Deborah enjoyed the thrill of the hunt, but Alison was going to be the one to step in and finish him off.

***

It sputtered and stalled, but Jeannie's car had done that a million times before. Alison muttered unintelligibly to herself. Jeannie stopped turning the key, and glared at her. "O.K., so my car's not new and doesn't have a fancy, push-button ignition."

"It sounds like it doesn't have an engine. How can you ride around in this death trap?"

"I have a better question. How can you? Why don't you cough up the money to have it fixed, your highness?"

"Sorry, Jeannie. I'm nervous, I guess."

Jeannie shook her head, and her face softened. "I'm sorry too. I'm nervous for you. I feel like I'm going on the date, too."

Jeannie tried the ignition again. Nothing...

"Just in case things don't go so well, I'm counting on you to get me out of there. Look, your car won't make it home and back again to pick me up. If I buy you some take-out and a bottle of wine on the way, would you be willing to park the car in his neighborhood and wait for me until it's time to leave? For me? For love and adventure?"

"*Shit!*"

"Please? *Pleeeeeease?*"

"All right, all right! Stop begging. But we have to have a signal in case you need to make a hasty retreat."

"How about a text?"

Jeannie's eyes widened at the thought of adventure until she remembered the signal was only in case of a misadventure. "O.K., text me the letter 'E' if you need to escape."

Alison gave her a final instruction. "Park up the street a house or two, and I'll meet you there."

Jeannie sighed and turned the key. This time the engine turned over. She hoped her heap of scrap metal would make it there and back.

\*\*\*

Ringing a doorbell had never been so exciting. Not even on Halloween.

"Hi, I'm glad you got here O.K." David flashed her a winning, whiter-than-white smile.

Deborah extended her hand. David grabbed it and pulled her into an embrace. This wasn't going to be as easy as Alison had hoped.

"I got here just fine." Deborah's eyes roamed the apartment. It was beautiful!

*He's either very successful or a thief.*

David was off to the kitchen. "I have to check on dinner! Have a seat in the living room."

He pivoted and whisked a bottle of red wine off the half-counter that served as a barrier between the kitchen and the dining room table. She considered doing it there, on top of that counter, with all its little bottles and containers swept to the floor.

"What do you do, Dave?" Deborah was in charge again. She wandered around the living room lightly fingering the brick-a-brack.

"A little of this and a little of that. I.T. stuff, mostly." He tried his best to look self-deprecating.

Deborah loved it. She leaned into his ear and tickled it with her breath. His erection was instant. "I'll bet you're a big success, David. I just *love* successful men. They make me go all loosey-goosey. Would you mind pointing me in the direction of the bathroom, big guy? I want to freshen up."

David was on red alert. It looked like he was going to have dessert first. "Down the hall, second door on the left."

The handbag she carried was stuffed, but she didn't think it looked suspicious. All men knew that women carried everything from first aid to camping tents in their handbags. Deborah allowed Alison to inventory her handbag.

*Smokes. Check.*

*Lighter fluid. Check.*

*Candle. Check.*

*Knock out drops. Check.*

Deborah stood behind David, watching him cook for a moment. "I'm back." The spatula flew across the room.

*I am sooo liking this power trip! I should let Deborah out more often.*

"Care for a smoke? I have some *righteous* weed with me."

"Great!" He was putty in her hands. He knew it, and she knew it, too.

"So, tell me, Davie, why on earth are you available?"

"She...she got sick. It was fast."

"Oh. Sorry." Deborah took a hit, but Alison decided David must have abandoned his sick girlfriend. This had to be his crime.

"I could ask the same thing. I bet you get all kinds of invitations." He opened the oven door.

"So many invitations, so little time..." Deborah threw her head back and giggled. Alison, buried deep inside of her, was full of envy.

"Well, for better or worse, the first course is ready." David grabbed a towel to lay over his right forearm. Then he bowed. "Right this way, madam."

Alison was depressingly unimpressed.

*Oysters? Really?*

Deborah raised her wine glass and sipped. "Oooh. It's wonderful!" She licked her bottom lip delicately.

David served her the best looking piece of chicken on the platter. He spooned vegetables with sauce onto her dish. "Don't be polite. Eat like you mean it." He stabbed a leg as if it might jump off his plate. "This is the best part of cooking."

Deborah's eyes sparkled. "Oh, you're not done cooking, yet, David. I'm going to light your fire. How about I pour us another glass of wine?" She picked up the two glasses and went into the kitchen. With her back to him, she emptied the contents of a vial of liquid into his glass and returned to the table with it. They talked and laughed and sipped.

David emptied his glass, and asked for a refill. They got up from the table and moved into the living room to relax. Within a few moments David's speech became noticeably slurred; he slumped forward in his chair. Alison slid the joint into his mouth. His eyes were as glazed as the chicken.

David coughed and spit it out. "God! My lungs feel like they're made of glue!"

"Oh, honey, are you all right?"

He shook his head from side to side.

*I'll take that as a 'no'.*

She placed her handbag on the table, unzipped it and removed her candle.

David seemed mildly curious.

"Two neurotransmitters—gamma-aminobutyric acid and glycine—are starting to kick in, David, that's all. There's nothing to worry about."

Imitating Deborah's light teasing banter, she lowered the boom. "You wanted to go all the way tonight, didn't you, baby? Your wish is my command. I think someone needs a..." She paused for emphasis, raising a lighter from her bag. "...*light*." David's eyes widened but that was all.

The candle was hard to stuff down David's throat. His paralysis made it damn near impossible, but she managed it. Pieces of food and liquid gushed up as she pushed it further down. David's eyes had rolled to the back of their sockets and his lids fluttered furiously.

"And now for the big finish..." She poured lighter fluid and the rest of his red wine down the front of his body, making his white shirt look like a candy cane. Then she blew him a kiss and torched him.

Inside the roaring flames, David appeared translucent. The fire consumed him quickly, but it must have been a long, agonizing death. Alison, rooted to the spot, looked on in morbid fascination.

*I wonder if it's morning yet...*

She stacked the plates and glasses into the dishwasher, just in case the fire didn't burn every trace of her D.N.A. Next, she made a quick inspection of the apartment for any other evidence she may have left behind, and finally, she slinked out the back door before the blaze set off his fire alarm. Dressed in black, with black stockings, black shoes, and a black coat, she walked up the block in silence.

Jeannie was there, waiting. "Come on, get in. How was it?"

Alison laughed. "It was one *hot* night."

A tall, dark figure hiding in the bushes wrote down the license plate number and smiled to himself as the old car chugged down Ashbury Lane.

# Chapter Six

Today Carter was busy unpacking boxes in their small, exorbitantly expensive apartment. Stumbling over a particularly heavy one, he decided to sit down and unpack as many as he could while Jill was out at the lab.

*Jeez! There must be fifty boxes of junk to go through. How'd we ever collect it all?*

He reached down into a box of books and lifted one out.

*I remember this. Jill gave it to me when we first met. We even had lines from it quoted at our wedding...*

It was a beautiful hardbound copy of *The Rubaiyat of Omar Khayyam,* its thousand-year old quatrains a death sentence for the author in the place and time they were written. Carter felt drawn to the poetry because it was a not-so-subtle reminder to live in the moment and to accept the joy of earthly pleasures as much as he embraced spiritual ones. Carter re-read the lines he remembered so well:

"A Book of Verses underneath the Bough,

A Jug of Wine, a Loaf of Bread—and Thou..."

It all boiled down to that, didn't it? Our everyday hustle and bustle and all our burning desires and ambitions were meaningless without knowing the comfort and contentment of simple, quiet moments of peace and companionship with bread and wine and a really good book to share.

*I want more of those moments with her. But that's not the reason she wanted me to read it. The lines also meant that I should always try to recognize and celebrate those moments whenever they presented themselves and that if they didn't, it was because I wasn't looking hard enough for them.*

The ring of his cell phone jarred Carter back to the present.

\*\*\*

Seacrest had some news for him, but she couldn't send it to him by text message or email. She wanted Carter to come to the lab. Seacrest enjoyed his looks of impatience and perplexity when she presented her lab findings to him. Carter loved that about her and would never consider robbing her of her big reveal, so he grabbed his coat and raced to the lab.

\*\*\*

Jill held up a gray sneaker with streaks of white and maroon on the sides. "For those of us not so athletically inclined, this is a *Stridewell.*"

"The killer wore sneakers inside the armor? *Stridewells*? Are you sure?"

"Yes, I'm sure. The pattern of the bloody shoe print on the floor matches this exact make and model. We lucked out, Carter. There's not much call for these shoes anymore. If you can put some men on it, we need a list of all the places in the tristate area that sell these *Stridewells* in a men's size 11, and if they have it, a list of people who paid with a card. The register tape will tell us when the purchase was made and at what register. We'll use in-store videos to try to spot our man."

Carter paced while he thought out loud. "Since we know he likes the Upper West Side, I think we should start there, don't you?"

"Yup. He was wearing the sneakers when he took off the armor and walked out the door that way."

"He's an amateur, then." Carter frowned.

"You think this was his first kill?" Jill placed the shoe carefully back in its evidence bag. It was being shipped to Washington for a more complete forensic analysis. Seacrest wanted to get some blood samples for D.N.A. tests before she sent it off.

"I do. These babies look expensive, Jill. Either he likes to live well, or he saved a long time for them. I'll bet he still has them."

Jill was excited. "If we can prove he purchased them and if he still has them, these sneakers, along with positive D.N.A. identifications on both the victim and killer tie him to the scene. Definitely. Now, we just have to find the right guy."

"We'll find him, Jill. Nice job."

"Maybe you should tell my supervisor that. I'm already off on the wrong foot with him. I didn't know I was supposed to get his signed permission to use tread-tracking equipment. Well, what's the big deal? I have to do my job, don't I? Honestly, what a baby!"

"Blame the shortcuts on me."

"I already did." Jill fought to keep a straight face.

Carter's phone rang. He put his hand over the receiver and whispered to her, "It's the deputy director. Another murder—in New Jersey. I wonder why he doesn't want their own people on it. Anyway, he wants me in his office in five minutes. Here we go again!"

Carter pecked her on the cheek. "Gotta go."

Curious as hell, Seacrest watched him walk away.

*** 

Fischetti stood behind his desk, hands on his hips and a sour expression on his face. "What do you make of this, Agent Carter?" Fischetti flipped the photo around for Carter to see.

Carter leaned in from the opposite side of the desk to take a look. The victim was nearly eviscerated from the top, down. A headless corpse was seated on a chair. Its legs were in what looked like pieces of a pair of men's slacks. The remains of its feet were disconnected from the body but were still located under the legs where feet should have been. In the far right of the photo a skull rested on the stump of a coffee table, staring at what had become of its body.

"Do you have cause of death, sir?"

"Well, it's not spontaneous combustion, Agent Carter."

"It could be anything at this point, sir, unless you have some facts you haven't shared yet. Have you ruled out accident? Suicide? *And* spontaneous combustion?"

Fischetti smiled. "I appreciate your open mind, Carter, but the fact is the Department of Justice thinks this is another thrill kill or a copycat. They're not ruling out the possibility of a serial murder or a spree, either. Are you familiar with the difference, Agent Carter?"

"Yes, sir. A spree killer differs from a serial killer in that he or she allows no cooling off period between murders."

"We need hard evidence that shows a pattern of thrill kills and copycats, serial, or spree murders. The local P.D. wouldn't know a murder if they saw one. The scene is compromised, and we've been asked to step in and clean up the mess. I need your team out there. Now."

Carter turned to leave the office.

"Carter, do not, under any circumstances, share our theories with Agent Deeprose, at least, not yet. I don't want her assuming anything just because the D.O.J. is. She'll be trained by the book, but for now, just keep her reigned in. That's all."

Carter nodded, realizing that keeping this kind of secret from Deeprose wouldn't exactly ignite a trusting relationship.

***

Carter felt Deeprose staring at him from the passenger seat as he drove. It was like being scanned by a laser. He cleared his throat. "You'll meet Special Agent Seacrest today. She'll be there to go over the scene for forensic evidence and gather lab samples."

Deeprose eyed the photo of the charred victim. "Sounds like she was in on the briefin' or had one of her own. Ah'm glad it's all under control, sir."

*Ouch.*

Carter peered into the rear view mirror to monitor his expression. He'd known this was coming and decided now was the right time to discuss it. "The scene is under the jurisdiction of the New Brunswick P.D., and the media is already all over the neighborhood. It's going to be a long day, and we won't have a chance to talk in private once we get there. You want to talk about it?"

"Yes, sir, Ah do. Why wasn't Ah part of the briefin'?"

"There wasn't much *to* the briefing, other than the photo you're holding."

"Ah'm not telepathic, sir, and Ah should have been there."

Fischetti wants this to be a training exercise for you. He figures the less you know beforehand, the less likely you are to have preconceived notions or biases. It also gives us a measure of control on the team—you'll have a more objective viewpoint than the rest of us who've been doing this for years. He has faith in you; I'm certain

45

of that. In fact, he asked me not to mention it to you, but the cat's out of the bag, now. I'm going to be much more of a mentor than a partner on your first several cases. You'll start out the right way, using the right tools and methods before we analyze the evidence, develop hypotheses, and draw our conclusions. O.K.?"

She sighed. "Ah guess it'll have to be, sir. So, y'all want me to go in there and ask only the occasional question."

"That's the gist of it. The less you say, the more you'll see and hear. This bunch is already going to have a chip on their shoulder when we walk in. Let's give them the satisfaction of telling us, in their own words, just how badly they screwed up our crime scene. It'll save us a lot of time today if you can act a little more like a kid just out of John Jay. Any time the feds have to step in to assist local police with its superior lab service or anything else, their nose gets out of joint. They're not equipped for something like this, and they know they've compromised the scene already. They'll have to play it off to save face."

"That's one thing about the service Ah don't miss. Sir, this photo seems to imply spontaneous combustion. Why not just send lab personnel to the scene and send us out on another lead?"

"Honestly, Agent, I don't know. Fischetti wants us here to assess all the possibilities, no matter how it looks or what we're told today. If I'd worked with him for any length of time, I might understand why he wants us to be flies on the wall for now, but I don't. We're both rookies in this regard, so I think we'll just go in, see what there is to see, and discover what there is to discover. Agreed?"

Deeprose perked back up. "Agreed."

Carter smiled knowingly. "Agent Deeprose, I'm going to ask you to do something difficult for me, today. We're stepping on enough toes as it is, and I don't want to push any unnecessary buttons because of your, uh, your…" Carter flushed and coughed.

"Ma *what*, sir?"

"Your…oh, damn it, your *accent*. I want you to hang back a little. Don't try to squeeze anything out of the boys. I want your eyes and ears on everything and everyone. There *are* preconceived notions at work here, and I want to know if I'm being intentionally pushed in a particular direction. If I am, I want to know why. While I'm interacting, I want you monitoring. Is that clear?"

46

"Yes, sir."

A cold, clammy, miserable rain kept them company during the rest of the drive. Deeprose shivered. She didn't care for ugly, gray skies.

When they finally arrived, the commanding officer, Captain Morelli, looked irritated and uncomfortable. "Who are you?"

Carter showed him his identification and introduced them. "We're here to assist you in any way we can, Captain. Agent Seacrest will be here momentarily with a crime scene crew to conduct a forensic investigation."

"Well, aren't we the lucky ones. Hey, listen up you guys! The feds just arrived on a white horse to save the day. Let's show them a little appreciation for helping us out, eh?"

Several men gave Carter the finger. Others treated them to loud, sloppy raspberries before turning back to their work.

"Agent Carter, my men have already been all over the crime scene. There's nothing there. Zip. Nada. What happened in there is anyone's guess. If you think you can find something we haven't, go ahead and knock yourselves out. If there's anything *we* can do to help *you*, why, you just let us know."

If word got out they'd bungled the job, Morrelli might never recover the reputation it took him fifteen years to build. He might even be busted in rank. That would be even worse than being transferred to *East Bumfuck*, Idaho. He decided it might go better for him later if he cooperated a little. "We need your forensics to confirm the victim's identity. We also need to determine if it's suspicious or accidental."

* * *

Deeprose's eyes grew to twice their normal size. Despite the gruesome photo depicting what looked like spontaneous combustion, she was surprised it hadn't already been termed suspicious. Morrelli must have been told that the D.O.J. was pushing to conclude this was another thrill kill. Carter was glad now that Agent Deeprose hadn't been filled in. As a rookie, the last thing she needed was to get tangled up in department politics.

The thing was, Deeprose knew the possibility of a thrill kill could be tossed out right now. Something else was going on.

*Why is the D.O.J. goin' out of its way to make this an open and shut case? Why do I get the feelin' we're supposed to hand them the findin' they seem to want so much? If these are thrill kills, I'll eat my hat. They may be completely unrelated. They probably are! But neither murder was done for the thrill of it. Right now, our best chance of breakin' these two cases depends on whether the killer or killers are amateurs, because amateurs make big, sloppy mistakes.*

Carter pulled out a notepad. "Can you give us time of discovery? Who reported it?"

Morelli sighed. "A neighbor called the fire department when she heard the fire alarm go off and smelled smoke outside. Ms. Rivera said she smelled a strange, offensive odor more than she smelled regular wood smoke. We kept the details of the case from the neighbors and press. The victim had no family." Morelli gazed intently at Carter, who kept his eyes on his notepad.

"Did she know the occupant?"

Morelli looked at him like he was a moron. "You know neighbors; they never know anyone once the cops arrive! The name of the occupant is David Florio. No, we don't know if the victim is also the occupant. We asked him, but in his current condition, he was unable to answer. He's twenty-seven and single. You better write that down in your little notebook, Agent, or you might forget."

"I know this is your baby, Captain. I'm here only to offer you our services and nose around a little to see if it ties in with any of my other cases. That's all. I have the authority to take over the case right now, and you know that, but I won't. I have bigger fish to fry, and I'm not interested in stealing your thunder."

Morelli looked dubious, but he relented. "All right, all right. What else do you want?"

Carter looked the captain in the eyes now that they'd come to an understanding. "In high-profile cases like these it's better to give the media as much information as possible without blowing the details only the killer would know. More information tends to jog the memory of witnesses. The more information we can put out there, the less secure our killer will feel. He'll make rash decisions that'll lead to mistakes, or someone will turn him in."

Morelli blew his cork. "*Just hold on one damn minute!* There's no way I'm going on the six o'clock news to tell this town that what we have here may be an accident or a suicide or a spontaneous Goddamn combustion when I know damn well it's a murder! And I am sure as shit not going to tell the world that two separate incidents in two separate states might be thrill kills *related* to each other. That's just what I need—a panic! Look, Agent, I have five more years to retirement, and that means I can't afford to make a wrong call. If you want it on the news so much, one of your own people can make the statement."

"You know that isn't possible, Captain. Our cover can't be blown. That'll either force their hand, which we don't want just yet, or scatter them to the four winds, in which case these two murders will go cold before winter sets in."

Agent Seacrest pulled up to the investigators with her window down. She had seen the local cops going in and out of the apartment and was already hopping mad. Oblivious to any authority that wasn't her own, she flashed her badge at the captain as if he was a clumsy waiter and barked an order at him.

"No one is to enter that apartment without my approval. Do you understand me, officer?"

Morelli turned purple. "Look lady, you can't just fly down here on your broomstick, flash your badge and tell me how to handle my own crime scene! Who the hell do you think you are? These are *my* men, and *I* put them there! *Per regulation*! They know their job, for God's sake; they're wearing shoe covers."

"I don't care if they're wearing fairy boots!" Seacrest slammed the car door shut and marched herself into the home. She used her thumb hitch-hiker style to wave them out. "Everyone out! And I said **NOW**!"

***

Carter was highly amused but he kept his mouth shut and wore a straight face.

*She certainly is something to see in action, unless you're on the receiving end. Poor guy, he had no idea what his day was going to be like when he got up this morning.*

Morelli ran after her. "Now listen here, you…"

Seacrest turned slowly, and spoke in her executive tone, which was dangerously low and level. "I am certain you want to cooperate with me, sir. I am equally certain you do not want to be responsible for having contaminated my crime scene. Furthermore, if your men have destroyed my chances for obtaining any useable evidence of which there should be a prodigious amount, I will make sure it is your ass that swings on national television. Are we clear *now*?"

She stood her ground and gave him a look that clearly dared him to challenge her. Seacrest knew the only thing a bully understood was a bigger bully, so she stared him down and counted silently. *One, two, three, four...*

"O.K. O.K. Keep your skirt on." Morelli spat on the ground and spoke into his shoulder mic. "Get everyone out of the apartment. Now."

Deeprose whispered to Carter. "Wow, Ah like her! How'd the two of you ever get together? Ah mean..." She turned red with embarrassment.

"Relax, Agent. I know just what you mean. If you ever figure it out, let me know."

Inside the garden apartment, Seacrest employed optical spectroscopy via camera to view the flooring area, particularly around the remains of the body. Carter stood in the doorway. He could hear Seacrest making exclamation points with her *Ah-hah's* and *Uh-oh's*. She was onto something.

Deeprose hummed as she examined the outside windows. Carter couldn't help notice the different ways both women behaved when they were concentrating.

*Interesting.*

Deeprose interrupted his thoughts. "There's no evidence that a door was kicked in and no marks or scrapes on the window sills. Ah think if there *is* a killer, he or she knew our victim. The lack of forced entry supports the accidental death and suicide argument, but y'all can't really think this is anythin' but a murder, can you? It seems to me that neither one is in the slightest way related to the other. There is no similarity in the style of the kills, the victims, or the locations. Sir, what in the heck is going on here?"

Carter made a steeple with his index fingers. "Remember, Agent, no assumptions. First, we need to know cause of death. Until Agent Seacrest can tell us that, there's no point in spinning our wheels. If she can definitively rule out accident and suicide, the only other

50

possibility is murder. The second most important piece of information is the identity of the victim. Once we have that, it won't be hard to determine whether or not this murder was personal, serial, spree, or thrill-related."

Seacrest appeared at the front door. "I think I found something."

Luminol was a spray that revealed any sign of blood on a surface, even after the blood was washed away. There was a lot of it on the chair where the body was found. "I'm hoping there are at least two different kinds of blood on this chair. I'm going to look around some more." She eyed the floor. "Give me a few hours to collect more samples, and then we'll let the mass spectrometer tell us what might have happened to our victim."

Seacrest raised a purple, gloved hand in Agent Deeprose's direction. "I'm Agent Seacrest. Welcome to the team. I'd shake your hand, but..."

Deeprose was all smiles. Seacrest, it seemed, had an admirer. "No worries, Agent Seacrest. Ah'm Agent Shania Deeprose, and Ah want you to know it was a pleasure watchin' y'all give it to that big bully in the parkin' lot. Can you rule out spontaneous combustion at this point?"

"No, I'm afraid I can't; it's simply not that easy. There are many factors that will determine what goes into my report. I will say one thing, though; in cases of spontaneous human combustion, the surrounding area doesn't burn easily, but this place has been completely torched. On the other hand, there is something called a wick effect which occurs when body fat burns as if it were a candle. It can burn for several hours due to the way fire consumes fat, and in that respect, the evidence supports the S.H.C. theory. But most incidents termed spontaneous human combustion are ones where there is no other plausible explanation, and according to the latest studies, there may be no such thing at all.

"There could also be a host of external sources of ignition responsible for an accidental suicide. For instance, maybe he fell asleep while smoking. Perhaps he consumed flammable drugs or dabbled with explosives. He could have been drinking alcohol excessively, perhaps inadvertently exposing it to leaking gas. The possibilities are endless."

Deeprose looked morose. "Ah guess Ah didn't think of all that."

"Don't look so down-in-the-mouth, Agent! The best way to determine the cause of death is to let science tell us."

# Chapter Seven
*Seven Years Earlier in Afghanistan...*

Although his vocabulary was limited to speaking Dari, one of two languages spoken by Afghans, the prisoner seemed to understand the American serviceman guarding him. He was telling him to run.

The guard had volunteered for the D.A.R.P.A. (Defense Research Projects Agency) experiment and was certain the prisoner understood him. The prisoner must have been imagining freedom, home, and family—all the things most men longed for.

The next stage of the experiment was for the guard to inject himself with a drug that was supposed to change him from an ordinary soldier into a killing machine. The prisoner was his prey and the chase began today.

The prisoner, sweating and stumbling, faced his guard with one question on his face. The guard nodded his answer and used a remote control to unlock the gate of the Parwan Detention Facility in Bagram. The Afghani wasted no more time. He ran hard and fast, plumes of dust rising in his wake.

The guard ran to the gatehouse first to report the escape and give the prisoner a sporting chance. He stuck a needle in his thigh. It hurt, but the pain became ecstasy almost immediately. On *Hyzopran*, he felt like God, and God was very, very angry today.

*I am invincible. I will capture my prisoner, and he will die.*

He heard the awe-inspiring voices of angels. They promised to guide him directly to the doomed man. In seconds he watched as a map unfolded inside his own head, complete with longitudinal and latitudinal coordinates. The guard was the blue dot and the Afghani was the red one.

The angels sang, "You are the executioner. No one may stop you!"

His strides grew more and more elongated until he thought he might bounce off the planet. His body was as weightless as his conscience. In less than half a minute, the escapee was in full view. He didn't have to wonder what the prisoner was feeling; he knew, but he felt no concern or responsibility for what he had to do to the enemy when he caught him. He would kill, and the prisoner would die. That was all.

A hunting knife tucked into a small leather case tethered to his waistline found its way into his hand. He grabbed the prisoner from behind and spun him around. The prisoner's screams died with him as the guard stabbed him viciously and repeatedly. The prisoner crumpled to the ground holding up his hands as a last defense, but they both knew this was the end. The guard lifted him half off the ground by his hair and sliced his neck open like a ripe melon. Fountains of blood arched ten feet above them before falling back down on the soldier roaring and beating his chest. It was both sublime and monstrous.

A new, more expedient type of warfare for the U.S. military had just been born and would soon be used all over the world. Numbers of prisoners would plummet. Resources used to keep them alive would be used to feed our own people. Death rates would rise like the sun. The use of *Hyzopran* meant no one ever had to go home emotionally damaged for doing his or her duty ever again.

The guard looked up at a camera drone hovering in the sky, and screamed his rage and triumph until he had no voice left.

### McLean, Virginia

Clayton Artemus Montgomery stroked his beard while watching a video recorded by a camera drone in Afghanistan one month earlier. "This video brings your thesis to life, Dr. Blake. This is the argument that will convince the board that your project is critical to ongoing and future war efforts."

"I still have reservations." Dr. Katherine Blake, a promising, young biochemist, shook her head as she watched the guard butcher an escaped prisoner with nothing but a hunting knife and an enormous dose of *Hyzopran*.

"What kind of reservations?" Montgomery didn't wait for

Blake's answer. "Remember, you can't show any weakness in your presentation."

Scopolamine, a natural hallucinogenic compound discovered in the wood of the South American Borrachero Tree, had been blamed for causing victims to surrender their bank account numbers without hesitation. A chemically altered and refined version of the drug was said to be responsible for making its victims 'zombies'. Montgomery was fully aware that *Hyzopran* was styled along those lines, but further refinement would allow humans to perform murderous yet necessary tasks without the crippling burden of guilt and shame which usually followed. It was a brutal solution, but not as brutal as the slow death of a prisoner of war or a lifetime of extreme anxiety, depression, and isolation.

Montgomery believed in Blake's dream. He was a Proposal Manager for the Meese Corporation, a non-profit organization that contracted with the Department of Defense, the overseer of D.A.R.P.A. Located within the walls of Meese was a government think tank of top theoretical physicists and professors known as the board of approvers. They gave the green light to projects needing more funding. But the board was hiding a much darker secret; their real name was the *JASONS*, named for the Greek hero who sailed to the end of the world to search for the magical golden fleece of good fortune.

The *JASONS* were founded in 1960, two years after D.A.R.P.A. began deciding which projects would receive further funding and development for government utilization. The *JASONS* would take over that process—at least, that was their original purpose. Naturally, the group was top secret, so top secret that no president was ever informed of their separate identities. Just in case the shit ever hit the fan.

The group had access to limitless funds. After the first few years, they realized accountability was a non-issue since no one knew who they were, where they were housed, or how they operated—no one, that is, except a chosen few, like Montgomery. Since money was no object, the *JASONS* based their decisions on the ideas that appealed to them rather than cost/benefit or risk analyses, and once they'd had a taste of ultimate power, there was no going back.

Blake was a rising star at Meese. Her synthetic version of

scopolamine was sheer genius. If she delivered a weak presentation now and was refused further consideration, it would mean the end of her career.

Montgomery rubbed his hands together. "Think of *Hyzopran* as your baby. Would you hesitate to bring a beautiful and gifted child into the world?"

Blake allowed herself to smile. It softened her face and warmed up her eyes. A blush painted her skin baby-pink. She turned to watch the video on a 72-inch screen. "It's the example we're using to sell the idea that I have a problem with. It shows the very type of brutality we are trying to stop. And if *I* have a problem with it…"

"Ah, I see, the board will too. Well, they won't. Unfortunately. War is far more brutal without *Hyzopran*. If the drug does half what you say it can, the only thing they'll care about is how soon you can roll it out. Believe me.

"There's something else, too. The moment you started working for Meese, your project became their intellectual property. You know that. You knew that. These old codgers are no boy scouts, Katherine. They might have been, back in the 60's, but with the money and power they have now, they're nothing short of demigods. If they like an idea and they decide to fund it, research it, and use it, well, they can do any Goddamn thing they want to with it. It's top secret, so you have no recourse whatsoever. And if you get in their way, I guarantee you'll end up in a federal prison wearing a number for a name. You have to decide right now if you think this drug is important enough to humanity to fight for. If you do, stow your scruples. Look, the board is only a means to an end, Katherine. Once the drug is developed and eventually mainstreamed, they won't care what you do with it. So what do you say, Katherine? *Hyzopran* for humanity?"

She shook his hand. "*Hyzopran* for humanity."

"Let's knock the ball out of the park, kiddo."

Montgomery cared for his protégés as if they were his own children. They might not be perfect or behave the way he wanted them to all the time, but he did his best to influence and guide them. Their purity of intention and altruism kept him on his toes and on the straight and narrow when he might easily have become a self-serving elitist.

When he was a young man, Monty inherited a fortune of 8.7

million dollars from an uncle who'd been an art collector and who'd once told him that money was like fertilizer; you had to spread it around to make things grow. He could have spent the rest of his life doing nothing, but instead, he chose to do everything. He became a philanthropist and a humanitarian.

There was a special place in Monty's heart for the Impressionists. The artist painted things the way he saw them—not necessarily the way they really were. A million dots and dabs of light and shadow looked messy and grainy up close but became perfectly smooth and clearly defined from a distance. One of his favorites was Cezanne's *Still Life with Fruit Basket.* The basket overflows slightly to showcase abundance, good fortune and largesse. That was how Monty felt about life and his waistline.

***

Arleen and Monty liked to read in bed.

"*Scientific American*? I thought you had the audible version."

"Dr. Blake gave it to me before I left. There's an article I want to read on South American insects that use venom to daze..." He sighed. "Never mind; it's just bug stuff. Nothing."

"*Yugh.*"

Monty tossed the magazine in the direction of a chair. Turning slowly toward her, he growled. She giggled uncontrollably.

Montgomery turned out the light. "*Umpf!*"

"What is it, baby?"

"Nothing."

"Umm, hmm. C'mon, *give.*"

"How do you know something's on my mind?"

"The same way I know everything that goes on in your mind, dear. I'm clairvoyant. Now come on, really, what is it?"

"Well, it's Dr. Blake. She made a proposal to the board. It could be a miracle drug, Arleen, but it has to be studied on a much wider scale and for a much longer period of time. You know that if they approve it, they own it."

"Yes. Everyone knows that. You mean to say she's balking *now*?"

"Well, a little. She's worried about it being misused, but she made the pitch today, so it's out of her hands, now. Do you think I did the right thing by convincing her to make her presentation to those twelve lunatics?"

"Who made the final decision, Monty?"

"She did, of course."

"Monty, you remember that *Cezanne* you love so much?"

He nodded.

"Haven't you said a thousand times that when you view it from further away it comes into perspective? You're standing too close. Take a few steps back."

"You mean you actually listen to all the crap that comes out of my mouth?"

"Not all the time, dear. Now listen to me; she's a big girl! You made her aware of all the arguments for and against the approval, you told her what the negative aspects were if she moved forward with its testing and development, and she made the choice. It's not yours to make, and that's the long and the short of it. At least she has you to look out for her, and you have a degree of oversight. If you can't live with that, Monty, then quit. So now that you're standing far enough back to see the big picture, you blockhead, go to sleep."

"Yes, dear." He hugged her tight, kissed her good night and rolled onto his stomach, but he didn't fall asleep for a long time.

*Arleen's right, but she doesn't know the whole story either. And I can't tell her. If she knew what these geezers were capable of, she'd think I was out of my mind. If she ever finds out what this compound is for and that I helped it along the pipeline, she'll leave me, and I won't blame her.*

*I want to quit, but I have to stay. I need to document everything I know so far and make them understand that I'll be documenting the rest of it, too.*

# Chapter Eight

Alison grabbed the blanket with a balled fist and screamed. She'd just woken up from a nightmare.

*What a horrible dream! What was the name of the guy? Oh, right—David something...David...Florio! That was the name. I must know the name from school or something. He must have been a real monster if I wanted to kill him so much. It seemed so real!*

A loud ring sent a jolt through her.

"What do you want, Jeannie? I don't feel good, and I want to go back to bed."

"You don't have to rip my head off, Alison. Look, a strange phone number keeps showing up on my caller I.D. It's the same number you used last night to text me for a ride home. I figured you accidentally brought home the wrong phone, but when I tried calling it back, no one answered. No voice mail. Nothing. So I decided to try calling your regular number, and you answered. What's going on?"

"Going on?" Alison asked with creeping apprehension.

"Allie, I called you back several times this morning on a number that turns out to be foreign, like *overseas* foreign."

"I must have dropped my phone at the *Collective* and picked up someone else's. I haven't been out since then."

"Huh? Then what do you call last night's adventure?"

Alison thought she might faint. "Last night's...*what*?"

"Oh for God's sake, Allie, quit fooling around! You said he was so hot he practically burst into flames."

"Flames?"

"Yes, *flames*! What about the cell phone, Allie? Do you think it came from his place? Geez, what was his name again?"

"I have to hang up."

"But what about the..."

Alison punched the off button and threw the phone across the room. She ran to the computer to check the headlines. If anything in her dream really happened last night, she'd see it there.

\*\*\*

Carter read Deborah Decker's dating profile a dozen times or more on a window left open on David Florio's desktop computer. The message thread implied that David and Deborah had met. Had she visited him last night? She left a phone number for Florio in her last text. Carter dialed it, hoping she'd agree to talk to him. No one named Deborah Decker lived within 500 miles of the victim, but he called the number over and over. It was repeatedly forwarded to voicemail that did not identify its owner.

Later, the local New Jersey P.D. turned the laptop over to the F.B.I. who traced the address to Switzerland. They discovered quite easily that the I.P. address used to create Deborah's dating profile also originated overseas. Too easily, in fact. The true owner of the I.P. address was counting on that. He was right under their nose and hiding in plain sight. It was really very simple, so simple a child could have done it. He used the V.P.N. browser on his cell phone to send the lab team off on a wild goose chase while he used another one, and *voila*!

\*\*\*

Carter met Deeprose in a local hole-in-the-wall café for a cup of coffee and an update meeting.

Deeprose shook her head. "This Deborah Decker mighta been an overseas scammer lookin' to steal our victim's I.D. It could be unrelated to the crime, Agent Carter."

"Maybe, but we don't want to make the mistake of overlooking something that might be important. No assumptions, remember? In any case, we know Florio was murdered and that's something." Carter looked grim this morning. There wasn't much to go on.

"You mean the lab has determined the home's occupant was the man who burned to death?"

"I can't begin to give the kind of detail Agent Seacrest could, but in a word, 'yes'."

60

"How'd she pull that off? Most of the victim was bacon."

"She had his teeth and pulled a blood sample from his foot, which was, surprisingly, still intact. They were a match with Florio's medical records. It's David Florio. Positively."

"Did she find anything else from the scene that would help us, Agent Carter?"

"She most certainly did. There was no murder weapon, of course, but from a forensic standpoint, we have reason to believe Florio's death was suspicious. Jill discovered some pretty interesting organic compounds at the scene using chromatography."

"What's chromatography? How does it work?"

"It's a method of separating and analyzing mixtures of chemicals by flowing them over or through paper, glass, or gas. First, the mixture has to be dissolved in a liquid. We'd found the remnants of a liquid that dried on the victim's pants. The lab crew placed the particles in airtight containers and got them back to the lab so Jill could use a process called gas-liquid chromatography to separate the gas from the original liquid. The compounds in the liquid form turned out to be lighter fluid."

Deeprose eyed her cold coffee with disgust. "Still, it coulda been a suicide."

"That is a possibility, of course, but would you kill yourself by setting yourself on fire? I can think of a half dozen better ways to go. Besides, the other liquid found at the scene was red wine, also spilled on the victim's pant legs, as well as on the dining room floor."

Deeprose stared absently out of the shop's window, mulling over this new information. "Red wine and lighter fluid. Hmm. If he did have a dinner guest, she mighta doused him with lighter fluid to ignite the fire and with wine to feed it. Ah suppose he would have let a stranger in if he thought he was gonna get lucky. Ah don't think this is suicide, sir, but Ah don't see any evidence pointin' towards a thrill kill or a copycat, either."

Carter pursed his lips. "Not so fast, Agent. Have you considered any other possibility besides murder, like an accident?"

"An accident, sir, with lighter fluid and red wine poured all over the victim?"

"O.K., so you're pretty convinced it *is* a murder. Let's think about that. If it's just another murder, why are we here? After all, we have our own murder to investigate at the *Cloisters*. The only reason for us to be here would be to confirm whether or not it connects to the museum murder. By the way, you might want to start taking notes."

Carter cleared his throat and dove into the conundrum. "Now. Fischetti more than suggests both are thrill kills; a thrill kill has a high possibility of tying together two seemingly unrelated murders. One doer could have committed two completely unrelated crimes for no other reason than the high of having done it. The victims could have been randomly chosen.

"However, if there are multiple and unrelated doers, which we now think there are, why are we here? Fischetti knew the possibility was strong that we would conclude they were separate and unrelated. We've done that. The possibility that *both* murders are thrill kills is extremely low—*not impossible*—but it would be a million-to-one shot. That leaves one remaining possibility."

"And that is, sir?"

"He wanted to be certain he could rule out thrill kills but he thinks the two murders are still somehow connected, maybe by one entity—like the mob or some other group or individual. What's your take on it now, Agent?"

"We're pretty sure there are two separate killers from the differences in victims, crime scenes, and the method of murder. One was planned much better than the other. Mob hits or organized crime? Ah don't buy it. We'd have heard all about it on the street by now. Would you mind tellin' me a little more about thrill kills, sir?"

Carter was in his element and loving it. "Thrill kills are not fad murders committed by people out for kicks on a Saturday night; they are committed by disturbed individuals looking for the self-gratification they can only get from taking a life. If he does it again and again, he's a serial killer, but there's one major difference between this type of serial killer and the ones we usually see; he chooses the victim at random, and there is no relation to or any feeling toward the victim, whatsoever. It's rare, but it happens."

"Can you give me a concrete example of thrill murders, sir? Actual cases?"

"In 2003, there was a string of thrill kills in New York. There were also several sniper shootings in Washington, D.C. the same year. There are three basic profiles of thrill killers. First, if the doer is a deeply disturbed individual, like a returning war veteran or a student who opens fire in a classroom full of kids, this type is usually prepared to die or commit suicide once it's all over.

"Second, the doer might be a highly intellectual, even brilliant person who kills to show his superiority over the victim and the authorities. This person has delusions of grandeur, a super inflated ego, and seeks only to prove he is smart enough to pull off the perfect crime.

"Third, and this is by far the most likely, the doer has a constant feeling of inadequacy, and what drives him to kill is a need to wield power so that he can feel powerful. This killer also has serial potential. So what do you think our next move should be, Agent?"

Deeprose frowned as she leafed through her notes and tried to figure out what to look for next. "Well…we can still try to find the person whose photo appeared on the dating site. And we have that dark, grainy camera shot of the museum perp. Maybe the lab has some answers by now."

The teacher in Carter was having a bang-up time. Deeprose was fully engaged and her brain was humming. Slogging through all the facts to come up with a suggestion for the next step of the investigation was a good habit for her to get into on her first case. It had always helped Carter see the issues, the possibilities and next steps.

"Both the name and profile are phony. Deborah Decker doesn't exist. What makes you think the person in the photo is real?"

"Agent Seacrest's discovery of the accelerant, sir. Ah found no container in the home or in the garbage cans which might have contained the lighter fluid."

Carter looked at her with pride. "Aha! You think someone took the evidence away. Good job! But why a woman?"

Deeprose raised her cup of cold coffee and grimaced before taking a swig. "Because we have no other suspects except her, so we have to hope against hope that the photo matches a real person and that the video of the museum murder reveals a face. Besides, Ah just don't see a man killin' another man this way. This one was done by a woman."

"Exactly."

Carter dug his cell phone out of his suit pocket to read a text from Jill. "You will come to find that Agent Seacrest doesn't like sharing information over the phone. She requests our presence at the lab."

\*\*\*

Seacrest held a photo in her hand like a trophy. "We've got a partial print from the New Brunswick, New Jersey crime scene."

Carter hadn't realized he'd been holding his breath. It came out in a whoosh of relief. At the same time, Deeprose sucked in her breath sharply and held it, waiting to hear if there was more.

"We also discovered a shoeprint in the yard. Carter, it matches the *Stridewell* shoe print we found at the *Cloisters*."

Deeprose let out her breath looking just as deflated as she felt. "So there is only one killer for all three murders after all? If we can find the museum killer, will the shoeprint be enough to place him at both scenes?"

Seacrest placed the photo in Carter's hands. "If he still has the shoes, yes. Agent Deeprose, I'm a scientist. My primary function here is to collect and analyze the evidence and give then you my professional opinion based on the test results. Solving the case is up to you and Carter."

Deeprose sighed and raised her hands in surrender. "Ah apologize, Agent Seacrest. Pardon ma bad manners. Ma coffee fix was less than spectacular this mornin'. At least we have more to go on. Perhaps one of them will make a mistake and show their hand."

\*\*\*

Michael Santiago knew by the next morning the Cloisters murders had been real and that he'd committed them. He saw the breaking story on *ABC News* and in the newspaper. He knew withdrawal when he felt it. As dull as he was, he knew he'd been drugged, and that it could only have happened at the *Collective*.

The thing was, he didn't care. He felt great. He wanted more of that drug, and he wanted to feel that power again.

*I'll get another invitation for next week's meeting in a day or two, but I'll bet no one gets dosed twice. It's too big a chance to take.*

*They probably pick first-timers only. I'll bet it was in the drinks. They invite the newbies backstage one by one to meet the team, and...bingo! The newbies are killers.*

*I wonder what their game is. Maybe they'd be willing to give me more of that drug to keep me quiet. Nah, that's asking for a bullet between the eyes. ...Know what? I'm just gonna mix myself a very large vodka tonic, relax my brain, and think about it a little...*

An hour and five cocktails later, Michael had his answer. There had been a girl at the meeting he followed home to Jersey. She was invited backstage which meant she'd also been assigned a murder. Her name was...*Alison. Alison Whiteway!*

*I remember now. I followed her and her friend back to New Jersey. They must have been driving to the victim's place. I was still outside when the other girl came back for her. I'm going to scare the hell out of that girl. I'll threaten to blow the whistle on her. She has no idea who I am; she has no idea I did a murder myself. She'll do anything I tell her to do. And what she's gonna do is distract the Silver Man's team at the next meeting just long enough for me to find their stash of drugs, grab them and run.*

In a drunken stupor, he nodded off and slept like a baby, without regret, fear, or shame.

# Chapter Nine

Deeprose pulled up her email and noticed one from her father. She bit her lips.

*Every time Ah try somethin' new, he thinks Ah'm doin' the wrong thing. Always judgin'. Always criticizin'. Ah can imagine what's in that email—either Ah should come on home and find a husband or take that local P.D. job and take care of him.*

Retired Colonel Deeprose was her only family now. Her mother passed on when she was a teenager, and she had no brothers or sisters. His long absences were hard on her. When her mother got sick, she took care of her and eventually, buried her. After that, her relationship with her father became more and more strained. His life was a lonely one. She knew he wanted her to come back home, but she just couldn't do it. Deeprose wanted to live before she died.

In her apartment way up in the sky, she stared out at the busy streets below. On the other side of the glass pane was adventure. She placed her hand on the glass and felt the reverberation of life teeming outside. Inside, she was torn up by her father's reaction to leaving home. She recalled breaking the news of her F.B.I. application to her father over dinner at his favorite restaurant, the *Rattlesnake Saloon*. He was deeply disappointed. "If you'd stayed in the military, you would have had a stellar career. Now, you'll have to start all over again. Right from the bottom."

Maybe he was unaware of the power he had over her, but she didn't think so. He'd use any weapon at his disposal to win a war.

*Shoot! Ah have one life to live, an' Ah'm gonna live it!*

Dear Daddy,

I'm happy here, and I'm taking a bite out of the Big Apple. I've been told by my superior that my interviewing technique is on point. I can't discuss my cases any further, but rest assured your little girl will always get her man.

Love,
Shania

Her duty done, she allowed her thoughts to wander back to the museum investigation. She had a strange feeling about the acting curator. His hasty retreat when they met seemed odd to her, but then again, he was new; maybe he was just busy and didn't want to get involved. She also thought about the man whose hazy face they'd captured on the museum video camera. She rose from her chair with renewed confidence and, after a moment of reflection, decided to put Jill Seacrest's lab skills to the test.

\*\*\*

Alison was confused and hungover, but her mind would not let her rest. The excitement and hope she'd felt at the *Collective* was gone. The new day was a reminder that her life was over. As the morning wore on, she spiraled down into a deep depression. By mid-afternoon, all she wanted to do was turn off her brain. That meant only one thing to Alison—moonshine in a mason jar. The thought of getting it broke through her usual lethargy, so she got herself together and set out for the bus. Her favorite liquor store was in a mall in Old Bridge. It was the only one that carried her brand, *Everclear*.

Alison caught the N.J. Transit's number 68 bus as it passed by her building. One other person got in after her. He followed her as she pushed her way through a crowd of teens and dropped into the only seat left. He stood up with everyone else, hanging onto a horizontal rail high over the passengers' heads. Had she noticed him staring at her, she would have recognized him from the meeting, but Alison, who was used to being invisible, treated everyone else as if they were, too.

She pressed her cheek against the window to soak up the last warm rays of the afternoon sun.

The passenger standing over her whistled as he breathed. Normally, she would have found it annoying, but today it was comfortably familiar. She couldn't recall where she heard it, but she knew she had.

When she finally arrived, the store was empty, except for the cashier. Alison forced a small smile. "Credit or debit?" he asked.

"Credit. Definitely credit." She slid her card into the machine to pay.

Outside, someone tapped her on the shoulder from behind. She pivoted, gripping the bag containing the heavy glass mason jar. "Who are you? Don't come near me!"

Stepping closer, a young man who couldn't have been older than twenty-five, spoke to her in an insultingly familiar tone. "I want to talk to you, Alison. I saw you at the *Collective*. And the night after that."

"Well, I didn't see you there or anywhere else. How do you know my name? What do you want?"

He grabbed the bag out of her hand and hurled it at the pavement.

She heard the glass break. "Are you *crazy*?!" Don't come near me!"

*My liquor!*

He took another step closer. "Lower your voice, Alison, or you'll attract attention, and a murderess can't afford to call attention to herself."

She heard that same whistling noise as he spoke.

*I know I heard him whistle like that on the bus, but where did I hear that sound before today? Oh, God! He's not lying; he really was there.*

Alison looked around frantically and opened her mouth to yell, but his hand shot out and gripped her entire lower face with it. With his other arm, he pulled her in close as if they were a couple. People flowed around them towards the bus stop, showing no interest at all. "See that? No one cares. Go ahead and scream your head off if you want the cops so bad. While you're at it, you can fill them in on your trip out to Florio's place."

She looked scared now.

"That's better. Now, let's get this straight; I saw you at the meeting. I followed you home and to the scene of the crime last night.

I saw you go in and come back out. That's right, honey. It was all over the news. One word from me places you at the scene. I bet the cops are panting for a lead."

Things were unraveling at lightning speed. Alison kicked him in the shin. Hard.

"*Owwwwwwww!!*"

She made a dash for the bus stop where she thought she'd be safe among the crowd, but that didn't stop him. Michael pursued her right into the middle of the crowd milling around, grabbed her wrist and squeezed. When she finally stopped struggling, he dragged her around the side of a building and forced her to her knees.

"You're hurting me! Let me go!"

"Not happening."

He pulled her up by the hair. It hurt terribly, but she neither cried nor looked him in the eye. Only someone who'd suffered a lifetime of abuse could have taken punishment like that without flinching. She could tell he liked inflicting pain. He let her go, but there was clearly no getting away, so she tried another approach. "All right, I give up. What do you want?"

A menacing smile spread across his face. "I want you to help me get my hands on their stash." Michael shoved her up against the wall.

She seethed. "You must have done a murder, too. You'll get *caught*! Why pick on me? *Why me?*"

Michael had her by the shoulders. His legs were spread apart so she couldn't kick him again. She jerked her head to the left and right, but there was no avoiding him. His mouth came crashing down on hers in an assault that split her lip. Then he gave her a final shove and stood back. "That was just as bad as I knew it would be. Come on. We have work to do."

They both stood there, angry and out of breath. Alison's lip was already swollen. Warm blood and salty tears raced each other to the ground.

In surreal silence, she placed her hand in his, and they headed for the number 68, together. His raw brutality was strangely erotic to Alison, who'd been taught that those who cared for you, beat you.

\*\*\*

69

Carter hoped to join Jill for a late dinner, but she was stuck at the lab and didn't expect to get home until late at night. He'd been looking forward to a quiet dinner with her all day and was disappointed.

Fischetti's attitude and strange behavior put him on his guard. He didn't want to burden Deeprose with his misgivings, but he knew she wasn't fooled into thinking everything was fine. At the lab, the friction between Seacrest and her supervisor was already reaching the boiling point. Carter needed to relax and empty his mind, because there was something about this that just didn't feel right. He could smell it in the air. Something was circling above him like a vulture over a dead carcass. Carter admitted he felt vulnerable and resentful because he knew Fischetti was holding out on him.

*Maybe we should just pack up and get out of here.*

He gave his cell phone a verbal command. "Addresses and phone numbers. Buddhist temples near Federal Plaza, N.Y."

***

The *Mahayana Buddhist Temple* on Canal Street greeted Carter with a splash of red and gold. Its awnings were lined with scripture the agent could not decipher, but he knew it was probably a message of peace and welcome.

The statue of a gigantic elephant was just inside, near the altar. It seemed out of place to him.

*Perhaps it represents my inner trumpet.*

Carter smiled at the thought. He brushed past the statue to take a white candle from a nearby table. It was meant to serve as a tool for defeating inner turmoil. Gazing steadily at the flame, he peeled away a layer of confusion and conflict that was clouding his vision and made an attempt to identify and understand the issues before letting them go.

Carter came away feeling there was only one issue he had any power over—his and Jill's relationship with Agent Deeprose. He decided to ask Seacrest to make more of an effort to get to know her. He felt she needed a friend as much as a mentor. He'd have to try harder, too.

Carter told himself the same thing he always did when faced with something he didn't understand.

*I'll file it away under 'New Case, New Partner' for now and take a look at it later. Maybe it'll make more sense then.*

Carter thought of himself as a master of emotion and turmoil, but the truth was that he was unable to cope with either. At some point, his mental filing cabinet was going to get too crowded, and when that happened, he'd have to come to terms with a lifetime of putting off until tomorrow what he should have examined yesterday.

Settled in a taxi and on his way home, his attention was drawn to a small T.V. screen on the windshield. A crowd of people were fighting over a hot, new toy. The news clip zoomed in on a policewoman separating two men who'd become violent over the last video game on a shelf. Her partner cuffed them both from behind. The driver glanced at Carter in his rear view mirror. Jabbing a finger at the screen, he said dryly, "I see the peace and serenity of the Christmas season has hit New York particularly early this season. *What a surprise.*"

# Chapter Ten

Although it was still dark, and very, *very* early, Deeprose was already waiting in line for coffee, shivering. She had Seacrest on her mind and thought a friendly gesture, like bringing her a coffee, might make her a bit nicer to work with.

*Ah'll bet she drinks mocha cappuccino or a double chocolate java latte. Definitely high maintenance.*

She giggled to herself because she had absolutely no idea what either of those things were. She drank coffee. Period. A half hour later, she walked out, disgusted.

*Ah'll never understand why these folks stand in line in the cold and dark for a half hour or more to be served a lousy cup of coffee at an outrageous price by a sociopath.*

Deeprose decided that Seacrest was right; she could interpret the evidence but it was up to Carter and Deeprose to catch the killers. Now was not the time to play it safe, or for that matter, too nicely. Seacrest could be a hard potato to boil, but Deeprose didn't pass the F.B.I. exam without proving she knew how to manipulate her suspects as well as her colleagues when it was to her advantage to do so.

She ambled down the hallway to the D.N.A. lab with a very hot cup of coffee in each hand.

*Shoot! They had to choose this mornin' to discover their coffee is always cold.*

The doors to the lab swung open just as she was about to walk in. Caught off guard, she scrambled out of the way and mumbled, "Mornin'."

Seacrest's smile was disarming. "Are one of those for me, I hope?"

Deeprose handed her the fancy coffee hoping she guessed right.

72

"Ah thought we could discuss an idea Ah have about our museum murders, that is, if y'all have the time." Deeprose felt a bit intimidated by Seacrest.

"Thanks! *Ummmm, coffee, coffee, **coffee**!* I need to get my supervisor's authorization to continue an examination of the blood from the Jersey victim, but I'll be glad to hear your idea if you care to walk with me."

"Sure!" To keep up with the tall, willowy blonde, Deeprose had to take two steps for every one of Seacrest's.

*Good thing there's enough chocolate in that coffee to stop a freight train.*

Seacrest glanced quizzically at the cup. "'*M*' for murder?"

"'*M*' for mocha. Ah hope that's O.K. Ah made a guess."

Seacrest sniffed the beverage through the lid. "As long as it's not decaf, it could taste like baked beans and I wouldn't care."

"Got a vendetta against decaf, Ah see."

"And it goes way back. The first time Carter suggested I switch to a decaffeinated anything was also the last. Let's just say chamomile tea is not the best way to start my day."

"Ah feel you." Deeprose sympathized. "My daddy says decaf oughtta be outlawed."

"Now there's a man I'd like to meet— the no-nonsense type."

Deeprose sighed. "You couldn't coax him out of Alabama for all the coffee beans in Colombia, and especially not up *here*."

"Sounds like you miss him." Seacrest threw her a quick glance as they walked.

"He's all the family Ah have, Agent Seacrest. That's why Ah want to get off to a better start with y'all than Ah have. Ah want to apologize for houndin' you about the cases yesterday. Ah'm just a little frustrated, Ah guess. So far, we're chasin' our tails and gettin' nowhere. Ah plan to make my home here, an' Ah could use a few good friends."

Seacrest came to a sudden stop. "I'll tell you what, Agent Deeprose, we're all working too hard and not playing enough. Why don't we start discovering the city together? Do you like jazz?"

"Yes, ma'am!"

"Then it's a date. We'll firm it up later. Now, I've really got to hurry. What did you want to ask me?"

73

"Ah was hopin' you would try to lift some prints from the inside of the gloves the killer wore at the museum. The material is not latex."

"Already working on it. I just have to convince my supervisor to spring for the budget and authorize the procedure. Underneath the metallic sequins, the material consists mostly of leather."

"So, it's a possibility?"

"Yes. I'll give it one out of three chances of producing a usable print. I'll need to find good ridge detail if I'm going to find anything at all."

"Why doesn't your boss want to authorize the test and the budget?"

Seacrest clenched her jaw. "Because the gloves are irreplaceable artifacts, because I can't guarantee a usable result, and because he has no balls."

Deeprose turned away so Seacrest couldn't see her smile.

"I'll get the approval, no worries, Agent. I usually get what I want when it's that important. The gloves escaped blood damage. The killer tossed them off as he ran from the scene. They were found halfway down the hall from the body. I was about to exclude them from further examination, so if we go for this procedure, it will mean cutting them up into a few pieces."

"What process would y'all use, exactly?"

"Essentially, I'd be using the Ninhydrin-Heptane Carrier process. We dip the gloves in a solution first and then cut them up to observe them both inside and out. Hopefully, in a few hours, ridge detail might be revealed, but I doubt we'll capture enough to prove the same perpetrator carried out both crimes."

"That's just it. Ah don't believe there is only one killer."

Seacrest glanced at her watch, sucked in her breath and resumed her walk in double time as she answered Agent Deeprose. "Unfortunately, we won't know the answer to that question until we finish examining the evidence from both scenes."

"Have you found any prints in the Florio home that aren't his own?"

"We have at least one other print found in the victim's bathroom, but we haven't been able to identify it, yet. If it belongs to the killer, he or she has no previous record. The cleanup job was almost professionally done, so the murderer was clever, like she'd done it before. Then again, we found traces of an accelerant and wine on the body. Not so clever. It's strange, you know? It's as if it was done by an amateur who was given instructions for most of the things she did and none for others. All we can do now is what we do best—stick to procedure and hope for a miracle."

Seacrest chugged her coffee and looked behind her to make sure Deeprose was still jogging along. "I have to wonder, though, how the victim sat still for his own execution. He wasn't tied up or anything, so my question is, was he given something to make him feel pleasure instead of pain or something to make him feel nothing at all? There's not enough left of him to autopsy, so that piece of the puzzle may be lost forever."

Deeprose stopped walking and turned to face Seacrest head-on.

"The Jersey killin' tells us much more than the museum murders do, which were half assed compared to it. Ah don't know about the other one, but this one was definitely premeditated. *Ma* money's on Deborah Decker for the Jersey case. If she really was there, she can't have slipped in and out that easily. Someone must have seen her. In ma mind there are two different killers. One is pretty dumb, has big feet, and either didn't plan this at all or was set up. The other one's smart, obedient, and hates men. Ah mean, *really* hates 'em."

"It may seem that way, Agent, but psychological profiling doesn't always fit the perpetrator in question, and investigations have a way of becoming much muddier before they become clear. Keep an open mind. Listen more than you talk. You can watch Carter's back better by keeping your eyes and ears open."

Deeprose finally got to the crux of what was bothering her. "Ah'm not rootin' for the killers to be two different people, Agent, but based on both crimes scenes, Ah think they are. The thing is, for whatever reason, the Bureau seems to *wanna* hang this all on one fella, and in my estimation, they want him to be a serial or thrill killer."

Seacrest's face flushed. "I see. So that's why you're pushing so hard for the glove test." Seacrest turned and walked down the hall in her usual fury of motion. "Agent Deeprose, Carter's the best. You'll learn a lot from him. Oh, yeah, thanks for the coffee."

*\*\*\**

Michael drove Alison to his apartment on the Upper West Side. It was slightly larger than a walk-in closet, and it was a pigsty.

"Sit down." He cleared the books off his leather couch with a sweep of his arm.

Alison eyed the ripped leather and wondered how it got that way. She knew everyone wished someone dead once in a while, but she was no killer. Michael, on the other hand, was a different story. The moment had worn off. She didn't feel safe here.

Michael sat in a chair facing her. "Let's get down to business."

She glanced at the books scattered on the floor to see if one of the hard covers might be heavy enough to knock him out.

Michael knew exactly what she was thinking. "I didn't bring you here to kill you. Like I said before, we have a future together. Call it a limited engagement." His smile was cold.

Alison was feeling sick again. "I don't feel good, Michael. I need something for it, but I don't know what."

"Calm down; you're *Jonesing*. It hits you big time the next day."

"*Jonesing?*"

"Yeah, you never heard of it? Alison, you took the drug one time and you're already addicted. You need more of it, and so do I. That's why we're going to team up. We're going to steal their inventory, keep some, and sell the rest. They can't do anything about it, Alison, because they can't go to the cops. It's a piece of cake."

*I do miss the voices and that wonderful sense of being filled up with acceptance and approval. It was like having my own cheer leading team inside my head. I want that feeling again. But just the feeling. I don't need to take drugs and kill people to get that feeling. But he does.*

"Once you're done helping me, I'll let you go. You have no choice, Alison. I saw what you did, and I have the license number of the car that left the scene."

"What about you? If you got dosed, you did a kill, too."

"You don't know that, Alison, and you have no proof, anyway. Go ahead. Call my bluff. It's only a couple of hundred years in prison for you if you guess wrong." He shrugged. "The point is, they knew or guessed we'd get addicted to it. I can't figure out why they'd take that chance unless they wanted to use us again, which makes no sense, or they hoped we might overdose. But we didn't and now we need more, so we have to get it without them knowing who took it and without getting caught. If we're caught, we're dead."

"You're not a man; you're something that crawls on the ground, Michael. You and I are *not* alike. I will turn your ass in and throw myself on the mercy of the court if I have to. I was drugged and coerced. I won't be held responsible—at least I hope not—but whatever happens, I'd rather take my chances with the cops than team up with you."

"I saw you at the meeting, Alison. Don't lie to me; you loved the message. Admit it, you agree that the only way to live better right now is to take what you want from the people who have it all. It's not murder. It's a war."

"O.K., I knew the *Silver Man* was talking about taking what we should have had all along and being willing to defend it if we had to, but I thought he was speaking in hyperbole. It was the message that was important, not the method.

"I know nothing's gonna change, not for me in this lifetime. I know crime pays, for some people, but not for me. I'm not going to help you deal drugs for profit. I don't have to kill to get what I want. I went to the meeting to meet people like myself. I was interested in the message too, until I realized what I did at Florio's the next night. The *Silver Man* did far more than talk about his viewpoint. He forced it on me, and now I'm a murderess!"

She sighed. "But, as much as I hate to admit it, I guess you're right; if it'll give me the proof I need to clear myself, I guess I have no choice. I'll help you, but when this is done and you have your bag of drugs, I walk away clean. I don't know you, and you don't know me."

He stalked out of the room and left her there. She heard his bedroom door slam. Alison curled up on the couch without a blanket or a pillow and cried herself to sleep.

*** 

Michael filled her in on his plan the next morning as they sat eating Captain Crunch with milk that smelled highly questionable. "I found someone else who was dosed at the meeting and tracked her to a bar downtown. She never did her kill."

"So? Good for her."

"Alison, don't be dense. Do you think these are just a bunch of crazies dosing people at their meetings for kicks? They sent us out to murder people, you dope! They must be watching us. They must know who did their murder and who didn't. We aren't safe as long as they know who we are and where we live, and *they* aren't safe until they're sure we can't connect them to the meetings, the drug, and the kills. That means we're on their hit list. We're not useful anymore."

"No kidding! Did you figure that out all by yourself? So why do you care about this girl, then? How does she figure into this?"

"We have to find her. We'll go to that bar again and see if she turns up or if the bartender knows where we can find her. She still has her assignment and the drug takes 48 hours to wear off. They'll still be expecting her to do her kill. That's our chance, Alison."

"Huh?"

Michael looked at the ceiling and rolled his eyes. "Look, if we're lucky, she'll still remember who she's supposed to kill and where to find him. By tomorrow, she'll be climbing the walls for another dose. If she bought into the idea of killing for what she wants in life, it won't be hard to convince Eliza—that's her name—to help us out of this mess and get more of the killing drug at the same time."

"Michael, *I'm* not climbing the walls. You don't seem to be in such bad shape today, either. It's possible that not everyone who takes it gets addicted to it. Why should she help us, anyway? She hasn't done anything except resist a drug and a post-hypnotic suggestion."

"If she remembers what happened then she'll know that her own life is worthless, now. The only way to keep herself safe is to help us expose them. We're going to get her to tell us who she was supposed to eliminate so we can convince that person to help us in return for our protection. Her victim is a walking bull's eye, now. Besides, Eliza is the other half of our proof. She's the only one we know of who was dosed but hasn't killed. That makes hers the only testimony anyone will listen to. The *Silver Man* gets busted, we're free and clear, and I have their entire stash as compensation. Plus, we get the undying gratitude of an entire nation."

"The drug will be out of Eliza's system in 24 hours! She'll have no proof that she was dosed, stupid! If you take their stash, there's no proof they ever had it in the first place, either. Who's going to believe this girl?"

78

"Thought of that, already. We'll leave the *Silver Man* with enough of the drug to cover the next meeting. Once we have our samples, the cops'll listen to us and the *Collective* will be too hot to touch us. Her intended victim will back up Eliza's story once she realizes who wants her dead. I'll bet she can tell us a lot more than we already know. We have to stick together and see this through. There's no other way."

Alison broke down and cried. She couldn't trust him. She hated herself for what she'd done over the past few days, but she couldn't bring that poor man back to life. The only thing to do was to expose this killing *Collective*. She couldn't do it alone. Like it or not, they had to work together. She knew full well that all he wanted was their help stealing the drug, but to get it and keep it, he'd have to help her get justice. It could work.

When she'd cried herself out, Alison looked Michael in the eyes. "I hate to admit it, but the plan could work. You found the flaw in his operation, so I guess I should say thank you. Even if Eliza and her intended victim won't help us, just knowing who Eliza is, keeping her from doing her kill, and getting those samples should be enough to save ourselves."

"You see? We're already a team. We'll go to *McGee's* later on to see if she's there. If not, maybe the bartender will know where we can find her."

Alison got up and went into the bathroom to wash her face.

\*\*\*

Michael watched her walk away, thinking.

*God, that was easy. If the other two are as gullible as she is, I'm home free. Yes, Alison, it is a good plan. It's a great plan. Too bad it's not the one we're going to use. After I get the bag of drugs that sicko owes me for the money I left in that hole, all I have to do is make an anonymous call to the Silver Man's people and tell them Alison, Eliza and this third person stole their bag of drugs. The three of them will disappear, the drug will never be found, and I'm living on Easy Street.*

When she came back, she turned on the television. "There may be more news on our kills, and if there's been another murder since then, we need to know about it."

79

\*\*\*

Carter thought Agent Deeprose was going to meet him at the office when he got there, but all he found behind her desk was a computer in sleep mode.

*She must have begun the day without me. Oh boy, that's not good. I hope she's not going it alone because she thinks I've been steering her down the garden path. Even I don't believe these murders were done by thrill, serial or multiple serial killers. Please tell me she's not the type to take unnecessary risks. I so don't want to mentor another Seacrest...*

# Chapter Eleven

Deeprose took a deep breath before walking into the museum. The temporary curator, Mr. Moreland, had been there less than a week when he was replaced. She was here today to meet the new permanent curator, James Alquist.

She flashed her badge and extended a hand to him. "Good Afternoon, Mr. Alquist. Ah'm Special Agent Deeprose. Thank you for your time this mornin'. Do you know, sir, why Mr. Moreland chose not to stay on? Ah' mean, temporary positions are usually a formality, aren't they?"

"He was unable to stay on permanently. Mr. Moreland contacted me a few days ago. He said he'd met me about a year ago at one of his lectures on Impressionism and remembered me. You see, we spoke afterward. My daughter had scarlet fever at the time, and I remember him talking about working with a team of scientists who believed that curing disease was far less effective than eliminating it from the human genome altogether. However, the point is, Mr. Moreland remembered me, and that's how I'm here today."

*A temporary museum curator who also works with scientists messin' around with D.N.A.?*

"Mr. Moreland sounds like a fascinatin' man. Ah didn't have a chance to talk with him last week. Do you know where Ah might find him?"

"He said he was planning a series of lectures in several different countries; sort of a world tour."

"Thank you, Mr. Alquist. We'll follow up on that later. If you don't mind my askin', have y'all decided to let us test the gloves the killer used for finger prints?"

"Yes, I have. I've already spoken to the board of directors. You now have permission to use any materials you deem necessary to close your investigation. The gloves are priceless, but we'd rather sacrifice them than keep them if it means catching a killer and saving this museum from financial ruin."

"Ah truly appreciate that, Mr. Alquist." Deeprose noticed something unusual on Alquist's desk. As she spoke, she removed her Smartphone from her jacket pocket. "Ah see y'all have a book on Impressionist art on your desk. Does it belong to Mr. Moreland?"

"It did, but he left it here for me. In fact, he donated a painting to us which I'm sending over to the Metropolitan Museum of Art. Impressionist art doesn't fit in with our medieval theme. I just wanted to brush up on my knowledge of it before contacting the Met."

"Ah'd like to take a look at the paintin', if possible, Mr. Alquist."

"Certainly. Let's take a walk and view it together."

"Ballerinas! How beautiful they are!" She came as close as she dared to the precious painting to study the dancers at their rehearsal.

"It's a *Degas*." Alquist framed the painting with his hands. "You can *feel* the drama."

"They look worried."

"Yes, worried about their performance, I imagine, and more worried about not pleasing their master. That's what makes a *Degas* so special. His subjects were almost always ballerinas. I think he was fascinated by performance art. These ballerinas had one chance to get it right every evening, and when they could no longer perform, they either faded into obscurity as a fat man's mistress or they starved to death on the street. It was a hard life."

"Ah'm sure. Would it be all right if Ah took a photo of it?"

"Go right ahead, but please don't use your flash."

*Why would Moreland donate a painting done by a master of 19th century Impressionist art to a museum dedicated to medieval art? Ah don't know...the fear in those faces is unmistakable, even to someone who knows nothin' about art. They all seem so afraid. What are they tryin' to tell me?*

"Well, thank you for your time, Mr. Alquist. It was a pleasure meetin' you."

She read a text message from Carter as she left the building. He was worried about her. She texted back, "Ah went to the museum to meet the new curator. Ah think Ah'm on to somethin'. We'll talk later."

\*\*\*

Michael and Alison got off the train at 59th Street and Columbus Circle and walked along for a few blocks until he recognized the bar where Eliza sat drinking the night before.

"She won't believe us, Michael. She was able to resist the drug, so why should she believe us? She may call the police; then what do we do?"

"Calm down! We have leverage, Alison. She's in a lot of trouble; she just doesn't know it yet. Whether she completes her kill or not, she'll be next, just like we are. Her only choice is to help us, so for all our sakes, she needs to be convinced that helping us is the only way to help herself. She has to believe her life is in danger, because it is, so don't blow it."

Michael opened the door to *McGee's Pub* and looked around. He spotted Eliza at the bar right away. They seated themselves next to her and gave their order to the bartender.

Eliza was a mean drunk. She obviously came here often because she knew the bartender by name. "Gimme another, Jimmy."

"You've had enough, Eliza. It's time to go."

"I said *give me another drink*!"

Alison saw her chance. "We know her. We'll take care of it. Come on, Eliza, let's all sit down and have something to eat."

Eliza squinted at them. "Who the fuck are you? I don't want any food. I want another drink."

"All right, all right, but let's all sit down where we can talk. We'll take you home, don't worry."

They steered a weaving Eliza over to a table in the back of a section partitioned off by a brick wall. It was empty back there—the perfect spot for what they were about to tell her. Alison had the waiter bring them a pot of strong coffee. She poured just enough Irish whiskey in each mug to mollify Eliza. After several mugs, she seemed a little more coherent. "I think I should take her to the ladies' room to splash her face with some cold water."

As they cleared the doors, Eliza turned green and started to sweat. Suddenly, she went into a rage, kicking in stall doors and punching the mirror. "*That bitch*! I'm going to kill her for what she did to me! I hate her! She has to die. She has to …" Eliza passed out in Alison's arms.

*Wait a minute; she's not drunk at all! It's that drug...*

Alison half carried and half dragged Eliza outside, signaling Michael as they passed through the dining room. He got Eliza's address from the bartender, paid the bill, and told him they'd take her home. Outside, they searched her pockets and found her car keys. "We'll get her home and make sure she doesn't leave until the drug wears off. When she wakes up from the nightmare and sees us, I think she might be more willing to listen."

"I hope she lives alone."

"Jimmy said she's a loser with a gutter mouth—no job, no friends. She goes in there almost every night and drinks until she's stoned. He usually winds up cutting her off and calling a cab."

*Great. Another one. This is all I need.*

Eliza kicked and screamed all night. It took both of them to hold her down. The bed was soaked with sweat, but they didn't dare let go of her to change the sheets. When morning finally came, a very crass, very nasty woman opened her eyes and stared at Alison for a moment.

"Who the fuck are *you*? What are you doing here?"

"We know you from the *Collective*. We saw you at *McGee's* last night, and the bartender asked us to bring you home. He thought you were drunk, but you weren't." Alison told Eliza the whole story. "I don't know how you did it, but you went to that bar instead of killing your target. We tracked you down and took you home. We've been here all night."

Eliza reached under the bed and produced a baseball bat. "You get out of here right now! I don't know you, and I don't know him. Whatever you're after, you can just forget it. There's nothing here for you to take, and it's not my place, anyhow. If you're not out of this apartment in five seconds, I'll beat you both to death with this bat."

"Eliza, *think*! Didn't you dream you wanted to kill someone? Someone who you thought was a terrible person? In your dream, didn't you know her name, her address, and your entire plan of attack? Listen to me! If we hadn't brought you home and sat on you all night, you might have woken up a killer, guilty of first degree murder. *Think!*"

Eliza lowered the bat and shut up long enough to try to recall her dream. She sat up in bed and began to think. "Yeah, I did dream I killed someone last night. And it *was* a woman." She slapped the cold cloth out of Alison's hand. "Get that thing off me."

Michael went out of the bedroom and came back with three cups of coffee. Alison began again and explained Eliza's position to her. She told her there was a way they could save themselves. Eliza nodded, and Alison explained Michael's idea, who was oddly silent. Michael wasn't good with strong women in the first place, but this one made him want to cross his legs. He thought it would be better all-around if he kept his mouth shut.

"First, we're going to talk to the woman you were assigned to kill. She needs to tell us and the cops why the *Silver Man* wants her dead. Once they find a valid motive, they'll start digging into our assignments and hopefully find similar ones, and when we get samples of the drug they used on us and turn them over to the police, all we have to do is tell them where the next meeting is so they can search the hall, and we're all free."

"I need a drink. Hand me that bottle on the dresser."

"I don't think you should be drinking now, Eliza. We have a lot to do."

"Give me the damn *bottle!*"

Alison gave it to her, not knowing what else to do. If Eliza was an alcoholic, she'd need it to keep away the D.T.'s.

"Look, Miss Nicey-Nicey, don't get all 'Come to Jesus' on me. I'm in. No one's gonna force *me* to live on the run or kill anyone I don't already want dead." She took a long swig of whiskey straight from the bottle and shuddered. "That's better. What's next?"

Alison continued. "We need you to tell us everything you can about the woman you were sent to kill. Once we talk to her, we help Michael get the *Silver Man's* stash of the killing drug. You're the only one we know of who was drugged but didn't do the kill. We're guilty, Eliza, but we didn't do this voluntarily. You, your target, and that drug are going to prove it for us."

Eliza closed her eyes to think. "She's a ballerina. Her name is Clara."

\*\*\*

Special Agent Deeprose scheduled a meeting with Carter and Fischetti. She wanted to tell them about the painting left behind by Mr. Moreland.

Fischetti was livid. "Do you mean to tell me that just because a temporary curator made a gift of a valuable painting to a museum, you think he's involved in some plot to have ballerinas killed?" There were veins popping out on Fischetti's neck; he looked like a balloon ready to burst. "Agent Deepose, will you please wait outside for a moment? I'd like to talk to Agent Carter, privately."

"Yes, sir. Ah apologize if Ah came on a little too strong." Deeprose realized too late she'd done this the wrong way. She should have discussed it with Carter first. Now, neither of them were likely to give any credence to her idea. Humiliated, she rose and left the office hoping she wasn't going to be fired.

"What in the holy hell is going on here, Carter?"

"Sir, I apologize for Agent Deeprose's overly enthusiastic approach today. I'll make sure she understands the importance of checking with me before she takes action. However..."

Fischetti's eyes widened. "Don't tell me you *agree* with her, Agent."

"Well, it *is* a little out of the ordinary, sir. Moreland shows up on the scene as a temporary curator. He seems desperate to avoid questioning. Less than a week later, he's gone, having found his own replacement—a man who tells us Moreland was involved with high-level scientific projects concerning D.N.A. What this has to do with anything is not my concern. It's just that it doesn't make sense that a man of scientific importance at the national level also happens to be an international lecturer on Impressionist art. Or so he says. Where would he get a genuine *Degas,* sir? Why in the world would he give something like that to the *Cloisters* as a gift? It's not medieval. Why would a temporary curator with a great opportunity dumped right into his lap, leave? Agent Deeprose absolutely went about this the wrong way, sir, but I think she's on to something, and I'd like to follow up on it."

Fischetti sat back in his chair, amazed. "You think there will be more murders, don't you? And you're suggesting a ballerina is the next target."

"Yes, sir. We're close to confirming our first two were not committed by the same perps. Still, something seems to be leading us from one to the other. I can't help feeling that they're separate but related. I agree with Agent Deeprose's assessment. We're looking for a ballerina being stalked or already dead."

Fischetti gave his permission to move ahead and dismissed

Carter. When his office was quiet again, he swiveled his chair around to face the wall of windows behind his desk. He lost track of how much time he sat there staring at nothing and drumming his fingers on the window sill.

# Chapter Twelve

Eliza didn't like Alison. "Stop whining; you wanted to meet new people, didn't you? Well you did; just not the kind you figured on. I want another drink before we start looking for the ballerina."

Balled fists confirmed Michael's fear of losing leadership. "The *Silver Man* never wanted us to behave like a community. To be a real community, you have to care about your neighbors. He wants to keep us angry and divided; that's how he got us there in the first place. But once we're off the drug and away from his influence, we can think for ourselves again, so what's happening here, right now, is something he didn't count on. That mistake will cost him."

"Cut the crap. We're a temporary alliance, Michael, and that's all. Look, I'm not risking *anything* for the two of you or anyone else. All I have to do is call the cops on the *Silver Man* and it's over. They can test my blood for the drug; I'll bet it's still in my system. No one's following us. No one has any diabolical plan. This isn't Goddamned Russia, you know. How is it you two never thought of that, Mike? Or did you?"

Alison dropped her coffee mug on the hard kitchen floor.

"I bet that never even *occurred* to you, Alison, did it? God, you're a moron. Look, all he wants is help getting the killing drug and the minute he gets it, he'll ditch us! He needs *us*; we don't need *him*!"

Michael picked up a chair and heaved it down on the tabletop no more than an inch from Eliza's head. She never moved. "So I was right. Neither of you know which end is up. All right, then, I'm in charge, now. Alison helps us or we kill her, plain and simple."

Alison started to cry again.

"Michael, I'll help you get the drug, but I get half the take. We'll leave just enough there for the cops to find. After that, you're on your

88

own and I'm outta here. Alison and Clara can worry about themselves. None of you idiots better even think about double-crossing me. The *Silver Man* may or *may not* be interested in you anymore, but I'll find you wherever you go. You'll all just have to watch your back as long as you live."

Alison was nearly hysterical. "If you want to call the police and turn him in, do it. I don't want any of those killing drugs, and I don't want to be around either of you any longer than I have to."

"But I don't want to turn him in, Allie. I liked the way that drug felt. I liked it a lot. With a whole bag of it, I can do anything. I'll have one big fling, take everything I ever wanted, live like a queen, and die like a gangster."

***

Carter issued an order to canvass all the ballet schools and academies in the tristate area. They were looking for a student who hadn't shown up to class, might have mentioned having an enemy, or seemed afraid.

Deeprose pointed out the *Florence Gould Hall* on a map of Manhattan. "There. That's the school we want, sir."

"It's the last one on the list. Let's head over there now and talk to this, uh..." Carter scanned his list for a name. "Uh, Clara Dumont."

The pretty, petite dancer was shocked to find they wanted to know who she'd been mentioning to the other girls in class. "I don't understand why this is important. I had a falling out with my girlfriend. I told a few friends she blamed me for something I didn't do. Big deal! For goodness sake, why would she want me *dead*?"

Deeprose tried a different approach. "Ah'm Agent Deeprose, honey. We're not lookin' for your friend. We're askin' everyone the same thing—if they have any real enemies, that's all. Is there anyone in your life that y'all are particularly afraid of for any reason?"

"No ma'am, there isn't."

"Can you tell us what the fallin' out was about so we can cross her off our list?"

"Sure. I suppose so. We've known each other for years. We trained together. Several months back we both auditioned for the

American Ballet Company. It's a very big deal, you know. She fell during her performance and broke her ankle. It ended her career. I was invited to join the troupe next season, so she got angry and stopped speaking to me. I guess I'm a reminder of what she can't have." Clara shook her head, looking very sorry for the girl.

Carter and Deeprose looked at each other.

"Ah'm so sorry to hear that, Clara, but like you said, it wasn't your fault. You worked hard to make the pros. Congratulations on your acceptance. By the way, since she was a dancer too, we should really ask her the same thing we've asked every other dancer in God's country. Would you give us her name and address, please?"

"Sure. I can give you the address I have for her, but I heard she moved. She may not be easy to find, Agent. She has no family, and she keeps pretty much to herself. But Abby works for an organization called the *Collective*. She's very devoted to their ideas, whatever they are. I'm not sure where their headquarters are, but maybe she'll show up at their next meeting."

Back out in the fresh air, Carter and Deeprose did a high five. "I'll get a team together to track down the girl, and we'll check back with them later. For now, let's take a ride around the Upper West Side. Jill did a great job enhancing the photo of the museum killer, but whoever he is, his face doesn't match anything on file. No priors. If he lives around there, maybe we'll get lucky and spot him on the street. At any rate, it's a beautiful day. We can look for him and sightsee at the same time. Want a hot dog?"

Deeprose did a little happy dance. "With everything, sir."

***

Eliza told him to drop them off, park her car and wait until they came back. "Let someone else do the thinking for a change." Eliza slammed the car door in his face and the two girls went into Clara's building on West 59th Street.

Clara opened her apartment door for a special delivery. Alison and Eliza introduced themselves on her doorstep as they pushed their way inside.

"Hey, hey, what's this? Who are you?"

Alison began. "We came to talk to you about Abby, the girl

90

whose ankle you broke after her audition. We know she works for the *Collective*, and we know she tried to have you killed. She'll try again, Clara. We're here to help."

"Is this a joke?"

Neither woman answered.

"Well?"

Silence.

"You are...joking, aren't you? Is she trying to scare me or something? Look, who are you two and what do you want?" Clara moved slowly backwards while she talked, buying a few precious seconds of time to reach her stationery desk and a letter opener.

"Eliza was supposed to kill you two nights ago. Michael and I tracked her down, brought her home and stayed there until this morning. When she came out of it, she remembered everything about you and the reason she was given for killing you. It had to do with the girl whose ankle you broke after her audition."

Clara looked incredulous. Her eyelids fluttered, and she became very pale. Alison knew just how she felt. "Where in the world did you hear a thing like that? I wasn't responsible for her broken ankle! She knows that! It was broken during her audition, not after. Who told you it was broken afterward? If this is a joke, it's not *funny*! I think you two need to leave. Right now."

"Clara, if we leave now, someone else will be given the assignment, and this time he may succeed. Eliza was given your name, photo and address. They know where you live."

Clara dropped the letter opener and fell into an arm chair like a graceful sack of potatoes. She cried piteously, "This can't be happening!"

Alison knelt on the floor at Clara's feet. "We're going to help you. I swear it. Eliza knows how we can help the police catch the *Silver Man*, but we need your help to do it. We won't let you down, Clara, but you're going to have to trust us. Trust me."

After a long moment, Clara took Alison's hand and sniffled. "What about Abby? I can't go to the police with a story about a woman with an intention to kill me; that's no crime, and I can't wait until she tries it, either. You'll help me, won't you, Alison? Because I'm so afraid. If I help you and the police capture this...this *Silver Man*, will you both help me to make sure this girl doesn't hurt me ever again?"

Eliza chimed in. "Hold on. Why are you afraid of her if her

91

accident wasn't your fault? Did you do it, Clara? Is that why she wants you dead?"

Clara burst into tears. She cried herself out and then told them the truth. "All right, she did break it afterward. I was picked for the troupe, and she wasn't. We had an argument, and it got a little ugly. We were about to go down the stairs to the subway when she shoved me. I shoved her back. She fell down the stairs and broke her ankle. But it wasn't my fault! It's not my fault that I was chosen and she wasn't, and I didn't mean for her to fall and break her ankle. Alison, pleeeaase! Don't let her kill me! We have to get her before she gets me. Be my friend, Alison; be my friend!"

Alison had been waiting to hear someone say that to her for a lifetime. "I'll help you, Clara. Don't worry, but listen to me; Abby had a reason for taking you out, but it's the *Silver Man* who must be choosing the targets. It *must* be! And if that's the case, then we have to figure out why he wants you dead, because even with Abby out of the picture, you're still in his sights."

"So what happens now?"

"Call her so she knows you're still alive. Ask her to meet you somewhere private so you can talk things over. Tell her you want to apologize. If she shows up, we'll make sure the cops catch her. That ought to be enough to get an investigation going. If a new killer shows up instead, the cops will catch him in the act. First, though, Michael is downstairs in Eliza's car. He wants us to help him steal the killing drug. If we take away the drug, we take away the *Silver Man's* power over us. We'll leave just enough there to incriminate him."

"Who is Michael?"

"He was the first one to realize he'd been drugged and where and when. He remembered who he was sent to kill. Then he found me and Eliza, and we found you. Right, Eliza?"

\*\*\*

Eliza stared straight through Clara with those cold, dead shark's eyes of hers. She was thinking about the killing drug and about Clara's thinly veiled request to help her commit a murder of her own.

*I understand that one, all right. She never once mentioned speaking to the police. What she wants is to get that girl before the girl gets her. As long as she helps us get the drugs, I'll play along, but I'm not lifting a finger for her. If Alison is so hot to make a friend, let her learn the hard way that there's no such thing.*

"You got any whiskey?"

Clara shook her head. She looked fresh as a daisy now that Alison promised to help her. "Nope. I never keep it around. Too many calories can ruin your figure, you know."

Eliza snorted. "Right, like that's your biggest worry right now. I'm going out to meet Michael and get a bottle. We'll come back and wait for you both in the car. Alison, tell her all about Michael and why he's going down once he helps us get the drug."

She left without another word.

"What did she mean by that?"

*** 

"Ooooo! *Zabar's*! Ah could eat my way through there from one end to the other and still want more."

Carter and Deeprose were driving up West 59th Street in an unmarked car. "You and Jill would have a ball together."

"What makes you say that, sir?"

"Same appetite for life."

"She invited me to go to a jazz bar with y'all after work someday soon. She says we need to play a little more."

"Looks like you made a conquest."

Deeprose answered nonchalantly. "Oh, it was nothin', sir. Ah owed her an apology anyway, so Ah bought her a coffee with lots of chocolate in it, ate a little crow and asked her a whole lotta questions Ah already knew the answers to."

Carter shot a surprised look at her.

*I tried that once, and she knew I was full of it in one minute. How'd Deeprose manage it?*

He scanned the sidewalks as he drove. The out-of-body sensation he experienced before a shootout began to overwhelm him, but he didn't want to alert her to it.

*Breathe slowly…in through the nose. Hold it for one, two, three, four, and five. Out through pursed lips, one, two, three, four, and five. Again…*

\*\*\*

Deeprose pointed at an electronic billboard. "Hey, there's an ad for the *Cloisters*. Ah wonder if the killer got his idea from that billboard. Sir, Ah appreciate your backin' me up after Ah pulled that boner with the deputy director."

"I always have my partners' back." Carter peered back at the billboard in the rear view mirror. It had changed to an ad for *Bustan's*. The idea that a billboard or any other kind of suggestion could have prompted a murder was on his mind.

A few blocks ahead, Carter slammed on his brakes and pointed to his rear view mirror. A man with dark hair rested against the front of a liquor store. "There he is!"

Deeprose shot out of the car. Carter was stuck in a traffic jam but he put on his siren, called for back-up, and said a prayer for patience as he crawled along after her.

She sprinted toward the suspect who bolted in the opposite direction. Carter forced himself to remain tethered to the vehicle despite his concern for Deeprose. Horns blared at Carter from all sides.

*They're honking at me! Unbelievable!*

The suspect ran across the street about two hundred feet behind him. Deeprose attempted to cross the street but was stopped by a passing car. Carter saw her reach for her weapon and beeped his horn to distract her. Firing a weapon on a crowded street was against protocol. In the moment it took to honk his horn and get Deeprose's attention, the suspect disappeared from sight.

*He might have gone into a building or store. He might have even gotten into a...*

Carter opened the window and shouted to the rookie. "He's in that parked car! Shoot the tires if you can! Back-up's on the way."

Deeprose zigzagged across the street and took cover behind the bumper of the car parked in front of her suspect. She sat tight and waited for him to make his move.

Carter turned on the car's loud speaker. "F.B.I.! Move out of the way! F.B.I.! Move! Now!!"

*These people wouldn't move for an ambulance carrying their own grandmother to the hospital!*

Carter made an executive decision. He gripped the wheel and drove up onto the sidewalk, vaguely aware of screaming men, women, and children running into shops and scrambling to take cover in doorways. Carter yelled into his car radio, *"Where the hell is my back-up*?! Block off 10th Avenue between 40th and 72nd in all directions!"

# Chapter Thirteen

As she turned the corner, Eliza saw Michael catapult himself into her car.

"Get in!"

With no time to think, Eliza simply did as she was told. She heard the click of the door lock as soon as she got in.

He threw a vial under the car seat before slamming the car into reverse and crashing into a fender. Then the car leaped forward again smashing a back bumper. It was the only way to get the car out of its parking spot.

Eliza's head flew forward and hit the dashboard. "*Shit*!"

As her car flew back and forth over and over again, she was shocked into silence. She hadn't gotten a chance to put on her seat belt and the constant bucking threw her around like a rag doll. She wrenched the passenger door handle to jump out, but it wouldn't budge. "Unlock this door!"

The car finally jerked free. Michael threw the car into 5th gear.

"No, Michael! Stop! There's a police officer right in front of us! You'll get us killed!"

"*Shut up*! I can't get caught now. I found a vial backstage the other night and took it before I found out what it was. It's under the seat, so hang on to something and keep your mouth shut."

An unmarked Ford 4X4 raced up behind them and crushed the trunk like an empty soda can. "*Screw the man*!" Michael roared.

"Michael! There's nowhere to go! *Stop*!" Eliza screamed, holding onto the dashboard and the car door for support.

A voice on a loud speaker ordered Michael to stop his car.

He lowered his head and said quietly, "We're going for it." Once more he gunned the engine, but the weight of the Ford was too much for Eliza's car. The tires squealed and smoked but went nowhere.

"O.K., you wanna play? *Let's play!*" He slammed into reverse, pushing the Ford backwards into a parked vehicle. It reared up just enough to free the trunk; Michael raced the car forward again.

Eliza began thinking about what she was going to say and do when Michael was finally caught.

*I'm not going down with him. I had no idea he took a vial of that stuff. It's my car, but he's driving. I'll say he grabbed me, took my keys and threw me in the car when he saw that cop chasing him.*

Suddenly, something that looked like a big black bat swooped over the hood of the car and landed on the windshield. Hard.

Eliza screamed, "What the hell is *that*?!"

"*Goddamned sonofab...*" Michael slammed on the brakes but the giant blob on the hood couldn't be thrown off.

"Stop the fucking car, Michael! *Stop the car!*"

Michael's right hand connected with her left cheek. Eliza's head flew into the passenger side window so hard it ricocheted back off it. She was bloody but calm. That was just what she needed for a get-out-of-jail free card. Eliza heard the roar of a large engine and braced herself.

A nearby hotdog stand was suddenly flooded with customers. Everyone could see what was about to happen and those closest to the vendor were buying food and soft drinks so they could watch the show in relative comfort. A large utility truck was approaching the intersection from a side street. Here and there people murmured, *'Oh my God!'*, but continued eating and watching.

A woman holding an infant screamed, "*Stop! Stop!* You're going to hit him!" Michael was momentarily distracted by her, and that was the precise moment the truck slammed into them. The thunderous impact of metal screeching and scraping against metal could be seen on the face of every onlooker. But, as with all things, when the momentary shock passed, the crowd disbursed, quickly. The show was over.

The blob with hands finally tumbled off the hood of the car. Michael shook off the impact and threw open his car door, ready to run. Eliza didn't fare as well. She came close to being crushed to death by the metal that hemmed her in on all sides.

Deeprose flashed a badge at Michael and ordered him to stop. Michael charged. She waited until he was almost on top of her and then stuck out her foot and tripped him. "Ah will not hesitate to shoot you."

Even Michael could see the game was up. "What the hell were you chasing me for? I didn't do anything!"

The agent placed handcuffs around the suspect's wrists. "You disobeyed several orders to stop, and y'all nearly killed me with your car. I thought you mighta stopped with a human bein' ridin' on your hood, but Ah see now that was wishful thinkin'." The agent sighed.

Eliza's heart jumped up into her throat. She decided it was a good time to play the victim card. "Officer! Help me! This man kidnapped me in my own car! Look what he did to my face! Look what he did to my car!" Eliza projected her voice so she'd be heard by as many witnesses as possible.

A man rapped at her window. He wore a badge on his belt and was dressed in a rich, chocolate brown suit. Eliza gazed into the man's brown eyes and was sure he would believe her story. It was her word against Michael's, and after all, he was a killer.

"Are you hurt? Don't worry, you're safe now."

She nodded, tears streaming down her bloody, swollen face.

Two uniformed officers dragged Michael to his feet. His mouth was bleeding from the impact of his fall. Agent Deeprose addressed the officers. "Please read the suspect his rights. He's a suspect in two murders. We don't want any technical slip-ups on this one."

"How'd you hang on to the hood like that?" Carter was in awe.

Deeprose removed a stray strand of black hair from her eyes. "The windshield wipers! That was better than ten carnival rides put together."

Eliza knew both their names by now. It took a few hours to cut her free of the metal twisted all around her. She remained quiet, listening to as much of their conversation as she could hear.

Carter squinted. "That was the most *amazing* thing I've ever seen. Now that's what I call tenacious!"

Carter turned to the ambulance crew. "Let me know if they decide to keep her at Columbia Presbyterian for testing or observation. She'll need stitches and she's pretty banged up. I want to know if she was sexually assaulted. We'll question her after she's been treated and calms down a little. Agent Deeprose, what made you do a crazy thing like that?"

"Ah wanted him to think Ah lost him in the crowd, so Ah walked up the street while he was fumblin' with the vehicle. Ah noticed a lovely display of shawls, and well, Ah sorta *borrowed* one. Ah figured if I tossed it over the windshield and held it there, he'd have to stop. Ah wanna reward that vendor, sir."

"Agent Deeprose, I'm going to make sure the expense is covered by the Bureau. That was really something. Not one fatality or major injury. You threw a simple, black shawl over the windshield and blinded him while you were perfectly safe and having the time of your life. They're going to love this at the academy. Who would ever think of such a thing?"

"Ah would, sir." Deeprose beamed with pleasure.

***

"What is this all about?" Michael slammed his cuffed wrists on the interrogation table.

Carter used meditation to face rage without becoming enraged himself, but all he ever managed was a veneer of calm. Everything else was swallowed and stored away. Essentially, he put on a very good show. "Such negative energy! Calm down, Michael, that won't work here. Care to give us your last name?"

Michael stared straight ahead.

"We've had a look through your wallet. It doesn't appear you were carrying a license."

Michael shrugged. "I must have lost it."

Carter looked at Michael head on. "I'm here to make a bad situation better. Help me, and I'll help you."

"I told you. You have the wrong man."

Carter folded his hands and leaned forward a little. "You were ordered to stop, but you tried to run. Why did you do that if we have the wrong man? Michael, you're in trouble. If there are others involved, give me their names. If you can give me a solid lead, I can help you get out of this. I can protect you, Michael. You don't have to be afraid. Just give me the names." Carter paused to peer under the table. "Nice shoes! *Expensive.* Do you happen to own a pair of *Stridewells?*"

Silence.

"Look, if we have the wrong man, can I borrow a little of the blood on your shirt to prove it?"

Michael exploded. "Take all the fucking blood you want! I'm not the guy in the video!"

"Video? What video?'

"The museum video!"

"Oh, *that* video! See, it's very interesting that you mentioned that, Michael, because that information was never leaked to the press. You never saw it the papers, but you saw it on the way out of the museum, didn't you? Sure, you did. But it was too late to go back for it. Here's what I think: I think you visited a museum called the *Cloisters* a few days ago; I think you took two husbands away from their wives; and I think you should help me understand why."

Carter smiled. "No answer? O.K. If you prefer to remain silent, it'll be for a very long time. A vial of clear liquid was found under the driver's seat of the car. The owner told us she saw you put it there when you jumped in. Our lab is analyzing it now. The F.B.I. lab, Michael. Let me clue you in on something; you stumbled into the wrong operation, and now, you're a part of this investigation whether you like it or not. Here's something else to consider, too; whoever you ripped off is going to get to you no matter where you are. So what's in the vial, Michael, and where'd you get it?"

"It's hers. It was in her car when I got in it. She's lying." Michael raised his chained hands. "Test her blood. You'll see."

"Ah! So it's a drug. Thank you, Michael. I appreciate the information. Does it have a name? What's it for? Where'd you get it?"

Carter sighed. "More silence? Michael, just because a drug is not inside you doesn't mean you can wiggle out of possession. I have you on kidnapping, assault and battery, resisting a federal officer, possession of a stolen car, possession of that chemical, and on suspicion of two murders. Testing your blood to see if you ingested the chemical is of no interest to me whatsoever. I'm not looking for a drug dealer, Michael, unless he's also a killer. Maybe you're him. Maybe you're not. Maybe the real culprit put you up to it. Unless you talk to me, I'll never know.

"Still not talking. All right, if it's the last nails in the coffin you need to see before you decide to save yourself, I'll show you two. First, the killer left a bloody shoe print at the scene of a double homicide. Size eleven. You wear a size eleven, don't you, kid?

Anyway, the brand are *Stridewells*. Expensive! The exact model was traced to a store just around the corner from where you live. We're going to search your apartment, and we'll find them, Michael. You left the museum with blood on those sneakers; we're going to match it to the bloody prints and the victim's own blood. You can't fight forensic evidence, Michael. It's impossible.

"It might also interest you to know we recovered D.N.A. and finger prints from a glove you left behind. That blood sample you were so quick to volunteer is the clincher. We're closing in on you, Michael, and when we do, we'll have justice for those dead men and their widows. If there were other people behind it, Michael, don't throw yourself into the fire for them. Why don't you get rid of all that bad karma and tell me who's really behind the two museum murders? I know full well you don't have the brains it takes to be a professional killer, but you know who does."

"Back off, Buddha. I want a lawyer."

"Certainly; that's your right. As long as you understand that once I walk out that door and you lawyer up, there won't be any more deals. The way things stand now, your goose is cooked. I don't understand your silence, Michael. The evidence is piling up against you, and yet you refuse to defend yourself. No lawyer can save you if you take a vow of silence."

"Why don't *you* take a vow of silence?"

"I think everyone hears better when they are silent, Michael, but sometimes it's necessary to do the talking."

\*\*\*

Agent Deeprose was at the hospital visiting Eliza. "Here's a tissue, honey. Go ahead and let it all out."

"Thanks." Eliza blew her nose and wiped her eyes. "I thought I was going to die. He ran up to the car and just went crazy. I thought he had a gun, so I got in. When I found out he didn't have one, I tried to get out, but I was locked in. And, well," Eliza sobbed, "when I tried to escape he punched me in the face and my head hit the window."

Deeprose assessed the damage to Eliza's face. The punch appeared real enough but she wondered if the woman would back up her story in court. "Are you willing to press charges and testify?"

"I don't know. How can I be sure I'd be safe?"

"We can provide you with protection."

Deeprose observed Eliza. The car was hers, she wasn't suspected in either of their cases, and a quick check of her name and address proved her identity. Although she had no priors, Deeprose still wondered if she knew the guy she said kidnapped her. If she had any connection to Michael Santiago, Deeprose needed to know it. "Is there anyone we can call for you?"

Eliza scratched her nose. "No. I just want to go home. I need a drink. Can I leave if the nurse says I'm free to go?"

"You may. Ah want you to take my card, Eliza. Call me right away if you remember anything else. Here, give me that tissue to throw away for you."

Eliza got out of bed. "Excuse me. I need some water."

Deeprose waited until Eliza was out of the room to stuff the used tissue into her handbag.

*Ah hope for your sake your tears are real, Eliza.*

\*\*\*

Alison was worried. Michael and Eliza weren't downstairs, and the car was gone; neither of them were answering their cell phones.

"I don't have a good feeling about this, Clara. I think we better stay right here until we hear from one of them."

"Fine with me. I'm starving! Can you cook, Alison?"

"I'm pretty awful, but I know how to make omelets. You want to have dinner with me? Why?"

"Because I like you, that's why. I don't think one in a million people would do for me what you did today for a total stranger. I want to be your friend, Alison. I think you need one, and frankly, so do I. Now look, I can't cook at all, and there's nothing in the fridge. Would you mind going down the block to pick up groceries for the omelets? Oh, and we can use a nice bottle of chardonnay and something sweet for dessert. I've been so upset today that all I want to do is relax in a hot tub. Here's the key."

Alison accepted it with reverence. "Thank you! I'll have to find an A.T.M.—I don't have my credit card on me—but that's no problem, really! I'll be back in about an hour. You just take it easy, and when I come back, we'll have a feast."

Clara hugged her and sniffled a little. "Oh, Alison, you're so kindhearted. Anyone can see that! I'm glad we met today, even under these circumstances. That other girl—Eliza—she's a horrid brute, isn't she?"

Alison seemed very flattered that Clara chose her as a confidant. "She's sick in the head, Clara. Cold and mean. Don't worry, I said I'd protect you, and I will."

Clara turned her baby blue beams on Alison. "I know you will. Hurry back."

Clara's smile faded as the front door closed and then vanished altogether.

*What a piece of work! I'm not surprised she has no friends. Who could stand all that fawning and begging? She's exhausting to be around, but I need an ally, and I can already see she'll do anything for a friend. Well, Allie, meet your new best friend.*

*That other one is too smart in some ways and dumb as an ox in others. She's going to be trouble. I'll just have to ask Uncle for enough money to buy her help and silence. I'll tell him it's for a new costume. He'll never know the difference.*

*I also need to come up with a way to get one of them to get rid of that bitch for me. Then I can breathe again. I'll think about it in the tub. Oh, I wish I'd broken her neck instead of her ankle!*

She padded off to the bathroom thinking about what scented bath oil she wanted to use.

\*\*\*

Alison and Clara finished their dinner and were sitting in the living room sipping white wine.

"I'm getting worried, Clara. Where is Eliza? I don't care about Michael, but we need Eliza to tell her story to the cops. I can't do it. I'm guilty."

"She'll turn up. You know, Alison, being a prima ballerina with the A.B.C. is a much bigger deal than you think. I'll get to travel all over the world sharing the love of art and culture. I'm also going to be an ambassador of peace."

"An ambassador of…peace? You?"

"Why not me? I speak several languages, and I'll naturally be

103

invited to all the state dinners. Uncle has friends in the United Nations who owe him some very big favors. He called in a few of them, and now I've been officially asked to help improve international relations with Russia, China and the Middle East, and all I have to do is be beautiful, graceful, entertaining, and polite. That will speak for itself."

"I guess I won't be seeing you much after next season, then." Alison looked down at the carpet, frowning. She was already losing her new friend.

Clara thumbed through an address book as she answered. "Nonsense, Alison. You're a friend. All I ever had were competitors. We'll be besties after you help me get rid of that horrible creature who wants me dead, won't we?"

"Really? Really, Clara? Will we really be best friends from now on?"

"What? Oh, yeah, sure. I think this shade of lipstick is a little too dark. Don't you?"

*Poor Alison. Sure, I'll be your bestie.*

# Chapter Fourteen

Seacrest invited Carter and Deeprose to the lab to discuss her findings so far. "I'd like you to meet Dr. George Riker, our latent fingerprint expert. He flew in from Washington to present us with his findings. I think we've got enough of a match for him to provide us with professional testimony. Dr. Riker, I'd like you to meet Special Agents Carter and Deeprose."

Dr. Riker shook hands with both agents before inviting them to sit down. He took out a thick, brown manila envelope containing copies of the evidence and his notes. "You see, even with a full print, the image must be carefully edited by our technicians to remove everything that isn't really a fingerprint, such as dirt and digital noise. Failing to do so reduces the accuracy of the process by about 30 percent. Partials, of course, are even harder to identify, and it's a painstaking process even before I sit down to do my part of it.

"We ran the partial print through the I.A.E.F.S. (Integrated Automated Fingerprint Identification System) database of 53 million files, which took us close to two hours. We also added 'elimination prints' of everyone who had legitimate access to the crime scene.

"The system can handle a partial print as long as it is big enough to include five separate distinguishing points. However, even if the suspect's prints are found in the system, they cannot always be matched to the evidence print if the part of the fingerprint on file is blurred or smeared. Ultimately, the system provides me with a list of the most likely matches, including the one taken when the suspect was taken into custody and booked.

"So, you see, in the end, if it finds anything similar at all, the system can only produce a small set of prints and partials to compare. No computer can make a definitive match. That's where I come in. A human being must always look at the prints on a lighted screen, side-by-side with the sample print, to determine which one is really a match. Unfortunately, only about 26 percent of the cases received by the lab include identifiable fingerprints."

Carter knew all this already, but he was glad Dr. Riker explained the entire process for Agent Deeprose's benefit. "And?"

"And I believe we have a match on the museum murders." He brought up the electronic records on Seacrest's monitor and displayed a split-screen comparison of the partial prints obtained from the museum gloves and the prints taken following Michael's detainment. Carter and Deeprose looked on as Seacrest pointed out exactly where the partial print matched Santiago's full print.

"I should also say you don't have to rely on probability; you have something far better. The database contains the prints from incarcerated criminals that are supposed to be deleted if a prisoner is exonerated, but very often that doesn't happen. It also contains prints provided voluntarily for the purpose of conducting background checks for new jobs. Your suspect obviously had no priors, because there was no match found in the system for convicted criminals.

"Almost half of all the searches done now are for background checks or child protective purposes, so it was fairly easy to obtain the necessary permission to check the database for prints from employment records. In other words, I got lucky." Dr. Riker handed Carter a file. "The name of your suspect is Michael Santiago, of New York City, New York."

Carter and Deeprose high fived each other. Carter shook the doctor's hand. "Thank you, Dr. Riker. You're a miracle worker!"

"Yes, I am something of a miracle worker at that." He smiled, nodded his head, excused himself and walked back into an office to attack a two-foot high stack of folders on his desk still waiting to be investigated before he flew back to the home office.

Seacrest moved on to the next piece of evidence. "I'll have a definitive blood analysis completed within the next few hours. Until we can get regular blood samples and lots of them, I'm using the blood from his shirt to see if it's a match for the blood in the shoe print. Anyone could have worn the shoes, of course, but I'm hoping against hope that some of his own blood is also in the print. If so, the forensic evidence will positively place him at the scene. That will strengthen Dr. Riker's professional opinion regarding the print. You have enough now, though, for an arrest."

Carter nodded. "Michael refused to provide a D.N.A. swab, but we recovered a sample from under the nails of the woman he put in the hospital—Eliza Bitner. He doesn't have many chips left to bargain with."

"So Eliza didn't know him?" Seacrest asked.

Deeprose answered. "So she says. Oh! Ah forgot to give you this. It's a D.N.A. sample from her from a tissue she used in the hospital."

Seacrest whisked it out of her hand. "Good, going, Agent. This may come in handy later on. You never know."

Carter added, "Now that we know who he is and have enough for an arrest, we can get a warrant to search Michael's home for the sneakers. If we find them, and even if he tried to wash away the blood, it'll still be there, and you can prove it for us with Luminol. That'll be the end of the ballgame for Michael."

Seacrest talked over her shoulder as she rushed away. "You'll have to excuse me. Time's wasting! Come back in a few hours, after you've searched the home. I should have a much more enlightening presentation by then, and I want those sneakers. I only hope he wasn't smart enough to get rid of them or burn them."

Carter and Deeprose heard the door to the blood lab slam behind her. She turned to him as they walked out of the lab. "Does she always present her findin's with so much…drama?"

"Depends on how many cups of coffee she's had."

\*\*\*

A few hours later, Carter had his answers from the lab. The blood on Michael's shirt matched one of the blood types Seacrest found on the sneakers Carter retrieved from his apartment. They still had the victim's blood all over them. It had been a very lucky day.

There were no viable prints recovered from the Jersey crime scene, however, where the death of David Florio still remained a mystery. It wouldn't be easy to connect the two murders even if there was a connection to be made. Carter knew Agent Deeprose didn't believe they were related, and he was inclined to agree. What she didn't yet know was that Fischetti *did* want thrill kills and serials ruled out. Seacrest's findings would take care of that.

Before they confronted Michael, Carter sat down with his new rookie, alone. "Agent Deeprose, have you ever heard of linkage profiling?"

"No sir, Ah haven't. What is it?"

"It's a process by which the various aspects of multiple killings are compared to each other to discern if there are any repetitive patterns or styles of killing that can tie them together—things like ritualistic signatures left on the bodies or commonalities in the victims themselves. There are all kinds of factors to consider. The point is, there are only a few experts in the country qualified to do this, and one of them works with us. I'll receive his official report sometime next week, but he's fairly sure, right now, that the murders were *not* committed by the same person."

"Ah *knew* it!"

"Hold on, Agent…That doesn't mean the killings weren't done by two different people sent by the same entity."

"Y'all are still thinkin' these were contract hits, sir?"

"It doesn't matter what I think. It has to be ruled out definitively. But we're one step closer. These were two different killers, but I suppose it's still possible Michael may know something about the murder in New Jersey, and if he does, he has only one chip left to bargain with. Let's go rattle his cage and see what happens."

***

"Mr. Santiago, I'd like to introduce you to my partner, Agent Deeprose. I believe you're already acquainted."

"So you know my name. Congratulations."

"That's not all we know, Michael. We've matched your blood and finger prints to the crime scene at the museum. Your blood and the victim's blood were both found in the sneaker prints you left behind. We also found your sneakers at your apartment with the blood still on them. Again, not the brightest of moves. You have one chip left in this game before your lawyer arrives. Tell us everything you know about the homicide in New Jersey and who's behind both hits. Do it now and I'll make sure you get off with no more than five years in prison and another five on house arrest. That's my final offer."

A court appointed lawyer entered the interrogation room. He set his briefcase on the table carefully. "Good Afternoon, Agents. Now that you've made formal charges, my client is invoking the Fifth Amendment. I'm so sorry to ruin your fun."

Carter waited for the lawyer to take a seat. "Mr. Stevens, we have all the evidence we need to convict, and we still haven't gotten the report on the substance found underneath the car seat. He'll get life without the possibility of parole, so if he wants to try to negotiate for a lighter sentence, he needs to tell us the whole story right now. Tomorrow the deal comes off the table, permanently."

Deeprose had some questions of her own. "Mr. Santiago, do you know the woman you allegedly kidnapped? Is there some kinda connection between y'all that you're not tellin' us about? Because she threw you so far under the bus, the second axle is about to run you over. Why protect her if she's guilty, too? *Do* you know her, Michael? Are there any others besides her involved?"

The attorney smiled icily. "Good try, Agents, but no cigar. Michael, don't say anything."

Michael stared straight ahead, looking at no one and seeing nothing.

Carter played his last card. "O.K., Michael, have it your way. But before we wrap up here, I want to make certain you understand me. We have everything we need for a hands-down conviction on two premeditated murder-one charges. You look surprised; did I forget to mention that earlier? Yes, in fact, your prints were found all over the security guard you buried alive as well as that bag of money you left behind. Someone made real sure you'd never walk out of here. Have it your way."

Michael glanced at his lawyer. "We're done."

Deeprose slammed a fist on the table. "Trust me on this, Mr. Santiago, you don't want to live in prison with career criminals. My partner, here, Special Agent Carter, believes souls can be saved. Me? Ah don't think you were even born with one. Ah'm gonna be workin' real hard on this case to see that y'all rot in prison until you don't remember what life was like before you were put there."

Stevens laid a hand on Michael's shoulder. "Let's go. The Department of Justice will take it from here."

Michael whispered in his lawyer's ear. He was starting to sweat.

"Agent Carter, you admitted to having in your possession a substance found in the young woman's car, and that you are asserting it belongs to my client. I'm sure you don't have to be told that's illegal search and seizure. This vial you have is more than likely hers. You'll have to prove it belongs to my client, and I don't think you can. I'll save the rest of my arguments for the preliminary hearing."

Carter knew a preliminary hearing would only become necessary if the client intended to plead 'not guilty'. He tried one more time. Looking Michael in the eye, just inches from his face, he said in earnest, "If you plead 'not guilty', you're going to be swallowed up by the system. There will be no reprieve. No hope. If you tell the truth now and give me a name, I can help you."

Michael swallowed hard but kept his mouth shut.

"All right, I tried. I have no idea what's in that vial, but the woman you kidnapped and beat will testify that it was in your possession when you forced her into the car—yes, forced her—don't look so surprised. Just because we didn't recover a weapon doesn't mean you didn't point one at her and ditch it later or make her believe you were pointing one at her to get her into the car as a hostage. She will testify that she saw you throw the vial under the front seat of her car. *You* were the driver, Michael, not her. She's not the one on trial. Who do you think the jury's going to believe? Either way, it should be pretty simple to find out who the vial belongs to, what's in it, what it's used for and where it came from. Once we follow the trail, I'm betting it'll lead straight back to you and whoever you got it from."

***

Alison fumbled in her pocket for her phone to see if she'd gotten any messages. "Where are Michael and Eliza? It's getting late! Clara, if something happened to them and they don't come back, we have to have a plan of our own. I'm still on the *Silver Man's* radar, and now I'm probably wanted as a fugitive, too. Your own killer is out there too, and this time I don't know who it is or if he'll be able to resist the killing drug.

"We have to figure out a way to save you first, and then go to the police so you can back up my story. Michael's worthless to us. Eliza

110

hasn't done anything against the law, and soon the drug will be out of her system. The locations of the *Collective's* meetings are secret, so even if she offers up her invitation and the address of the last meeting, she can't prove she was ever there. We have to find out where they're meeting next so we can take some of the vials as proof of what they did to me and tip off the police; they'll find the rest of them there. If we can time it so that they get there at the start of the social hour, they might be able to catch the waiters passing it around in the drinks. Don't forget, we also want to make sure *Galatea* is caught red-handed giving new members their orders to kill. If we can manage all of that, we'll have leverage."

Clara sashayed over to her closet, rummaging around for an outfit she threw in there a few years ago and had forgotten about until now. "Sure, Alison. Leverage. So, how are you going to help me get rid of *my* killer? Right now, that's the only thing that matters to me. I can't help you until you help me, honey. You know that. Friends 'til the end, right?" Clara flashed her a great, big ingratiating smile.

"Right." Alison blushed all the way to the roots of her dirty brown hair.

"We can figure out all the rest later. You know, I don't need any leverage, I only need protection, but like I said, you help me and I'll help you. If Michael comes back, we'll send him out to the liquor store or something, make an anonymous call to the police and have him picked up. If Eliza comes back, we can still use her even if the drug is already out of her system. Like you said, the *Silver Man* knows by now she didn't kill me. He'll be after her, too. She *has* to help me. I mean, *us. Us.*"

She sat behind Alison on the bed and began to braid her hair. "Oh, Allie, I could introduce you to all the best people. You'd have invitations pouring in every weekend. You know what? I should do your hair for you! Let me give you a completely new look. I'll cut it into the latest style, get rid of that mousy color and make you into a racy redhead. What do you say, bestie?"

Alison was aware that she had to change her look for her own protection, but she never made *any* changes, and she wasn't sure she wanted to make such a drastic one now. "I don't know, Clara, it's kind of a lot to think about."

"Come on, Alison, you need to look like a different person or you won't last a minute outside this apartment, and you certainly can't go home to get anything. You can wear something of mine until we can get you some new clothes and anything else you need. You do have money, don't you? I can't afford much, I'm afraid."

Alison was becoming overwrought again. She bit her nails right down to the quick while considering what to do. "Yes, I have some money. I suppose you're right. I do have to change my look. All right, let's do it."

"It'll be fun, Allie! We need a diversion anyway or we'll worry ourselves to death. I'll get us another glass of wine and we'll play Cinderella."

Clara left the bedroom and went into the kitchen for the wine. Once there, she let out her breath in a whoosh of relief, rolled her shoulders and arched her back. Playing this part was becoming a strain on her delicate body. Maybe it would have been easier for her if she liked Alison or even respected her, but Clara didn't know the meaning of the words. She spent her life putting on false faces to get what she wanted, and it had always worked before, so she saw no reason to change her methods, now.

Clara had been perpetually rewarded and admired for her selfish, willful machinations by '*Uncle*', a man of wealth, power, and social standing. Several months after her father lost his job and could no longer support the toddler, Uncle decided to take her in. He raised her as his own when Clara's mother passed on shortly afterward.

She'd grown up in the elderly man's home spoiled and privileged beyond reason. He was a proud and ruthlessness Machiavellian and a brilliant lawyer determined to win at any cost. Wildly successful in the business world, Uncle was neither admired nor envied. He was feared as a sly, calculating, trickster without remorse or pity. Uncle taught Clara that justice meant nothing; winning the case created its own justice. Everything was about winning.

Clara was the jewel in his crown. Alone and lonely, he had no one to coddle or brag to other than her. The little girl grew up every bit as self-serving as he was. She learned early on that her grace and beauty emitted a blinding light even he could not see through. She learned quickly and well that money and power could buy anything. Men were ridiculously easy to hoodwink. Women were much harder to fool, though, so she generally had no use for them.

The old gentleman was in his dotage now. He was smart, but not smart enough to see that Clara had become a carbon copy of himself. She wanted all the things he worked so hard for—money, a nice home, a glamorous life, high-class friends, and the best of everything. But, as the years rolled by, her desires often clashed with cold, stark reality; his money wasn't hers. She had to pamper his ego and tease him playfully for every nickel she got, and he squeezed those moments out of her like oil from a grape seed.

Clara might have seen a lot more trouble in her life if he hadn't continually bailed her out, and perhaps that would have been a good thing, but he did. He could never say no to her, so she spent most of her time and all her energy hurtling towards disaster at lightning speed.

Tonight, Clara was exhausted, friendless and frightened. She couldn't go to Uncle with this problem; he'd know in an instant that she was responsible for the ruin of that woman's career. She couldn't risk being disinherited. Alison was her only hope.

The irony of Clara's assumptions were in how she went about using Alison, who'd *offered* help willingly before it was even asked for. She asked for nothing because she expected nothing. She gave what she had without expecting anything in return.

Armed with a fresh bottle of wine and a plate of cheese and fruit, Clara pulled herself together and plastered a smile on her face before walking back into her bedroom to face a night of girl talk and beauty makeovers. Alison, whose bravery and altruism outshone the brightest stars in heaven, sipped, ate, and laughed with Clara, who served her up nothing but artifice.

\*\*\*

Carter sat in his office thinking about the billboard advertisement for the *Cloisters* that Deeprose had pointed out to him in the car. She really did entertain the possibility that Michael might have been influenced by someone or something. But he's not smart enough to understand much, let alone be influenced by anyone.

*I'm looking at unrelated murders that seem related, but not to serials or thrillers. Unrelated yet related. What could tie separate murders together besides the person obviously pulling the strings? What if he wasn't influenced by a person but by a chemical? That would make a lot more sense where Michael's concerned. Could the stuff in that vial be the connection in these cases? Is this all about drugs?*

The still unidentified substance didn't appear to be anything they'd ever seen.

*The death of the curator and the guard didn't seem to be about money. Nothing was missing. Could Michael have killed for drugs? But, if that were the case, wouldn't he have taken the bag of money? And why would anyone leave a sack of money in a grave unless they were under the influence of...something?*

Carter relaxed his mind and allowed his consciousness to float through the rooms of the museum. Deep in meditation, he could hear every conversation he'd had or heard concerning the crimes there. Suddenly, he opened his eyes. He remembered that Deeprose believed the near-priceless painting, donated by the odd and absent temporary curator, Arthur Moreland, was a clue.

*And it is! But, if Mr. Moreland knows something, there were a thousand ways he could have let us know it. Why leave behind a painting that no one would think about twice? Why run away and hide?*

*What was it Deeprose said? It didn't belong at the Cloisters. It was from a different period altogether—Impressionist. But Moreland left it there just the same, hoping it would lead us to that ballerina – Clara.*

*... We have to find Mr. Moreland.*

***

Agent Seacrest knocked on Carter's office door and barged right in without waiting for an answer. She was as excited as a child playing *Show and Tell*. "Pop this flash drive into your P.C., Carter, and bring up the video on it. Sorry I didn't bring any popcorn, but I promise you one hell of a show."

"Let's wait until Agent Deeprose gets here, shall we? Whatever it is you have up your sleeve, I want her in on it."

When everyone had their coffee and was comfortably seated, Seacrest turned the screen so that it faced the three of them, and pressed 'play'. She narrated a gruesome story as an unsuspecting cockroach became a two-car garage for a wasp determined to raise its young inside of it.

"What you are observing is neuroscience in all its terrible glory. The wasp has injected its venom directly into the roach's brain to take control over it. See how it moves away from the roach for a period of time? That's because she's waiting for the drug to take effect. Notice now that the roach is obsessively cleaning itself. The venom induces it to create a germ-free environment for the wasp's offspring. The roach has now stopped all motion and sits docilely, allowing itself to be dragged by an insect many times smaller than itself into a safe place she has already chosen and one from which the roach will not try to escape. He has become a zombie—an unwitting, yet willing victim. He will play host to the wasp's egg, without caring that it is being eaten alive little by little from the inside out."

"The venom is used for mind control?"

"Indeed. And it's done that way throughout much of the insect kingdom. The roach might be physically able to crawl away from its fate, but he won't. His brain has been altered to accept anything that happens to it. He may even experience euphoria in this altered state. We don't know for sure. But we can surmise that the wasp's venom is as powerful as any drug known to man. Maybe more."

Carter raised a hand. "I assume we're watching this because it relates somehow to our case. Am I right?"

"Go to the head of the class. Certain behavioral responses may be shut down when a drug, or venom, mutes specific neurons. Our wasp was born with venom that shuts down just the right centers of brain activity to immobilize the roach. Humans experience the same loss of control when they ingest certain inhibitors, like Rohypnol, known as '*Roofies*'; Gamma Hydroxybutyric Acid, known as '*Liquid Ecstasy*', and Ketamine, also known as '*Special K*'. These are the most commonly used drugs in date rape, where the victim is conscious but can't move or talk or resist in any way. Additionally, the same way some drugs can make us docile and unable to resist an attack, other drugs, like *Angel Dust*, might make us extraordinarily aggressive, or, like Scopolamine, open to suggestion. These drugs all come in pills, liquids, or powders."

Deeprose jumped out of her chair. "Liquids! You mean the liquid in that vial we found?"

"Maybe, but I can't find anything about it in the national drug database. It may be a synthetic replica of a naturally occurring substance like the one inside the wasp, or it may grow on a plant or a bush or tree. It may come from half way around the world. We don't know yet, but once we've completed analyzing it using the mass spectrometer test and identify its compounds, I think we'll find it has similar properties to the classes of drugs I just mentioned. Until then, we can't even guess what it's meant for or to what degree it affects men, women, children and people of different sizes, ages, and weights—or for how long."

Carter interrupted. "Just a second. Let me wrap my head around this, Jill. Did you show us that video because you think this substance we have might be one half of a *set*—the other half of which we don't have? One drug to pacify the victim and one to suggest a plan and increase the aggressiveness of the perpetrator? Am I correct when I say that what we think we *do* have in our possession is either a stolen prototype or one that's been reproduced into God knows how many doses? And that someone is going to have to ingest this thing to find out what it does before we can begin to guess what its companion drug does—if there even is one?"

"Carter, we have no idea what we have, yet. It was found in a murderer's possession and it's an unidentified substance we've never seen before, but...I'm fairly certain that we'll find it's something like what you described. There may not even be a companion drug. Yes. I'm guessing there are two, but maybe there's only one. It may be that the killer only uses it to subdue his victim. Or maybe he uses it himself to come down afterward. We just can't know until it's tested."

Carter was beginning to get a headache. "And it may be that whatever this drug is, it has nothing to do with our murders at all."

Seacrest talked out loud as she paced around the office. "I'm waiting for test results from Michael's blood to see if it's still in his system. If he was dosed and forced into doing this, then no matter what we think of him, he's a victim, too. If he took it knowingly, well, then that's a different story—motive being that he knowingly took it to feel a high that would encourage brutal, and even murderously aggressive behavior. And killing that old man wasn't done on the spur of the moment. It was a half assed plan, but it was definitely *planned* and by someone *other* than Michael, right down to the buried security guard and the bag of money.

"The fact that the substance is so hard to identify makes me almost positive it was stolen—if not by Michael, then by the ones who gave it to him. It's not a new street drug; we'd know that in a minute. It must have originated in a private or government-sponsored institution. Michael would never have access to a drug like that; I'm sure of it.

"No, our thief is someone at a very high level of authority in the government or the private sector who reports to and is funded by the government. He knew what he was taking, and where and how to get it. And he took it for a reason. We need to know what that reason is and whether or not it's related to the murders."

Deeprose crossed her arms over her chest. "Let's assume everything y'all just said is correct. If one or both companion drugs affect the morality or judgment centers of the brain, and the killer can prove he was dosed without his knowledge or permission, he can plead extenuatin' circumstances, like temporary insanity or hijackin' of the mind. Maybe he got dosed originally without knowin' it, but Ah'm bettin' he had it in the car because he already knew what it could do and wanted more. That's what we'll have to prove to get a conviction that can't be overturned, and that's gonna be damned near impossible."

Carter got up and grabbed his overcoat. "I'm starting to understand the reason Michael won't tell us the 'why' of the crime; no one would believe a story like that, and as dull as he is, he knows by now that if he talks, he's dead."

# Chapter Fifteen
*Seven Years Earlier...*

The *JASONS* were a secret that had been around so long they'd become mythical. The 1957 launch of Sputnik caused a knee-jerk reaction throughout the United States' Department of Defense (Directive Number 5105.15). Their new immediate goal was now to ensure we would be the initiator, and not the victim, of unexpected strategic technological leaps. They created the Defense Advanced Research Projects Agency (D.A.R.P.A.) shortly after; the *JASONS* were the men who comprised its executive board.

Working with innovators inside and outside of government, D.A.R.P.A. produced game-changing military capabilities such as precision weapons and stealth technology, the internet, automated voice recognition and language translation, and G.P.S. receivers small enough to embed in cell phones.

More powerful than any government or agency on earth, the *JASONS* acted quietly and under the radar. Their strength was not in numbers; it was in their absolute authority to approve or deny D.A.R.P.A. projects that would result in breakthrough technologies for national security. Approval was based on a unanimous vote, ensuring that one person always had the power to shut down dangerous proposals or unscrupulous board members. Therefore, it took only one vote to scrap a proposal.

The *JASONS'* true identities were never revealed to the public, even after the Department of Defense abandoned their sponsorship. The majority of their proposals were submitted to the D.O.D. by a non-profit organization called the Meese Corporation, in Langley, Virginia. Meese conducted scientific research and development for the government and had done so for decades. They were naturally

118

above suspicion. It was the perfect hiding place for the *JASONS,* known only as the Board of Approvers at Meese. The D.O.D., always hungry to gain an advantage on the battlefield, focused on projects that were weapon-based. However, the secret committee of *JASONS* focused on a much bigger picture. No battles ever won provided a permanent, or even a long-lasting, peace. The *JASONS* considered it their responsibility to keep humanity from becoming extinct, any way they thought viable.

Decades before a single newscaster talked about acid rain or global warming, the *JASONS* were studying its effects. The computer and electronics-based battlefields of today actually grew out of ideas generated in the early 1970's. They were not implemented until years later, when the *JASONS* finally agreed that technology was at an optimal level to bring war to a swifter and less destructive end. However, some members were bent on non-militaristic endeavors, which led to friction between them and the D.O.D.

Dr. Katherine Blake, a bright, young biochemist, hoped the committee would understand and appreciate the short-term and long-term implications of the new drug she called *Hyzopran.*

"This, gentlemen, is much more than a drug. It is a way to transform soldiers into killing machines one hundred percent of their time in the service, without any second thoughts or after-effects. I know that may sound fantastic on first consideration, but let's take a look at the facts. We expect every enlistee to be a killing machine when they emerge from training. Like automatons, they are expected to receive and carry out orders without hesitation, without fear, and without having to come home feeling like murderers or cowards. But that is simply not a realistic expectation. We've had to accept that a percentage of our soldiers will wash out from battle fatigue, P.T.S.D., and various other psychological impediments. We've had to admit that we are unable to transform soldiers into assassins without paying a life-long price."

Dr. Blake began a video presentation depicting one of the many human subjects helping to test the drug. The soldier practically leapt through the air in his relentless pursuit of an Afghani prisoner intentionally allowed to escape a detention center as part of the experiment.

One board member turned his eyes away from the screen.

119

*This is not a depiction of war. It's a slaughter! The soldier is crazed, not in control of himself. Anything could happen with a drug like that in a real conflict. And what about the legal implications? My God, what we spend now on behavioral care is a drop in the bucket compared to what we'd have to pay for psycho-pharmaceutical side effects, addiction, permanent damage, or...death.*

*It wouldn't matter if we poured years and millions into its development; you never know what'll happen with a drug. I don't care if her study purports a 100% efficacy on every subject. There is no such thing. I'm opposing it; I don't even want to hear any more about it. It's far too dangerous.*

\*\*\*

Completely unaware that several members bristled or looked away while it played on in a continuous loop, Dr. Blake plunged ahead, going boldly forward with her presentation.

The victim's dying breath, his wasted attempts to shield himself from repeated stabbings, and his needlessly gruesome death was captured in high definition by a drone camera. "Notice our test soldier suffers from no distractions. He displays not one ounce of guilt when he slaughters the enemy."

Blake purposely pushed her black-framed eyeglasses further back on the bridge of her nose, in a nonchalant act of clinical detachment. Her boss and mentor, Clayton Artemus Montgomery taught her that using this psychological tool would make her appear emotionless and very, *very* smart while presenting her argument.

Less than an hour ago, he'd been giving her last minute instructions. "If you should be turned down, let it go, and start working on a new project. Accepting set-backs and going back to the drawing board are the stuff of champions. Every failure is one step closer to success. Remember that, Katherine. These old gents can smell desperation a mile off, so keep your cool. You are a scientist and a seasoned professional. Stick to the facts; they speak for themselves."

With a final pat on the back, Monty sent her off to win the *JASONS'* approval. He bit his nails and waited in silence outside the boardroom.

Chairman Karl Watson met Blake's direct, impersonal, gaze.

"We are all very excited about your proposal, Dr. Blake, and enjoyed your presentation immensely. While we believe *Hyzopran* would be an expedient measure, unfortunately, not all of us agree that its implementation would be wise from a business standpoint, for the following reasons:

1. We could not approve further research and funding simply on the strength of the data resulting from one small study done over a limited period of time and on so few human subjects.

2. To prove that this drug is safe and effective over time, widespread clinical studies conducted over several years and vast amounts of data would be required.

3. We'd need assurance that it is not addictive, won't cause any side-effects and that no physical or psychological issues would occur after discontinuation of the drug.

4. The real problem with the use of a drug to control behavior is that no matter how much testing is done there's always a long list of side effects and disclaimers when one is finally approved.

5. Where there is no sickness, we cannot condone the use of a pharmacological remedy.

6. Ordering military personnel to use it would be a monstrous misuse of authority.

7. This project would cost much more money and take far longer time than we care to spend on it, and in the end, there would be massive legal snags and ramifications even if, by some miracle, it was ultimately approved.

"Dr. Blake, we seek a far more predictable and less expensive solution to this problem without having to worry about lawsuits and settlements. I'm very sorry." Watson sighed. "We hope to see you at our roundtable again, presenting many more ground-breaking ideas. Because we value your work so highly, Dr. Blake, at this time, our lone dissenter would like to speak briefly about his reasons for not sanctioning this project."

Katherine was stunned. Her mind began to move in slow motion.

*What? The project is canned? One dissenter? One?! I've got to change his mind. I'll have one shot at it when he's done speaking. If I can make him understand the sheer magnitude of military lives that can be saved, he'll change his mind.*

Lost in thought, Blake didn't notice Bill Pressman rise. His eyes were stunning, ice-blue glaciers, and his hair was a thick, brilliant, shiny silver. Pressman rose from his seat at the head of the table to introduce himself. Unbuttoning his blue-gray jacket in a smooth, swift motion, he took his seat once more.

"I would like to begin by thanking you, Dr. Blake. I know you've put a lot of hard work and more than a few years of your life into developing this drug and conducting the initial study. This committee applauds and appreciates, to an inestimable degree, your motivation for and dedication to its development. I am truly sorry that I do not see a future in which any human being, civilian or military, should be subject to behavior modification by a drug unless they've been diagnosed with an illness requiring it. Even then, the patient has a choice. Yes, we've sometimes had to resort to its use in extreme situations of interrogation, but certainly not as the norm. We cannot invest time and money on a product which is inevitably unpredictable. The drug is supposed to provide soldiers with limitless amounts of confidence and self-control, but what I see in this video presentation is a soldier consumed by viciousness and aggression and who has absolutely no self-control. That frightens me, Dr. Blake.

'We feel there are other, less costly and more controllable and predictable ways of achieving the same goal. But when we do decide to move forward with this project, we'd like you on the R&D team."

Kate was astounded.

*Have they already heard another presentation and decided that one was more viable? Wouldn't Montgomery have known about another team? I don't understand what's happening here…*

She raised a hand. "Mr. Pressman, the data bears out the assertion that the benefits of the drug far outweigh any of the risks you mentioned. *Hyzopran works.* Right now, this is still the best solution for a problem that is growing and will only get worse over the years. Then there's the cost of a lifetime of aftercare.

"Wars over politics, religion, land, food, and other precious resources have been going on for thousands of years, and they'll go on for a thousand more if we let it! The things soldiers see, the things they have to do—every experience follows them home.

"The number of deaths due to hesitation or battle fatigue has the potential to go down by as much as seventy percent and more. Dollars saved on mental and emotional healthcare for veterans will drop to almost nothing. Until you figure out a way to fight wars without using people, the next best thing is to help them do their job more effectively and efficiently and without lasting emotional effects.

"This drug is ready to go right now. It can be studied while it's being used. Soldiers can be invited to volunteer for trials, understanding all the benefits and possible risks, and decide for themselves if they want to participate. We'd ask them to sign a legal waiver. This is war, Mr. Chairman, and we can't continue losing good men and women without trying to help them with everything we've got, and what we've got is *Hyzopran*."

Pressman shook his head. "I'm sorry, Dr. Blake. It's out of the question. Technology will take us where drugs could never go. We already have someone in mind Corcy Holt. Dr. Holt contributed, in great part, to the precursor of Google Glasses. His eye wear allows soldiers to see many spectrums of color and light, including infrared and U.V. Our soldiers can now see the enemy coming, Dr. Blake, and that makes him a lifesaver. He's working on something now that will have one hundred percent efficacy, can be externally controlled and terminated at any time with no risk whatsoever. Technology is in, Dr. Blake, and pharmaceuticals are out."

"Is it a weapon, sir?"

"It's an implantable Nano-chip that will have the exact same effects as the ones you described, Dr. Blake, with one exception—we'll have absolute control of the thoughts and feelings experienced and remembered with zero risk of side effects or exposure."

Dr. Blake was aghast. "What you're proposing is nothing short of hijacking a body and brain. A drug wears off. Nothing is left behind. Doses can be adjusted. But once you can control a brain through technology, free will goes with it; even if you don't abuse the power, the power is there. You decide how it's programmed, and you choose whether or not to remove the Nano-chip. Once it's installed, you'd have unlimited access to and absolute control of that brain and body. *Until its death!* It's not a step forward, Mr. Pressman, it's insanity!"

Pressman flushed. "You don't believe we have a conscience. I assure you, we do. The details have already been worked out and approved. It will work, and it will open the door to a new solidarity among Americans. A new understanding. We plan to move on this as soon as possible. You can join us or watch from the sidelines, Dr. Blake; the choice is yours. Thank you for your time, and good luck to you."

\*\*\*

Montgomery raked a hand through his hair. "Have you forgotten everything I ever told you?! Have you completely lost your mind?! Whatever their decision, whatever their plans may be, you had *no* right to sound off like that. You don't realize who you're dealing with, Kate. This is not some small-time, rinky-dink non-profit organization that doesn't have the power of decision, the brains to make a better mousetrap or the money to fund you. For God's sake, these are the big boys, and you blew it! In a situation like this you thank them for their time and consideration, keep your mouth shut, and let *me* take it from there. Je*sus Holy Christ, Katherine!* You've made an accusation they can't ignore, and that's dangerous for both of us."

Kate raised an eyebrow. "This whole thing came out of left field, Monty. Who is Corey Holt, and why are they convinced his magic dream machine is also a magic bullet? Did you know anything about this before today?"

"I did not. Holt *is* a genius, although his motives are often less than humanitarian. He likes to live large. I'm pretty certain he cares far more about his patents and royalties than the ethical applications of his inventions."

Blake looked straight down at the ground. "Do you think there's any chance at all of repairing the damage done today and getting another chance to change their minds?"

"No, Kate, I don't think so. You pretty much called Mr. Pressman a Fidel Castro with mind control technology. The project is scrapped. It was funded by Meese, and all your intellectual property belongs to them. If they ever decide to use that idea, they can. And they can have someone else do the research and testing."

"Oh no they won't, Monty. All my notes are at home in my safe. I've never used their computers, and I have the only copy of the presentation. I'm going home to burn it—*all of it*—right now. Let's see them recreate the drug without the formula."

After she cleaned out her desk and left, Dr. Blake's sole focus was the destruction of her research notes. She forgot there was one vial of the prototype still locked away in the Meese lab.

***

At home, Arleen Montgomery stood at the top of the stairs, grinning suggestively at her husband. "Wipe that glum look off your face, sir, or suffer the consequences."

"I vote for the consequences, my incorrigible girl! What's my penalty?"

After all these years, Arleen could read him like a book. She knew he'd had a rough day as soon as he walked in the door, so she tried her best to divert him. He let her.

"I suppose the punishment should fit the crime. Perhaps a spanking, for starters..."

He rubbed his hands together in anticipation and bounded up the stairs two at a time. "Oh, I've been baaaad, verrrry, verrrry baaaad. I *should* be punished!"

"Come here, my bad boy. I'll show you some tricks even your geniuses don't know."

As distraught as he had been earlier, Arleen's love was a restorative to him. Her very presence affected him deeply. She lived in her own universe, floating along in a bubble, incapable of being burst. And she carried him along with her. She was the only one he trusted to navigate rough weather and lay him down softly again on the ground.

He pulled her to him and kissed her long and sensuously. Finally, he looked down into her face and choked up. These were the moments that made life everything it should be.

"I don't know what I'd do without you."

# Chapter Sixteen
*Present Day...*

Like the fall storm brewing outside his office window, Deputy Director Fischetti's thoughts were scattered and blew every which way, leading nowhere. Tension strummed the muscles on the back of his neck. Pigeons and seagulls huddled together on the window sill.

*You guys have it good. I rather be subject to the whims of nature than the whims of man and government.*

*Shit.*

It was Friday evening. He should have been on his way home to Long Island by now, relaxing in the Corinthian comfort of a Lincoln Town Car that picked him up and took him home every day. He looked forward to seeing his usual driver, sipping a rare and wonderful scotch whiskey and staring out at the night with Segovia softly serenading him in the background.

As he waited for U.S. General Breen to arrive, Fischetti thought about the verbal lashing he was about to receive. He just wanted it over with; it had been a rough week. Even sitting on the Long Island Expressway in gridlock was preferable to this, but Fischetti had his orders, so he waited and worried.

He'd been instructed to provide almost no details of the Michael Santiago arrest to the media, but that was impossible in a world permanently plugged into the web. Internet videos that captured Agent Deeprose leaping onto the suspect's getaway car like some kind of giant bat went instantly viral. He had the authority, of course, to pull them down, but it was too late; the damage was done. Fischetti snatched up several sheets of waste paper, crumpled them into a large wad and squeezed.

The ping of a text informed him that General Breen was on his way up and that he should clear his office of all ears but their own. That part would be easy. Even Liz had already gone home. He tossed the squashed mass of paper he'd been squeezing into the trash can and braced himself.

Breen walked in, ignored Fischetti's proffered hand and took a seat in front of his desk. He cut right to the chase. "I just got in from D.C., Deputy Director. It's late, I'm tired, and my request is short and sweet. I want the investigation of the museum killings, and any other related murders, kept quiet. My main concern is this vial you confiscated. Whether or not your lab has already identified it, I'm taking it back to Washington with me on Monday. Those are my orders, son. Sorry, I don't get paid to give a rat's ass about the rest of it." The general leaned heavily into the backrest of his cushy, leather chair and sighed.

"On whose authority, sir?" Underneath the large rosewood desk, Fischetti began to flex his right fist. Something was going on, and he wanted to know what it was. "The last time I checked, the D.O.D. was not in the business of conducting murder investigations."

The general stared out the wall-sized window behind Fischetti. "I'm not at liberty to provide you with that information." He paused for a moment before continuing. "Look, there's a hell of a storm brewing out there. My advice is to bend with the prevailing wind, and right now the prevailing wind is coming straight out of Washington D.C., so do what you're told, son. In any event, the law is clear. The D.O.J. and the D.O.D. play nicely together when they have a shared interest."

"I can't tell my lab team to halt all further analyzation without an explanation of any kind." Fischetti rose from his seat to pace. "That's going to raise an immediate red flag, sir. If you can allow us some time to find out if this drug is linked with our murder investigations, we can stop any more from happening."

"I fully understand your concerns, Deputy Director Fischetti, but your role in this investigation is to provide the D.O.D. with whatever it requires. This is a highly-classified investigation. Therefore, you *will* have your lab, voluntarily, hand over the vial and all existing data regarding it. If it helps you sleep at night, remember, this is in the interest of national security."

Fischetti wasn't giving in that easily. He had his agenda, too. "I need more than that, General. I'll agree to keep our lab findings under wraps, but unless and until my superiors order me to stand down, this is still a local investigation in my jurisdiction. I have a responsibility to this city and the families of the curator and security guard."

Fischetti stopped pacing, looked Breen squarely in the face, and put his cards on the table. "Sir, if you already know what's in the vial and what its capabilities are, I respectfully ask that you share that Intel with us *now* and help us do the job we're here to do."

"I admire your moxie, Bill. In your place, I would probably demand the same thing." The general slowly tapped out a march on the hat resting on his knee. "But I'm here to confiscate that vial. I can't share any more with you than that. Hell, *I* don't even know any more about it. The decision's already been made. You're out of it. Period."

"I'm afraid it's not as simple as that, sir. You're going to need a court order to take that drug from me, and I don't think it'll be as easy as you think. Further study *is* in the interest of national security. No court of law will disagree with that."

Fischetti, glanced at his watch. "War is hell, General, but so is Friday evening traffic. It's getting late, and I'm sure you're anxious to get to your hotel."

Breen raised his eyebrows. "O.K., Bill, we'll play it your way. I'll be back Monday morning, but no later than that. *Think, man!* You don't want to make a stand over *this*. It's not a mess you want to look at from the inside out. Take my advice son, and back the hell *off.*

"I'll let you in on a little something; this request comes straight from the Commander-in-Chief. I don't need a court order. All I need is to get to Washington with that vial by end of day, Monday."

With that, General Breen abruptly stood up, carefully put on his military cap, and gave the visor a small tug. He turned and walked out without saying another word.

Fischetti turned back to his window, losing himself in thought as the howling wind battled an army of party-colored leaves.

\*\*\*

*Earlier that day...*

Alison woke up feeling much better than she had in years. She stretched, and it felt great! Clara came into the bedroom as soon as she heard her moving around.

"Good morning, sleepy head. I brought you a cup of coffee. Scooch up against the headboard and sip while I tell you the latest news. A man suspected of committing two murders has been caught."

"What?! Is it Michael? Two murders? Where's Eliza?"

"That's all I know, Allie, sorry. They aren't releasing any details, but we're safe for now."

Alison shoved the mug into Clara's hand and shot out of bed, tearing off her nightgown and looking around frantically for clothing. "Clara, you're wrong! If Michael is the one they caught, he'll tell the police about me to save his own skin. We're trapped if we stay here. We have to leave. Now!"

"Wait a minute, calm down. I've thought about this all morning. If he's the one they caught, he can't tell them anything about you, me or Eliza. He can't tell anyone about you being at Florio's unless he admits that he was there himself and did nothing to stop you, Allie! That makes him an accessory! He doesn't even know me. I haven't done anything wrong and neither has Eliza. The drug's got to be out of her system by now, and he can't tell them about that either! He can't hurt us. He's out of the way."

Clara shoved the mug back into her hand. "So sit back, drink your coffee, and then take a nice, hot bath while I get breakfast ready. We have some planning to do."

*** 

Carter promised Seacrest he'd join her and Agent Deeprose after work at a local club called the *Jazz Standard* for some hot jazz and cold beer. He sat in his office thinking about Michael Santiago's refusal to cooperate. Something was nagging him that he couldn't let go, but he couldn't put his finger on it. A big chunk of the puzzle was missing.

*What is it I'm not seeing? If Michael clearly has the power to save himself, why is he so willing to take the fall? To protect himself from something worse; that's why. Michael is more scared of turning in this person than he is of a life sentence.*

Carter looked at his watch and sucked his breath through his teeth. He was seriously late, but there was something he had to do before he headed to the club. Carter had an appointment with one of the city's best cognitive behavioral psychologists. He was hoping she could help him understand Michael a little better.

*Jill will have a field day with this when I tell her about it. She'll tease me about it, but she's right; I should've done this for myself a long time ago.*

He climbed up the steep stairs to the lovely brownstone building on East 25th Street. Dr. Andrea Lewis greeted him warmly, shook his hand and asked him to take a seat.

"Dr. Lewis, I need to try to understand the motivation and actions of a suspect, or in your terms, his thinking and behavior. As you know, his identity must remain private. We don't know a lot of the facts yet, but I can tell you what I know so far. The police don't need a warrant to obtain his medical records since he's considered a suspect and possibly a victim as well. But under the H.I.P.P.A. law, we can also get a copy if we feel there is a reason to suspect the crime is related to international terrorism. This murder may very well turn out to be the result of a mind-altering drug given to the perpetrator without his knowledge or permission. If that turns out to be the case, international terrorism is definitely on the table. As long as I have to wait until Monday to get those records, I thought it might help me to speak to a behavioral psychologist who also provides expert testimony in high profile murder cases. I want to try to understand the suspect's frame of mind prior to the crime."

"Agent Carter, I'll certainly do my best to help you in any way I can, however, even in my capacity as a professional, any conclusions I might draw would be based solely on his profile and your description of the circumstances and the suspect. I don't know if I can be of any real help, but I'm willing to listen. But first, if you don't mind me asking, why are you so interested in my insights? Your suspect is already in custody. Your participation, at this point, would usually be limited to gathering evidence for a conviction. I don't mean to be blunt, but this is the kind of thing I would usually expect from prosecution and defense attorneys. Do you have some kind of personal stake in this? I'll be able to help you much more if you can tell me why you need to understand the 'why's' so much, and what makes you need to know them at this particular time and in this particular case."

Carter smiled uneasily, realizing he did, indeed, have more than a professional interest in Michael's case. Dr. Lewis was extremely astute. She knew it was unusual for a detective to seek her help to understand a suspect. He certainly wasn't fooling her. In fact, he seemed very troubled by the nature of this crime.

Carter flushed. He didn't like acknowledging that he might not be as enlightened as he ought to be; he could find no peace or satisfaction in finding the bad guys and bringing them in. Period. No questions asked. "Maybe I should back up a little and tell you about myself and why I think you may be right about my coming here for both professional and personal reasons."

"Dr. Lewis, I believe everything is made out of the same stuff and all connected. Perhaps because this case has brought it to the forefront of my mind, I need to know something important, and it can't wait. If it's O.K. with you, I'd like to talk to you about that first and then move on to trying to understand my suspect's motives."

He began to tell her a little about his understanding of the world according to the teachings of Buddhism. As he spoke, he began to realize that the ideology and philosophy gave him peace because it explained how the universe operated according to cause and effect, and cause and effect gave us the 'why'. For a pragmatist, those answers worked quite well; kind and helpful actions created positive force, and hurtful and selfish actions created negative force. He believed in karmic reward and debt rather than heaven and hell because those concepts provided a vastly more optimistic view of man's quest for total enlightenment. For the Buddhist, there was always another chance to reach Nirvana. When the debt was paid and the lessons learned, there was still a chance to evolve once again.

Even supposing his transgressions warranted regression to a lower form for the space of one lifetime, that was justice, wasn't it? The Buddhist accepted devolvement as a chance to live again in any form. And learn. Within the confines of traditional Christian dogma, if one missed out on all earthly chances to reform, hell was the absolute and only last stop for all eternity. That was too depressing a prospect for Carter to consider.

"So what's the problem?"

"I have to know if I'm a good man. I need to know why I am here, and what my purpose is in life. Will I evolve, devolve or simply be judged and damned? Buddhism tells me that laughter, simplicity, meditation, acceptance, equilibrium, moderation, and respect for all life are the ways to Nirvana. It tells me that whatever I do, as long as I believe in and practice these ideas, any path I take is the right one. Christianity tells me, on the other hand, that the eternal struggle between good and evil, sickness, suffering, atonement and penance pave the path to heaven. If I confess my sins and contribute to the poor box, I'll be forgiven. The teachings of the Buddha fill me with a feeling of calm and lightness of spirit that I don't feel in the Catholic Church. How can I? It focuses almost entirely on the fundamental corruption of the human form. What if I've made the wrong choices, got on the wrong path and damned myself? Can a man be guilty of having thought, said and done awful things as part of his job and still be considered a good man? Or will that keep me barred from salvation no matter what I do to retain my essential goodness?"

"But you came here tonight already understanding that there could never be a definitive answer. So, why isn't it enough for you to choose your own purpose for being and your own road to walk? If there is a plan and it always works out, doesn't that mean that any choice you make will still lead you to the right place in the end?"

"I suppose. But what I mean is, I don't know where the finish line is, either. What I'm doing now…it just doesn't feel right to me, anymore. Do I stick with it anyway or make a life change?"

"Let's back up a moment, Agent Carter. You said the choice no longer felt right. Why?"

Carter began to shiver and shake. "Because I never thought twice about having to understand people and what motivates them. The thought never crossed my mind! I was a cop. Stewing about the reasons there were perps and victims wasn't going to change anything. I tracked them down and brought them in. It was so much easier to do the job without feelings getting in the way. Now, though, I'm beginning to realize I don't understand the first thing about the people in my everyday life, either. Did I destroy that capability when I decided that thinking was too dangerous a sport to indulge in? I want to be a better friend and a better husband. The *best*. I don't want to be the guy who thinks he has all the answers when he doesn't even know what questions to ask. All of a sudden, I know I have to understand myself so that I can be there for them and allow them to be there for me."

"And how will that help you with your cases?"

"The new job assignment requires far more insight into how people think than I ever had to have before. If I can learn to understand all the stuff I packed away in my mind, and if I can learn how to go about understanding every person I meet, I can do far more than track down the suspects and haul them in. But first, I need to know if it's even possible for me to gain insight into people. Maybe I should be back on the local force."

"You say you want to know what motivates people, and yet when faced with opportunities over the past several years, you say you shut down because that was more comfortable for you. Why?"

"I guess the truth is I never really wanted to know. It took too much time and energy. It was a lot easier to believe I had all the answers, and it was easier to turn everything into cause and effect rather than feelings and emotions, which never made any sense to me, anyway. Now, I'm sure I'm sending out nonverbal messages to people that shout, 'find someone else to talk to'. The truth is, the lids won't stay on the boxes anymore; the confusion and unrest is affecting my relationships and my work, doctor."

"Affecting work and relationships in what way? What's forcing the lids off those boxes?"

"This suspect is making choices I don't understand. In this case, understanding his motive is critical to solving the case. I need to understand why he's burying himself alive instead of helping me catch the people who put him in jail. He also has the power to save himself and several others, but he won't. I can't believe that's the 'master plan' at work. I think the plan is for me to understand what makes him tic and get him to open up."

"Why explore your own thoughts and behaviors and those of your immediate friends and family if they already love you for who you are?"

"Because I need to return the favor. People are my business, now. They want wisdom, answers, direction. I think I should understand every one of them and love them for who they are, too. I don't know the people closest to me because I never bothered to ask them what made them tick. I'm dead certain I've never shared a tenth of myself, even with Jill. I want people to know that I'm listening to them and that even if I don't get it, I care.

"Then there's Jill. We moved to New York just a few weeks ago.

133

She's been very worried that we might have made the wrong move for the wrong reasons. She tried to get me to talk about it for months and months, but I wouldn't. I told her the universe had a plan for me, or that my gut told me it felt right. We both know that's nonsense. I do need to know why I made this move, and so does she. I know she feels there's a part of me that's always separate from her, a part of me to which she is not privy. I want her to know that door is now open, and I want her to help me sort through all those boxes. It's the last barrier between us. I'm ready to tear it down, doctor, but I don't know how. I have to learn how people tic, and that scares the crap out of me."

Dr. Lewis laughed. "Agent Carter, if even one percent of all males could identify and verbalize an emotional problem as well as you just did, there might still be hope for the human race. You are not alone in those feelings. People skills do require understanding; you're right. There are tools I can teach you to use to help you document encounters, how you respond, how the other person reacts to your response and how the situation made you feel and why. When you see me, we'll take a look at your chart, discuss it and decide whether or not their feelings, yours, and your responses were objective, valid and appropriate. If so, we will discuss why and let them go. If not, we will practice ones that would have been appropriate and discuss why they might have been better choices. And that's it!

"Exploring and understanding an exact situation after the fact will become easier and easier, allowing you to plan how you want to behave the next time it happens. When you behave differently, I promise you will experience a different result. Once you see a different result, your mind and heart will change. *Truly*. We can't alw///////////////////////////////ays control other people, but we can try to understand what buttons they push and why, and we can learn how to control and change both."

Carter looked like a weight had been lifted off him. "O.K., so anyone can do this. Thanks, Dr. Lewis. When this case is wrapped up, would you consider taking on mine?"

"My door is always open, Agent. Before we move on to business, you mentioned that your work relationships were also becoming a problem. How so?"

"I'm breaking in a rookie who is on her first case, and it's a big one with lots of possible repercussions both politically and professionally. She's my responsibility. I should have been paying a lot closer attention to her than I have; now she's beginning to pull away from me and act on her own, which could be dangerous or fatal. She needs to learn protocol if she's going to move up the ladder, and I'm blowing my chance to bond with her and mentor her correctly."

"Now that you've heard the problem stated out loud, Agent Carter, do you have any idea how to repair the damage?"

Carter looked miserable. "Well, my wife invited her to join us this evening to hear some live jazz. That's a start, but it was Jill's invitation, not mine. I guess I need to look for moments to have conversations that will open her up to me and to my direction and guidance. I suppose I'll need to open up to her, too."

"Good work. You just described one instance in which it is critical to spend quality time and energy on getting to know all about someone else; she is your professional responsibility and she has to learn the tools of the job. You have to be able to count on her as a member of the team, too, and to that end, she needs to be motivated to listen to you, trust you, and talk to you. Find those moments. Think about conversations you want to have before you have them. Celebrate your victories as a team, and blow off steam together when things get frustrating.

"One more thing, Agent Carter; practice using open body language in front of a mirror. Maybe you should even try video-taping conversations you have with your wife so you can see how you look when you're relaxed and receptive.

"You have to give a little to get a little, Agent. Encourage people to ask you about yourself and tell them what they want to know about you. It is imperative you make the time to listen to them when they need a sounding board. You don't have to know the answers or any of the questions. Just listen, and they'll discover their own answers in their own time.

"Maybe that's what your suspect is waiting for. Why should he open up to you when he knows you don't care about him? If you want to be connected to the universe, start with the people in it. All of them. Observe. Ask. Tell. Listen. Learn. Tolerate. Accept other points of view, and for goodness sake, keep your philosophies and opinions to yourself.

What's next on the agenda, Agent Carter?"

135

Carter stabbed the air with his index finger. "O.K., on to the business side of motive. Do you think it is possible to turn crowds of deeply disturbed individuals into murderers by using rhetoric combined with a drug to create a sense of invincibility and aggression? I mean, if I said I thought it was possible for someone with massive amounts of power and money to create a cult of murderers, would you say that was possible?"

# Chapter Seventeen

Seacrest scanned the drink menu at the *Jazz Standard* with the same intensity she applied to her lab experiments. Carter had sent her a text earlier saying he was going to be a little late. The two new colleagues were both tired, so they decided not to wait on the cocktails.

"Go ahead, Agent Seacrest, you pick the first round. Make it a signature drink."

Happy to oblige, Seacrest ordered them a round of Manhattans to start. The old-time favorite was dark red and sweet. It came with a cherry, and it packed a wallop.

When the waitress left, she threw back her head and closed her eyes. Running her fingers through her hair, she gathered it all up in one mass and lifted it off her neck to enjoy the breeze from the ceiling fan. After a moment, she sighed and let it tumble back down. "Ahhhhh, that felt good. Long day!"

The club, a landmark and jazz den located beneath a restaurant called the *Blue Smoke*, had been renovated recently. Seacrest suggested a night out on the town, and Deeprose chose this spot hoping it might pick up their spirits. It didn't pretend to be anything other than what it was. The décor was no nonsense, but the talent was unbelievable, and the crowd was even better than that.

Deeprose was mesmerized by the hundreds of tiny stars dangling above her, sparkling gold and silver against a pitch-black ceiling that she could almost convince herself was the night sky. Deeprose noticed Agent Seacrest was also looking up at the stars, except she was frowning.

*She's still thinkin' about the case...like Ah am.*

The jukebox blasted a whole string of Duke Ellington classics, and Seacrest called out the name of every one of them. Deeprose was impressed; she would never have guessed that Agent Seacrest had a passion for World War II oldies.

The *Jazz Standard* showcased all kinds of jazz, from acid to big band and swing to mainstream, cool, fusion, and avant-garde. Here, you could kick back, avoid the tourists, and hear a pianist whose *Rhapsody in Blue* left you with your mouth hanging open. Then, if you were invited, you could stay after hours and listen to the band blow their heads off until dawn.

Deeprose clapped with enthusiasm when the band finally came on.

"Ready for another Manhattan, ladies?"

Deeprose answered, "Not just now, ma'am. Just some water. What's in those things, anyway?"

"Three parts bourbon and one part sweet red vermouth. And a cherry."

"*Good God!* Is that what Ah've been drinkin'?"

Seacrest rested her chin on her right hand. "This time I want something, a bit more…I don't know…*wild.*"

"How about a *Red-Eyed Zombie?*"

Seacrest sat straight up. "I *like* that idea. Bring two, please."

"Ah haven't had a stiff drink since leavin' Alabama. Ah have a feelin' Ah'm gonna regret this…"

"No regrets tonight, Shania. Can I call you that outside the office now?"

"Ah'd be pleased if you would. I wonder where Agent Carter is."

Seacrest turned toward the stage to watch the band. "Not going to worry about that! Carter's a big boy."

"It's pretty amazin' that y'all are so different but still work so well together."

"It's a pain in the neck, sometimes, but mostly it's very nice. Very nice, indeedy-do."

"Ah hope Ah get along with my husband like that." Deeprose looked sideways at Seacrest and burst out laughing. "But first Ah gotta catch 'im!"

Seacrest glanced around the room. "Maybe it's not going to be as hard as you think. There's a nice-looking gentleman at one o'clock who's got his eye on you."

"One o'clock from where?"

"From where *you* are. To your right and a few feet behind me." Seacrest picked up the drink menu again, and with downcast eyes and a frown of concentration, furtively checked him out by way of her compact mirror. "I think you should go for it!"

"What makes you think that fella's lookin' at *me*?"

"Why not, Shania? He's certainly not looking at *me*. You can see my wedding ring from space." Seacrest held up her hand to reveal a magnificent Vera Wang diamond and sapphire engagement ring and matching wedding band. "This is the only jewelry I wear except for my necklace. See the pendant? It's the sky. The disk is made of Lapis Lazuli, and the moon and stars are diamonds. Carter gave it to me six months after we met. When he put it around my neck, he said that it would remind us always to look up. Then he asked me to promise him that if anything ever happened to him, to search for the brightest star in the sky and say a prayer that wherever he'd gone, he was content." Seacrest became misty-eyed.

"Agent Carter said *that*? Ah didn't think he had that many words in 'im."

"Still waters run deep. Look, why don't you visit the restroom so you can walk past the guy? When you clear him, take a quick look back. If he's been watching you walk away, he's as good as hooked. Carpe diem, Shania."

"Maybe after another one of these zombie things. It's *hot* in here!"

Seacrest knocked Shania's menu off the table. "Ooops!"

Deeprose bent to pick it up and took the unexpected opportunity to glance at the chocolate-brown man wearing a lime button-down shirt with a matching tie so deep in color, it was almost black. Slightly nervous, she began winding a strand of black hair around her finger. "But do ya *really* think he's my type?"

"Wouldn't know. But he's in the band. Ever date a musician, Shania?"

Deeprose scanned the walls without moving her head. Sure enough, he was featured on a poster holding a saxophone and smiling like he really meant it.

"Men are a little slow on the uptake, Shania. If you don't grab him with both hands, it could be a long, lonely winter."

"Ah see." Deeprose giggled. "Is Agent Carter thick too?"

"Oh, yeah." Seacrest rolled her eyes. "Top of the list." She nodded her head. "You don't know how many coffee dates I had to sit through until the light finally dawned on him. Thick as a brick. Some Zen Master!"

"Dear Lord, that gentleman's headin' this way. Keep an eye on my *Red-Eyed Zombie*. Ah'll be right back."

***

"Before I answer your question, Agent Carter, tell me about how you caught your suspect."

Carter gripped the arms of his chair. "I studied the video of Michael taken by the security camera at the museum, until I could mimic, in my mind, his gait and posture. I tried to crawl into his head with the little I could guess about him, but we hit pay dirt when we took a chance the murderer might be hanging around the area where the crime was committed. I know it sounds ridiculous, but that's what happened. I just tried to get a feeling for who he was and we found him. I haven't told Jill or Agent Deeprose about it yet, and I'm not sure I should."

"It doesn't sound ridiculous to me, Agent Carter. Women do it all the time. We plug into social consciousness pretty much the same way you do, except that we don't have to think about it.

"Agent Carter, you caught your suspect because you looked outward into his mind, which is a fabulous start if you really want to change. Your nut to crack is that you look inward. A lot. You've done your best to ignore people, and now you worry about not understanding them and about them misunderstanding you. You see where ignoring them has gotten you; your body language, voice, and demeanor now clearly discourage people from approaching you."

"Really? I thought I was so much better at that now. You know all that about me just from me being here and telling you this story tonight?"

"Textbook, Agent. Do your best not to think about yourself when there are people around. Work on open and welcoming body language and your tone of voice. Engage the world. Force yourself to be interested in others, try to like them for who they are, interact with them, ask questions and give honest answers. Be interested in their problems, joys and sorrows. Get involved. Paste a face on it; if someone's crying on your shoulder, don't push her away.

"Now, tell me everything you can about the facts of the case. Let's see if there's anything helpful I can add."

Carter explained everything he could to her, in detail.

"Regarding how likely it is for a group of angry or fearful people to ignite into a raging mob, the answer is 'very likely' if the combined elements are present in the right proportions at the right time. From a psychosocial perspective, hate can be said to be a contagious disease because it travels through a live social system infecting everything in its path, like cancer devouring a body. Have you ever heard of the *Contagion Theory*?"

\*\*\*

Deeprose extended her right hand to Wilson. He took it in both of his and smiled back at her.

"You have beautiful green eyes, pretty lady. We match tonight."

"Thank you. My name is Shania. Ah saw your name on one of the posters. Wilson, isn't it? Are you playin' tonight?"

"I am. I am." Wilson patted a hand on his chest. "Best saxophonist on the East Side, if I do say so myself."

"Ah've always heard that musicians and bartenders are a great judge of character. Do you consider yourself a great judge of character?"

"Funny you should ask that question! Yes, I consider myself an excellent judge of character. I'm pretty good at knowing the real stories from the bull, but tonight I overheard a conversation that made me wonder if I know anything at all. A bunch of college-age kids were talking about a meeting they went to. I gather it's a part social, part political organization called the *Collective*. They seemed to be pretty freaked out by some of the ideas they heard. To tell you the truth, hearing some of the rhetoric freaked me out a little, too. Do you think they were just jerking my chain?"

"Are they still here, Wilson? Can you point them out to me without using your hands? I'd like to ask them a few questions; it's important."

"Sure. They're sitting three tables to the left of yours—just there,

141

against the wall—the big, round table with all the twenty-somethings. Don't let them know I eaves dropped and spilled the beans, O.K.? They're potential fans." Wilson beamed at Deeprose and pointed at the stage. "Excuse me for just a little bit, Shania; I have to start warming up for the next set. I hate to be so forward, but I'd like to see you again. Can I have your number?"

"With pleasure, Wilson. Maybe you can even put me on your mailin' list."

Wilson grabbed a pen off a nearby table and wrote it on the back of his hand. "Stick around a while. I'll find something real special to play for you."

Shania smiled to herself. She was beginning to feel more at home in New York, and she liked that.

*** 

Dr. Lewis pointed to the T.V. screen hanging on the wall. "If you take a look at the screen, you can read all about *Gustave Le Bon*, a French psychologist, who proposed that crowd psychology differed from that of the individual." She returned the remote to a small table beside her.

"I would rather hear it from you, Dr. Lewis." Carter smiled attentively.

"Certainly. Crowds can radically alter the individual's mindset and subsequent behavior, at least within a very short window of time. Le Bon believed that the influence of the crowd could make a sane and very moral person do things, as part of a crowd, that he would never do as an individual or anywhere else. However, there are some who favor the *Convergence Theory*, which states that individuals join a certain crowd because they want to behave in a certain way and influence others in the crowd who already share their beliefs. It is the 'strength in numbers' principle. Freud believed in something he called a circular reaction, where each person repeats the bad behavior of another, allowing the perpetrator to keep his influence resonating. Because this is a stimulus which generates an almost automatic reaction, individuals might be able to abandon logic or morals, even for one momentary thrill."

"Dr. Lewis, could contagion or convergence theory work on

huge numbers of people? Could it be used to influence people on a national level for political, social, and economic purposes? I'm trying not to go there, but...is that a technique that would have been employed by a man like Hitler on crowds of thousands?"

"Yes. Definitely."

"Doctor, how could this speaker affect a crowd so easily and in so short of a time?"

"He would indicate that he's one of them and that he understands their pain, give them a reason for their suffering that seems plausible, encourage and inspire them to hate and punish, and promise them a better life or after-life if they put his ideas into practice. Men like that have even convinced their followers to commit suicide."

"Do you think people are still as susceptible to manipulation as they were in the past? Could it still happen today?"

"Absolutely. And today, a crowd can be connected technologically; they no longer have to be physically present to gather together. Now you can easily communicate with so many more people at one time and deliver audio-visual effects that are captivating, even theatrical. As long as the techniques used are pretty much as I described, and assuming the audience is affected by this person to the degree that they become passionate to join the cause, anything is possible—from simply joining a club to meeting like-minded people to riot and revolution. Effectively manipulating people and exerting one's will over them in the modern world requires only access to their eyes and ears."

"What about a drug? Could a drug be used to exacerbate the effects of the *contagion* and *convergence* theories enough to make an individual want to....kill?"

"Yes. However, if 'wanting' becomes 'doing', no matter how strong a drug is, we still have free will and can choose whether or not to resist it, with an exception. If a person is unaware he's been drugged, he may not be able to distinguish fantasy from reality. Drugs can be used to control brain activity and hormones, but you never know what else you may be letting out of the can when you use them. A drug would be considered, by anyone administering it, only a temporary measure or a safeguard.

"Le Bon suggested that in a period of widespread discontent, the actions of a mob serves to destroy an old order in preparation for a new one. Social movements help to build the new order, but really, it doesn't matter what's discussed at the large gatherings we're describing. The speaker doesn't care about anything other than getting people there and keeping them there because he has plans of his own for them."

"Unbelievable. I truly appreciate your insights into social behavior in general as well as my own. This has been most enlightening, Doctor."

Dr. Lewis glanced at her watch. "I hate to say it, Agent Carter, but we're just about out of time for today. Would you like to schedule another appointment?"

\*\*\*

Carter hustled through the foot traffic, abandoning his cab to make better time. He was excited and disturbed by Dr. Lewis' explanations, but that would keep until tomorrow. He raced to the jazz club, ready to kick back and let go.

\*\*\*

"Nice of you to show." Seacrest stood up, teetering slightly on her heels. She offered Carter a mighty scowl. "We waited all night for you. What could possibly have been so important?"

"Really, Jill, it *was* very important and *very* last minute, or I never would have been so late. I promise to explain the whole thing to you later."

Deeprose was tapping Seacrest annoyingly and persistently on the shoulder.

"Explain it to me now, big guy. For goodness sakes, what *is* it, Shania?"

Deeprose maneuvered them toward a bunch of millennials at a large table next to the wall. "Y'all just gotta see this for yourselves."

A man with shockingly red hair and a baby blue sweater waved his cell phone in Carter's direction. "Maybe you can settle this for us." Carter smiled and nodded at the young man. "Sure, buddy. What's a night out with friends without a good debate?"

144

It was obvious that Deeprose wanted them to talk to the kids, so Carter pulled up a chair and invited the two ladies to sit down. He blushed as a tipsy Seacrest trailed her hand along the thigh closest to her.

The red-haired man smiled. "Dude, that chick really likes you."

"You know, I think you may be right." Carter whispered in the man's ear. "Think I should ask her out?"

"Yeah, but have a drink first; she's way ahead of you."

He showed Carter a video he'd recorded earlier that night. That was the subject of the debate. After he saw it, Carter nodded to Deeprose, who rose to follow him. "We'll be right back, everyone. Don't finish the party without us."

Someone yelled, "Look man, now he's got another one!" The party roared with laughter.

"What's going on, Agent Deeprose? What is it you think they can tell me? All I saw was a replay of a video of a speech given by some evangelical-type of man. I'm not connecting the dots. Can you help me out, here?"

"These people may have just broken our case, Agent Carter!" She quickly described to Carter, in detail, the event they all attended earlier this evening. "They told me, Agent Carter, in their own words, that as soon as they realized this man was talkin' about real violence, they bolted."

Carter had to acknowledge to himself that when it came to enthusiasm, socializing, and charming information out of people, Deeprose was truly gifted. And as it turned out, she was right. She'd spied out a group of attendees and flushed out a promising suspect like it was all in a day's work.

"I think I know where you're going with this; you think this speaker may be connected to Michael and the drug we confiscated. All right, let's run with it and see where it leads. We'll have to tread lightly, though. We don't want to scare them off. I want a closer look at that video. Agent Deeprose, you're a natural when it comes to putting people at ease. Do you think you could get that redhead to let you borrow his phone?"

"Piece o' cake, sir." Turning to her new friends, she said, "Ah think Ah can settle your debate now, Red!" Deeprose tousled his hair and he blushed furiously. "How 'bout Ah spring for a round o' drinks

145

for y'all, an' you can tell me all about it? Ah'm all ears." Deeprose
gifted the man, now known to her as Red, with a thousand-watt smile
he'd never forget.

Millennials, one and all, raised their glasses, and shouted,
"Cheers!"

Deeprose motioned to the waitress, who flew over to the group
and quickly took their order.

"O.K. Ah'm ready to listen to all your arguments and decide
who has the stronger one. My decision will be considered final.
Commence, Red."

Red looked like he would willingly lay down and die for her. It
was pretty obvious that he liked people and they liked him back, but
he didn't seem to be especially suave with the ladies. He'd be telling
this story for months to come. Carter was glad for him.

*Good thing you thought to video tape that meeting, Red.*

Waving his phone around while it replayed the video, he
continued. "I recorded it at tonight's meeting of the *Collective*. They
call themselves protectionists, whatever that is, and they talked a lot
about their enemies in this country and around the world. The enemy
was everyone and anyone and no one. He just made us angrier and
angrier about how we live and told us our enemies made it that way. I
never heard one specific name mentioned, though. It felt like one of
those radical hate rallies to me. Here's what happened. I got an
invitation by email to attend, so we went. I think the speaker in the
video is a senator, but I can't recall his name. My friends think I'm
crazy."

"And he is. Nice to meet you. I'm Linda." A young woman
extended her hand to Deeprose. She was the West Village artsy
type—no makeup, long mousy-brown hair parted straight down the
middle and huge pointy eyeglasses with black rims.

Agent Deeprose shook Linda's hand. "Nice to make your
acquaintance, Linda. Was it a senator you saw there, or do you think
it coulda been someone who just looked like one?"

Linda answered. "It had to be a look-alike. Why would an
important politician agree to host a fanatical political meeting that
encourages people to tear down a society of just about everyone but
themselves to rebuild a better America defined by himself? I mean,
the guy actually suggested eliminating the "wrong thinkers" for the

good of the American community. That was *exactly* what the man said. Am I right? It's got to be a joke or something. Tell Red he's dreaming if he thinks a senator would cut his own throat in public. Whoever it was, he wasn't actually there, anyway. Seriously, it could have been anybody." Linda began to bite her nails.

"So he was on a screen instead of being there in person, but it was still a live meeting." Red leaned way across the table pointing to the video for emphasis.

Linda frowned. "How do you know? He didn't take any questions or speak to any of his support staff during his speech. It could have been prerecorded. And what makes you so sure that he really meant all that crap, anyway? Maybe he was trying to make a point and we ran out of there too soon to hear it."

"I'll tell you what makes me so sure; I'm not deaf. This man was not exaggerating to make a point. He meant what he was saying! I left because he scared me, yes, but not until the end, and I have it all on tape. He was really out there, you know? Nuts! What I wanna know is, what's in it for him? What happens when some nutball takes him seriously and starts attacking people? I'll tell you one thing, I'd know him if I saw him again. I'm telling you, none of this makes sense!"

Red was way too smart and way too curious for Carter's comfort. The agent decided it was time to step in and tell them who he was and what he was after. "Well spoken, Red. Allow me to introduce myself. I'm F.B.I. Special Agent Carter. This is my wife, Jill, our lead forensic scientist, and our partner, Agent Deeprose."

Suddenly, Red looked like he was about to lose his dinner. A general commotion broke loose, and everyone began talking at once. Carter became momentarily nonplussed.

*New Yorkers! Everyone talks, no one listens.*

"Hey, everyone, calm down. Red, here, is a pretty smart fellow. He may be on to something, but he may not. Let's not get excited. It's possible this was just a giant misunderstanding. We're talking about a senator, after all." Carter didn't want to alarm them unnecessarily, and he certainly didn't want them spreading their ideas any further than this table. Red looked crestfallen. "Red, I promise you we'll still dig around and see what there is to see."

"Really? Cool! This is the only place on earth you can listen to a lunatic in an auditorium that seats hundreds, run into the F.B.I the very next night in a neighborhood dive, and see the film on *Netflix* by next year."

Carter seized the opportunity to gain their cooperation while they were still all revved up. Once they went home, they'd begin to think. "Red, Agent Deeprose would like to borrow your phone and examine it. You'd be doing the city a big favor. Is it O.K. with you?"

"Sure. I mean, no." He rubbed one hand over his forehead, flustered. "Yeah, anything dude. I thought the National Security Agency would have already pulled this info off the web and shut him down, but, hell yeah, you can look at it all you want. Just don't let anyone know I gave it to you. I'm not entirely sure it was cool to film it."

Having learned a little lesson from Deeprose tonight on making friends out of strangers, Carter gladly shook on it.

While they exchanged phone numbers, Deeprose slid the cell phone off the table and into her purse.

Carter guided a very tipsy Seacrest back into her chair while Deeprose, in fifth gear and nearly unstoppable, rattled off ideas. Carter was proud of her and told her so. "Let's get Jill situated. We'll talk about all this later. O.K.?"

Seacrest shouted in Carter's ear. "Shania met a man, tonight— the sax player! And I found him for her!"

"*Shhhhh!* Stop yelling, Jill, it's a jazz club, not a rock concert; everyone can—Wait; did you just call her *Shania*? How much did I miss tonight?"

Seacrest leaned over to whisper in his ear. Unfortunately, she broke the sound barrier again with a huge sonic boom. "A Lot! *Shania met a man*. Did I forget to mention it?"

Actually, it was nice to see Jill finally letting her hair down. Carter put his arm around her shoulders and gave her an affectionate squeeze. He'd made a promise to himself to try to inject a little more fun into their lives when they could manage to snatch the time, and the time, apparently, was now. He pasted a smile on his face, but didn't feel it yet; he was too keyed up.

Seacrest motioned for the waitress. "Excuse me! Over heeeeere! My husband's thirsty. I think he needs one of those *Red-Eyed Zombies*." She smiled wickedly at her husband and winked. "Your forfeit for being late is two of these, Carter. Pay up."

One *Zombie* in, Carter looked around the room in a glow of good cheer. The stars drifted and dazzled in the night sky, and he could actually feel Deeprose *shimmering;* romance was definitely in the air. His attention turned to the dance floor. It was packed with couples swinging to a Glenn Miller classic. He supposed it had become tradition to sing along with the refrain. After each verse he heard the ring of an old fashioned telephone followed by a number shouted in unison by the entire audience— *'Pennsylvania 6, Five Thousand!'*

He'd never seen a swing band or this type of energetic dancing. It was done with incredibly professional precision and great enthusiasm by old and young, alike. Now *that* was blowing off steam! Carter considered taking dancing lessons with Jill. He watched her as she looked around the room taking in everything at once—sound, movement and rhythm that finally drove her right out of her seat.

"Whaddya think of *this*, Carter?"

"I think we should have done this a long time ago. Would you like to give it a try?"

Seacrest beamed. "We don't know how to dance like that! But…what the hell, let's go!"

As they rose, she caught the waitress's attention. "Another *Zombie* for my husband, please. He has a lot of catching up to do. Oh, hell, *Zombies* all around. Come on, Carter; I feel the need for speed."

When they finally sat down again, sweating, exhausted, and very, very, happy, Carter toyed with his second drink to pace himself. The first one hit him hard. Seacrest was having none of that. "Drink up, my love. The purple dusk of twilight time is stealing across the meadows of my heart."

"What does that mean?"

"It means we're not getting any younger. A toast to the night and songs of love!"

*Oh boy, she's gonna be really hung over, tomorrow.*

When the band took a break, Seacrest put some coins in the old-fashioned juke box and chose several slow ones. "Shania, I see your saxophone player walking this way. Why don't we all dance? I picked songs that are slow and timeless. Let's all make a memory tonight."

It was pure magic. Even Carter couldn't deny the dreamy quality of romance wrapping him in its old, familiar embrace. He wished he could capture it in a jar and keep it on his dresser.

*This is what life is all about. This moment. This feeling.*

They danced to every song that old juke box gave out. It occurred to Carter that the melodies and lyrics from back then were much more direct and poignant than today's. Those were the World War II years, when lovers came together for one brief moment if they had the chance, knowing they might have to live on it for the rest of their lives. Moments like those were terribly important. They were memories that became indelibly linked to a single night, a scent and a song that said it all, beautifully.

The last song was *Stardust*, a hauntingly beautiful melody written by Hoagy Carmichael and Mitchell Parish sometime in the 20's—the 1920's, that is. They'd chosen it for the first dance at their wedding reception. There was something about the song that tugged at their heartstrings every time they heard it.

Wilson inhaled the scent of Shania's hair and looking into her eyes, thanked her for the dance. The club was about to close, and the next few sets would be played for the band's own pleasure. He needed to get back to them, so regretfully, he placed a light kiss on her lips and said goodnight.

Carter couldn't help but notice the bemused look on Wilson's face as Deeprose left the dance floor. He seemed to be under a spell.

*Jill did something extraordinary tonight when she decided to play those old juke box records.*

"Ladies, I think we should get some food into us."

Deeprose, amazed, pointed at Carter. "You're right! An' Ah know just the place."

With half closed eyelids and a softness of voice Carter never heard before, Seacrest asked Shania. "Would you rather stay here, honey, and wait for Wilson to take you home?"

Deeprose seemed touched. "He has my number, Jill. I'll wait for his call before Ah consider letting him take me home some other time. Ah'm enjoyin' romance far too much tonight to turn it into a booty call." Smiling, she rose from the table. On their way out, she stopped, shot a long look at Wilson, and winked. Whooping it up and finishing the last of their drinks, late night revelers shouted catcalls at her. A man in an expensive-looking tux with a girl on each arm and a magnum of champagne in each fist projected his voice clear across the room. "Oh yes, oh yes…It's gonna be a hot time on the old town *tonight!*" Then he howled like a wolf. "*Ahwoooooooooooo!!*"

150

Deeprose curtsied in return. Lovers in the dark recesses of the club playfully booed and hissed at Carter as he inched them toward the door. He was mortified.

Seacrest kissed him. "Well, you sure know how to bring down the house, Carter."

Outside, Carter inhaled deeply several times and then had a coughing fit. Seacrest couldn't resist ribbing him a little. "Carter, I told you, you can't swallow this air without chewing it first. One deep breath too many and you'll wind up in the hospital."

Deeprose raised a hand to hail a cab. It came to a screaming halt directly in front of them. "Well, whaddya know? Ah'm on *fire* tonight! Ah just snagged us a cab in under a New York minute!"

"It seems the heavens are smiling down on you, Agent Deeprose. Where are we headed next?"

"For a New York pizza baptism, complete with thin crust, oozin' cheese and oil drippin' out onto paper plates and napkins. And *Cokes* all around!!"

Carter opened the door for Seacrest and would have gotten in after Deeprose, but she'd already scooted around to the other side of the cab and scrambled into the back seat. "Driver, take us to *Ben's Pizzeria* at 123 MacDougal Street. Google says it's a favorite late night spot for N.Y.U. students, an' Ah must say, any campus with its own *Krispy Kreme* knows good food."

The driver, used to out-of-towners, was a good natured man. From the sound of his accent, he hailed from somewhere in India. "Yes ma'am. I know just where you want to go. No problem."

He hit the gas and the little cab obligingly achieved warp speed. Deeprose shouted, "*Yeeeee haaaa! Wooooo Hoooo!*" Seacrest looked a little sick. Carter's face was so mashed up against the window, he couldn't speak, but he thought there was a definite possibility the cab could fly.

*I hate to be the one to rain on the parade, but we've got to start focusing on a new plan of action. Tonight. The next inning is coming up. Deeprose can't afford any strikes, and I can't afford to lose the game.*

"We have arrived." The cabbie parked on a dime and turned his head to smile at them.

It was obvious he was highly amused by the three contorted

151

faces mashed up against the glass partition separating them from himself. As they worked their way out onto the sidewalk, Carter paid the cabbie in cash, something that astonished him. This time he wouldn't have to report the tip. "Thank you, sir. Thank you!"

"Everyone's gotta make a living. Thanks for getting us here in one piece. For a minute, there, I had serious doubts."

The cabbie laughed. Just then, the clouds moved, and the moon struck him full in the face, revealing a visage so handsome it was beautiful. Reverently, he said, "I love America! I am working very hard to become an American citizen, too. It's not so bad driving a cab; I enjoy driving *fast*." He grinned and took off.

"Come on, darling, baptize me. I'm a willing convert." Seacrest was beginning to revive herself now that she'd gotten off the car-plane. The idea of eating out at one in the morning appealed to her.

***

Carter drank in the heavenly scent of tomato sauce, cheese and pepperoni as soon as they walked in. A chef expertly tossed the dough in the air, catching and stretching it into a bigger and bigger disk with every throw.

"That is amazin'!" The pizza chef nodded at them, in a gesture which clearly meant he was ready to take their order. He never took his eyes off the dough, not for a second. "Ah call that real talent! How about we all start with a slice of mushroom and three *Cokes*? No sense in gettin' a whole pie if we want to try *everything*. Next choice is on y'all."

Seacrest gave her the thumbs up. The chef nodded once again, still tossing and turning the ever-growing circle of dough. Carter steered them into a booth. He let out a long, slow, breath and launched into the topic he'd been waiting to discuss all night. "First of all, I want to apologize for being so late tonight. It was because I thought there might be a way to find out why our killer behaved the way he did during the kill. He might have taken that drug he was caught with to help him commit the murder, but according to Jill's lab findings, the curator wasn't given anything that would make him docile, the way Florio was. That's one more inconsistency. "

Deeprose sat completely still for a second, and then, threading her fingers together until they were white-knuckled, she leaned half-way across the table, all attention.

"Here's what I found out. In a nutshell, explosive, vicious, fanatical behavior can be 'contagious'. A person who might never ordinarily conceive of doing something cruel or violent, who understands the difference between right and wrong and who might even be highly intelligent is definitely susceptible to *catching* the excitement of a mob gone wild, even to the extent of joining in their collective behavior. Violent behavior is both highly convergent and contagious when there's a catalyst that sets off an entire group of people. There is a compulsion to let go of thought and inhibitions and to participate and share. When that happens, people are liable to do anything, and they don't have to be under the influence of a drug, either."

Deeprose chimed in. "Sure, it was just the same over in the Middle East with every damn fundamentalist leader and his henchmen."

Carter recalled those bold, American World War II soldiers who risked their lives on the principle that no one had the right to persecute, imprison, deport, torture, or kill people simply because a madman said it was O.K. to do it. The unmistakable parallel of the influence the speaker had over the *Collective* and Hitler's influence over the majority of all Germans hit him like a freight train. "That senator has to be found and questioned."

Deeprose had a thought about the speaker being visible only on a movie screen. "Imagine what it might be like if that same leader gave the same performance, over and over again, all around the country, without ever havin' to leave his own livin' room. Then, imagine havin' a hallucinogenic drug distributed to the audience afterward to push them into fulfillin' his agenda. Every single listener could become a potential murderer and suspect."

"Let's get back to Michael Santiago for the moment. I'm fairly convinced that someone else besides himself orchestrated the museum murders. We've got a blood sample showing trace amounts of something we can't identify. Once the drug he was carrying is done being analyzed, we'll know if that's what we found in his system. We'll also know if he took it prior to the murder. If Michael went to a meeting of the *Collective* that night, he couldn't have known he'd be in for anything else but an ear-load of crap. Suppose, after the speaker got them there, he gave some or all of them that drug to make them willing victims *and* perpetrators, all in one shot. Nice and neat, except for one thing—Michael needed, *or wanted*, more of it after he made his kill. That's why I think he had an unused vial on him. I think he stole it."

Deeprose had more to add. "The speeches are only a way to get the audience into a place where they can connect with other like-minded individuals and a speaker who seems to understand them. He whips them into a frenzy and then either gives them the drug or has them drugged without them knowin' it. But why? What is it? He's got a premeditated plan. Michael didn't even know the old curator, so we can assume the murders aren't personal. That's what has me stumped. If Michael didn't even know the victim, why did he kill him? Why kill a little, old man who worked in a museum his whole life?"

Seacrest wanted to know where Carter learned about the contagion and convergence theories. "How about sharing your source, *Double-O-Seven*? Where were you, tonight?"

"I went to see a cognitive behavioral psychologist." Carter raised a hand expecting a barb from his wife. "I know the *Contagion* and *Convergence* theories might sound crazy at first, but no crazier than people, in general. These are accepted psychological theories, backed up by scientific research and data, on collective violent social behavior, like the peasant revolts during the French Revolution."

Their order was ready. Reluctantly, Carter rose from his seat to retrieve it. "Oh well, let's get back to this later. Right now, we've got some food for the soul coming up." He carried the slices back to the table on a large, round, tin tray. Eager hands pulled at the gooey slices, and for the moment, everything else was forgotten.

Seacrest shot her husband a glance. "Come on, Carter, eat up. Take a walk on the wild side, for a change. Look at all that cheese! Those horribly bad-for-you carbs are calling your name! Give in and enjoy it." She hiccupped.

Carter was hungry, so his standard protest sounded halfhearted, even to himself. "But you have to wonder what all that is doing to your insides."

Deeprose waved a hand in dismissal. "Shoot, as long as no one can see my insides, Ah don't give a damn."

They polished off the slices right down to the crunchy, half-burnt crusts. Seacrest raised her eyes toward heaven, and shouted, "Hallelujah! I've been saved! Thank you, New York, my taste buds are doing the happy dance."

She dabbed sauce off Carter's chin. "Really, Carter, I can't take you anywhere. Who's up for pepperoni?" Seacrest clapped her hands like a child with a new toy. She gestured to the waiter, who plated the steaming slices and delivered them to their table.

Carter lifted an index finger. "We have three theories to consider: Someone gave Michael a not-so-gentle push; the video supplied by our friend, Red, tonight, may confirm there is a definite hub and a person to investigate; and New York City pizza may be the best on this planet. Pretty good for a night's work."

"Yes, *sir*!" Deeprose took another bite and closed her eyes in rapture. "You're so right, Jill. This *is* heaven. Ummmmm!" She swiped the face of her Smartphone intending to check messages, but saw something else instead. "Wait a *minute*! See that right there? That's a photo of Senator Bill Pressman from Langley, Virginia. Look like someone we know?"

Carter heard his own phone receive a message just then and stopped eating to fish it out of his coat pocket. "It looks like Deputy Director Fischetti's been trying to reach us; there must be some new developments. I'll contact him in the morning to get the ball rolling."

"What does the message say, sir?"

"He wants to meet with us tomorrow morning."

Seacrest raised her *Coke*. "On Saturday? Crap! Oh well, it's still *tonight*, so, let's enjoy our last supper."

Carter nodded. "Agreed."

Seacrest frowned. "I'm sure there's an explanation for why the murder victims were chosen, but if all of the attendees received the drug at their last meeting, why haven't we discovered hundreds of murders over the last twenty-four hours? It seems apparent that not all of them received it or the programming, either. I wonder why? And another thing. Neuroscience only goes so far; the ones who do receive the drug still have freedom of choice. They can resist it if they want to. That means it doesn't work on everyone. I'm sure he must have chosen a select few who seemed most likely not to fight it and who'd also be scared to tell anyone afterward, but the only sure way to find out who the *Collective's* killers are is to get the name of every single person who ever attended a meeting. If we can't get the locations, how do we get the names? We don't even know if there are any existing records of these meetings."

Seacrest was overwrought and overwhelmed by the enormity of the issue, and the *Zombies* hadn't helped any. She looked down at the table a moment and then whipped her head back up. "Hey! Red and his friends walked out, Carter. *They walked out!* Isn't the speaker afraid they'll blow the whistle on him? There must be others who did the same thing, too. Carter, those people might know too much now. Red or any of his friends could be on a hit list."

Carter jerked to attention. "Jesus, we forgot all about him and his friends! I'll make arrangements for protection. For all of them. We can talk to Fischetti about it tomorrow morning. That's why I love you, angel; you're the brains of the outfit."

"Thank you, darling. It's high time you admitted it."

Carter shook his soda cup and watched the bubbles bounce off each other. Something Deeprose said earlier suddenly struck him.

He banged the table with his hand. "Random, yet not random. Unrelated, yet related! And by one man—the speaker Red caught on video. Someone's got to talk to Senator Pressman, but I think the deputy director should phone him first to pave the way. Our next step has to be the notification of law enforcement agencies in every single state to send us a blood sample from every murder suspect they've arrested in the last month and ongoing. We'll see if any of them contain the same unidentifiable compounds we found in Michael's blood and the vial he stole. There's got to be someone out there who remembers everything and is still willing to talk. Our case may depend on that person."

***

Alison knew she should be feeling guilty about what might have happened to Michael and Eliza, but she didn't. She'd never been close to anyone before, and until now, she never knew how *good* it felt to feel good. Her phone rang. The identity of the caller came up as "Unknown", but she answered it, anyway.

It was Eliza. "I'm calling from a burner phone, and I can't stay on long. Are you still at Clara's? I'll come over and tell you what happened."

"Hold on." Alison muted the phone. "It's Eliza. She wants to come over. We need her, Clara. She's mean and coarse, but we need all the help we can get. Don't forget she's in trouble now, too, because she didn't follow through with her order to kill you. What should I do?"

# Chapter Eighteen

Carter sucked on his mint, hoping it might help alleviate the whammy the *Red Zombies* laid on him last night. He observed his wife, seemingly fine and sitting with perfect posture, waiting for Deputy Director Fischetti to explain his cryptic text. Agent Deeprose sat to Carter's left, looking, if possible, worse than he felt.

Fischetti grumbled and massaged the back of his neck. His clothes, the same ones he wore the night before, looked all mashed up. Deeprose asked him if he felt all right.

Fischetti glanced over Carter's shoulder at his office couch in answer to her question. "I figured it would be easier to sleep here than to go home and come back again in a few hours." With a grim look of determination, he plunged ahead. "I've got some bad news, and it can't wait. I felt it was only right to share it with all of you, in person."

Fischetti provided them with the details of General Breen's visit and his demand for the vial and all the data compiled from their lab tests by Monday. "We've got until tomorrow night to test it. Agent Seacrest, starting right now, you're in the lab for one thing only—to find out exactly what this compound is and what it does. After that, unless you can pull a rabbit out of your lab coat, we're done with this investigation. You have carte blanche to use any lab equipment necessary and any personnel you need. I'll be blunt; I need you to work around the clock until the deadline. I'm not asking, Agent Seacrest."

Fischetti read and answered a text message before pursing his lips and nodding his thanks to her.

She rose from her chair and made for the door. "May I please be excused for just a moment?"

\*\*\*

Fischetti continued once Seacrest returned. "Now, down to cases. We are faced with highly unusual murders connected, we think, to an unclassified drug. Suddenly the D.O.D. is involved and obviously doesn't want us to know anything more than we already do. That tells me it was made for a purpose, possibly by them. The info is classified; they won't tell me a thing. These murder investigations trump national security, but we still don't have a leg to stand on. I made every argument I could." Fischetti squeezed the bridge of his nose with his thumb and index finger.

"Sir," Carter cleared his throat. "We do know Michael attended a meeting of the *Collective*. We found traces of an unidentified substance in his blood and this morning confirmed that it matches the components in the vial we took from him. The two museum murders were committed within 72 hours of the meeting he attended. It's circumstantial, but it's still a good, solid lead. Agent Deeprose has uncovered a possible connection between the drug and the *Collective* and it's captured on video. I think you should see it right away."

Fischetti suddenly came to full attention.

Deeprose piped up. "We know of at least one meetin' hosted by way of virtual technology, by someone bearin' an uncanny resemblance to Senator Bill Pressman. We have a video taken by one of the attendees on his cell phone. He's been very cooperative, sir, loanin' us his phone an' all."

Fischetti's eyes sparkled. "I begin to suspect your talents have been slightly overlooked, Agent Deeprose. Come on....let's see it. *Christ*! A solid lead!"

Carter was cautious now. "Sir, we can't be sure of the senator's involvement. It may be a lookalike or an attempt to frame him."

Fischetti waved a hand toward Carter. "We can pursue that lead at the same time we infiltrate the *Collective* and investigate their possible link to the drug and our murders. Right now, we need to verify that the video is real. I'll get this down to the cyber team."

Fischetti continued after he'd sent Liz to the cyber lab with the cell phone. "I asked her to come in this weekend to help out. Sometimes I don't know what I'd do without her." Fischetti coughed. "I'll set up an interview with Senator Pressman. This interview has to be done with just the right kind of finesse, the kind that comes across as honest and inexperienced. If he feels safe enough, he might make a mistake while he's talking. It needs a woman's touch. Agent Deeprose, this one seems to be right up your alley. Pour on that southern *'little old me'* act and charm the socks off him. Do whatever you think'll work, but I want any Intel he might have, and I want it yesterday. Remember, any information we get from the senator, at this point, is purely voluntary, so no hardball."

Carter was surprised that Fischetti was on to her.

*Well, well, well....she can't use that one on him anymore...what a shame.*

Seacrest began to squirm in her seat. "I think I should get right down to the lab, sir. Agent Carter, I'm going to need your help. Will you come with me?" The feisty agent looked hard at Carter. Marriage came with all kinds of hidden signals between couples. She wanted to see him alone.

"Certainly."

Carter raced to keep up with Seacrest, who was already out the office door. "Jill, what's going on? Why do you need me in the lab?"

Seacrest punched the elevator button. "No big deal, I just want to show you something. Don't *worry*, Carter! I'll explain when we get down to the lab."

Carter knew that breezy tone of voice and overly innocent look. She had something up her sleeve. She always did. Carter followed her into the elevator, resigning himself to whatever came next.

*** 

Fischetti nodded into the phone and scribbled something on a notepad. "Right away would be best. This is an urgent matter. I appreciate your cooperation, Senator."

Ripping the paper from his pad, he handed it to Deeprose. "Looks like you're flying to D.C. this afternoon. Go home and get some overnight things together. We're done, Agent. Get going."

"Alone, sir? You mean...*alone?*"

"Certainly. Don't worry about a thing. Be yourself." Fischetti laughed for the first time since she'd met him. "Boy, I'd love to be a fly on that wall."

*Has he lost his doggone mind? Ah'm a novice, for pity's sake! What could be more important than havin' Agent Carter lead the questionin'?*

\*\*\*

"Jill, what could be more important than staying for the rest of the meeting? What good am I to you in the lab?"

"You were always a good catcher." Then she fell—face, first.

Carter lunged. "Jill! What's the matter? Your pupils are dilated!"

"Are they? Take me home, Carter."

He looked at her face again and began to sweat. "Tell me you didn't."

"I did. But only half the vial. We still have something to turn over to the D.O.D."

"I'm supposed to be heading out to Washington with Agent Deeprose right now!"

Seacrest's eyes were glazing over quickly. "When Fischetti gave us the lowdown, I sent him a text right there in the meeting to let him know I was going to take half of it. He *knows*, Carter. This is the only way to test the drug before Monday morning. He didn't like the idea but he agreed, and he knows you have to take care of me."

"What?!"

"We don't have a lot of time, Carter. You have to get me home."

This was becoming too much for Carter. He went over the top. "Are you both crazy?! Do you realize *anything* could happen to you? Brain damage? Death? You practically dropped dead in my arms just now!"

"Don't be so dramatic, Carter. It was my decision to make."

"It was not! You're my wife, Jill. You can't jump out of an airplane without a parachute without discussing it with me first. Jill, *why*? Why did you risk everything?"

"For the same reason you risk everything on the job every day, Carter; it's the right thing to do, and the only thing to do."

He clutched her tightly. "Don't you ever, *ever* do something like this again, do you hear me? *Ever*! If anything happens to you, Jill, I…I don't …"

Safe in his arms, she faded away into oblivion.

161

\*\*\*

Deeprose picked at the pills on her sweater for the thousandth time during her flight.

*Ah guess Agent Carter received new instructions requirin' him to stay behind. Why wasn't Ah told what they were? It just doesn't feel right, and now Ah gotta do this interview all by maself.*

Deeprose assumed politicians were every bit as tight-lipped as the big brass were in the service. Everything was on a need-to-know basis, and it was a matter of course that you never needed to know.

She couldn't imagine a senator having anything to do with a group like the *Collective*. What kind of past did Pressman have? There were no records of him prior to taking office, so she'd have to tread lightly.

*What kind of leverage would get me some candid answers?*

\*\*\*

Carter settled Seacrest into a cab while hoping against hope they wouldn't have the kind of ride they had last night.

*Will this turn her into a murderer? Maybe I should be ready for it, just in case.*

"Hey buddy, my wife is ill. I'd appreciate a smooth ride, if possible." Carter handed him a ten dollar bill from his suit pocket.

The cabbie smiled into the rear view mirror. "No problem, sir. Smooth as silk."

Carter was scared to death and hopping mad.

*No mantra ever invented could help me in a situation like this. Wait—now is exactly the time to use the calming mantra. Stop. Think. She doesn't need anger now; she needs me to get her through this. Now, get a hold of yourself before we get home.*

Seacrest slumped against his shoulder, so he pulled her across his chest and enveloped her in his arms. When she closed her eyes, he plunged himself into positive, rational thought. Carter was neither self-indulgent nor selfish; he knew that it was absolutely necessary to clear his mind of all thoughts of himself if he was to function on all thrusters for Jill. He slowed his breathing and inside his mind, he spoke the mantra.

*Worry serves no purpose; it won't change anything. I can feel the worry leaving me with every outward breath. I am human; I acknowledge these feelings, but I choose not to be ruled by them. Planning is better than worrying. Show her compassion and quiet strength. Let her know your thoughts lie solely on her.*

"Are you O.K., honey? How do you feel?"

She answered shakily. "I'm O.K. I just want to get home." She closed her eyes again and sighed.

*That's the way to do it. Better, Carter; you're doing better.*

*Now, to continue.... Outward and inward displays of anger, fear, and control are selfish, useless and hurtful. They are distractions that solve nothing. They cloud my brain. Venting will not give me the relief I think it will. It adds to my problems and creates them for others, resolving nothing. I will not create bad karma when I need to generate all the help I can from a willing universe. With every outward breath I feel anger, fear, and the need to control leaving my mind.*

*Focus on Jill. Only on Jill. She needs me; she is my only concern, not myself. I feel all my fears leaving me with every outward breath so I can fill myself up with helpfulness. I am not in control of some things, but I can try to control the outcome of this situation. I can. I will. I feel the calm entering me with every inward breath. I can do whatever I have to do.*

"Is there anything I can do to make you more comfortable, Jill? Do you want to stop for some water?"

"No, just get me home."

"Driver, is there any way to speed up the ride? We'll sacrifice a smooth ride for speed."

New York cabbies are the keepers of the sacred secrets of cutting through heavy city traffic at any time and on any day; it's a trick of the trade on which they pride themselves. Enthusiastically, the driver replied, "Yes, certainly, sir! On a Saturday, the fastest way to get to the Upper West Side is by taking the F.D.R. Drive on the *East Side* and then cutting over. I'll get you there in less than 15 minutes from where we are now."

The taxi took off like it was being chased by the cops. Carter braced himself and hung onto Jill. If it was a fast ride she wanted, a fast ride was what she was going to get.

*There, now. I kept the lid on it, asked her what she wanted and calmly asked the driver if he could help. I'm going to have to remember that the tools work the best when you don't want to use them at all. Now, where was I?*

To stay focused on the moment, he imagined himself filling up a glass with all his anxieties, and then, in his mind's eye, watch himself pour them out onto the ground. He saw his worries seep into dry, thirsty soil, and he felt some relief. By the time they got home, Carter's heart rate had come back to normal, and he was ready to focus on whatever lay ahead.

\*\*\*

Deeprose settled into a seat before Senator Pressman and presented him with her most engaging and open smile. She'd done her homework. Pressman began his career in the military. "It's an honor to meet you, sir. Your service to our country is truly appreciated."

Pressman looked first surprised and then pleased. He relaxed his posture and smiled. "I'm happy to make you're acquaintance, Agent Deeprose, and thank you. Am I really getting that old, or are agents getting younger and younger all the time?"

The dance had begun. She waved a hand in the air while subtly removing the phone from her pocket with the other. "Shoot, you're in the prime of life, Senator. We'd appreciate it awfully, sir, if you'd allow me to ask a few questions pertainin' to an ongoin' investigation. We're hopin' you can shed some light on somethin' that's not makin' sense to us."

"I don't know how I can help, but go ahead and ask."

"What you're about to see on this video might be shockin', but Ah need you to be as forthcomin' as possible when it's over. Your thoughts might lead us in a new direction."

As he watched, the blood drained from his face but returned in a flood when he started yelling. "Where did you get that garbage? Is this some kind of joke? I may be fair game during an election year, but this is outrageous!"

Pressman was so red in the face, Deeprose thought he might have a stroke. She held up a hand as if she was a crossing guard. "Calm down, sir! No one believes this is really you, but Ah'm here to try to find out who it is. This is not a joke, Senator. Will you please confirm that this is *not* you on this video? Why do you think someone would use your likeness and voice as a front for this operation? Sir, is there any chance you're bein' framed? Ah need to know everythin' you can tell me."

"*Of course*, it isn't *me*! I have no idea who the hell it is! Why hijack *my* identity? Oh God—it must be all over the web by now! This will *ruin* me! Agent Deeprose, I'm going to have whoever is responsible for this strung up so high he'll be wearing his balls for a hat!"

"We have reason to believe these meetin's are incitin' people to murder. If you have any idea who could be behind it or why he'd want to make you the fall guy, it would be best if you told me now."

Deeprose regretted the words as she soon as she spoke them.

*Shoot! Ah practically accused him of collusion. Carter's so much better at goadin' people into confessions.*

Pressman leapt from his seat and paced. His maroon leather chair spun in circles like one of those scratchy, old records her father still played. Deeprose watched it turn, hoping that if the senator was going to unravel, he'd do it as quickly as his chair did and get it over with.

"I can't think of anyone out to get me, if that's what you mean." He wrapped a hand around his chin. "Even if I had a name in mind, I can't very well give it to you without something more than suspicion."

"This video has already gone viral, sir. If you're not goin' to help us, y'all are just shootin' yourself in the foot. Ah don't think you have a choice. Ah need to know anythin' ya think might be relevant to this case; *we'll* worry about interviewin' our leads and collectin' evidence."

"Agent Deeprose, you don't know the depth of the water you're treading. My past is a matter of national security."

*His past? Ah didn't say anythin' about his past. Come to think of it, Fischetti mentioned that General Breen said over and over again that this was a matter of national security. Could Pressman know we had a visit from General Breen? What else does he know?*

"Sir, do you know of any new drugs that were designed or used to stimulate feelings of murderous aggression and fearlessness in an individual or a group of individuals?"

"What? No! How could I?" Pressman thrust his hands into his

pockets. He turned toward the window, and in the light, she could see shiny beads of sweat glistening on his forehead.

"Sir, Ah have it on good authority that some kinda drug is bein' slipped to attendees that encourages them to commit murder." She knew nothing of the sort, but it couldn't hurt to fish a little.

"I already told you I know nothing about this!"

"Then why are they usin' *you*, sir? Don'tcha think that's more than a little strange? More than a coincidence? Don'tcha have any idea why you're bein' set up and by whom?"

"This interview is over, Agent Deeprose. I expect this video to be buried. It should have been pulled the minute you found out about it! I want you to go straight back to New York and tell Fischetti to pull that video, and leave this problem to the big boys. If he has to do damage control by calling it a hoax, then that's what he has to do for the sake of national security. This has to be kicked upstairs to the D.O.D. If you're right about this, it's out of your purview now."

"Thank you, sir. Ah apologize for upsettin' you, but unfortunately, it's part of the job. Ah hope our lab can provide definitive proof that the man on the video isn't you. Good day."

*O.K., Mr. Senator, have it your way. Ah gave you every chance to come clean or to help us. Now all bets are off.*

She snatched up the cell phone and headed for the door.

"Agent Deeprose!"

She turned.

"I'm doing this for my country, damn it! You're too young to…"

She left without hearing the rest.

***

Seacrest tossed and turned on the bed while Carter raced around their apartment looking for extra pillows and blankets. He hoped they might keep her from falling off and hurting herself. Just after they got home, she began saying there was someone she had to kill for everyone's good. Carter tried to minimize it for his own sanity.

*She only took a half of a dose. She probably experimented with things like that in college, anyway. She's trained to control her own behavior in the event that she's given mind control drugs, so come on, Carter. No 'what-ifs'.*

166

Carter stroked her sweat-soaked hair. "Remember your training, honey."

The drug was turning his wife into a monster. "He has to die, and I have to do it. He doesn't deserve to live!" Spit flew from her mouth with the vehemence of her screams.

*I can't stand seeing her like this. When this is over, she has to learn caution and self-control. She has to! I can't live with not knowing what crazy thing she'll do next.*

There were moments when she struggled to remain rational to record the effects of the drug, but in other moments, she pounded her fists on the bed and ranted at some boy she must have known in school. "I'm going to wrap my hands around your neck and squeeze it into *Silly Putty*, Tommy Gardner!"

Carter admitted to himself the full scope of Seacrest's situation. It was going to get far worse before it got better. If it got better. He was ashamed of what he was about to do, but it was for her own safety and protection. He removed his handcuffs from his belt and grabbed his wife's left arm. The click of the cuffs sent Seacrest into a rage. Her mouth dove at anything closest to her. She bared her teeth, sank them into Carter's hand and smiled in satisfaction.

"*God!*" Before he could shake it off, Seacrest dive bombed his free hand again. He barely evaded her attack. Throwing himself onto her, he used his own weight to restrain her as he struggled with the cuffs. A few dicey seconds passed until he heard a confirming click.

*One hand successfully cuffed.*

Carter eyed the bedpost to gauge exactly what he'd have to do to secure the other hand without bloodshed and a tetanus shot.

"If...you'll...just...*cooperate*..."

Jill spat in his face and howled. "Everyone knows you hunt for stray dogs and shoot them in your backyard! I saw you do it myself! I'll kill you, you sick bastard! You killed those poor animals and *liked* it! You don't *deserve* to live!"

Carter dragged her other arm to the bedpost and fastened it there while she was distracted.

*At least, now, you won't fall out of bed, or hurt yourself....or me.*

Somehow, they made it through the night. Seacrest screamed for blood and Carter mopped her face and helped her drink as much water as she could take. By morning he was a wreck, and she was

167

incoherent and vacant. The cell phone never left his side in case they needed an ambulance, but he'd already asked a neighbor to drive them there if push came to shove. He knew full well you could die in New York City before an ambulance got to you.

Seacrest started screaming and tugging on the cuffs again. This time, the outwardly unflappable Carter disappeared altogether. His Zen tools went right out the window, completely forgotten. He walked in circles, trying to decide if they should stay in the apartment or go to the hospital when he noticed the metallic clinking of handcuffs against the iron bedpost. It gave Carter an idea.

*Sound!*

He bounded across the room and began searching for the wireless speakers Seacrest gave him for Christmas last year. When they didn't readily appear, he started grabbing boxes and dumping them out on the floor in piles and heaps.

*Ah! Finally!*

Carter commanded his voice assistant to play something very special. The assistant obeyed, and the speakers came to life.

# Chapter Nineteen

Seacrest stared at Carter with empty eyes as if he was a stranger. She knew her own name, but not his. She croaked, "Who…who are you?"

Handcuffed to the bed and sweating profusely, restless and disoriented, all she could do was turn her head from side to side and jerk on the cuffs.

*"It's me,* honey, Carter. You're O.K. You're safe, home and in bed. Listen to me; I'm going to help you. The agitation and confusion you're experiencing are caused by too many neurons firing at once. I'm playing isochronal tones for you. They'll help your brain waves re-stabilize from a beta to an alpha state. Concentrate on the beating of the tones, try to relax your body, and breathe slowly. In through the nose and out through the mouth."

"Where am I?"

"Jill, do you remember being in the jazz club on Friday night?"

"Huh? Oh yes!" She tried to sit upright. "Why am I handcuffed? Did I make some kind of a scene? Am I under arrest?"

"No, honey. Yesterday morning you volunteered to take the drug we confiscated, remember? It should wear off by tomorrow, I think…I hope. By then we'll know exactly how it affected you and what happens when it wears off. You took a *terrible* risk, Jill."

"Oh, right. Right. I remember. How'd I do last night?"

"Pretty bad. I had to handcuff you to the bedposts for your own safety. You had crazy superhuman strength, you were completely out of control, and if I hadn't stopped you, you might have, well, let's just say you were incredibly angry at some kid named Tommy. You lost a lot of fluids and most of your voice, but you're doing a damn good job of resisting the drug. When you feel better, we'll talk. I'm recording the whole experience so we don't have to bother about documenting it or forgetting anything. For now, honey, just focus on the sounds. Try not to think too much. I'm here, and nothing's going to hurt you. I promise."

"I hated that twisted sonofabitch so damn *much*! Did I kill him, Carter?"

"Who? Tommy? No, no you didn't." He smiled reassuringly.

"Oh…that's good. I wanted to, though. I really did. This music is weird. Are we still at the club?" She was drifting from one place to another.

"No, sweetheart. You're here with me. Home."

"I didn't really want to hurt anyone." Jill whispered. "Come closer." When Carter cuddled up to her, she made a confession. "I *saw* you in my dreams. There were all these people inside my head, and they were chanting. They wanted me to do it. I knew it was wrong, and I tried my best to ignore them, Carter, but I couldn't. It was like I actually became rage and vengeance." She whispered in horror, "There wasn't anything that could have stopped me, Carter, if I hadn't been chained up. I might have killed *anyone* thinking it was that boy!"

Before he could answer, she faded away from him again.

This time, she was floating on the soft ripples of a pond surrounded by tall grass. The voices called her, but she couldn't see who they belonged to. Passively, Seacrest noticed that everything she saw pulsed to the rhythm of a pounding sound she didn't like.

*I can't move.*

The water rose and fell with those tones, rising so high it terrified her and plunging down so deep she felt swallowed up. The last thing she remembered was seeing Carter walking along the horizon; was he walking toward or away from her? She couldn't tell.

*I shouldn't have made so many important decisions over the years without talking to him, first; everything I do affects him. Why didn't I realize that before?*

But she knew the answer, already.

*Because he never told me so, and I have to hear the words.*

***

Deputy Director Fischetti rolled over in his bed, fighting to recall where he was and how he had gotten there.

*What time is it?*

Glancing at his Rolex, he realized with enormous relief that it was early on Sunday morning. A quick stumble out of bed brought him face-to-face with a standing mirror. Wearing only his boxer shorts, a white T-shirt and navy blue dress socks, he inspected his body.

*What a mess!*

The stubble of his beard made him look like one of those 1940s murder mystery detectives he liked to watch on cable. All he needed was a trench coat and a fedora smashed down over one eye. His clothing had been thrown over a chair. He usually kept everything neat and folded.

*Must've had one Scotch too many, last night.*

Fischetti scrubbed a hand back and forth over the stubble on his chin and thought back to the day before.

*Crap! I've got to check on Carter and Seacrest. Please God, let Deeprose get a hot lead from Senator Pressman. She is really something, that one. I bet she's got the goods on him already.*

A long, hot shower was the first order of business. He'd stayed in a hotel over the weekend to save commuting time and had his heart set on a treat for breakfast at *Ess-a-Bagel,* his very favorite café, on First Avenue near 20th Street.

*Nothing like a good old fashioned garlic bagel and a schmear— the breakfast of champions!*

It had been a while since Fischetti allowed himself to eat freshly made New York City bagels, which, when it came right down to it, were the *only* real bagels in the world. The thought of a hot pastrami and Swiss on marbled rye brought on such a feeling of longing that it was almost painful.

*Choices, choices...Oh, what the hell; maybe I'll get both.*

Fischetti had already blown some big money staying at the *Millenium,* but it would wind up on his expense report, anyway. The Bureau could thank General Breen for that. With righteous indignation, he shaved and then began to make himself presentable. He made sure his tie was knotted expertly—it only took him three tries and a couple of curses to get it right. Fischetti walked outside and shook off the chill of another overcast morning.

*You'd think we could get one day of sunshine in this crummy town. Just one God damned day!*

He stood still for a moment, trying to decide if he should walk, take the subway or hail a cab, but his mind wandered back to food...

*Definitely a bagel for breakfast and hot pastrami for lunch. I'll take a cab and worry about my waistline tomorrow.*

For a man in his 50's, being away from home for the weekend was a mixed blessing. He missed Amelia, his live-in girlfriend, but he'd been married before for several years and was somewhat set in his ways.

*Maybe this live-in thing wasn't such a good idea.*

With fiendish delight, he looked forward to breaking the rules.

*I'll take a nap if I want one, too.*

His habit of needing naps after a big Sunday breakfast was the real reason carbs were off the menu at home. That, and his growing belly, really got under Amelia's carefully protected skin.

*I hate to say it, but she's right. On the other hand, life's short, and sometimes a man's just got to have a God damned pastry without it becoming a federal case.*

Walking along Church Street searching for a cab, Fischetti recalled his first wife, Angela, and how she loved to walk with him, early on Sunday mornings, to their favorite Italian pastry shop. It was one of the few things they really enjoyed together.

Then, as now, his work took a serious toll on his relationships. It was pretty much the same for all officers of the law, and most certainly for the ones that got ahead and were assigned to positions of importance.

*But the work is more than important. It's critical. If she can't compromise a little, she'll just have to decide what she wants to do, and do it. I sacrificed too much to give up my big chance, now.*

But, it wasn't an easy choice to live with. He often felt lonely and alone, with no one to talk to who really wanted to listen, and no one who gave a damn enough to help him through the rough patches. He needed someone to love him and to save him, but he knew Amelia was only interested in saving the world from a safe distance. He also knew he'd never ask her to move out.

A man in a dark blue *Lexus* slowed down and lowered his window. "Good morning! You're in luck. Hop in." It was an unmarked livery car, and the driver looked about twenty years older than himself.

Fischetti was instantly on the alert. "No thanks. I'll wait for a yellow cab."

"I'll take you anywhere you want to go, Deputy Director, free of charge. You can't do better than that."

*Shit.*

He suspected he'd been put under surveillance since his meeting with Breen, so he wasn't all that startled.

"Who are you? What's this all about?"

The old gentleman possessed an elegance and rakish charm that came naturally to him. Intelligence sparkled in the depths of his eyes. He had a dazzling lopsided grin that made no secret of his penchant for devilry. "Please. Get in, make yourself comfortable, and I'll explain. I promise you, there's nothing to worry about. As you see, I am a harmless, old man. And you? You are very famous in this neck of the woods. I'm here to give you some help and guidance from the sidelines, but if you want it, you'll have to get in." He glanced in his rear view mirror and back to Fischetti.

"*Shit!* All right. I'm armed, so no sudden movement."

The old man chuckled and pulled a dark blue fisherman's cap closer down to his eyebrows. "I'll keep that in mind."

Fischetti knew the D.O.D. wanted him off the case, but how far were they willing to go to make sure of it?

The car pulled away from the curb and maneuvered into the growing downtown traffic. "So, what's this all about, Mr.—I didn't get your name."

"With all due respect, that's because I didn't give it to you. I've worked behind the scenes for a long, *long* time, and that's where I have to stay. Consider me a ghost." He looked at Fischetti in the mirror again and smiled, revealing an entire regiment of crinkly laugh lines that ambushed his eyes every now and then. Fischetti looked into the mirror as well and made his decision. "Have it your way, *Mr. X.* I can dig, too. And I will."

"All you need to know is that I'm an ally. I know about General Breen's visit, the murders, the drug, and the video you have of the *Collective* and Senator Pressman. I can help you catch the people organizing it all. After that, it will no longer be an F.B.I. issue."

"How do you know...?" Fischetti paused. "You must have hacked my phone and bugged the office."

He seemed amused. "I *did* do a little eaves-dropping. I apologize. In any case, it wasn't very difficult to put the pieces together once you got a visit from the D.O.D."

*The son-of-a-gun is enjoying himself!*

"Just who are you, Mr. X, and what's your interest in this mess? And no more cloak-and-dagger nonsense. I want to know."

"It's about time we restored a little integrity to the F.B.I., don't you think?"

"Restored the integrity of...what the hell do you mean by *that*?"

"I'm implying that the F.B.I is mixed up in all of this."

"Look, you haven't told me one damn thing I don't already know, and I still don't know who the hell you are or what it is you're after. So, let's start with something else. What do you know about Senator Pressman? Is he involved in this?"

"I'm not certain yet, but there are a few other things I think you should know. The drug was probably developed by a foundation that serves the military. Take a look at Meese Corporation in Langley, Virginia. It would have been approved and funded by a top-secret government-sponsored think-tank called the *JASONS*."

"The *JASONS*? Are you *kidding* me?" Fischetti pressed fingers against his temples. "Look, Mr. X., we're officially off this case as of tomorrow, as I'm sure you already know, so I appreciate your offer to help us catch the mythological *JASONS*, but I think I've got it under control. However, the city thanks you and so do I."

*Crackpot.*

The lopsided grin returned. "I'm sorry I can't give you more than that right now, but you're on the right track. Keep pushing along, and you'll get there. I'll be around to help when you need me. I don't care much about consequences anymore. There's very little left they can do to an old man like me."

He winked into the rear view mirror. "The drug and all the documentation concerning it must be destroyed when you find it. If we don't end it now—quickly and completely—we won't be able to stop it at all. Now, where can I drop you?"

\*\*\*

"First and 20th."

They rode along in silence for a few minutes.

*He seems like a nut, but he knows a little too much. He didn't meet me on the street by chance, either. I'm knee deep in this investigation now. If Agent Seacrest is forced to take a drug test, she'll go to prison.*

*If the military wants to screw with me, we could all be arrested for high treason by Monday night. And if an anonymous entity and the government are colluding in an operation involving drugs and murder, they won't bother arresting us. They'll just kill us.*

*Well, at least the lab's inventory programming is only capable of cataloging the dosage as a single unit, so tomorrow morning when I hand it over to General Breen, there's no way of proving we ever recovered more than half of it. That ought to burn his britches.*

"You have a nice smile when you use it, Deputy Director Fischetti. We're going to get along just fine." At the next light, Mr. X twisted around in his seat and extended his hand for a shake. "Don't worry, I've got your number. I'll be in touch with you. Soon."

Fischetti nodded, extended his hand and left the car feeling…deflated.

*I only wish he was the real deal. I could use some help from an old-timer with all his marbles.*

Mr. X lowered the front passenger window. "Don't trust anyone. Not your colleagues, not even me. It's going to get ugly, Deputy Director. I'll be watching."

Fischetti stared at the car until it disappeared into the traffic. He felt like he'd just seen a U.F.O. Who would ever believe a story like this?

*Who the hell is he? And whose side is he on?*

***

Later on, Fischetti received an email containing preliminary news about the video footage from the last meeting of the *Collective*. As he scanned the message, he wondered how many other eyes and ears had already been privy to it. How many more men like Mr. X were listening and watching?

The report indicated that technology was used to create the "talking head" of Senator Pressman. Any good film editor could have done the job much better.

*Whoever did it knew it would lead straight to the Senator's door and keep us running in the wrong direction. Pressman is a blind.*

The buzzer outside his office interrupted his thoughts. He sighed and pressed a button underneath his desk to unlock the door.

175

*Is there anyone left on this planet who hasn't figured out how to get past Liz? What does she do out there, anyway?*

Agent Deeprose's lavender sweater whispered hello. He liked that color; it was calming.

*I wonder if she chose that color on purpose.*

"Well, Agent Deeprose, you're a sight for sore eyes."

Deeprose smiled quizzically. "What'd Ah miss?"

"Oh, conspiracy, murder, mind control, high treason...you know, the usual."

Deeprose made a beeline for his coffee maker. "Would you mind, sir? Ah just gotta have a decent cup!"

"Help yourself. I want to talk about your trip to Washington and fill you in on Carter's end of things, but I also have a piece of news. We might have an ally."

\*\*\*

Agent Deeprose delivered her report to Fischetti.

"Too bad you didn't catch the rest of what Pressman was yelling about when you left. He was in the military, and he says his past record is classified, so the drug must have been developed for military use. We'll keep an eye on him. Once he starts to think, he's going to get good and scared. Then he'll come to us."

"Yes. Sir."

"Agent Deeprose, I don't want to give you the impression that I run this office as if we were shooting it out at the *O.K. Corral*. We're, very regrettably, engaging in *highly* questionable protocol I would never sanction if I thought we had any other choice. If we survive, we won't be thanked; we're more likely to find ourselves executed. You have a rare talent for dissembling that we could sorely use, but you're also a rookie; you haven't even completed your field training yet. I have no right to ask an untried agent to engage in this operation, *but I do ask.* If you want out, no one will blame you, but I need your decision by the end of the day."

"Then Ah suggest y'all quit wastin' time, sir. Ah'm *in*. What's next?"

Fischetti cleared his throat and nodded his head once in an awkward attempt to express his thanks. "It's imperative we make the most of whatever we find out from Agent Seacrest. She took a God-awful chance for us. It has to count."

He opened a drawer and handed Red's cell phone to Deeprose. "Why don't you pay a visit to our young hero to return this and give him our thanks? When you get back, your priority is to focus on a company called Meese. See if you can tie them to our museum murders. I have work to do, Agent. That's all."

"Yes, sir. Is the lab still workin' on the Pressman video?"

"Yes, but they have what they needed from the phone, so it can be returned now."

Deeprose was half way down the hall when he called her back. "Yes, Sir?"

"Remind Red not to speak to *anyone* about this. We've got him covered by plainclothesmen, but I don't want to spook him, so don't tell him the extent of the danger he could be in. That'll just make it worse for everyone. Just tell him to keep an eye out for anything out of the ordinary and to call us right away if he obtains any further information. Let him know we value his cooperation and that we're working on getting him compensated for his help. There are still some decent kids out there; I want him to know his contribution is noted and appreciated."

⚜⚜⚜

Now that she knew Fischetti felt she'd done a good job with the senator and wanted her on the team, she was able to relax and enjoy the pretty drive to Westchester, where Philip Dean, or 'Red', as she called him, grew up and still spent his weekends.

She parked the car and looked around the neighborhood.

*It's so quiet around here that I feel like whisperin'. No wonder he let his friends drag him to that meetin'.*

The door opened almost before she rang the bell. "Oh, hi! Agent...Deeprose. Right?"

"Live and in color!" Deeprose flashed her I.D.

Red led the way to the kitchen. He opened up a couple of cans of soda, and they settled themselves at the kitchen table to chat. "My parents are away, so we can talk without being overheard. They're snow birds—you know, they travel to warmer places when it gets cold. I love the seasons." He stopped short and turned beet red from his forehead down to his shirt collar. "I'm rambling, aren't I?"

177

"Not at all, Red! Ah think y'all are a very charmin' young man, and Ah enjoy your company very much."

"About the other evening. I was a little smashed. What I mean is, I'm not usually argumentative or insistent. In fact, I'm usually kind of invisible, except for my hair. I hope I didn't make an ass of myself." He stared at a spot on the table.

*He looks like he's waitin' for the earth to open up and swallow him.*

"Red, you are the bravest man Ah have ever met. Y'all knew somethin' wasn't right, and you spoke your mind regardless of what anyone mighta thoughta you. That's the stuff that heroes are made of. You are *anythin'* but invisible, and your whole bright future is right out there in front of you like a red carpet, just waitin' for you to start your journey. Y'all don't cut loose enough, if you ask me!"

"Thanks. I appreciate that. You know, going without my phone for the past few days has been serious cold turkey! Never wanna do *that* again. Can I have it back, now?"

"Here it is all safe an' sound. Ah hope you don't mind, but the Bureau thought it'd be best to remove the video from your device."

"Uh, sure. Was I right about the host? Was it Senator Pressman?"

"Ah can't discuss it with you, Red, even though y'all deserve to know. After the case is closed, we'll talk again. You know, we'd still be in the dark if it wasn't for you."

She paused briefly and then plunged on to her real reason for visiting. "Red, wouldja help us out just one more time? It'd mean a lot to our investigation if you would; you can help us break it wide open. How about directin' us to the next place the *Collective* plans to meet?"

"I don't know if I can. I mean…" He looked away for a moment. Deeprose watched him struggle to come to a decision. When Red turned back, he slammed a fist on the table and answered her in great excitement. "Yeah. Sure I can. Hell, yeah!"

*Golly! He just grew up right in front of my eyes...*

He explained the problem to her. "It's just that you're not allowed to attend any meetings without an invitation, and I highly doubt I'll get another one. They're held in a different location every time they meet, so I'll ask my friends to respond to the next one they get. After that, I'll be able to tell you the 'when and where'. Cool?"

"Cool. But promise me that none of y'all will attend any more of those events. It's trouble all the way."

"I promise." Philip raised his right hand. "So, we really uncovered something criminal, huh?"

Deeprose cocked her head. "Again…open investigation…"

Red laughed. "Yeah, I forgot. The thing is, *it's* so *cool*. I've always had pretty good instincts, and trouble does find me wherever I go; that *must* mean something, Agent Deeprose. The answer's been right in front of me my whole life!"

"The answer to what?"

"To what I want to do with my life. I picked the wrong major; I should've chosen criminal justice. I considered applying to Quantico, but I wasn't sure I had the right stuff. If I could turn back the clock, I wouldn't think twice; I'd do it."

Deeprose was amazed. The goofy college kid was gone. In his place was a man who knew what he wanted.

*Ah hope Ah never forget this moment.*

"That's a wonderful idea, Red, and you don't have to turn back the clock; we can use all the help we can get, but think it over carefully. Once you make that choice, you won't have much time for yourself or your friends an' family, anymore. It's not an easy road, but it's a rewardin' one. C'mon, walk me to the door."

***

When Deeprose finally got home, she was worn out, but the deputy director had made it clear that he needed her to research a company called Meese to see if there was any connection between them and the museum killings. She made a big pot of coffee to re-energize herself. A quarter of a can of *Reddi-whip* sweetened her steaming mug.

The internet was a vast jungle of misdirection and misinformation, making it difficult to find real answers. It was also a haven for thieves, spies and modern day pirates who used the web as both vessel and hiding place. A natural snoop, Deeprose was also an expert researcher, so if there were any answers to be had, she'd find them.

She found Meese easily enough; it was a corporation in Virginia.

179

Then she did search after search looking for something that might connect it to the *Cloisters*.

*Nothin'. No mention of the victims or our suspects. Ah need a new startin' point. What can Ah try next?*

Deeprose realized she hadn't yet started her routine background checks on Michael Santiago, David Florio or the now-absent temporary museum curator, Arthur Moreland. There hadn't been any time for that, yet. She crossed her fingers and looked for Michael's history.

*No surprises there!*

Next, she moved on to Arthur Moreland.

*That's funny. Nothin'. It's like he sprang up out of nowhere.*

Deeprose began to feel the familiar excitement of the hunt. Her gut told her she was onto something, so she redoubled her efforts and started again. The F.B.I. database of criminal records was available to her at home, so her next move was to search for any mention of his name in the major newspapers in the past twenty years. Maybe he had a prior conviction and changed his name. That wasn't a crime. She looked for Moreland mentioned as an alias, too.

*So he doesn't have a criminal record. O.K., Mr. Moreland, Ah don't give up that easily. There's one more thing Ah can try. It'll be a miracle if it pans out, but before Ah even consider askin' for an A.P.B. and pullin' you in for questionin', Ah just GOTTA have somethin' on you that'll scare you to death. If Ah assume Moreland IS connected to Meese but not by the name we know, the only way Ah can make a connection is through a visual identification. Ah'll search the Virginia newspapers and state public records for anythin' mentionin' Meese that includes photos of their employees over the past twenty years.*

There were no photos of Meese employees in the business or society sections of the local papers. Several cups of coffee later, bleary-eyed and hours into the dead of night, she hunkered down and started again.

*Maybe he's dead an' we've been talkin' to a corpse.*

Her eyes opened wide in a sudden flash of genius.

*Obituaries! Why didn't Ah think of that before? Maybe he went missin' and was presumed dead. He could have faked his own death and left the state. Or maybe he assumed the identity of someone who really is dead.*

The truth was even stranger than she supposed. It took only twenty minutes to find her answer. There, on the very last page of hits for death notices printed in all the local Virginia papers over the last twenty years connected to the keywords "Meese Corporation", was the face of Arthur Moreland, staring right at her.

*Except his name is listed as Clayton Artemus Montgomery. He's younger, thinner, and has different color hair in this photo, but there's no mistakin' it. Mr. Montgomery and Mr. Moreland are the same man.*

Deeprose read further along and clamped a hand over her mouth, horrified. His wife, Arleen, had been brutally murdered in Forest Hills, New York. Shortly after, he left Meese. According to the article, he suffered a fatal heart attack a few years later. That was where the public trail went cold.

*He mighta been involved in an accident, lost his memory and simply been presumed dead. No. Too soap opera. Or, he mighta deliberately faked his own death, changed his name, and moved. Again, too soap opera. Ah wonder if anyone at Meese knows he's alive. What if that death notice is a fake? One thing is sure, anyway; Montgomery, a.k.a... Moreland IS alive, and Ah won't find out what's goin' on or where he's hidin' himself unless I do a little fishin' in Meese waters.*

Deeprose slammed the laptop shut and let loose a rebel yell. Her head barely touched the pillow before she fell into a deep and very satisfying sleep.

# Chapter Twenty
*Three Years Earlier...*

Arleen Montgomery loved her occasional shopping trips to Manhattan. Of course, living in Langley, Virginia didn't mean she didn't have access to the very best, but New York was *New York*! It was like nowhere else in the world, and she loved it.

She wrapped the scarf tighter around her neck and leaned into the wind sweeping down Fifth Avenue, pushing and shoving her way down the street like a Sherman tank. By the end of the day, Arleen was dead on her feet but still set on having dinner at Morton's, on Fifth Avenue and 45th Street. Settling herself in a cushy curved booth, she surrounded herself with bags of the spoils of war and promptly ordered a large glass of sherry.

She'd been looking forward to this sinful encounter for months. Tonight she would toss caution to the wind and eat all her favorite comfort foods as only Morton's could prepare them. She devoured her filet mignon with her eyes closed in ecstasy before turning them ravenously towards a sea of creamy twice-baked potatoes au gratin daring her to take the plunge.

The heavy meal combined with several glasses of fine sherry produced a quality of warmth and deep satisfaction that flooded her mind and body like the afterglow of great sex. Arleen sat back and allowed her mind to wander where it would. When dessert arrived, she took her time polishing off a mountain of chocolate cheese cake and a cappuccino.

Full and sleepy, she no longer felt like going out to Forest Hills Gardens to visit her old college roommate.

*But I can't cancel now; that would be unforgivable. I'll feel better when I get outside.*

She gathered her bags of loot and left the restaurant. As she negotiated the door, a welcome blast of cold air hit her in the face. *The Weather Channel* had predicted an uncharacteristically cold storm this evening and, for once, they were right. She hurried to the corner where a black limousine was already waiting for her. The driver watched in admiration as bags and boxes, expertly aimed and launched, flew from the street to the inner reaches of the back seat. That done, she propelled herself inside the cozy cave and yanked the door shut before the driver had a chance to do it for her.

Arleen was headed to a wealthy neighborhood in Queens this evening, bordered on all sides by dirty red brick apartment buildings, all of which were lined with fish, meat, and fresh vegetable shops along the street level. Arleen dozed while the driver battled evening traffic.

An hour later and close to their destination, Arleen suddenly remembered she hadn't bought a hostess gift, but knowing that old neighborhood like the back of her hand, she quickly spotted a florist shop, asked the driver to park at the next corner, and gathering up her parcels, dismissed him. Years later, Monty would still be wondering what made her decide to get out of the limo in that neighborhood at night in the cold with all those bags.

The wind had turned to sleet, and it plastered itself onto Arleen's hair and cherry red face. The last of the commuters, looking beaten and resigned, exited the F train and hurried past her with coat collars up and heads down. Arleen remembered how it felt to be steadily ground down into nothing, day after day, year after year. She gave silent thanks that life had treated her well.

As the last straggler rushed by, the usually bustling area became eerily silent. Very few cars passed by, and those that did went steadfastly on their way, the drivers refusing to see anything but the road ahead. Without another thought, she headed towards the florist shop.

Some businesses were still open. Their shop doors threw squares of light on the sidewalk here and there, but most were already closed, leaving the normally bustling area dark and deserted. The black recesses of doorways were considered a no-man's land, being the favored hiding spot of muggers. All native New Yorkers were well aware that one never walked close to the buildings after dark, something Arleen had forgotten about.

Absorbed in thought and hurrying along, she was an easy target for the man wrapped in a hooded winter parka. As she walked past, a hand shot out from the void, grabbed her by the arm and jerked her off balance. Gasping, she dropped everything and fell to the ground. He grabbed a fistful of her hair and bashed her head hard against the cement. Something wet and sticky oozed into her hair; she supposed it was blood. The whole thing happened so fast, and yet, for Arleen, it lasted an eternity.

Without a word, she was dragged deeper into the recess of a shop door where no one would see him finish the job. He drew a ferocious looking knife from his belt and with his hands still buried in her hair, pulled her head sharply backwards. In one motion, he slit her throat from left to right. Arleen died horribly but quickly in a hot pool of her own blood. The man disappeared with her jewelry and money.

***

A teenage boy opened the door of the florist shop and took a cautious look around. He had been about to make his last delivery of the day when he saw the woman outside being brutally assaulted. Scared stiff, he turned out the lights and hid under the counter until the man was gone.

He knew there was nothing he could do to help; it was over. He made the call to 911 but declined to provide his own name, locked the door of the shop and ran home as fast as he could, hoping the man hadn't hung around to see if there were any witnesses.

***

Arleen's attacker was a professional; knowing he had nothing to fear, he never looked back. The knife, minus his finger prints, would be tossed into the East River where nobody would ever find it. His coat, pants and shoes would be burned up in one of the many trash can fires that dotted the streets of the South Bronx. Jumping into a stolen car, he turned the key a full three times and almost flooded the engine before the engine stopped coughing and grudgingly began to move.

*Thanks for the nice getaway car, you fuckers.*

184

***

F.B.I. Special Agent Frederic Dawkins had been slugging back bourbon after bourbon in a dingy and dilapidated bar not far from where Arleen was attacked. As he began to feel the rush of liquid courage, he became increasingly abusive to the small, slender bartender.

"What do you mean I've had enough? I'm paying and you're serving."

She shook her head and looked at him without blinking. "The bar is *closed*, Agent Dawkins. I can't afford to lose my license. It's time to go home. If you can't drive, I'll call you a cab. The drinks are on the house."

Dawkins gave her dirty look, but kept his mouth shut. She reminded him of his superior officer, Natalie Rodgers. There were certain women who could wither his balls in public with one glance. The kinder ones avoided him. Dawkins was a democrat; he hated them all equally.

Kicking over a tableful of empty glasses on his way out, he apologized, facetiously. "Oopsy. Looks like I made a mess."

His car, conveniently parked in a handicapped space, took a minute or two to warm up. The police radio was on even though he was not on duty and not on the police force. Dawkins just liked to keep his finger on the pulse of things.

Then his eyes lit up. They were reporting a homicide on Queens Boulevard near Austin Street. That was only ten blocks away. "Yeah, baby!" He put the pedal to the metal and squealed out of the lot. The car swerved in and out of traffic at dangerous speeds, slicing the side view mirrors off several parked cars.

*I've been wanting to transfer to the N.Y.P.D. anyway; I might as well leave the Bureau with a bang.*

The police radio described the victim as a middle-aged woman. Her skull had been crushed and her throat slit. He set his mouth in a grim line, ready for a final showdown.

Suddenly, he slammed on the breaks, as did every car behind him. A steady stream of re-directed drivers cursed at him, giving him the finger as they passed by. Oblivious to it all, Agent Dawkins leaned his head out the window and listened. A siren about three blocks ahead convinced him he was on the trail of the suspect.

Dawkins saw a blue sedan in the left lane blow through the next red light without stopping and thought he was on to something, so he threw the car into 5$^{th}$ gear and got into the middle lane. When he got right up alongside the car, he yanked the steering wheel hard to the left, broadsiding it. Both cars skated onto the raised median dividing the six-lane boulevard, taking sizable chunks out of the old trees planted there a hundred years ago.

When the noise and chaos finally died down, Dawkins scrambled out of his car without his badge or gun. "Hold it, shitbag! Don't move! Put your hands on the steering wheel. *NOW!!*"

The driver kicked his door open and tried to run, but Dawkins launched himself into midair and landed on him.

He regained his wind and then head-butted the man he was sitting on. "I told you to stay in the car! Now look what you made me do!"

The man grabbed Dawkins by the forearms and threw him over his head. Dawkins landed on his back. Hard. "*Oooof!*"

The man got up and spat on him. "This just isn't your day, *Clint.*"

The suspect turned to run, but Dawkins was able to grab him by the forearm, twist him around and throw a roundhouse punch at his temple. He hit the man so hard that he dropped to the ground, unconscious.

\*\*\*

The sudden burst of a siren brought Dawkins back to reality. He stood motionless, trying to remember who, exactly, was the one being pursued. Then it came back to him. He imagined shaking hands with the mayor and receiving the key to the city, if they still did that kind of thing.

Dawkins shouted to the two men in blue, "Gentlemen, look what the cat dragged in…"

Both officers trained their guns on him. Dawkins' triumphant smile faded rapidly, and he began to look confused.

"Get down on your knees and lace your hands together behind your head!"

"Listen, you knuckleheads, I'm an F.B.I. agent, and I just did your damn job for you. Your suspect is over there, unconscious."

The two men traded uneasy glances. One of them spoke again. "Remain where you are. We repeat, get down on your knees, lace your hands behind your head, and don't move. We won't say it again."

Dawkins sighed and got down on his knees. He looked up and muttered, "Don't bother thanking me, guys. You're entirely welcome." He swayed back on his heels and then pitched forward. Locomotion brought him to rest at the feet of the men in blue. Dawkins turned his eyes up at them with an expression that said 'Oh well'. He shrugged and lost his dinner on their shoes before passing out.

\*\*\*

*One Year Later...*

The dull light of late afternoon blurred the edge of the world where sea and sky met. Montgomery was at Virginia Beach, grieving. He turned in his chair to retrieve his sunglasses from the table, took a sip of his sherry and thought about Arleen and how they used to have a glass of the sweet wine together after a long day. It was a daily custom, one they never broke. It felt wrong drinking alone in what was always their special place.

His mind drifted to the elements. Arleen had been a fiery little imp. She was the sun. Raising a glass to his lips, he toasted her. Then he began ruminating on other aspects of his life. When Arleen passed away last year, Monty took on the role of a senior consultant and stepped down as project manager.

*Let someone else do it now, someone anxious to make his mark on the world. I'm tired of fighting. Nothing I say makes a difference, anyway. Kate's career was finished after the board turned it down. No pharmaceutical company or organization would ever consider funding it after that. Then she killed herself.*

Monty fantasized about walking back into Meese and doing something about it.

*I'd love to get my hands on those rotten bastards.*

Montgomery picked up his glass and knocked back its contents in one huge swallow. He shouted as loudly as he could, "Take that, you sons of bitches!"

Sitting back, he remembered that after Pressman defeated Dr. Blake's research project, Monty started scheduling proposals which even *he* found ludicrous. He went home every day laughing his head off.

*I wonder if they ever caught on to that. Ah, well, screw it; they're lucky that's all I did.*

After he resigned and moved to Virginia Beach, he heard the board had been disbanded. The rumor was that the D.O.D. wanted to take control of the appointee process.

*Gee, what a shame. I guess the animals are no longer in charge of the zoo.*

As sunset began, Monty's thoughts drifted. It was time to make a change and get on with life, but he couldn't go back to the old routine. That was out. Thanks to the money left to him from his late uncle's art collection, Montgomery was a wealthy man.

*Maybe I should go back to my first love—art history.*

Armed with a Master's Degree from 30 years ago, a wealth of knowledge, and an incredible amount of influence in all the right places, he thought working in a museum might be just the thing he needed to pull him out of the dumps.

The sun, almost gone now, flooded his eyes with an explosion of burnt orange. Monty felt it was a sign from Arleen to move on. The iron band constricting his chest eased up a little at the thought. He'd been so angry for so long. A botched investigation forced the District Attorney to throw out the case against Miguel Ramirez, the man arrested for allegedly murdering his wife. He had Agent Dawkins of the F.B.I. to thank for that. Besides failing to read the suspect his rights, Dawkins also beat him half to death, costing the city an estimated one million dollars in compensation when a high-priced attorney sprang up out of nowhere to represent him.

*He could never have afforded that kind of help. Someone else was paying.*

Day settled into dusk, and Monty decided it was time for a stronger cocktail and some dinner. He was about to raise his hand to summon the waiter when he noticed the young man already standing at his side holding a sheet of paper folded in half.

"Who gave it to you? Can you describe him to me?" But the waiter said it had been left on the bar with written instructions. No one saw who left it there.

Monty thanked the young man and ordered a whiskey sour and the New York Strip Steak. He waited until his drink arrived before opening the note. As he read, he moved from disbelief, to rage, to fear. The note slipped through his shaking fingers and floated off into space. With a shaking hand, he grabbed his drink and tossed it down his gullet.

When he knew he wasn't going to upchuck, he picked up the note again. Still unable to believe what it said, he forced himself to read it again, slowly and carefully. If this wasn't a sick joke, he was finished.

*My Dear Mr. Montgomery,*

*Your wife's death was an intentional warning to stay out of Meese's business decisions. While that may have satisfied your enemies before, it won't save you now. The stakes have risen, necessitating the elimination of various individuals. In case you don't fully comprehend or appreciate the gravity of your situation, let me make it perfectly clear; you are a dead man, so be smart, for once in your life. Make a change of name, location, and line of work. Disappear into a big city somewhere. Anywhere.*

*I am not the enemy; I am vengeance. Do not discuss your association with the Meese Corporation with anyone. I promise you I will be watching. Leave now, Mr. Montgomery, while you still can.*

*- Mr. X*

All the half-formed thoughts that had been dogging Monty's nightmares suddenly screamed one word.

*Conspiracy!*

The word tore through his body.

*Arleen was murdered as a warning to me! What would make me such a threat that they'd kill Arleen to keep me quiet? Why not just kill me?*

Monty tossed a handful of bills on the table to cover his drinks and uneaten dinner and raced to his hotel room to pack.

*I can't take my car or use any credit cards or my phone. What's the best way to get out of town without creating a fuss or any notice?*

*The bus. Yes, I'll take a bus into Manhattan, buy a burner phone and arrange to have the bank bring my safety deposit box to me at the Radisson Martinique Hotel on 32nd and Broadway. Refurbished or not, no one's going to look for me in a building used as a welfare hotel until the 80s.*

Monty dumped everything he could into a suitcase as quickly as possible, never questioning the authenticity of the note. It was real. His wife's death had made no sense to him before, but it did now. She was deliberately hunted down and slaughtered because of something he did, knew, saw, or even possibly possessed. He had no way of knowing.

In the wall safe was a pile of cash and his valuables. He took a last look around the room, paid his bill and took a cab to the bus station. Once Monty was on the Greyhound heading for New York City, he began to relax slightly and remembered, with deep regret, that he hadn't eaten dinner. To take his mind off his rumbling stomach, he began to think about an alias. He'd already solved the problem of where to go and what work he could use as a disguise. After only a minute or two, he settled on the surname of Moreland. It had been Arleen's maiden name, and it would keep her close to him.

*What kind of a name would an art scholar and museum geek have? I have it—Arthur. I like it. It's meek and innocuous, yet medieval and majestic.*

# Chapter Twenty One
*Present Day...*

Agent Deeprose rushed to her meeting with Deputy Director Fischetti on Monday morning.

*Don't come off as over eager. Don't get excited. Be professional...*

Thanks to Fischetti's mysterious *Mr. X.*, Deeprose believed she had successfully tied Arthur Moreland, a.k.a. Clayton Artemus Montgomery, to the Meese Corporation.

Bursting with excitement, she squeezed herself into an elevator that traveled directly to the top floor of the F.B.I. headquarters. No one bothered to make room for her, so she used her body as a plow.

*Remember to start at the beginning. Keep your voice low and level. Take your time. Montgomery had access to Meese's scientists and labs. So, the way Ah see it, the sixty-four thousand dollar questions are as follows: Is Montgomery responsible for the development and distribution of this drug? If so, why would he intentionally leave us a clue that might solve the crime? Why was he hangin' around the museum incognito? Last, but in no way the least, why would he want to point the finger at a senator? Oh shoot! My brain hurts.*

The soft *ding* of the elevator announced their arrival, but Shania was concentrating too hard to notice. A few men made an obvious show of frowning at their watches and sighing with impatience, but a small-statured stinker elbowed her in the ribs.

"Y'all have a super day, now!" Deeprose took a perverse pleasure in annoying her fellow New Yorkers with her perkiness and thousand-watt smile. Especially in the morning.

*What this city needs is a dose of good manners. And an enema.*

191

Walking quickly past Liz, Deeprose mouthed, "Ah'm expected".

Liz, Fischetti's first line of defense, was middle aged and single, statuesque, and stunningly beautiful. Her custom-made suits hugged long, lean curves in colors that whispered class and style. She had porcelain skin, sable hair, and lips that matched her fingernails perfectly. And she was absolutely loyal to Bill Fischetti and the Bureau, in that order.

*Ah just hope that after a lifetime of workin' fifteen hour days, nights and weekends tryin' to land him, her tombstone doesn't wind up readin', 'She gave at the office.'*

Deeprose ignored Liz's habit of treating her like something that crawled out of the sticks. As a rule, she exuded chilly condescension to everyone, if only to remind them who had the power to let them in and show them back out of the executive office. At first, Shania accepted it with her usual good grace, but it got old, fast.

Liz shot out of her chair, her voice achieving new stratospheric heights as Deeprose raced by. "Wait just a moment! You can't go…"

But Deeprose had already cleared Fischetti's office door and let it slam closed behind her. Smiling a hello, she dropped into the seat opposite his desk, allowing herself a momentary and slightly petty delight in the sound of Liz's muffled outrage.

He was winding up a phone call, so she got back up and made a pot of his gourmet coffee, thinking about her report. Not long after, he hung up, rubbed his eyes, and sighed. Attempting a smile that looked far more like a grimace, he helped himself to a fresh cup and nodded. "Good. I've been waiting for you, Agent Deeprose. Did you get anything we can use?"

"Yes, sir, Ah sure did!" Ignoring her own advice to remain calm and professional, she plunged right in, talking a mile a minute. Waving the news clipping around for emphasis, she blurted out the results of her online search without explaining how Moreland, the obituary of Clayton Artemus Montgomery and Montgomery's late wife Arleen had anything to do with Meese. "This is all too coincidental!"

She also left out the bit about not being able to connect any of it to their investigation at the museum, the drug or the hate-driven meetings known as the *Collective*.

Fischetti made several desperate attempts to ask questions.

Finally, he had to raise his hand to stop her. "Agent Deeprose, just who in the hell is Montgomery, why do I care if his wife was murdered in Queens, for God's sake, and why is this all *too coincidental?* Now, start from the beginning and *go slowly* for those of us who haven't seen the episode yet."

*Oops.*

She gave him a copy of the obituary, sat on her own hands and told him the whole story again, this time from the beginning and in perfect order.

"O.K., I'm following you, so far. You think the temporary curator, Moreland, was actually Montgomery, a career man with Meese, come back from the dead. And you think he deliberately steered you toward the ballerina painting, knowing we'd think it was a clue that would lead us straight to Clara, our ballerina. I want the low-down on that ex-friend as soon as you find her, Agent. We need to know if she has any connection to Michael or the *Collective* or their meetings. Well, well…very neatly done…"

She looked slightly worried. "Ah don't know yet exactly what part he plays in all this, sir, but Moreland—uh, Montgomery—*did* leave us that clue deliberately. Ah think Ah should check in with Agent Carter and make my report to him, sir. Ah really shoulda done that before Ah came up here."

Half lost in thought, Fischetti rubbed a hand across his razor stubble. "Yes, yes… I mean, *NO!* You did the right thing coming to me, first; Carter can wait. Until we know if and how Michael, Montgomery, and the drug all fit into the picture, Agent, we know nothing except a bunch of facts we can't tie together, whether your gut says so or not. And for God's sake, Agent, from now on, let's just refer to him as Montgomery. It's too confusing to keep using both names.

"Did you say his wife was murdered?" Deeprose nodded as Fischetti plowed on. "That could be motive and opportunity right there, you know that? If he thought Meese and the government were responsible for her death for whatever reason, he would have had motive to steal the drug and the opportunity to try to frame them. Maybe worse. We need to know why he'd have reason to believe that and if it's true.

"Look here, Agent, a man doesn't simply walk away from a

career like that, fake his own death, and create a new identity just because he's grief-stricken unless the place he worked was the cause of his grief. The connection has to mean something. Just *has* to! I wonder which of their holding companies he worked for. Agent Deeprose, you're heading to Virginia on a fact-finding mission."

"Yes, sir."

Fischetti nodded once more. "We're on shaky ground here, and we have to tread lightly. I don't have to tell you we have absolutely no evidence to back up an official visit. You'll have to pretend that we believe Montgomery is really deceased and gauge their reaction.

"Try to find out what they know and don't know. I want you to ask for the manager of the personnel department when you get there. Do *not*, under *any* circumstances, speak to the head of human resources or public relations, and do not contact them at *all* before you show up at the front desk of their corporate headquarters. Are you writing this down, Agent Deeprose?"

"Yes, sir. Writing."

*Do not, do not, do not...*

"I have it, sir."

"Middle managers are very cautious, Deeprose. They're not easy to manipulate unless you luck out. We're going to have to hope that the manager of personnel will tip Meese's hand unknowingly, will actually volunteer information she should not divulge, or will leave you with the definite impression that she is truthfully in the dark. If she really has nothing of value to share with you, we're screwed.

"Since you're new here, and this case is extremely unusual in nature, I'll spell this out for you, Agent. No illegal search or seizure will be tolerated. You're going to be savvy. Subtle. Make your contact a *friend*. Are we crystal clear, Agent Deeprose?"

"Perfectly, sir. Ah apologize for losin' my cool with Senator Pressman. It won't happen again."

"Yes. Well. All right, Agent. I'll have Liz email you the plane tickets and Meese's address in Langley. Remember, speak to no one but the manager of personnel, make sure no one else sees you walk into or out of that office, and keep H.R. and P.R. out of it. If those idiots know anything worth mentioning, they'll only gum up the works trying to put their own spin on it. We don't want to tip our hand.

"I want you to confirm that Montgomery worked there under his legal name. Use the news clipping as a visual reference; it'll give you more credibility. Find out if he resigned or was fired. If you think you can do it without raising a red flag, find out why. If you can't find out why, find out if there was some tr ouble between him and management or anyone else there. I also want confirmation that he's listed as deceased on his personnel record and whether or not the manager seems to believe that's the truth. Are you keeping up with me, Agent?"

"Writing, sir."

"If Personnel clams up and wants to send you to the head of Human Resources, thank them for their time, and make a clean exit. I'm hoping they'll warm up to you and dish a little. Your main concern is to make sure the person you speak to is not afraid to open up. They need to believe that what you want to know is not that big of a deal, there's no reason to bother management with it, and there's something in it for them if they help you out. Use something that would appeal to their sense of vanity. Make them feel important.
Then, if we're very, very lucky, we'll know which way the wind is blowing and have enough to bring Montgomery in for questioning."

Deeprose hesitated.

Fischetti looked up. "Questions? Concerns?"

"It's just that Ah thought our asset, Red, might have an address for the next meetin' by now. Maybe Ah should check in with him before Ah leave town. Ah don't want him to leave a message, text or email. Shouldn't Ah pay him a quick visit before Ah leave, sir? He's probably back in the city by now, seein' as how it's Monday an' a school day for him."

"No, Agent. Your orders are to proceed to Virginia, immediately. Red and Carter can both wait a day or so."

"Can Ah at least take a few minutes to see how Agent Seacrest is doin'? Is she down in the lab, or…?"

"She's in the lab getting her blood tested. I want Carter there when she figures out exactly what that drug is and what it's for."

Fischetti broke off and began talking about what he'd allowed Seacrest to do for them. "God only knows what that fucking drug did to her. If there's any lasting brain damage or side effects, it'll be my fault. My responsibility."

195

Then, just as suddenly, he cleared his throat and was all business again. "You have your orders, Agent Deeprose. You will go to Meese alone. There's no need to burden Carter with this, now. I'll fill him in once we know Seacrest is out of the woods. If she doesn't…well, if it goes south, it won't make any difference to him whether he's been briefed or not.

"And the D.O.D. will just have to be satisfied with the half dose we're giving them this morning. I couldn't care less whether they believe we have the other half or not. Happy Monday, Agent Deeprose."

Deeprose knew she'd made a mess of her report this morning.

*He didn't thank me, but he sure as hell didn't fire me, either.*

She slipped out the door, doing her best to ignore the smug look of satisfaction on Liz's face.

*That miserable little eaves-dropper!*

Shania knew better than to disappear again without saying anything to Carter or Seacrest, so against Fischetti's orders, she went down to the lab.

*Ah hope Jill's all right…*

Peeking through the small, square windows of the swinging doors on her tip toes, she saw Carter stroking Jill's hair. It was a tender moment, and she didn't want to intrude.

*How could she volunteer to take that drug not knowin' what would happen? Ah'm sorry, but duty doesn't include poisonin' herself to death to push along an investigation. That's a little too nuts, even for me. My God! What am Ah gonna say to her? Ah don't think there's a Hallmark card for somethin' like this…*

Seacrest initiated the conversation, saving Deeprose from making an ass of herself. "Agent Deeprose, it's good to see you." She was surprisingly lucid.

Deeprose bear-hugged her. "Ah'm *that* glad to see you, Jill! How are you? What happened?"

Seacrest wiggled uncomfortably out of the embrace. "Well, I made it; I'm O.K. I was a little over the top, according to Carter. He had to cuff me to the bed. I remember feeling madder than I ever felt before. It was rage, really. Fight without the flight feelings. I remember an *irresistible* urge to kill and the feeling of being unstoppable, but it was all directed toward some kid from my past that I barely knew.

196

"Something else had to have been used to direct that impulse to a specific target. If there's no companion drug, they didn't need one. There was a small window of time between ingestion and psychosis when I felt like I was slipping into a dream state. That's what makes this drug so valuable; the subject can be programmed through the use of a post-hypnotic suggestion during that window of time. The result? One human killing machine to be aimed at anything desirable with little or no memory, guilt or remorse afterward. If Michael remembers most or all of it, we have to get him to admit where he got it, and hope he knows why he was sent to kill the old curator."

"You see, I think some people will be able to resist the drug, but most won't without the kind of help I had last night. Of those that don't resist, some will remember what they did, but again, most won't. If the user resists the programming and goes after someone else, our chances of finding it out are slim to none.

"There are potential hordes of 48-72 hour killers out there, and our only way of finding even a small percentage of them is to get the names of every murderer arrested in every state for the past few months and hope that some of them remember being at a meeting within the correct timeframe of their respective murder. But getting that drug out of circulation is only half the problem; we have to make sure it can't be duplicated, and that means finding the scientist who developed it and destroying any existing documentation that describes where the natural compounds were found and how to reproduce them synthetically."

Carter had a depressing thought. "Jill, getting a list of past attendees may not help as much as you think. The ones that remember anything won't have the drug in their system anymore. That's their only proof that they actually attended a meeting if—and that's a big *if*—we can prove the meetings were the only place to get it. Even circumstantially, we may not be able to tie those crimes to the drug or the meetings."

"But *some* of them will still have the drug in them, and those are the ones who can help us find the source of it all. We need a lot more to go on than what we have now, and the clock's ticking. Right, Carter?"

Deeprose was incredibly impressed with Seacrest's insight into her own experience and her ability to articulate a hypothesis and discuss its provability. The purpose for using the drug at the meetings

197

finally began to make sense. They knew now that the meetings were just a way to get a lot of angry, unhinged people together at one time all over the world. But it was the drug that gave the *Silver Man* an army to command.

When Seacrest finished speaking, Deeprose started to ask her more questions but noticed right away that Jill was staring into space as she responded. She spoke in a dull monotone, like an automaton. Then it was like a clock stopped ticking. Seacrest simply turned "off". Entirely mute, she stared straight ahead, expressionless. Deeprose and Carter exchanged a quick, terrified look. Before she could fall, he gathered her in his arms, and Deeprose sprang into action. She whipped out her cell phone and punched 911.

Carter stood rooted to the spot. Deeprose grabbed him by the shoulders and shook him. "Agent Carter, you have to do something; there's no time for an ambulance! *Carter!!*"

*Ice cold water on full blast might do the trick.*

He scooped up Seacrest, ran to the bathroom and dumped her in the shower stall. Deeprose turned on the faucet and stood by, ready to do C.P.R. if she had to, but Jill started to come around. "I was having *suuuuch*a nice dream. Summer in Boston. We were dancing on the lawn in the rain." She raised her arms in the air to feel the rain better. Then she started yelling. "Hey! I'm in the shower! Why am I in the goddamned *shower*?!"

Deeprose threw open the lab's many closets and drawers searching for something to dry her off and warm her up. Carter slipped down to the floor and clutched her to him.

"Get *off me*, Carter! I can't breathe! *Carter?*" Her voice was soft and filled with wonder. "Carter...you're crying!"

Deeprose plopped herself down on the floor, too, soaking herself. She hugged them both and said in earnest, "All for one..."

"And one for all." Seacrest laughed, but she meant it. At that precise moment a trinity, of sorts, was born that would never be broken. It was a trinity of heart, mind, and courage, cubed.

\*\*\*

Deeprose returned with spare sets of sweat pants and sweaters she scrounged up in the lab's locker room. Comfy and cozy, they sat around sipping really bad coffee. Seacrest said what all three of them were thinking. "I wish we had some whiskey."

"Amen to that. Oh shoot, Ah almost forgot! Deputy Director Fischetti said not to bother stoppin' here first, but as long as Ah did, Ah might as well give you an update before Ah catch my plane. Arthur Moreland, the temporary curator at the *Cloisters*, has somethin' to do with this."

Carter interrupted. "What makes you believe that, Agent Deeprose? If he knows who the killer is, why use a painting to send us a clue? Why not just tell us what he knows? Slow down and start again."

"Damn! Everybody's tellin' me the same thing today."

She reached into her pocket and pulled out a crumpled up copy of a newspaper article. It was an obituary. "Ah have here an obituary for a Mr. Montgomery, of the Meese Corporation in Langley, Virginia. Take a look at this photo. It's a few years old, an' he looks quite different now, but that's the spittin' image of Mr. Moreland, sure as Ah'm standin' here. Dontcha see? Montgomery is posin' as Moreland. Montgomery's wife was murdered a short while before he resigned; it was never solved. If he thought Meese had anything to do with it…"

Carter was confused. "Wait a minute. Are you saying he may have stolen the drug for revenge or blackmail? But then why would he want the curator dead? Why help us find Michael?"

"To point us in the right direction! My theory is that he helped us find the ballet school and Michael to lead us to Meese, the manufacturer, without involvin' himself. He couldn't have known Michael had another vial, but he'd have known Michael would still have it in his system when we picked him up."

Seacrest was all ears. "Okay, I'll bite. What makes you think the Meese Corporation had anything to do with Montgomery's wife's death? Why assume the drug came from there just because Mr. Montgomery worked there?"

"Deputy Director Fischetti told me to see if I could connect Meese to the drug and Montgomery's disappearance. He worked at the museum where Michael committed the murder; the fact that Michael was also in possession of a drug that could only have come from Meese's lab is too coincidental to be overlooked. Mr. Montgomery's wife died horribly. It may provide us with motive and opportunity, but y'all are right; we need to know why the curator was *specifically* targeted to understand what's really behind all this."

Carter stared at Deeprose and asked her in a soft, calm voice, "When did Fischetti tell you all this?"

"Yesterday morning when Ah got back from Senator Pressman's office in Washington, Ah came in to make my report. Fischetti said he'd received a tip from a source he referred to as '*Mr. X*'. After that, Ah headed straight home and started combin' the web to find answers. Ah came in this mornin' to give him an update on what Ah found, and all of a sudden Ah'm on my way to the airport again. This time to Langley, Virginia on a fishin' trip."

"That bastard! He intentionally kept me out of the loop. If you hadn't stopped down here by chance, I'd never even have known you left! Agent Deeprose, moving forward, I want you to keep me in the Intel loop every step of the way, and I want that Intel *before* the deputy director gets it. He's using Seacrest's experience this weekend as a convenient excuse to take advantage of your rookie status. He also knows you can't say no to him, and I don't like it."

He started to pace. "I am very concerned, Agent Deeprose. There are more questions here than you know. Why does the deputy director believe this tip? Who is this *Mr. X*? How can we be sure we can trust him? This doesn't feel right. Not right at all."

*Is this Monday, for heaven's sake, or 'Freaky Friday'? Did they switch bodies while Ah was in D.C. and forget to tell me? Carter's losin' it and Jill is grounded. This musta been one helluva weekend.*

"Agent Carter, Ah admit Ah had some serious doubts about Fischetti when Ah first came on here, but he stepped up to the plate for us, sir. He fought Breen, bullied Jill's supervisor for extra lab time and funds and broke the law six ways from Sunday to keep half of that drug for us to examine. Ah don't think we can dismiss that so easily.

"Ah'm not sayin' he isn't a fox in the hen house, but for goodness sake, give him the benefit of the doubt! The only reason you weren't filled in was because you had your own hands full. He's sick with worry about Jill. He said it was his fault if anything happened to her. Ah really don't think he's tryin' to leave y'all in the dark, sir."

Her words had the same immediate effect as a slap in the face. "I

200

apologize. You're right, of course, but he *is* responsible for letting her take that drug, and he *should* be worried sick about it. How can I be sure she's going to be O.K?"

He stopped talking to take a few slow, deep breaths. "All right. All right. I don't like it, but I have no say in it. Proceed with extreme caution, and contact me if anything—*anything*—happens that you can't handle alone."

Seacrest derailed them both with a new thought. "You know, it occurs to me there's another question we need to answer based on my own experience with the drug. What if Red only *thinks* he left the *Collective* without ingesting the drug? Remember, his friends left before he did."

Deeprose pressed her lips together; she was frightened for Red. "Ah see where y'all are headin' with this. He may have taken the drug, committed a murder and not know it; we have to face that. Ah'd like to be the one to check on his whereabouts before he came to the *Jazz Standard* on Friday night. It shouldn't be too difficult to retrace his steps."

"Fine. Oh! Before you go, I want you to have this." Carter rummaged around in his wet pockets.

Shania marveled at the sparkling brilliance of a deep green-black gem in Carter's hand. "Ooooo! What's that?"

"The stuff that stars are made of, Agent. This little stone was part of a meteorite that crashed here over a thousand years ago. It's called Moldavite, named for Moldavia, where it landed. It's almost completely mined out by now and very hard to get. I want you to have it because it's got an extremely high energy content—one you can actually *feel*. Here, hold it lightly between your thumb and forefinger in your non-dominant hand. Feel it? It is said to increase mental focus and clarity of thought. I want to know you're carrying it with you. We both do."

"Thank you!" She held the stone in her palm for a few moments, feeling its slight buzzing motion before placing it in her pocket. "Ah never believed in this crystal stuff, sir, but this feelin' is *real*! Thank you; I'll cherish it. Jill... take it easy, O.K.?"

As Deeprose left the building, she expected to smell dried leaves mixed with earth in the chilly air. Instead, she smelled the heady scent of garbage mixed with exhaust fumes from a million old cars jammed up on Church Street.

*Funny, Ah was the one who originally felt Fischetti had somethin' up his sleeve. Ah was sure he wasn't tellin' me what he was tellin' Agent Carter. Now Agent Carter feels that way, too.*

\*\*\*

Deeprose sipped coffee in Jane Kerrington's cozy, little office. She was Meese's personnel manager. The woman knew her business, and Shania didn't have to be a veteran to know she'd have to outsmart Ms. Kerrington if she was going to get anything out of her. It was against the law to divulge information from personnel records without a court order; they both knew that. Deeprose planned to come on very subtly using Kerrington's own sense of pride to soften her up and then her sense of sympathy and duty to open her up. It was a *fait accompli.*

*Ah hope.*

"Thanks for sittin' down with me today, Ms. Kerrington. Ah'm told y'all have teamed up with the surroundin' feeder colleges and high schools to develop curricula aimed at educatin' local residents so they can obtain 21st century government jobs."

"Yes, we have, and it's worked out better than we hoped."

"Reachin' out to the local communities meant makin' a conscious decision to put a name and face back on a relatively anonymous organization. How's that workin' out for y'all?"

Kerrington was surprised and flattered that the F.B.I. noted and admired her P.R. campaign at the school level. "Surprisingly well! We're also conducting presentations at local universities, advertising on online job sites, using job placement specialists, and utilizing social media for recruiting and staffing purposes. We're a true part of the community now."

Deeprose felt this was the time to come to the point. "Speakin' of the local community, Ms. Kerrington, perhaps y'all can help us out regardin' a current case of some importance."

"Me?"

"Ms. Kerrington, let's face it; the executives provide you with their input and a little face time. Maybe they even do a little one-on-one mentorin', here and there. But you're the real face of the Meese Corporation. Am Ah Right?"

Kerrington blushed outright. "Well, I guess you could say that..."

"This case has nothin' at all to do with Meese, but Meese could play an important role in helping us solve it. It requires a break in normal protocol, but this investigation goes up so high that Ah gotta be sure Ah can trust my sources, implicitly. Ms. Kerrington, the person who helps us break this case will receive the Congressional Medal of Honor."

"The *what*?!"

*Reel her in fast, Shania!*

"Ah need to verify the date of death for a past employee. One little date, and you'd be a national hero, Ms. Kerrington. If Ah go through proper channels, our man's gonna get away. Once Ah leave here, Ah can't risk comin' back. Ah need the date now. Will you help us?"

"I can't help unless I know who it is you're talking about. If it's commonly known information, I can discuss it without opening a file."

*She can? Holy shit! The manager of personnel is also the office gossip! Oh, pleeeeease let this be common knowledge...*

"His name was Clayton Artemus Montgomery. He resigned and passed on shortly afterward."

The color drained out of Kerrington's face.

*She knew him! Let's see what else she knows.*

"He's got no survivors and no distant relatives. You can help us get justice for him, Ms. Kerrington. If I can get the date of his death and the details y'all are obviously familiar with, Ah can help catch his killer."

Kerrington whispered, "*Killer*? You mean he was murdered?"

"Ah do, Ms. Kerrington. What can you tell me?"

"Mr. Montgomery left the company at least a few years ago. We don't keep files that old here. I'm sorry; I wish I could help you."

"But employee records, even that far back, were traditionally scanned into a database for easy access, weren't they? I mean, you can't call *Iron Mountain* with every historical question you have, can you? Wouldn't it be perfectly O.K. for y'all to go into the database lookin' for Bernard Montgomery and take the merest uninterested glance at Clayton Artemus Montgomery's record while you were in the neighborhood? Ah mean, that must happen all the time. Slip of the wrist."

Kerrington balked. "The thing is, Agent, non-disclosure law is very definite concerning personnel records. That information is protected even after the death of an employee. I could lose my job…"

*Hurry up, you're losin' her!*

Deeprose appeared to be completely without guile. "Yes, you could. And work for the highest bidder, instead. Maybe start your own high-end recruitin' and staffin' firm. Kick back and enjoy all those interviews you'll get on the mornin' shows and C.N.N. Or just write a book and retire." She rushed ahead. "Ah'm not tryin' to be facetious, Ms. Kerrington; all Ah need is a teeny tiny answer to my one and only question. How about it?"

"Well…what is it you want to know? I can't promise I know anything of value."

*In a pig's eye.*

"If you can't recall date of death, can you tell me anythin' about his state of mind when he resigned? Was he upset or angry about anythin'?"

Kerrington began to see the trap she'd set for herself and tried to back off. "He worked at one of our pharmaceutical research facilities, not here at the corporate office."

*Rush her with questions, and don't give her time to think before she answers.*

"Was there a misunderstandin', disagreement, or fallin' out between Mr. Montgomery and the folks he worked with? What was the nature of the misunderstandin'?"

Kerrington's face reddened. "There was no problem from a corporate standpoint. Back in his day, we maintained a board of approvers who voted in the projects to receive further funding to complete the research and development and testing necessary to present them to the military for purchase. However, it only required one vote to kill a project that would have already been deep in the preliminary stages of development. This practice was put in place strictly for fail-safe purposes; Mr. Montgomery was well aware of that. We wanted to prevent a majority vote from approving a project if even one member saw it as a potential danger. There may have been some ruffled feathers in the past between Mr. Montgomery and the board when a project was shelved, but it's their call and no one else's. In any case, they were disbanded a few years ago. Most researchers are able to move on to other projects when their own is rejected. Sometimes one or two don't bounce back, but that's nobody's fault."

*Don't jump on that one yet; get the dates she does remember, first.*

"Do you remember when this board you spoke of was disbanded? That might give me a time frame to work with."

"Oh, that was about two years ago."

"So, approximately two years ago Mr. Montgomery was still here. He left before they were disbanded. That helps. Who's on the board?"

"I'm sorry, I don't…"

"No problem. But you did say he resigned because one of his researcher's inventions was turned down for fundin'. Who was the scientist?"

Kerrington blushed. "I didn't say that at all. I just wanted to explain his position here as a project manager of military biologicals and the framework in which he operated. There would have been no reason, to the best of my knowledge, that Mr. Montgomery would have had any issues with Meese. His position was never in jeopardy even if his researchers' projects were rejected, and he moved steadily upward in the ranks of management. It would have been a very rewarding job, Agent."

*Ah'm sure it was…*

Deeprose paused and glanced at her watch. "Well, Ah think that's all Ah need for now, Ms. Kerrington. Thank you so very much for your time and help. It is most appreciated, and please feel free to contact me with anythin' else that comes to mind."

Kerrington looked vastly relieved. "That's all? All you wanted to know about was the nature of his job? Why, anyone who knew his title can find that out on our jobsite. There's no law against that."

The two women rose. Deeprose shook her hand and got the hell out of there before Kerrington realized what she'd just told her.

*Ah see they're still givin' out diplomas at Moron University. Hmmm, a mysterious board of approvers who had him by the short hairs combined with a favorite researcher who got the ax, followed by his wife's murder. Well, Now Ah finally know why Montgomery*

205

*resigned and when. It won't be difficult to find out whose project got the ax just before he left. There's always a disgruntled employee somewhere dyin' to give you the lowdown.*

She was antsy and wanted to get back to New York to check on Jill and to see if Red might have tried to reach her with a location of the next meeting of the *Collective*.

*He has an awful crush on me, an' now he trusts me, too. Ah only hope we don't wind up on the opposite side of the fence when this is over and done with.*

The sudden thought of a crush reminded her that Wilson might have been trying to contact her over the weekend. Deeprose hadn't checked her private messages in a few days. After searching her texts and email, she finally found his messages in her spam folder.

*Oh my, he's goin' to think Ah'm just terrible.*

Deeprose smiled. Sometimes it wasn't such a bad idea to keep a gentleman waiting.

*Guilty as charged.*

\*\*\*

The door to Clara's apartment flew open. Eliza cursed a blue streak and flopped down into a chair to tell the girls everything that had happened to her and Michael since the last time they'd all been together.

"I've been knocked around, given the third degree by everyone and their brother and sent to the hospital. There's a lady F.B.I. agent sniffing around, too. She's not so convinced that I don't know Michael from Adam. I'm hot, tired and thirsty."

Alison answered her as she walked into the kitchen to get her a glass of wine. "We still have a few big problems Eliza, even with Michael out of the way. The *Silver Man's* people will be looking for you, I still have to be cleared, and Clara's still being hunted. So, you're the only one of us who can get the next meeting address without getting killed or arrested. Can you get invitations to the meeting for us or not? They'll have to assume, if you answer the next invitation, that you don't recall being dosed or your instructions to kill. They'll be anxious to get you back there again, don't you think?"

"I received the link for their new website today. Hang on while I see if the invitation is there. Eliza flashed them a twisted grin. Oh, yeah. We're in."

Alison nodded.

***

Deputy Director Fischetti pounced on his phone. He'd been waiting all day to hear that special ring tone signifying an incoming urgent message. The call was from the Special Operations Unit. He began to pray.

*Please God, make it good news.*

"It's a go, sir. We have the location of the next meeting."

# Chapter Twenty Two

The trio hid inside the rhododendron bushes at the site of the next meeting. The plan was to snatch the bag of drugs from the *Silver Man's* assistant as she entered the abandoned warehouse in Yonkers. Proof the drug existed was Alison's only hope for exoneration. Eliza made it clear she had no intentions of getting herself embroiled in a crazy attempt to save the other two and Michael. She wanted those drugs. Period. Clara kept her mouth shut and let the other two call the shots. Her turn would come.

Both Alison and Eliza talked a little about the feeling of freedom they'd experienced on the drug. There were no boundaries, no judgment, no right and wrong—only the freeing catharsis of rage which felt so incredibly good.

Alison was worried about Eliza; she was a wild card—crass, criminal, and as dumb as a doorknob. It seemed to Alison that the closer she got to Clara, the more Eliza asserted her claim to leadership, but it didn't much matter anymore who the leader was; they needed to be a team right now, so Alison did as she was told.

The finality of autumn prompted Alison to think of what might lie ahead. Perhaps this was the end for her, but at least she'd go out doing something to atone for the crimes she committed under the influence of the serum.

*** 

Deputy Director Fischetti ordered the Bureau's Hostage Rescue Team (H.R.T.) to conduct the raid on the *Collective*'s meeting scheduled for tonight.

The unit rolled out in Chevy *Suburbans* armed with Remington shotguns and sniper rifles. Their mission was simply to round up all the organizers and attendees of what they were told was a Manson-type of cult who called themselves the *Collective*. Fischetti's team would take it from there. He gave them instructions to confiscate illegal substances and arrest anyone who had them. Fischetti could not officially tie Michael Santiago to the *Collective* or even to the drug he was allegedly dosed with, but that wasn't going to stop him from sending in the big guns. This was his big chance to prove himself worthy of the director's chair—whenever the old man finally decided to call it quits.

Suburbanites heading home during rush hour drove side by side with the army of Chevy's crawling along the *Cross Bronx Expressway*. According to Red's tip, the meeting wouldn't get underway for another hour, at least. Unit Commander Rosenfeld reminded his men by radio to take it slow and steady…slow and steady.

\*\*\*

Eliza's cell phone rang.
Alison whispered harshly. "Don't answer it!"
Eliza picked it up.

\*\*\*

The black vans moved like a conga line on the highway. Rosenfeld patted the .45 holstered on his belt and wondered if the attendees were primed to react to the threat of violence with violence of their own. From the sparse Intel he'd been provided by the deputy director, he understood only that there was one single speaker referred to as the *Silver Man*, who lectured by way of video conference and resembled Senator Pressman. The *Silver Man* spoke at every meeting, slightly rearranging his fanatical rhetoric so that it sounded new each time.

Rosenfeld had a teenaged son, so he'd made it his business to be familiar with every new social science theory, cult and hate group out there.

*This guy sounds like a real nut job.*

The commander's heart raced when the highway congestion finally opened up. It wouldn't be long, now. He swore to himself that he would have a heart-to-heart talk with his son on the subject of civic responsibility and right and wrong, as soon as he got home.

\*\*\*

Eliza sounded combative. "Yeah, well not unless you identify yourself."

"Eliza, hang up. *Hang up!*"

"*Shit*! Someone says he knows what we're doing. But how could he?"

Clara took Alison's balled fist in her own hands and kissed it. "Now, everyone take a breath. Let's all just calm down. There's no way anyone could possibly know what we discussed in my own private place, right?"

Alison nodded. "Cut it out, Eliza. Stop trying to scare us."

"Don't you want to know what he said?"

\*\*\*

The cars proceeded to Webster Avenue off the *Major Deegan Highway*, still maneuvering at an even pace. Commander Rosenfeld felt his heart sink as they approached the target.

*This isn't a warehouse; it's a party hall!*

Using sonar technology, Rosenfeld could also see that the hall was full of people. He jumped out of the lead car, but his unit remained inside waiting for his signal to engage. He trod on the loose gravel in the parking lot as lightly as he could and then peered into the soft, golden light of a window.

*It's only a bunch of teenagers!*

Above them hung a banner congratulating them on winning the junior varsity football championship.

Rosenfeld leaned into his mike and terminated the raid.

\*\*\*

At the real location of the *Collective's* next meeting in Yonkers, a black van rolled to a stop in a space close to the building. Eliza ran to the back of it just as its trunk opened, knocking her to the ground in stunned silence.

The masked woman, *Galatea*, emerged from the van with the bag they'd been waiting for. Alison leaped onto her back from behind, hoping weight and momentum would bring them both to the ground. *Galatea* jabbed her in the stomach but couldn't shake Alison loose.

If Alison was overpowered, they'd all be in for it, so Clara jumped over Eliza to kick the woman's legs out from under her. As she went down, *Galatea* hit her head on the side view mirror. She was unconscious and bleeding from the ear.

Eliza jumped up and got in behind the wheel. "Get off her, you two, and get in!"

Alison yelled, "We have to search her for the bag, first!"

Eliza held up a large black drawstring bag of vials and shook it. "It fell out of the trunk when it opened. Get *in!*"

She floored the gas.

The masked woman came around slowly as they drove away in her car. She called her superior for instructions.

"Let them go. We'll wait and watch."

***

Deputy Director Fischetti pounded his fist on his desk. "What do you mean it was the wrong address, Rosenfeld?" Fischetti didn't wait for an answer. He slammed the phone and called Agent Carter.

***

"I've got some news that can't wait. We attempted a raid tonight, and it failed. It looks like Red gave us a bad lead."

Agent Carter listened to Fischetti with his mouth slightly open; he paused before answering. "Deputy Director, why wasn't I made aware of this raid or any of the other developments in this case?"

"I promise a full rundown, Agent Carter, first thing in the morning. You needed to be there for your wife, and I needed to know you were there for her. How is she doing?"

"She's returning to normal. I think you should know that the lab results came back inconclusive. We don't know what this drug is made of, but it's most likely synthetic, which would make it nearly undetectable."

Seacrest waved a hand and took the phone away from Carter. "He's partly right, Deputy Director; it will take some time to analyze, but it can be done."

211

Fischetti's voice boomed over the speaker. "We don't *have* time! We need to turn our heads in another direction right now, anyway; there are other leads to pursue."

"But…"

"There'll be more of the serum to study when we make the next raid, Agent Seacrest."

Seacrest grumbled under her breath. "If the Bureau can manage to get the right address."

Fischetti barked. "That will be enough, Agent Seacrest." I want both of you in my office, first thing in the morning."

Carter kneaded her shoulders. "Just relax; I'll take care of this." He tucked away his anger, took the phone from her hand, and said good night to Fischetti.

*Either Red was given a bad address or Fischetti sent the H.R.T team to the wrong place intentionally. Why would Fischetti want to do that? And why would he want to discredit Red?"*

Doubt flooded Carter's mind.

*Fischetti needs to answer a few questions, beginning with Mr. X.*

"I'll run you a bath, hon, with those bath salts you love so much. You'll forget all about today."

Seacrest inhaled deeply before nodding. "You read me like a book, Carter. That is exactly what I need right now."

She settled herself at the computer table. He kissed her on the forehead and went into the bathroom.

"Carter! Come back here. *Quick!*"

He ran back out. "What's the matter?" Peering over her shoulder, he saw she'd been watching their wedding video on *YouTube*.

"I just saw a new comment."

Carter recognized the quatrain instantly. It was from the *Rubaiyat of Omar Khayyam* but was decidedly different than the quatrain read at his wedding. Carter read on:

'*I sent my soul through the Invisible,*
*Some letter of that After-life to spell:*
*And by and by my Soul return'd to me,*
*And answered 'I Myself am Heav'n and Hell:'*

# Chapter Twenty Three

Seacrest was running down a long hallway. She ran, not knowing from what. It was pitch-black and went on and on. She looked for a door but saw only her reflection.

*I see myself...but, there's no light to see by!*

Solid black walls transformed themselves into a green maze of tall, sturdy, bushes. A soft voice whispered her name. It was Carter. His eyes were cold and punishing.

"Carter?"

"I *myself* am heaven and hell."

*He's hunting me!! I can't move. I can't move!!*

In desperation, she slammed her eyes shut and prayed to something greater than herself. For once, Seacrest didn't need proof God existed. Faith was just as good. Maybe even better.

\*\*\*

Carter was shaking her. "Wake up, honey; you're having a bad dream."

"Carter, what did you mean by that?"

"Huh? Boy, that must have been some dream."

"It wasn't a dream; it was real."

"No, Jill, it was a nightmare, and the fact is, you never have them. I wonder if your dream was the result of a residual effect—you know, like a flashback."

"Maybe it's the drug and maybe it's something else. What do those isochronal tones do, Carter?"

"Binaural beats can cause very lucid dreaming. And in extreme cases..."

"What? What happens in extreme cases?"

"Sometimes they have been known to change eye color. Or cause seizures. But they also clear chakras, Jill!" He laughed.

"Uh huh."

"Well, I wish we had the time to stay in bed and talk, but we're supposed to be in Fischetti's office at nine, sharp."

"What time is it now?"

Carter flashed his watch and smiled. "It's time to get moving, my girl, that's what time it is."

"I think I'll skip the meeting. I have a lot of catching up to do in the lab."

"That's fine. I can handle Fischetti alone."

"Are you certain? You blew your top last night, you know. I mean, for you, that is."

"A small show of testosterone was all that was needed, my dear; he'll be putty in my hands from now on."

Seacrest tumbled into a gray dress and matching jacket and gazed at her reflection in the standup mirror. She felt herself being pulled into it.

*This is exactly how I feel when the subway rushes past me; its rushing, sucking wake is like the inside of a swirling hurricane. It compels me, forces me against my will, toward the edge of the platform. And over...*

Jill gasped and clapped a hand over her mouth. All of a sudden she was terrified of him.

*Stop being silly!*

She grabbed her coat and briefcase and met Carter at the front door. His face clearly indicated that he was mystified by how much time women take to get ready in the morning.

*See? The whole idea is just silly!*

She said nothing more about the dream. Now was exactly the wrong time to get into it again. Instead, she stopped short halfway out the door, tugged on Carter's lapels, and allowed her lips to brush against his. This was her reality. She hugged him tight. "I love you, Carter."

He raised his eyebrows. "I missed this."

"I know; so have I." She looked away. "Promise me you'll use that famous Carter calm and cool, today."

"I promise I'll handle the situation tactfully. Let's go."

\*\*\*

Deputy Director Fischetti was up before dawn hoping to get a jump on the day. He didn't want to be interrupted by Carter before nine, so he left a post-it on Liz's computer asking her to hold all his calls when she came in. He settled himself in his chair and reached into a drawer for a burner cell.

As he dialed the Meese Corporation's CEO, Tony Berringer, in Langley, he silently rehearsed the speech he'd memorized while tossing and turning in bed all night. This was an intricate game of chess, and it called for a very daring move.

\*\*\*

Tony Berringer was just settling in at his antique mahogany and chocolate brown leather desk for another enjoyable day in Paradise. When his personal phone line rang he frowned, annoyed. It was a well-established rule that under no circumstances should Mr. Berringer be bothered before he'd read his morning paper.

"Berringer." The voice was haughty and curt.

Fischetti decided to put a little respect into it. "Good morning, Mr. Berringer. I'm Deputy Director William Fischetti, of the New York City division of the Federal Bureau of Investigation. I'd like a moment of your time, if you don't mind, on a matter of great importance. I can send a man around to your office, of course, but I thought a phone call would be more discrete. For you, I mean."

*"What?!"*

"I wanted to thank you for allowing Ms. Kerrington to share Mr. Montgomery's personnel record with our agent. It might just give us that big break we've been hoping for." Fischetti held his breath and waited.

"What? Excuse me? She shared *what* with your agent?"

That was the part Fischetti always liked best. "You know, the history on Clayton Artemus Montgomery. He was a former employee of yours. Now he's using an alias and living right here in good old New York City. He's going by the name of Arthur Moreland. We wanted to double-check the reports of his death after he resigned, including your company records, but we didn't have time to get a

215

court order. It turns out you had him listed as officially dead, too. My agent was able to confirm everything Ms. Kerrington told her. Thanks. We owe you one."

"Why did you need to see his personnel records from Meese Corporation to confirm his death, if you don't mind my asking? Surely there were many other more simple ways to do that."

"Mr. Berringer, there is no death certificate on record for Mr. Montgomery with the coroner's office in Langley, Virginia or anywhere else. The obituary we found didn't give us much, but it contained a photo and mentioned that he'd worked for Meese, so I sent out an agent to confirm that your employee records contained a similar photo and listed him as deceased. I wanted visual confirmation, not verbal, and Ms. Kerrington was kind enough to share his file with her.

"I'm sure you understand I can't divulge anything more than that at this time other than the fact that there *is* a death notice in his file at Meese, but to our knowledge so far, no body. That could spell trouble if there's a co-conspirator inside your walls. We suspect he is alive and living in New York. It's no crime to change your name, Mr. Berringer, but it is a crime to forge a death certificate. The evidence Ms. Kerrrington shared with us is all we need to justify a warrant. We'll have to subpoena your records as evidence, eventually, so make sure they're kept safe for the time being, will you?"

\*\*\*

Berringer hung up and kicked the gym bag underneath his desk.
*Damn that idiot in Personnel! I'll hang her for this!!*
He launched himself out of his chair and walked as quickly and quietly as he could to the elevator.
*This is a fire that cannot burn!*
Berringer ignored everyone in the elevator as he rode down to the eighth floor in a panic. He strode up to the big corner office on the north side of the building and barked, "Is he in?"

Shocked at the look on his face, an executive assistant simply nodded. Berringer walked past her. "Hold his calls."

The door slammed shut, startling Greg James, the S.V.P. of Human Resources. "Well, I don't need a second cup of coffee *now*. Thanks."

Berringer's veins were standing out on his head and neck. "Whose idea was it to allow Kerrington to speak with an F.B.I. agent?"

"What are you talking about?"

"The deputy director of the fucking New York branch of the F.B.I. called me just now to thank me for sharing Clayton Artemus Montgomery's personnel records with one of his agents. He sent her here to confirm that Montgomery worked for Meese, that our photos confirm his identity and that our records list him as dead. They also know his resignation date and the reported date of death. He says the coroner has no death certificate, Greg. Then he told me that the bastard is alive somewhere in New York, and using an alias!

"He thinks one of two things—we did something to Monty and then faked that record, or he has a co-conspirator in Personnel who helped him out so that he could fake his own death after he left."

Berringer rapped his knuckles on Greg's desk. *"Which is it?!"*

"Wait a minute! Wait a minute! What's the problem, Tony? All he wanted to do is confirm that the man's alive and used to work here. He's looking for *Montgomery*, for God's sake, not *us*. The man must have gone off his nut. Maybe the F.B.I. is trying to protect *us* from him. Ever think of that? So the guy's alive and in New York. What do we have to worry about? Besides, it's been years since he came anywhere near here. Whatever Monty knows is old news by now."

Berringer stopped pacing. "Jesus! No wonder you wound up in H.R.! Who cares what he knows! It's what he *imagines* that has me shitting bricks! Do you realize that this psycho could turn up here and blow the place sky high for some imagined injustice to his former colleague Dr. Blake who committed suicide? And his wife! She was murdered in Queens, New York, of all places!

"Now, you listen to me; you're going to offer Kerrington a package *today* and transfer her to our office in Kansas. You will inform her that she should be fired and prosecuted for divulging the information contained in a personnel record, as she well knows, but that we will forgive and forget if she signs a nondisclosure agreement and honors it. Tell her she's placed us in a very bad legal position with the deceased's family, and say nothing else."

Greg tried to put an optimistic face on the problem. "I wonder if they know Montgomery had a falling out with the board. Christ, no one forced Blake to kill herself! No one here killed his wife, either! Let them investigate, Tony. You're acting like we did something wrong, for God's sake, when we know we didn't! I don't know... maybe he was having an affair with Blake and it went sideways. There's your reason for his faked death."

That was something Berringer hadn't thought of. "Anything is possible, I suppose. But I want to know every single detail of his work life here. Dig up what you can on the wife and financial situation. I also want to know where Montgomery's hiding. He's using the name Arthur Moreland, now."

"Look, the F.B.I is fishing, Tony. Why would they share that kind of information with you unless they wanted to see how you'd react? You didn't, did you?"

"Of course not, but we're involved now whether we like it or not. The publicity alone'll be a killer, and I don't plan on leaving this job in disgrace. Why couldn't Montgomery just stay *dead*, damn it? Greg, there are things you don't know about."

Berringer turned white and sat down. Then he told him everything he knew about Meese's connection to the *JASONS*. "You absolutely cannot mention the *JASONS* to anyone under *any* circumstances, do you understand? Not even to our own investigator. The *JASONS* are a myth to anyone outside Meese and the D.O.D. If their existence becomes fact, the White House is going to use our carcasses for charcoal at their next barbeque. Get it?"

Greg turned white and gulped. "Got it."

"I need to know what Montgomery's game is." Berringer stalked out of Greg James' office, slamming the glass door so hard that Greg winced.

***

Carter kept both hands folded and resting in his lap. He wasn't about to blow his career in a fit of pique over a petty dictator's decision to play both sides against the middle. He no longer trusted the man, but he'd play it cool, just as Seacrest suggested.

"Good morning, Agent Carter." Fischetti paused to take a large sip of coffee. "These meetings whip up hate for everything and everybody. That much is evident from what we pulled off of Red's cell phone. These con men invariably turn up when the economy is bad and people are looking for a scapegoat. This isn't news, Carter; it's been going on since the beginning of time. Unfortunately, it always will, people being what they are."

"I see. But then why send Agent Deeprose to Langley, Virginia to talk to a company called Meese?"

"Her visit to Meese may turn out to be nothing, Agent Carter, a tempest in a teapot. She discovered a photo of Moreland in an obituary written for a man named Montgomery who worked there, so I thought we'd jab them with a needle and see if anyone hollered."

"I understand, sir, but I was told that the reason she went looking for Intel on Meese was because of an anonymous tip you received. If the tipster thinks Meese is involved with the killings, does he think Meese is after Montgomery or the other way around, sir?"

"We're looking at all possibilities, Agent. Meese and Montgomery are a new focus of investigation, but unless we can connect the *Collective's* meetings to the drug dosing and organized assassinations, the only motivations we have so far are the fear and hate of its members."

Carter nodded.

"On another topic, your friend Red either intentionally gave us the wrong address or was fed the wrong Intel. I want to know whose side he's on."

Based on Carter's conversations with Red, he had a hard time believing the young man wasn't being completely honest with them. It was more likely he was fed the wrong information. He nodded again. "Sir, getting back to—what's his real name? Montgomery? I thought he left New York to travel internationally. Do you have any new Intel in that regard?"

Fischetti shrugged. "Not yet."

"The tip you received didn't mention anything concerning his whereabouts, sir?"

"No. I don't know who this tipster is. Maybe it's some crackpot or someone with an ax to grind."

"Did he mention anything about himself or his personal history? Did you get a look at him?"

"I could give a description to a sketch artist, but I doubt it would do any good. If he's the real thing, you'll never find a match; he hasn't survived this long because he's stupid. He's probably had his face changed and his finger prints burned off, at the very least."

Carter knew when he was being stonewalled and was beginning to feel very frustrated. He was deeply disappointed in the deputy director for treating him like a first-year rookie and for playing a shady game of his own.

It was unlikely the tipster would leave out any major details that would corroborate his story. He also doubted the tipster was a crackpot; he knew too much. No, the mystery man was the real McCoy, and they both knew it.

Fischetti tossed him a bone. "If you'd care to look it over, Agent Deeprose is in her office completing her report on her interview with Meese."

Carter took that as a not-so-subtle hint that the meeting was over. "Of course, sir."

On his way out, it struck Carter that Senator Pressman had suddenly become a distant object in the rear view mirror.

\*\*\*

Eliza took a long swig out of the bottle she bought on their way back to Clara's. "Scored the bag and ditched the ride! Well, ladies, it's been real."

Alison was worried. "Oh, no! You're not walking away from us that easily, Eliza. What about that phone call? You still haven't told us anything about it. I think we're being watched."

"Don't be paranoid, Alison. Now we're being watched, too? Your creepy father's *dead*. Let it *go,* already!"

Alison looked like she'd been hit in the face. "*You shut your mouth*! He *loved* me! He just didn't want me to turn out like my mother, that's all. Now be quiet; Clara can hear us from the bathroom."

"So?"

"So I don't want her to hear what we're saying, Eliza. She's not like me and you; she's clean and perfect."

"Why is Clara so important, Alison? You know she's using you, don't you?"

"There's a girl out there planning to kill her! She's using *me*? I like that! Look Eliza, I know you couldn't care less about Michael, although if it wasn't for him, the *Silver Man's* people might have already murdered you. I know exactly how you feel about *me*; you think I'm weak and needy, and you hate me for it. But I know something about you, too, Eliza. I know why you really helped us steal that bag; you want it for yourself, and I'm pretty sure you won't stop with taking the drug just to feel invincible. You're a killer, Eliza, without the courage to go through with it. You want that drug to make murder easy for you. You want to enjoy it, don't you? *Don't you, you sick bitch?*"

Eliza looked at Alison with something akin to respect. "Look who has a spine after all! That may become a problem for me, Allie, so don't push your luck."

"And one more point before we move on. I don't want to have this conversation again, so pay attention. Clara is important to me because she's my family, now. She genuinely cares about me. She could have avoided this whole thing by telling the police the name of the ballerina who threatened her life and going back home to her uncle, upstate. But she didn't. She stayed, for *me*. And God help us, for *you*."

Eliza smirked. "And if I take the bag and leave? What can you do about it?"

"You won't take it. You know Michael, and you got into his car voluntarily. You gave him up to the cops to keep yourself out of trouble. But now you've got an illegal street drug. One anonymous call from me, and you'll be right where Michael is, answering a lot of questions about the vial they found in the car. Maybe, just maybe, they'll decide it belonged to you all along."

"O.K., Allie, let's talk about Michael. Why aren't *you* trying to help him out of jail?"

"Because Michael is also a born killer. It's in your D.N.A. and his, and no one can ever change it. Your brain is wired up all wrong. You're turned on by power and control. You have no sense of right or wrong. You think if stealing is an impulse it's natural and what's natural is O.K. to do. But nothing about you is natural! You were the kids that killed insects with magnifying glasses and then moved on to drowning cats. That's who Michael is, and that's who you are."

221

"All right, Alison, if you're gonna choose this moment to grow the hell up, then here's a news flash; I have to make a kill, and it's an order. An *order*, Alison, not a choice!"

"Is that what the call was about?"

"I don't know yet. Look, you were right about the *Silver Man's* people, Allie. We *are* being watched, O.K? We broke the rules, and it can only end one way. Until then, I'm gonna live it up as long as I can, and I'll kill anyone who gets in my way, including you and Clara."

Clara emerged from the bathroom. "Did I miss anything?"

"Eliza's thinking about dumping us to go on a toot and kill anyone who gets in her way. Isn't that right, Eliza?"

"Shut up, Alison. Here's the deal; if I don't get another call, I'm on board with you." Eliza pulled her leather jacket off the back of her chair. "I'm outta here."

\*\*\*

When Eliza left, the two girls sat down to talk.

"We have to think up a way to scare your killer away from you without resorting to violence."

Clara perked up. "I've been thinking about that. I know a guy who used to have a serious crush on Abby. He's a nighttime security guard at a local micro-brewery. I'll invite her there for a little party and get him to open the door for us while he's on duty. Then, with him there as a witness and protector, we'll confront her and tell her that the cops are looking for her in connection with the *Collective* murders. He can control her if she loses it. What do you think?"

"It sounds fairly simple. But will she accept your invitation?"

"Nope. That's why we're going to deliver the invitation in person."

# Chapter Twenty Four

Eliza's phone rang just as she pulled the car into traffic. She dispensed with the niceties. "Give me a minute. I'm driving."

The caller was curt and commanding. "I have a message from the *Silver Man*. Pull over and park. You did not follow the instructions you received at the meeting. You stole our property. You have one last chance to prove that you are not an enemy of the *Collective*."

For the first time in her life, she was truly scared. This was the moment she had dreaded. Sweat soaked through the back of her shirt, making it feel like a second skin.

*Will they let me live after this?*

"I was going to do it, I swear. I'll do whatever you want." Frantically pleading with him, she heard her own voice as if it came from somewhere outside the car.

"Relax, Eliza, we know you're going to do your job. Why don't you have a smoke? They're in the glove compartment. I think we'll both get more done once you realize we're your friends. And you're going to help your friends by doing exactly what you're told. That's reasonable, isn't it?"

His voice was deep and rich, smooth and slick with culture and class—not at all what she expected. Eliza's fear increased until all she could register was sheer terror.

"Will you let me go after it's done? I have to know."

His answer was unmistakable; "Once you complete your assignment, you're done. We have no interest in cultivating this relationship beyond that.

"Go to the U.S. Post Office at 127 West 83rd Street and retrieve a key that is taped underneath box 1001. Open it, and you will see that it contains instructions and everything you need to do the job. Follow the instructions, and you'll be fine."

"Who is it this time?"

"Here's a little hint; who wants to kill a billionaire?"

\*\*\*

"Are we all set for tonight, Clara?"

"All set. Doug Meir is the overnight security guard at *The Ginger Man* on East 36th Street. I told him that you were my best friend and that you'd be bringing Abby there tonight to meet us for an after-hours party when the bar closes. I'll wait for you at the back entrance. It'll be unlocked. The fermenting rooms are the perfect place to scare the hell out of her."

She giggled and squeezed Alison's hand. "He's going to cut the feed to the in-house security cameras so no one will know we were ever there. He thinks he's got a shot at a three-way!"

"*Shut up!*"

"Abby hangs out at a bar called the *Pig n' Whistle On Third* on 55th Street every night without fail. The bartender is her cousin, so she drinks for free. He hates her guts." Clara smiled beatifically.

"Then what?"

"Get a seat next to her at the bar. When she's stinking drunk, walk out with her and get her into a cab. Have the driver drop you off a few blocks away from *The Ginger Man* and steer her to the back door. I'll be waiting."

"O.K., but…" Alison looked worried.

"But what?"

"I just thought we were going to do this together."

"We are! Alison, if I'm seen at the bar and anything happens we didn't count on, I'll be the first person they look for. They'll find out I know you and connect you to the *Collective*. Then it'll be all over, Allie. Victim of the drug or not, they'll put you away. Look, you're a stranger to her; no one's going to be looking at you. Besides, she can't say anything without incriminating herself."

"But what if the bartender sees us talking and remembers I left with her?"

"Don't do either one, Allie. Just watch and wait. Leave when she leaves. Clever, huh?"

"Yes. Clever." The thought made her uncomfortable. "What's the rest of it?"

"We'll tell her that we know about the *Collective* and have proof that she's one of them. I want to scare her so badly that she'll pack up, leave town and never look back. End of story. Do you think I should change my dress? I think black is more appropriate."

\*\*\*

Eliza found the key taped under box 1001, exactly where she was told it would be. She opened the mailbox and looked over everything inside it.

*You're kidding me. Austen Boyd? The bankrupt billionaire? The brainless wannabe whose mouth is his own worst enemy? I consider this a public service!"*

A full dossier lay inside the black folder. Before Eliza read it, she began to salivate over what else was inside the folder—a set of keys to a Lincoln Town Car and a big wad of money.

*Good afternoon,*

*You will be posing as a call girl, tonight. Billionaire Austen Boyd is the target. His valet has already made arrangements for an escort for this evening's festivities. Purchase a little black dress at Bergdorf's and present yourself as "Jolie Gaspar", tonight. Drive to the address you see here and park in the underground lot. Take the freight elevator and exit at the lobby level. The chauffeur will meet you there and escort you to Mr. Boyd's limousine. Boyd expects you to be up for anything he wants to do. He likes his cocaine, so play along but stay alert. He was going to make a speech tonight at an N.R.A. gala asking for support of his candidacy for president. You must stop him from reaching the hotel by blowing the enclosed bag of poison in his face. After that, you're on your own. Burn this memo before ditching the car, and don't get yourself caught. Remember, if you run away, no matter where you go, we'll find you.*

Eliza recalled her low end jobs, low end pay, and low end life style. She understood the *Silver Man*, now. Yes, it did feel good to be the one to eliminate a bastard like that. It would improve life for everyone.

*People have to learn that when they try to grab it all, they only wind up with a handful of enemies who'll fight or kill to get it back.*

\*\*\*

Alison had her first self-protective thought, ever.

*I don't have to go into the Pig n' Whistle, at all. I know who to look for; why risk being seen when I can just wait out here on the street for Abby?*

The bartender spoke to Abby without making eye contact. "I can't serve you another one. Rules are rules. You can catch a cab outside."

Abby nodded and stumbled out of the bar straight into Alison's arms. The two women got into a cab and headed toward *The Ginger Man* for the second round.

***

Eliza leafed through the literature one more time before burning it. Her weapon was *Fentanyl*, a dangerous narcotic responsible for a recent rash of overdoses. Despite its highly publicized death rate, *Fentanyl* remained wildly popular as a synthetic opiate mixed with heroin to increase its potency. Even touching the substance could be lethal. It was immediately absorbed into the body, causing the organs to fail within moments.

*This is my kind of kill. Quick and easy...*

***

*The Ginger Man* was impossibly crowded, but Clara made her way inside and found a seat at the end of the bar. It was close to last call, and the bartenders were frantically processing everyone's credit cards. She ordered a tray of extremely potent pints of black stout and paid for them in cash before making her way to the fermentation room. Doug had already disconnected the surveillance camera. When the last customer was gone, he locked every door except the back entrance. Hot and impatient, he went straight to the room containing four huge boiling vats of beer and grabbing at the glasses, downed one after the other.

Slowly, deliberately and from across the room, Clara slid one hand and then the other into her skin tight mini dress to adjust its strapless cups. His mouth went dry. Two more pints went down the hatch and then two more. Doug was going to be incredibly easy to handle, tonight.

226

She slinked her way across the room in four-inch stilettos and pulled him against her. Beginning at the base of his throat, she delighted him with little butterfly kisses that worked their way up to his mouth. He was almost mad with excitement.

"Where's Abby and your friend?"

"They'll be here in a few minutes. Where exactly is the video camera? I want to make sure it's off."

He pointed to a portrait on the wall directly in front of them. "It's right over there."

"Show me how you turned it off. I want to make sure I don't get you into any trouble, Dougie."

"Don't worry about that, Clara. I took care of it."

"Even so, I'd feel much better if you showed me it was done and how you did it."

"O.K." He shrugged, took the portrait off the wall and showed her how he turned the video camera on and off.

"Can we try some of the beer in the vat?"

"Sure, but it's not done yet. The fermentation process has to complete before it cools off."

"Let's taste it hot, right now, Doug. We can just lean over the side and fill our glasses. Whaddya say?"

"I don't know how good it'll be, but anything you say."

"Ah, my favorite words!"

Doug told her a little about the process as they peered down into the fermentation vat. Clara strolled around its perimeter, asking questions. When she stood facing him and had her back to the camera, deftly, she reached behind her back and pressed the start button.

"Come 'ere, big boy. The party starts right now."

He reached out to touch her hair but stopped short when he saw her begin to laugh. He looked confused. Then his face turned bright red. With a will of their own, his hands shot out and ripped the dress off her. He was beyond self-control. She knew full well what was coming and egged him on.

"Go ahead, Doug. Show me what a big *man* you are."

He beat her until her blood was all over him, and she stopped fighting back.

\*\*\*

227

Abby was passing out and Alison, who had to drag her for two blocks to the back of the bar, knew in her heart the plan was not going to work. You couldn't scare an unconscious assassin. That was when she heard Clara scream. Pulling Abby in front of herself as a human shield, she burst through the door just in time to see Doug hit Clara in the face. Alison had no time to think. All she saw was a naked and bleeding Clara and that was all she needed to see.

"Get your hands off her!"

Doug turned around when he heard Alison yell; that was his last mistake. She rushed him like a linebacker, knocking him off his feet and over the edge of the boiling vat of beer.

Abby, fully revived, flew at Alison. The two women fought in earnest, rolling on the floor, kicking, gouging and tearing each other's hair out. Alison fought for her life. She heaved Abby up into the air in an iron grip and tossed her over the side, where she boiled to death with the security guard.

In the absolute silence that followed, Alison gripped the lip of the vat and stared at the boiling bodies drifting in the tank and began to realize the implications of what she'd done. "Oh, my God. They're dead, Clara, and I did it! Why didn't you tell me the beer was boiling hot?! All I wanted to do was throw them in to cool off a little."

Clara looked at Alison but said nothing.

"Clara? Clara! Why are you looking at me like that?"

Alison understood. Finally. She'd driven the last nail into her own coffin for nothing.

Clara had been staring enigmatically into the vat until this minute when the mask she'd worn her whole life fell away. She looked...triumphant. *Resplendent*. And utterly evil. This was Clara. The innocent angel in distress was as hard as nails and as cold as ice. Alison couldn't take her eyes off that face; she'd never forget it as long as she lived.

***

Clara saw no further need to keep up the performance now that Alison had done her dirty work. Still naked and fiendishly beautiful, she turned towards Alison wondering how people could be so incredibly stupid.

She had been very careful to step to one side of the camera when

Doug started hitting her so that the police could get a very good, very clear look at Alison, her misguided protector.

* * *

Eliza had the *Fentanyl* in her clutch bag. She was barely inside the limousine when Boyd let loose. The man seemed to have eight arms, and every one of them was either clutching a breast or clamped between her legs.

"Hey, take it easy, lover. You don't want it to be over before it begins, do you?"

"I like the way you think, baby. How about some champagne?" Boyd pushed a glass into Eliza's hand, clinked his glass against hers and swallowed. "Can I offer you some blow?"

"Sure!"

She realized, just then, that she had forgotten to drink the killing serum, her little partner in crime.

*Now I'll have to kill him without it. Goddamn sonofabitch! It won't be any fun at all. Well, I might as well get it over with, then.*

She leaned up into Boyd's face and licked his bottom lip and tugged on it a little with her teeth. "How about trying some of *my* blow first? It's very high grade, Mr. Boyd. Almost impossible to get. Taste a little bit before you snort it. Come here, baby. Closer. Much closer. Now...open your mouth and close your eyes..."

Boyd's eyes sparkled. "O.K., I'm game, I'll play."

The instant he opened his mouth, Eliza poured the *Fentanyl,* all of it, directly onto his tongue. The black glass partition was up, so the driver could neither see nor hear anything that happened in the back of the car.

Boyd's hands flew to his mouth. "What the *fuck*?!"

He tried to spit it out, but it was already too late. His eyes bulged. Uncontrollable spasms racked the body already in death throes. Eliza squeezed her eyes shut, not sure what to do next.

In what was most likely the only act of kindness Austen Boyd ever showed to anyone, he unintentionally saved Eliza from having to make a decision. His right leg shot straight out, propelling her back against her door. A clicking sound initiated and the next thing she knew, Eliza was out on her ass in the middle of 5th Avenue watching the limo speed away.

# Chapter Twenty Five

Frustration mounted every hour, every day the cases stayed cold. Although Agent Deeprose stumbled onto a connection between Arthur Moreland and the Meese Corporation, the trail seemed to end there. Michael's refusal to talk spoke loudly; he'd been scared into complete silence. The public outcry was creating a pressure cooker for all of them.

Carter hoped they'd have better luck with *The Ginger Man* double homicide. He'd lost track of how long he stood outside the brewery studying the foot prints that lead from the sidewalk down a dirt alley and into the micro-brewery's back door. He was certain they belonged to three different people, one having been dragged along the ground. He was glad winter hadn't set in yet or the soil would have been too hard for them to show.

Carter reflected on the foot prints for another moment before going inside to see the crime scene. Killings were committed, for the most part, by men, but these prints were too shallow and small to belong to men. No, they definitely belonged to women.

By the time he entered the building, Agent Seacrest had already examined most of the area surrounding the fermentation vat.

"What do we have?"

"A couple of drunks in the drink."

"How do you know there are two victims?"

Seacrest jerked her head toward the vat. "Take a peek."

Carter observed two skulls floating in the nearly drained tank. The same brewery foreman who'd discovered the bodies six hours earlier had emptied the vat for the forensic team. Seacrest took samples of the liquid for analysis.

"It'll take a while to retrieve the remains, but I've got good news, Carter." She showed him a photo of dusted fingerprints. "This was found around the perimeter of the tank."

Carter wasn't as amazed as she expected him to be. "Another messy scene. That makes three. The Florio murder in New Jersey was tidier, but there was still that partial print left behind. Could that be my smoking gun? The murders appear unrelated, but they've all been committed by amateurs, some of them women. We haven't found any evidence of a payoff or even any attempts to escape the city."

"It's starting to sound more and more like an initiation rite or a cult thing, Carter. The murders were too vicious in nature to have been thrill kills, and a serial killer would most likely have been more experienced in the art of killing and disposing of a body. He also would have learned from his mistakes and gotten better at it, not worse."

Carter was on the same wavelength. "The *Collective* may be the common denominator between the previous two murders and these."

Seacrest held up the photo again. "In the meantime, I think this print is our best lead right now. If this hand print matches the partial in Florio's bathroom, we'll have proof that the same person was at both crime scenes. That could break everything wide open, Carter!"

"If we match both sets of prints to one person, find the two women that belong to the footprints outside and get one of them to talk, Jill, I'm taking you to Fiji for a month."

Seacrest laughed. "That's a deal. Just remember you said it."

He looked around the room again. "It appears the deputy director is correct in assuming these murders are tied together. If the *Collective* meetings are the motivating factor, these *could* be initiation kills. Believe it or not, I hope he's right. That would be a quick end to it, the *Collective* and the circulation of that damn drug. But if the truth goes deeper than that…well, we'll just have to burn that bridge when we get there."

"Carter, the foreman tells me he can't account for the whereabouts of his night watchman, Doug Meir. He should have been on guard here all night, and oddly enough, someone turned the video surveillance camera off and then on again. Maybe the footage will give us a hint at what went on here last night."

Seacrest surveyed the room again. "There's no sign of a forced entry, so my guess is he knew the girls. At any rate, he'd have been the only person who could have voluntarily let them in."

231

"What makes you think that?"

"The cameras weren't disconnected and no wires were cut. Nothing was damaged. He'd have known where the security camera was and how to turn it off and on. He may even have shown the girls how to use it before his death. There are no scuff marks outside the door, so he wasn't shoved or forced into this room. Someone was pushed across this room, but it wasn't him. He came in because he wanted to. Did the E.R.T.s find anything of note outside?"

"The prints are relatively small and shallow, which suggests they belong to women. They lead inside and come back out the same way. Two women came in together and two went out together, but not the same two."

"So there were three women here last night."

Carter nodded. "One set of prints heading inside shows that one woman was walking sideways. Two deeper parallel lines starting just behind her show that someone—perhaps one of the victims—was dragged along the dirt path and into the building. Two women went in together. However, the exit pattern shows that the two women who left together were both walking side by side. Neither set of prints are especially deep, so no one carried out the third woman. She didn't walk out on her own, either, so we can assume she's still inside. I think we're going to find that one of the skeletons is hers. The other probably belongs to the security guard."

Seacrest was flabbergasted. "Two women; that's a major change in pattern. Interesting. The foreman told us there are free beer tastings after their daily tours. Could the two women have taken a tour and then hidden themselves in here when until everyone else left?"

"It's possible, but not probable. Their footprints went in through the back entrance. Tourists don't do that. But employees do. They're being questioned now. If anyone here was involved or saw anything, we'll know it soon enough. By the way, where's Agent Deeprose?"

"She's not here, yet."

Carter raised an eyebrow. "Not here yet?"

"Carter, ever hear of a thing called a *personal life*? She texted me just before you came in. I think love is in the air, and it sounds a lot like saxophones, to me." She looked jubilant.

Carter looked slightly miffed. "I don't begrudge her a personal life, Jill, but I expected her to be here by now. Besides, she's great with the locals. She's our secret weapon, Jill. Men love her and women aren't threatened by her. It's absolutely mystifying to watch her work."

"For you, Carter. For women, it comes with the equipment. Hers is an age-old method that never fails, honey, and it's sooooo much easier than confrontation."

Carter had no answer for that one. She was right.

Deeprose breezed in with three coffees. "Watcha'll talkin' about? Agent Carter, you look flummoxed. And Jill, you look…smug. There's just no other word for it." Deeprose was rosy red from the cold morning air and in very high spirits. She put down the coffee cups and took off her coat. Carter and Seacrest exchanged a guilty glance before she turned back to them.

Carter cleared his throat. "Just discussing the new crime scene, Agent. Any particular reason for being late this morning?"

"A lady never tells. Isn't that right, Jill?"

Seacrest winked at her and resumed her examination.

"So, what do we have here, Agent Carter?"

Her eyes grew wider and wider as he told her what they'd found. When he was done, she tossed her red beret into the air. "Hallelujah, amen!" Then, she peered into the tank and sniffed. "*Yugh*! It's goin' to be a while before Ah drink draft again."

"Connecting the crimes to the *Collective* is still circumstantial so far, but the case gets much stronger every time we can make a connection between a murder and the hallucinogen. To fit the pattern, one or both killers should have been using the drug last night. Jill, can forensics determine if the drug was secreted from the killer's hands into the hand print on the edge of the vat?"

Seacrest shook her head. "Afraid not. It's much more likely we'll find D.N.A. secreted into the hand print, if we find anything at all. I'll call the Washington Bureau to see if they have anything we don't, but I honestly don't know if anyone could pull that off."

Carter frowned. "Well, if we can at least match the hand print with the partial from the Florio crime scene, we'll have enough for a warrant for search and seizure at the *Collective's* next meeting. I don't want any more sneak attacks on high school victory parties. This time we go in through the front door of the correct place."

"I think we already have enough of a print though, to make a positive I.D."

Agent Deeprose was intrigued. "Could we really get a D.N.A. sample from the hand print, Jill?"

"Theoretically. There's a technique I could use called '*Touch D.N.A.*'. It's popular in the U.K., but not here in the states."

Deeprose looked crestfallen. "But could we get the equipment we need to do the test? Ah wanna see if the print you have here matches someone of interest, but the only sample Ah have is also on something that's been touched. If that test can identify her D.N.A., and if Ah can match hers up to the D.N.A. left on the hand print here…*bingo*!"

Carter raised an eyebrow. "Who do you have in mind, Agent?"

"There's a loose end that's been botherin' me. Do y'all remember Eliza, the girl who was in the car with Michael the day we caught him? She claimed to have been an innocent victim—a *hostage*—and Michael never contradicted her. Even so, when I paid a visit to her at the hospital, Ah managed to get a D.N.A. sample from a tissue she touched. I gave it to you for safe keepin'. Remember?"

Seacrest nodded. "I sure do. It'll take a little more time, but if I can get enough cells from the hand print to compare with those on the tissue, it's possible."

Carter smiled. "If the cells are there, Agent Deeprose, she'll find them."

*** 

Eliza walked into Clara's apartment and immediately noticed a half empty bottle of liquor on the kitchen table. Alison was downing glass after glass of 151 proof rum. She also noticed that Clara did the pouring but not the drinking. "How did it go, last night, Alison?"

"What do you care?"

*Great! Clara's tossing Alison off the wagon with both hands.*

Eliza guffawed and dropped into an easy chair. "Good for you, Alison. One for the home team. I was just wondering why you're three sheets to the wind this early in the day, that's all."

"Yeah, well you quit us, so you can just keep on wondering. I have a question for you; did you make sure no one followed you back here from your own job last night? I don't want to hear anything about it, but if you left any evidence at the scene, we don't want you dragging us into it."

"There's no evidence to find, and no one followed me here, Alison. Get a grip for God's sake." Eliza flashed back to the limo. One second she was in the roomy back seat and the next she was out the door. Her clutch bag had her prints all over it, and the *Fentanyl* was still in the car. By now, the *Silver Man* was sure to know what happened.

*Did I scratch Boyd's face? It happened so fast I can't remember! Skin cells are easy to leave behind; anyone who watches those forensic crime shows knows that.*

Alison slurred her words, but her intense anger toward Eliza came from the heart. "You *traitor*! You were going to *help* me and Clara. All you did was help yourself to a bag of drugs that turn people into raving killers!"

*Shit. I forgot about that. Between that and my assignment last night, the two of them could ruin me if they want to, and they know it.*

Eliza began to sweat, and when she did, she always came out swinging. "Listen, your only concern is to watch your own ass and keep that big trap of yours shut."

Clara chose this moment to shock them both. "Hey, *hey*! Come on, now, you two; we still have to stick together, don't we? After all, if we lose our nerve now, someone's liable to get caught. Let's look at this thing logically; Alison's a drunk, and no one ever believes a drunk. However, she did commit a double murder last evening without benefit of the *Collective's* killing drug and has no other excuse or alibi as far as the police will see. She may have had an excuse the first time, but not this time. They'll send her up for life and forget she ever existed."

The room became absolutely silent. Alison stood staring at Clara.

"You've been using me the whole time! You, *you*…you're worse than Eliza!"

"Hey!" Eliza took exception to that remark.

"At least she doesn't pretend to be anything but an animal. You double-dealing, selfish whore! You only pretended to like me!" She put down her glass and buried her head in her hands.

Clara went on as if there had been no interruption at all. "And you, Eliza, you committed a murder last night also—or tried to. We may not know the details, but that doesn't really matter. Since it didn't take place directly after a *Collective* meeting, you can't blame the crime on having been drugged without your knowledge or consent. Since you didn't do your murder the night you did get dosed, you can't prove you were ever at a *Collective* meeting unless Michael talks, and we all know he won't. That leaves you holding the bag for possession, murder or attempted murder, with no way to blame it on the *Silver Man*.

"As for myself, well, I never heard of the *Collective*, and I never met either one of you—or Michael, for that matter. As I said, no one will believe Alison. She'd blame anyone to save herself. You? Don't make me laugh. You were in Michael's car. You're up to your ugly ears in trouble, and you've been in trouble your whole life. No one will have any trouble believing me over you.

"Then there's Abby. Abby was a member of the *Collective* and arranged my assassination. If Alison gets caught, they'll assume she and Abby got into a fight over the killing of the security guard and that Alison decided to get rid of both of them in one shot. If the cops find out Abby had a grudge against me, they'll be glad that my best friend Alison got to her before she got to me. Besides, of the three of us, I'm the only one with the right address and education. My uncle is a well-known defense attorney who hasn't lost a case in forty years. I'm a prima ballerina with a prestigious dance company and an international ambassador of peace. Let's face it; if anyone has the believability factor and the upper hand here, girls, it's myself."

Eliza lost what was left of her temper. "You rotten... miserable... entitled... lying... manipulative, **BITCH**! God knows there's no love lost between me and Alison, but what you did to her is worse than murder. She's the only one of us who gave a shit about saving your sorry ass. I may have had to be tough and mean to survive in the neighborhood I grew up in, but you're something straight out of hell; we shoulda let Abby have a second shot at you."

Clara laughed and made a deep curtsy. "I am a good actress, aren't I? Perhaps I should take on Hollywood after my dancing career is over. Then there's the book to write once you're all locked away for life. Well, what do you say? Shall we drink a toast to the gruesome twosome? After all, you may not have come from hell, but that's just where you're both going."

Eliza was worried. This one was no dummy.

*I have to be careful. I can't underestimate Clara again. I'll play along with her for now. Later on, when they're both off guard, I'll get rid of them. Then, I'm home free. No witnesses, no evidence, no worries.*

*If Boyd didn't survive, the only witness is the chauffeur. He only saw me for a second, at best, and the only evidence are my prints on the evening bag I left there. The only other thing in it is the Fentanyl. Unless I get arrested, no one has my prints or photo anywhere on file. If he did survive, he'll never come after me; he can't afford a scandal so close to an election. They can't connect me to the escort agency, and no one except the Silver Man knows my real name, address, or phone number. I paid for everything in cash and burned the dossier. Unless my picture gets into the news, no one will ever know about me. No one except for the Silver Man, that is...*

Alison looked up. "I don't like the look on your face, Eliza. There's something you haven't told us. What is it?"

"I might have left a tiny little loose end."

"*God damn it*! Can't you do one single thing without screwing it up?! If you get caught this time, you're on your own."

Clara looked stunned.

Eliza was also surprised at Alison's show of strength. "I thought it all through, Alison. There's no way to connect me to the job last night. But there is something we have to do together. That hillbilly agent is a liability. I was in Michael's car, and she's seen me and spoken to me at the hospital. If she has any reason at all to think I was in on it with him, she'll hound me until the end of time. I have no choice; she has to go."

Clara jumped out of her chair as if she was sitting on hot coals. "Now, wait just a minute! That's *your* fault and *your* problem. I'm done with both of you."

Eliza was practically begging, now. She needed help, and Alison was still her best bet. "Alison, you know we have to do this; you're in too deep not to help! If there was any way Clara could've set you up and framed you for those two murders last night, you can bet she did, but you have no record and you had no connection to any of the victims, so unless they can get your prints or any other evidence from either scene, there's no way they can tie you to them. You didn't leave any physical evidence, did you?"

"Of course not, you idiot. I was very careful."

*I hope she was…*

"All right, then, listen to me; Clara will turn us in to save herself, and you know it. It's only a matter of time, Allie, unless you do this one last thing with me!"

"Who gives a flying fuck about you, Eliza?! I'm sick of the sight of you. Getting rid of that F.B.I. agent won't keep Clara from talking, anyway. We'd still be looking over our shoulders for the rest of our lives. All I want to do is end this whole nightmare. I'm no killer; I want to confess. There are extenuating circumstances for me, but not for you."

Eliza turned a cold smile towards Clara. "Alison, she can't tell on us if she helps us, though. Can you, Clara? The way I see it, there's only one way out of this; all three of us have to have enough on each other so that none of us is able to turn on the other two. Doing a job together will make sure of it."

Alison trembled uncontrollably. "Look, all I did was protect Clara and myself from two killers; it was self-defense! And I wasn't morally, ethically or even mentally responsible for the first one because I was drugged! If I do this thing now, Eliza, then I really am a killer, and I'm not. *I'm not!*"

"O.K., then you'll go to prison knowing you're not a killer, but you'll still go. Is that what you want, dummy? God, Alison, for once in your life, face reality! No one is going to come to your rescue. You're going to have to save yourself. That's what the *Silver Man* meant. Killing to protect yourself is a natural instinct. There's no good or evil about it, Alison. I'm not evil. You're not evil. And your only responsibility is to yourself."

Eliza stuck a hand into the pocket of her jeans and fished out a business card she'd been holding onto, just in case. She slammed it down on the table. It belonged to Agent Deeprose.

# Chapter Twenty Six

Hours later, Agent Deeprose was still hanging around the crime lab, waiting and hoping for answers.

*Damn! Ah knew Ah shouldn't've had that fourth cup of coffee. Ah'm so jumpy Ah could hit the ceilin'! Come on, Jill, come on.....time's not on our side. The suspect could be long gone by now.*

The wait was driving her crazy, and now she was driving Seacrest crazy, too. The hand print left on the edge of the fermentation vat turned out to match the partial found at Florio's home, definitely placing one suspect at both scenes, but since they didn't match any prints already listed in the police and F.B.I. databases, the suspects remained unidentified. The evidence suggested that these were the suspect's first crimes, but since the second murder was much sloppier than the first, it still made no sense to any of them.

Shania's impatience finally broke Jill's concentration. "Why don't you get some food to go with that caffeine, Agent Deeprose? Waiting here for me to I.D. the bones won't make the process go any faster, and frankly, you're getting on my last nerve. I recovered both sets of teeth, so identifying the security guard won't be that difficult, just time consuming." Then she smiled apologetically. "Look, it's going to be a painstaking process, Shania. Go find something to do. I need to focus." Seacrest turned back to her work.

Deeprose cleared her throat. "But Ah thought you might do that *Touch D.N.A* test we talked about at the scene—the one where we can see if the cells on the hand print match the ones that belong to the girl Michael had in his car. Ah haven't ruled her out as a person of interest, yet."

"I'm aware of that, but priority goes to identification of the bodies, or in this case, the bones. I'm sorry. When I'm done, I'll talk to the deputy director about finding us more budget money for the D.N.A. testing equipment." She turned back to her microscope and forgot all about Shania.

Since Agent Carter was doing a last sweep of the *Ginger Man* crime scene, Deeprose decided to head over to the F.B.I. computer lab to do some in depth research on the Meese Corporation. It was probably what the deputy director would want, anyway.

She was swept forward by the crowd pushing their way onto the elevator and then back out again by those getting off. She felt the corners of her mouth rise.

*You'd think getting' to their next meetin' was a matter of life and death!*

While waiting for the next ride, she noticed a text message from Eliza. As she read, her smile evaporated, and her jaw dropped open.

"That day in the hospital you said to call you if I remembered anything else about Michael Santiago, the guy who pulled me into his car and tried to kidnap me. I assume he's still in custody, but I've been receiving strange messages from a man who won't identify himself. It can't be Santiago, if he's in jail, so it's got to be someone else; maybe someone he knows. The caller thinks I know something about that day that I haven't told the police, and he wants to know what it is. I don't know anything more than I already told you, Agent Deeprose. Who could it be? I'm scared to death!

"Please, *please* meet me at in front of a bar called the *Whiskey Trader* at 71 West 55th Street, between 5th and 6th Avenue, as soon as you can. Make sure to come alone, and don't tell anyone I contacted you. I don't trust anyone but you—not even the people at your office. Please. I need to talk to you. *Hurry!*"

A list of options flooded her mind. She could contact Agent Carter for instructions, bring her phone to the cyber team to try to determine the authenticity of the text, or meet Eliza alone without notifying anyone. It didn't take Deeprose long to make her decision. Carter was temporarily out of reach, and notifying Fischetti first was exactly what Carter told her *not* to do. Text analysis would take too long, and this opportunity might not be on the table for long. In the end, she left Carter a voice message saying she was on her way to Midtown for an appointment and would call him later.

It was certainly possible that Eliza was telling the truth, but Deeprose really didn't think so. She trusted her instincts. When she appropriated Eliza's D.N.A. at the hospital after capturing Michael, there was something about the stubborn set of her jaw, her hard voice and dull, shark-like eyes that aroused Deeprose's suspicion.

*I don't believe that cock and bull story for a minute, but she knows something. If she's the killer—or one of them, anyway—there's only one way to find out...*

\*\*\*

Deeprose pulled up in front of the *Whiskey Trader* and waited for Eliza to show up. Dusk was approaching, and the sky, steel gray, cast gargantuan shadows of the towering buildings over the pavement. She shivered, despite the warmth of her car, turned up the collar of her coat and adjusted her red wool beret.

*It's too quiet around here.*

All at once she didn't like the feel of the whole thing. Deeprose turned on the car radio and listened to the local traffic report. Several streets in the area were closed off due to a water main break.

*That explains why it's a ghost town around here. Ah wonder if that's really true or if they just say that when any ol' thing happens.*

*Keep it cool, girl. You can certainly handle one young woman. Be ready for anythin'. Don't take anythin' at face value. Call for backup.*

She never got the chance.

\*\*\*

A pair of headlights flashed behind Deeprose's car and a car pulled up behind her. She didn't want to spook Eliza, so she slid out from behind the steering wheel slowly and took her time shutting the door behind her. She kept one hand close to her holstered nine-millimeter *Glock* and waved to Eliza with the other. The windows of the black *Lincoln Town Car* were tinted to such a degree that it was impossible to make out anything except the outline of a woman in the driver's seat. She steadied herself, ready to assume a shooting stance.

*Ah know Ah should have demanded we meet at H.Q., but Eliza*

241

*would never have agreed to that; Ah gotta know the truth, one way or the other.*

The driver's door swung open, and Eliza hurried toward Deeprose. "God, it's cold out! I'm sorry we had to meet out on the street like this, but my phone's being bugged for sure, and if I'm being followed, I'd rather they catch up with me in a moving vehicle with you riding shotgun. Look, we can't stay here. Leave your car in the underground lot down the street, and I'll take you somewhere they can't find us."

Deeprose knew that if Eliza's phone was being bugged, it was also being tracked, so whoever had been calling Eliza knew where their meeting was taking place, anyway. Eliza didn't seem to realize it. "Ah think, in this case, it'd be safer for *you* to park your car and ride with *me*."

"I can't do that, Agent. What if those calls are coming from inside your own organization? I'm not even sure I can trust *you*, but I have to trust *someone...*"

She looked Eliza full in the face, speechless. Sure, Deeprose suspected Fischetti of not sharing all his Intel with her in the beginning, but he was a straight arrow; the accusation was preposterous. She blinked a few times, shook it off and gave Eliza the only answer she could. "Eliza, we don't operate that way. We only have the authority to question y'all if we have suspicions. As far as Ah know, your association with Michael Santiago does not warrant suspicion. Or does it?"

Eliza shook her head. "No, Agent, but I won't be safe in your car if the F.B.I's listening in, and we can't stand out here on the street, either. You can't know for sure that someone inside your organization isn't behind this. I'm not getting into your car. Period. Will you come with me or not?"

"O.K., Eliza, you win; let's go."

Deeprose parked her car and headed over to the passenger side door of Eliza's car. The tension mounted with every mile they covered.

"Pardon me for bein' nosey, but where'd this car come from? Ah mean, y'all don't have a job at the moment, right? Whadja use for money?"

"I raided the last of my savings when my aunt told me she was selling it." She laughed. "The old bag had no idea what it was worth."

As they drove along, Eliza's eyes darted from side to side.
*She's makin' sure we're not bein' followed.*

Deeprose observed a not-so-gradual abandonment of the damsel-in-distress pose and the emergence of pride mixed with equal parts of slyness and craftiness. "Family's important, Eliza. They come in real handy when the universe gives back what y'all put out there."

Eliza rolled her eyes, and Deeprose saw her do it.

"Eliza, you don't have to keep up the act for me, an' y'all can quit lyin'. Ah don't really care where you got this car. All Ah care about is the information you might have concernin' this case. What is it you think you know?"

Eliza reached inside her jacket pocket. Deeprose shifted in her seat, ready.

"I don't have a weapon, Agent, I'm just checking my phone to see if he left another message."

Deeprose studied Eliza's face. "Maybe these are just prank calls, Eliza."

"No. They're not prank calls." She answered much too quickly and decisively.

Deeprose started to close in. "How do you know that, Eliza? You sound pretty sure."

"I just know, that's all. I have a feeling. They have my name, for starters."

"Maybe you said your name when you answered the phone the first time he called, and you just don't recall it, but let's leave that one alone for now. There's somethin' that doesn't make sense to me, Eliza; even if Michael Santiago was tryin' to terrorize you to keep you from testifyin' against him, how would he have gotten your name and cell phone number? Ah mean, if he really is a stranger to you, he doesn't know either one."

"I—I don't know. But *someone* does." Eliza's volume rose with her agitation. "That's why I think your organization is trying to scare me."

"Why? For what possible reason? Oh, *shoot*! Where in the heck are we headed?"

"I'm taking you to *Dead Horse Bay*. It's an abandoned strip of beach off the Belt Parkway in Brooklyn. It's pretty cool - used to be a glue factory here when horses were still the only way to get around. Then it was turned into a garbage dump. I like it there."

Deeprose felt that was the first true thing she'd heard Eliza say so far. She smiled to show she understood the feeling.

*Ah can't let Eliza know her inner psycho is showin' or the game'll be up before Ah can find out anythin'.*

"It must be quite a place."

"It's *my* place; it belongs to me. No one can boss me around when I'm there, because when I'm there, *I'm* the boss." Eliza pulled up and parked. "We're here."

Deeprose looked around. "Eliza, this place isn't safe. There's nothin' but vermin an' drifters an' garbage here. Why, of all the places in the world, would y'all wanna come *here* to be alone?"

"Because I feel right at home here, Agent, that's why. *'Queen of the Garbage'*—that's me." The complete absence of feeling in her voice actually moved Deeprose.

*Jesus, Mary and Joseph, she must have had one hell of a life.*

"Look, you gotta make those calls go away. Listen to the message he left on my phone, today."

They were still sitting in the front seat of the car. Deeprose turned to her to accept the phone, making Eliza's job fairly easy. She used it to bash Deeprose in the face. Her nose broke instantly, spewing blood all over the car and herself. Her head flew back against the window.

Deeprose mumbled, "Eliza, killin' me won't make those angry, irrational thoughts go away."

"I suppose you're right, but as long as I'm screwed, I might as well enjoy the power trip while I can. Besides, it has to be done. You're our only threat, now."

Barely able to move, Deeprose could not draw her gun. Eliza saw her falter. Putting both feet up against her head, she rammed it into the passenger window with all her might. Deeprose heard the sound of her own skull crack at the same time everything went black.

Slowly, she groped her way back to consciousness, unable to remember what had happened or how long she'd been out.

"Ohhhhh, my *head!*" Deeprose was dizzy and nauseous. An irrational thought struck her as her hands flew to her pounding head.

*If Ah can hold my head together tight enough, maybe Ah can keep m'brains from spillin' out.*

Eliza sat next to her, waiting. "I knew you suspected me the whole time. I'm not stupid."

*Her phone is still on the seat of the car! If Ah can get a hold of it while she's talkin', Ah still may have a chance.*

"That's a matter of opinion, Eliza. What's your plan? Ah'd really like to know why Ah'm still alive an' talkin' to y'all right now when you coulda just shot me to death already."

"True, true, I did take your gun, but it's no fun shooting someone who can't shoot back. Now the game is more even." She guffawed. Menacingly close to Deeprose's face, she allowed her eyes to travel from the poor, broken face to the blood and vomit-stained shirt.

"Ah don't understand you. *Fun*? Is killin' *fun* for you? Does it give you that powerful, triumphant feelin' you get when you win a game or does it give you a little sexual thrill, maybe?"

"I've been wanting to do this for a long time, Agent Deeprose— to anyone! And I'm gonna enjoy it; that's what I mean. I live by the law of the jungle—kill or be killed."

"We don't *live* in the jungle, Eliza! And we don't live like animals, *either*!"

"Who says we don't? It's a different kind of jungle, that's all."

"Animals don't kill for enjoyment, Eliza; they kill to eat and to protect themselves and their territory, and that's all."

"How would you know? I didn't make the rules. If some rich bastard has to die so I can get a little something, why shouldn't I kill him and enjoy it?"

Deeprose answered her while using her left hand to slowly work its way toward the phone, still on the seat halfway between them. "Y'all may hate the fat cats of this world, Eliza, but no one's keepin' you from tryin' to become somethin' better and to make somethin' of yourself. You say you hate them for lordin' it over you, for screwin' with the rules an' for takin' the bread outta your mouth. All right, but committin' murder won't change any of that. And it won't change the outcome for you. You're sick, Eliza, and you need help. Let me help you."

Eliza was silent a long time before answering.

"I have to kill you. If I don't, it's over for me. But that's not all of it, I guess. The truth is, I always wanted to feel what it was like to have the power of life and death in my hands. You know what? I don't give a shit who has what and how much of it. I don't care who dies or why, and I never did. All I know is that I want to do it. I don't know why I love that rush of fear I get from people, but I do. Why is that so bad? Why shouldn't I feel the way I do? I've never felt any other way. If I was born that way, then it must be O.K. to do what comes naturally. *It's not sick; it is what it is.* Not good, not bad. Just different than most, but not all. There's lots of killers out there, so how can it be sick or unnatural?"

Like the eye of a storm, any rational thought she might have had was suddenly gone, replaced by the hard, unthinking, brutal beast she'd always been. "You're pretty stupid for an F.B.I. agent, you know that? You should never have gotten in my car. Oh, I expect to get caught, eventually, and when I do, they can do whatever they want to me, but not until I finish what I started. But, it'll be months before anyone finds *you*, and by then, nothing'll be left but what the birds left behind."

"Look honey, they won't hurt you if they know you're ill. Ah promise Ah'll make them help you, not hurt you. They'll listen to me, Eliza, but if you go through with this, there's no comin' back. Whaddya say?"

Eliza replied by mimicking Deeprose. "Ah say put yaw head between yaw knees and kiss yaw country ass goodbah." She threw back her head and laughed.

Deeprose closed her eyes. Even in excruciating pain, she turned her head away from that laughing face. Eliza was a born killer; she knew it, now. Just plain wired up that way. No amount of nurturing could have brought about a different result.

Eliza was born without the capacity for introspection. She knew right from wrong, but didn't understand why wrong was so very, *very* wrong. Her brain was simple. She did what felt good and took what she wanted. She was like the carrier of a fatal disease running rampant through a small, rural village; the only way to stop her was to contain her before she could hurt or kill anyone else.

Eliza finally noticed her phone laying on the front seat and knocked it out of Deeprose's reach.

*Shit! Now, Ah'll have to try somethin' else...*

She tried bluffing. "My cell phone, Eliza... It's been on the whole time. They've been trackin' us. They know where Ah am. And you too, honey."

"We'll be long gone by the time anyone gets here. *Honey.*"

"Who else is involved, Eliza? Where are they?"

"Never mind that. Just make sure you don't move. If you do, I swear I'll push your head right through the fucking glass." She tugged on a small hidden lever with her free hand, and the trunk popped open.

Deeprose struggled desperately to stay conscious. She spat out the blood pooling in her mouth. It tasted like tin. "Eliza, if someone put y'all up to this, he's the one Ah'm after. Understand? Not you. Now tell me what Ah need to know so that Ah can do my job."

Eliza stared straight ahead, unmoved.

*She's got the same stony look on her face Agent Seacrest did that day in the lab. Holy Mother of God! She took another dose within the last 48 hours!*

Her thought was interrupted by a knocking sound on both the driver and passenger windows. A delicate looking girl stood at one and a scared, sullen looking redhead stood at the other.

*Hey! That pretty one is the ballerina Carter an' I met at rehearsal. It begins to make sense, now. Clara was also at the Ginger Man. That's it, children, play time is over. If Ah'm goin' to make a last stand, it has to be now.*

With superhuman strength and a resolve that came out of thin air, she grabbed her gun out of Eliza's hand and aimed it right between her eyes. "Tell them to step away from the car and put their hands on their head. If they surrender now, Ah won't shoot, but if either one makes a move toward me, Ah'll kill you, Eliza. And them, too. *Tell 'em!*"

Eliza did something Deeprose could never have anticipated; she leaned forward and wrenched the gun back out of her hand. "The safety's still on. That wasn't smart, Agent."

Eliza turned her attention to the task at hand. "O.K., you two, I have her gun. She's already half dead. Open her door, Alison."

*Show no pain. Show no fear. Look for your opportunity. One moment is all you need...*

The redhead did as she was told. Deeprose tumbled out of the car and onto her back. The redhead apologized before stomping on her arm. Deeprose made no sound, but her arm was broken, maybe even shattered.

Alison hesitated, but picked the gun up off the ground where Eliza had thrown it.

"Christ, Alison, where are the balls you had on yesterday? You killed three people in cold blood! It doesn't matter that you were drugged the first time or that Clara tricked you into the other two and filmed the whole thing. You're going to jail for the rest of your life, you idiot! *They'll never let you out! NEVER!* Now cut the shit and do what we came here for."

Deeprose didn't yet know that the video camera at *The Ginger Man* had recorded Alison's crime, but she did know that someone turned the camera off and then on again, so she took a calculated risk and tried another bluff. "Don't listen to her, Alison. The two murders at *The Ginger Man* were recorded on their surveillance camera because someone turned it back on. You were double-crossed by Clara, and Ah can help you prove it, now."

They all waited to see what she would do. The gun shook like a leaf in Alison's hand. "Clara? You switched the camera back on? Oh, no. *No, No, No!*"

Alison looked at Deeprose with infinite sadness and regret. "I'm sorry; I wanted to help *end* all of this. That night at the micro-brewery, the plan was to confront Abby and scare her into leaving Clara alone. The security guard knew them both, so he let us in, but he got drunk and was hitting Clara when I got there. It looked like he was trying to rape her. I had to do something; I thought she was my best friend."

She shook her head in abject misery. "There was a struggle. Somehow, both of them wound up in the vat. No matter how you look at it, I'm guilty. I'm sorry, but you said it yourself; by now, they've all seen the video. You can't help me. Eliza's right; I have no choice; I can't spend my life in prison. If they're busy searching for you, it'll give me enough time to get away."

Alison took off the safety catch and used both hands to steady the gun. She aimed it at Deeprose.

*The only device Ah can use, now, is distraction.*

Using her one good arm and her two legs as weapons, Deeprose kicked dirt up into Alison's face. Using every ounce of strength she had left, she grabbed back her gun, catapulted herself into a mid-air somersault and used Alison as a landing pad. She stood up slowly, heaving and gasping. Alison remained on the ground with the wind knocked out of her.

"Don't make me use this, ladies."

"Please, *please* help me! Help!" Deeprose gazed in the direction of the voice. Clara was crying and screaming accusations at the other two. "These women killed two friends I was supposed to meet at *The Ginger Man* the other night. Then, they kidnapped me and threw me in that girl's trunk. I've been in there suffocating until now! They brought me here because I'm a witness, just like you are. That's all I know. I have no idea what they're trying to hand you, but I don't know either one of them!"

Clara put on quite a show of hysterics, but it wasn't good enough to convince Deeprose, who'd noticed she hadn't made any attempt to run away when Eliza opened the trunk earlier.

Intending to smash Clara's head in, Eliza came out from behind the trunk with an old hockey stick. Holding the stick horizontally in front of herself, Eliza walked straight toward Clara. She'd had enough. "I'll kill you for that, you lying sack of shit!"

"You heard her! You're a witness! She's a killer. They both are!"

Deeprose yelled, "Stop! Stop, Eliza, or I'll shoot you where you stand!"

Eliza just kept on coming, as inevitable as a tidal wave. Deeprose shouted a last warning and aimed for her knee when Clara let out a blood-curdling scream and ran straight at Eliza, who was twice her weight and size. The force of her own momentum knocked them both off balance and they fell to the ground. Clara grabbed the hockey stick. She knew Deeprose had no reason to believe her story, and seeing no way out, she swung it at Deeprose, who was forced to drop her gun so she could grab the stick mid-swing with her one good hand.

Clara stood like a statue with a sick expression on her face, knowing what was coming and knowing it couldn't be stopped. Deeprose caught the stick and returned the blow with great enthusiasm. She heard a few ribs crack. It was a very satisfying sound.

Alison knocked Clara to the ground and jumped on her. Eliza pulled her off to deliver a glorious right hook to her jaw, just for the hell of it. She'd been wanting to smack Alison since the day they met.

Deeprose held the stick up over her head and yelled, "Stop! Stop!"

No one heard her. She scanned the ground for her *Glock.*

Alison lifted a hand to her face to see if it was still there and then lowered it again. She'd been badly abused as a child. Eliza and Clara saw it and froze as if they were waiting for someone to snap a picture. The tension was unbearable. Alison stared at the blood dripping through her fingers, and suddenly shrieked, *"You fucker!"*

All hell broke loose again. The three girls rolled on the ground, ripping clothes, pulling hair, biting, kicking and bitch slapping. Deeprose had never seen anything like it—not even in Iraq. As she bent over to pick up her gun, Eliza saw the opening she'd been waiting for. Throwing the others off her the way a dog shakes off rain, she picked up her old hockey stick, and...*Wham*! Deeprose dropped like a stone when it connected with her head.

Eliza raised the bloody stick in the air and yelled, "Score!"

Alison dove to the ground, snatched up the lost gun and pointed it at Eliza's temple. "You should have kept your eye on the gun. You're both *shit* straight out of the gutter, you know that?! Neither one of you is worth saving. *You're...not...worth...it*!" Alison broke down and cried, still holding the gun.

Deeprose thought it was a good moment to intervene since Alison seemed like the only one of the three capable of rational thought. "Alison, honey, put down the gun. It's over. You're O.K. now."

Alison had begun to lower the weapon with trembling hands when they all heard a deafening boom. She looked down at it in disbelief; the gun discharged at almost point blank range, piercing Deeprose's right shoulder. With her last conscious thought, Deeprose pulled a small, sparkling crust of meteor out of a pocket. It was the stone Carter had given to her before her flight to Langley.

Alison was the only one left standing now. She saw the Moldavite reflecting its brilliance in the sunlight. As if the question came from someone else, she heard herself ask, "What is that?"

"It's hope."

Deeprose finally passed out, her body almost unrecognizable.

\*\*\*

A motorcycle roared past just then, and as it did, Alison felt a slight stinging sensation. "There's a dart in my shoulder!"

Seconds later, Eliza and Clara felt it too. All three were out cold in less than half a minute. The motorcycle stopped, and a man in black, with an equally black visor pulled down over his face, knelt beside Deeprose. He pulled out a handkerchief and soaked it in water poured from a plastic bottle. He gently squeezed it all over her face.

A voice whispered in her ear, "You're all right. You're going to be all right." He held the handkerchief to her lips to suck on. She lifted her eyelids slightly to see who it was.

"Agent...Carter?" Her eyes rolled to the back of her head, and she passed out again. The motorcycle man got back on his bike and roared away.

# Chapter Twenty Seven

At the hospital, Carter held Deeprose's hand in both of his. The parts of her that weren't in traction or a cast were taped up, bandaged or splinted. An I.V. dripped morphine into her body to block unbearable pain. The injury to her skull had caused swelling of the brain.

*This is my fault. She broke protocol because I let her run with her leads on her own.*

Sedated or not, Carter had to talk to her. He waited as long as he could to ask her what details she could recall of her ambush at *Dead Horse Bay*. Agent Deeprose had no recollection of anything except a man in black passing by on a motorcycle. She didn't recall requesting emergency backup, but supposed she must have. She was alive because someone wanted her to stay that way; that much was obvious. The tranquilizer darts did the trick; *The Unholy Three* remained unconscious until they woke up in handcuffs hours later. Carter thought the man who saved Deeprose might have been Mr. X.

She croaked, "Water, please?"

Carter retrieved a glass from the bedside table and helped Deeprose sip through a straw. It took all her energy to do it. "Thank you for saving me."

"You saved yourself, Agent. I'm sorry you had to."

"You mean…you weren't there?"

"No. I had no idea where you were. Someone else stopped to help you – someone with a dart gun who hit all three women and called it in anonymously. That was what saved you. We don't know yet who it was, but it could have been Mr. X."

"How could he have known Ah was there when no one else did? Unless he's been followin' me."

"We may never know. Agent, the only reason you're alive is

because Alison picked up your gun and refused to use it. It went off accidentally while she was putting it down. I'm convinced, from the statements the other two made, that if they'd been the ones to retrieve your gun, you would have been dead before the motorcycle man got there. The bullet entered between the shoulder and the collar bone and exited out the other side. No internal organs were hit. You were lucky, miraculously lucky, Agent. This is the last time you will investigate a lead on your own."

"Yes, sir."

"Alison told us the whole story. I wish she'd gone to the police right after the Florio murder, but I also understand why she felt she couldn't. The micro-brewery kills were in defense of the girl named Clara; the surveillance camera bears that out. She's ready to take whatever's coming to her.

"Clara is screaming bloody murder. Apparently her uncle is a big-time attorney she thinks will be able get her out of this. She's all hysterics but not one hair out of place. Clara maintains that she was an innocent victim who was kidnapped and forced to participate in the *Dead Horse Bay* attack on you. She's smart, but not smart enough. Her story has huge holes in it; it's already falling apart. She won't go down without a fight, but we'll break her pretty soon. You know, she never even asked about your condition—not once—but she's still pretty positive she's got you bamboozled. It's pretty sad, actually, because the only one she's fooling now is herself.

"Eliza's more like a caged animal than a human being. She's a sociopath—no emotion at all beyond the desire to party, kill, or be killed. All she'll say is that she never got to experience a single murder. She was also a victim of the *Collective* but resisted the drug and remembered everything, including not having gone through with her kill. She decided to go rogue, and, along with the other two, stole the serum for her own purposes. I don't think she's competent to stand trial."

"So what's next, Agent Carter? We still have to find out who the *Silver Man* is an' get those filthy drugs out of his hands and off the street. Ah haven't done a thing to solve this case, damn it, an' now Ah'm stuck in here for the doo-ration."

"Hold on! You pointed us in the direction of Arthur Moreland and the Meese Corporation. We'll get a line on the *Collective* through Alison; she's eager to help us capture the *Silver Man* even if the other two are worthless to us. You've done an enormous amount of work breaking this case. Let me run with the ball now. Your only job is to get well and rest up."

"Where's Jill? Ah thought she'd be here." Deeprose seemed more than a little disappointed.

"She's at the lab analyzing the tranquilizer darts. Maybe it'll lead us to the motorcycle man or Mr. X, or both. I'm beginning to wonder how many mystery men there *are* in this game."

\*\*\*

Carter raised his hand to hail a cab. He had no idea where he wanted to go, so he let the cabbie drive around Central Park for a while. He needed time to think about his next move. The D.O.J. charged *The Unholy Three* with conspiracy to murder a federal agent, attempted murder and kidnapping, but there was no evidence yet to support any other charges except Alison's own admission of responsibility for the murders of David Florio, the micro-brewery security guard and Abby. Alison and Eliza both stated they'd been to a *Collective* meeting. Until she'd met Michael, Alison asserted, she didn't know anything about the killing drug. At least his story was out in the open, now.

He began to focus on Clayton Artemus Montgomery a.k.a. Arthur Moreland. His connection to the *Cloisters* museum and Meese Corporation was too much of a coincidence for Carter to believe he knew nothing about the drug developed there and later stolen. Maybe he could lead them to the *Silver Man*. Senator Pressman had already spoken with the F.B.I. He was no longer a person of interest, but he knew more than he was telling.

Carter decided to get out of the cab and walk a little bit. Deep in thought, he began to formulate a plan to track down the man he now thought of as Montgomery, when a large, black *Cadillac* appeared alongside him and stopped. An elderly gentleman lowered his window.

"Good morning, Agent Carter. Please allow me to drive you to your next appointment." His tone was light and breezy and his blue eyes twinkled, but he was all business.

Carter stopped dead in his tracks. "Who are you?"

"I think you know who I am, Agent Carter. I'm here to help."

Carter felt his pulse quicken. Was this the infamous Mr. X? He hesitated a mere moment for show. Eaten up with curiosity, he approached the open window and flashed his badge.

"I'm a federal agent, sir. This is not a game. If you make so much as a short stop, I'll shoot. Got it?"

"Got it."

Carter walked around to the other side and got in.

"Your deputy director refers to me as '*Mr. X*'. Has he told you anything about me?"

Carter shook his head. "No, he hasn't. Suppose you do…"

"Officially, I don't exist. Many years ago, the Department of Justice created an organization that was, and still is, untouchable. They were supposed to play a key role in moving civilization forward—all civilization. The problems were the usual ones. How would they decide what initiatives were the best ones for all mankind? How should they be introduced into society? Was a better, safer future a justifiable reason for using unlimited wealth and power to put anything they deemed necessary in motion? I couldn't have answered that all those years ago, but I can now.

"I don't deny my complicity with them—at first—but, I gradually distanced myself from that particular group. Over time, the organization faded into obscurity, and they all went their separate ways. But make no mistake, Agent Carter, they've regrouped, resurfaced, and renamed themselves. They have access, once more, to the highest levels of protection and a vast fortune organized by a few people at the top of the government food chain. They plan to pick up where they left off, and, by now, they may already be unstoppable. That's why I'm here."

Carter was more than a little skeptical. "Look, even if I believed half of what you're saying, we're not aware of any such conspiracy. I want to know why you decided to risk your own exposure to help us close this case."

"Because the murders arranged by the *Collective* are neither motivated by fear nor arranged by anarchic haters. Their leader is most certainly mad, but he's the one pulling the strings, and those meetings are nothing more than a way for him to collect killers quickly and easily. No, there's a larger picture at play here."

"How so?"

"The political climate is forcing an explosion of fanaticism. Unfortunately, it's relatively easy to fan the fires of intolerance. All that was needed were advertisements targeting known extremists, the right words and the perfect orator. The drug was the real reason for the meetings."

"The drug? Why?"

Mr. X let out a long, frustrated sigh. "It's part of a larger plan. I can see now that Deputy Director Fischetti either ignored me or intentionally misled you. Either way, you're on the wrong trail. The men and women of the *Collective* are the unwitting participants of a double-blind study. They don't even know they're committing real murders until it's too late. When they do find out the truth, they're obviously too scared to come forward."

"We'll come back to the details of the experiment, later. Why do the murders seem random? What is this leader really after? What is he trying to prove?"

"He's trying to prove the short-term efficacy of a synthetic drug intended to produce temporary killers—ones with little to no recall afterward. After it's been ingested there is a small window of time in which the killer may be programmed to do, say or think just about anything, but the real jackpot is that it induces incredibly violent behavior along with an extreme sense of euphoria—a human war machine, if you will, with none of the after effects. As it turns out, the drug is also addictive. Some attendees find themselves craving more of it, but since they have no idea they've been drugged, all they know is that they felt better at the *Collective*, so they go back again and again. Others, the sociopaths and psychopaths who do eventually realize they've been drugged, want more. Either they go back to the meetings hoping they might get another dose, or they attempt to steal it for their own personal use. The rest are hiding, scared shitless."

"And the randomness of the kills?"

"They're not random, Agent Carter."

"Who is he, sir?"

"I can't tell you that just yet—not without compromising my anonymity—and I'll help you catch the killers, but we can't stop there. We must catch the *Silver Man*; he's the only one who can lead us to the organization we're after.

"As I said, the murders are not random. There's no time to waste hoping you'll chase a carrot you can't see, so I'm going to tell you where to look. Confiscate the evidence that was overlooked at David Florio's home, in New Jersey. If I'm correct, there's something there that will help you understand everything—almost everything, anyway. The curator may have been an intentional target, but Florio had to have been an unexpected liability; he doesn't fit the pattern I'm seeing. He must have stumbled onto something and died for it. The murders are all connected, Agent Carter. They are *not* random. Not by a long shot."

Carter was itching to get back to the Bureau to go over all the evidence again, but he wanted the whole story and thought he was going to get it. He asked a few more questions to test the waters. "So the *Collective* is testing this drug on humans as the first part of a larger agenda. What is the agenda, then? Do you know the name of the drug and where it came from? Is Clayton Artemus Montgomery or the Meese Corporation involved in any way?"

"All excellent questions, Agent. Now, go find the answers. Stick to the evidence connected to the killers you have in custody."

Carter decided to share some information in the hopes of getting more. "We've got the girl the Jersey cops found on Florio's computer from the dating site. She's our prime suspect. Can you tell me how she could come up with such a plan, even drugged?"

"As I said, as the drug begins to take effect, the subject is extremely susceptible to suggestion. My feeling is that they are programmed to commit specific murders in a specific way and for a specific reason. I'm taking a terrible risk helping you, you know, but no one lives forever." He then graced Carter with a wry grin.

"Suppose I do manage to get this evidence; how will I find you if I want to discuss it?"

"No worries, Agent Carter; I'll find *you*."

Carter tried to get one more answer out of the old man. "Did you save Agent Deeprose?"

Mr. X smiled and pulled over. "Good try, Agent Carter. Now, get a move on."

\*\*\*

257

The N.J.P.D. had long since turned over all their evidence to the Bureau, so Carter went directly to the evidence locker at headquarters and pulled out the one thing most likely to have contained information that was overlooked—David Florio's hard drive.

He walked it over to the Bureau's cybercrime unit, a bunch of square pegs delighted with the prospect of snooping around for what the police might have missed.

Tom, their self-proclaimed king, tossed back his straggly, dirty blonde hair and nodded with enthusiasm. "Cops are lunkheads. Real linear thinkers, know what I mean? I bet they missed a whole lot of stuff hidden away on this baby. I'll find the dirt for you, Agent Carter."

"This is just between you and me, O.K., Tom? Report anything you find to myself only."

Tom smiled mischievously and rubbed his hands together in anticipation. "Now I *know* there's something good on it."

The next day passed slowly. Carter knew that demanding an update every ten minutes wouldn't get him his answers any sooner. Deeprose would be in the hospital until nearly Christmas, and Jill was working in the lab around the clock. She'd finally identified Alison's print as the one left at Florio's home, and it matched the hand print left on the rail of the fermenting vat at the micro-brewery.

Carter knew that if he interrupted her now, he'd only get tossed out on his ass, so he decided to visit the Buddhist temple to try to regain his sense of calm.

Afterward, he went to pay Fischetti an impromptu visit, but Liz wouldn't let him into the office. Her voice was a little too sharp, even for her, and she avoided making eye contact. "I'm sorry, Agent Carter; he can't be disturbed."

*She looks worried.*

"O.K. Liz, what's up? I can't help him if you don't tell me anything."

"A couple of suits came in a little while ago with no identification. They knew there was another buzzer to his office door under my desk and used it to let themselves in without me notifying him first. They shoved me out of the way like I was a, a...*nobody*! I'm concerned about him, Agent. This breaks protocol."

"It sounds like someone above Fischetti's pay grade is pretty anxious about something. Don't worry, Liz. I'm sure it's all right."

*I wonder what that's all about....*

Carter knew he wasn't going to get into the office, so he checked in on the cybercrime unit, next. Tom uncovered a recent copy of Florio's resume which tied him to Meese as a short-term I.T. consultant. He also found a document that had been deleted the day of his murder. Florio would have known that it could still be retrieved. It might be an important clue.

"Keep at it, Tom. I want to know what's in that document. It may be nothing, but you never know. Contact me the minute you have something." Carter walked out whistling.

An hour later, he was back, staring at a document simply entitled *Burn List*. Carter emailed it to his home computer, printed a hard copy and dropped it in a mailbox for home delivery. That was his insurance. Tampering with the mail was a federal offense, so he was fairly certain that even if he was hacked, he'd still have a hard copy to bargain with.

*I wish I could be certain of Fischetti, but I can't chance it. Until I know more, I'll have to keep this to myself.*

The list was intriguing. It contained two columns; the names of various organizations, agencies, and companies were on the left along with specific job titles. Corresponding names were on the right. It was a list of people who held key, high level, or influential positions. They seemed to represent every walk of life and were from all over the world. He scanned the list looking for a common denominator.

## Burn List

| | |
|---|---|
| Justice, Supreme Court | Earl Statler III |
| Civil Servant, Environmental Protection Agency | Nancy Bodeen |
| Research Scientist, Area 51 | Steven Anderson |
| Internationally Known Talk Show Host | Candace Williams |
| Author/Poet, Pulitzer Prize Winner | Tamika Washington |
| Actor, Endangered Species Activist | Michael Francis |
| Philanthropist, Children's Hunger Foundation | Princess Stefanie, United Kingdom |
| Foreign Correspondent for the World News Press | Jennifer Powell |

| | |
|---|---|
| Director, Library of Congress | Anthony Scarpello |
| Lobbyist, Natural Gas and Oil | Kelly O'Reilly |
| Dean of the School of Medicine, Harvard | Dr. Arthur Sternberg |
| Living Saint | Mother Christina |
| Spiritual Leader, India | Maharishi Yogethartra |
| Spokesperson, Civil, Women's and LGBTQ Rights | Gretta Olsen |
| Founder and CEO, SmartComputer, Inc. | Eric Schmidt, Jr. |
| Fundamentalist Leader, Syria | Abu Rashad |
| Four-Star General, U.S. Air force | General Roger E. Rodriguez |
| Minister of Community Affairs, North Korea | Kim Jong-Un |
| CEO, Toro Electronics, Japan | Masayo Takamura |
| Secretary-General, United Nations | Ping Zhao |
| Human Resources Director, U.S. Department of Agriculture | Warren Houston |
| Lobbyist, Big Pharma | Dr. Harold Lucas |
| CEO, Big Blue Health Insurance | Louise Wicznefsky |
| Donation Coordinator, National Rifle Association | Robert Owens, Jr. |
| Research Fellow, Housing and Urban Development | Roberta Johnson |
| Secretary to the Pope | Giorgio Mastrantonio |
| Astrophysicist | Josef von Hubler |
| Philosopher | Jean-Michel Francois |
| Director, National Security Administration | Christian Phillips |
| Psychological Examiner, Department of Education | Kamal James |
| Executive Assistant to C.E.O., Solartech Industries, China | Chin Maigun |
| Government-paid Hacker, West Africa | Nsonowa Chibuzo |
| Mathematician, N.A.S.A. | Giuilianna Piccolomini |
| Security Guard, Paris Global Warming Summit | Jean-Claude Gilbouis |

| Secretary to the Israeli Prime Minister | Eliahu Ben Isaac |
|---|---|
| Grand Dragon, K.K.K. | Bobby Gene Stetsen |
| Operative, Russian K.G.B. | Alexsei Kuznetsov |
| Protest Singer/Songwriter | Molly Agar |
| Curator, the *Cloisters* museum | Dalton Wells |
| Prima Ballerina, American Ballet Company | Clara Dumont |
| Multi-billionaire and Aspiring Politician | Austen Boyd |

*There's Dalton Wells near the bottom! But how can he be of any real significance? And right underneath is Clara Dumont, the woman who claims she was next on the hit list. Hey, Austen Boyd's there, too! What could anyone want from that brainless twit except favors? Some of these others appear to be of no significance at all— a security guard, an executive assistant...even a poet! What the hell does it all mean?*

But he knew what it meant; this was a list of assassinations, and it was no fake. The tiny hairs on the back of Carter's neck stood up.

*Assuming Wells was murdered because his name is on this list, all these people are going to be, or already have been, assassinated. But why? Why?! How are we supposed to find out who the assassins are or will be? How can we stop an international conspiracy?*

*Wait a minute. Calm down. Breathe. David Florio found the Burn List while working for Meese. He emailed it to himself and then saved it on his home computer. And now he's dead. We've got to find a way to verify this information, but until we do, we have to warn these people right now and protect them.*

*I hope to God this is the only list. What the hell were these people doing—or going to do—that signed their own death warrant?*

# Chapter Twenty Eight

Working on the *Burn List* around the clock had given him little to no time to consult with the hospitalized Deeprose, workaholic Seacrest or the enigmatic deputy director. Carter was so bleary-eyed that when his home computer screen blipped on and off, he wasn't quite sure what he saw, if anything. It blipped again. This time Carter was certain he saw something from the corner of his eye, so he took a break from the list and pressed a key to take the screen off sleep mode.

*This many covert eyes and ears can't be possible. I'm getting as paranoid as my parents were after Watergate!*

There was a new comment on their wedding video on *YouTube.* Carter hated peeking into his wife's email but she was still out at the lab, so…he opened it. It was a phone number and one short phrase— *Limited time offer.*

There was no sense in playing a guessing game, so he punched the number into his phone and waited. Glancing at the comment again, he noticed the number and message were already gone.

*Nothing like breaking all the rules in one week... Here goes nothing...*

"Agent Carter, speaking. Who is this?"

He got no answer; the voice on the other end was a recording instructing him to come alone to a specific meeting place without any electronics or weapons. If he didn't obey, the offer was off the table.

*What offer?*

For once, he did the rash thing instead of the right thing; he grabbed his jacket off the back of a chair and ran out the door. The meeting place turned out to be an abandoned century-old police station directly underneath the Brooklyn Bridge on the Brooklyn side of the river. It was dark and creepy—the perfect place to dump a body. No sane person would come within a mile of this place. Half-walls crumbled under their own weight, and the roof was long gone.

*Man! I can't see a damn thing!*

Carter thought he heard the sound of a door being pushed open. "O.K., I'm here. Now you can hold up your end of the bargain."

A voice from somewhere behind him answered, "You will have all your answers tonight, Agent Carter."

"I'm unarmed and prepared to listen to your demands. Who are you? What is it you want in return for stopping the assassinations?"

"Nothing, Agent Carter. They cannot *be* stopped; 'I am both heaven *and* hell'." He took great care to pronounce each word slowly and clearly.

*The voice sounds like it belongs to an old man. Educated. Arrogant. Is this the same man who posted the YouTube messages?*

"What does that mean? Why am I here?"

"Because in your heart you believe you'll be judged someday by an omnicient being, and you're scared to death you'll come up short. For all eternity. But Hell isn't a place or a state of being to be feared after death. *For God's sake, hell is all around us, Agent Carter. We made it that way! We fucked it all up! But we can also fix it, if we want to.*

"You, more than anyone else, should be able to appreciate our great endeavor. The world is about to change. Hell is an archaic, superstitious concept designed to keep fools in line through fear and punishment. Man does not need to suffer so that he should know comfort and health. We can create heaven on earth and eradicate for all time the merest suggestion that man is a warlike being.

"But first, the old world must be properly prepared. There are certain changes in the population that must take place. We'll disarm, quite peacefully, those who would destroy this planet. Then we'll build something that will last forever."

"You mean you'll destroy a system that doesn't work for *you*. And build something that will serve *yourself.* I understand why you think that would be heaven on earth; that's not news, but don't try to tell me it would be one for anyone else. Hasn't history taught you *anything?* Even Hitler couldn't sustain his messianic dream, and neither will you. People will fight back like they always do, and you're the first one they'll come for."

"Yes, I suppose that would've been the case in the past, but that just won't be possible in the future, Agent Carter."

"What does *that* mean? Never mind. Look, I've got the *Burn List*. I know your plan is to assassinate people of critical importance—the decision makers, the movers and shakers and the ones with access to top-secret information. From the looks of it, you also plan to exterminate some of the world's most notorious dictators. That made no sense to me at first, but now I get it; you plan to stir up trouble so horrendous that the threat of a final war will distract anyone from noticing anything else. That's it, isn't it?"

"Something like that..."

"But how are you going to stop the trouble you started? I'll grant you it's easy enough to push us towards our end, but not back to a bright, new beginning. Once the destruction starts, it won't stop until there's nothing left, no one left to rule over, and no air to breathe that isn't poisoned.

"This hallucinogen you're testing out...even if it can control your assassins, how do you ultimately control them? Or do you eliminate them, too? Do you just keep killing and killing to maintain paradise? Because that's what we've been doing since the beginning of time. I thought you said your heaven could exist alone. I'm sorry; this would all be very enlightening if it wasn't the same old song that's been playing since the first megalomaniac roamed the earth."

"Agent Carter, these deaths are essential. They're blocking our path to a future that, quite frankly, they are not even capable of imagining. Anyway, the assassinations are nothing compared to what's coming next."

"But, if you're so all-powerful, why can't you achieve this miraculous change without bloodshed?"

The *Silver Man* remained silent.

"O.K., then tell me this; what is your plan for a Utopian future once these people have been killed?"

"I will tell you everything in just a few minutes, Agent, just a few more minutes. First, you need to understand something you refuse to face; the deaths that have already occurred will shape your investigation, but they will have no effect on its outcome. The government wants a quick and easy end to these assassinations, and they will have it. If you pursue us, I can safely promise you that *no* one—not your superior, your closest friends, the police or the media—will believe a word you say."

Carter felt a sharp pain in the back of his head. As he went down, someone caught him, dragged him somewhere and strapped him into a chair. When he came to, he was fighting mad.

"You strapped me into a chair? A *chair*?! Look, whatever you're planning to do…it won't work. I'm trained to withstand anything you can dish out, and I can get out of any trap you can set. A chair with straps will not stop me."

An assistant in a strange mask held up a handful of electrodes so Carter could get a good look at them. The *Silver Man* continued speaking conversationally from behind him.

"This device has been a long time coming, Agent Carter. We approved other experiments in the past, but they all failed miserably. We couldn't control every outcome, every time. With this little baby, though, we can. It's destined to become an implantable Nano-chip, and you're going to be our first test subject, Agent Carter."

Without a word, the assistant fastened the electrodes to his head. Carter heard a machine begin to hum. Seconds later, a small rubber ball was forced into his mouth. Just in case.

***

*Ten Years Earlier…*

It was Christmastime, and a man in an obscure and unpronounceable country halfway around the world sat rocking in his chair by a fireplace. He had one last gift to give the world, and it was the only gift it would ever need. He'd had the foresight and the ability to reconvene the *JASONS* for one mission only; the plan was a good one but the timing was wrong. He'd have to wait for modern technology to catch up to it.

Meanwhile, the *JASONS* faded gradually into obscurity. By the time they forced Clayton Artemus Montgomery, their last connection to any government entity, out of the game, not even the D.O.D. could find them.

He unwrapped a symbol of the change to come. It represented perfection by intentional design. Inside the small, gaily colored box was a miniature replica of *Galatea*, the mythic stone sculpture of a woman brought to life by *Pygmalion*, who fell hopelessly in love with his own perfect creation. She was breathtakingly beautiful, thought the man, as beautiful as his own country had once been.

Inside the statue, instructions for the transformation lay dormant. One day, when the time was right, he would crack it open and launch his plan to redesign the world the way he imagined it might have been at its birth. These instructions were a thousand times more powerful than any army or weapon made by man.

He caressed the beautiful statue. "One day, my love, you will lead us back to the path we were all meant to travel."

\*\*\*

*Present Day...*

"I'm going to give you a demonstration of how a mind—any mind—can be controlled perfectly or reduced to rubble, for the sake of peace and prosperity. We always knew the drug wouldn't be enough to do it, but for the sake of argument, we'll use it on you as well."

Carter felt the pin prick of a needle in the meaty portion of his right arm before he had a chance to knock over his chair and break it. Despite a trick he used to lower his heart rate, he was scared to death. He'd already seen what the drug had done to Seacrest.

*I know what this is. I can control it.*

But he couldn't. From far, far away, the voice spoke in a peaceful, even tone. His words painted visions of seething mobs inside Carter's head. There were riots, fires, looting.

Carter was unable to see the *Silver Man* standing just behind him, but his assistant, in the long robes of a penitent and wearing the ivory mask of a woman, stood before him.

*Who's wearing that mask? A man or a woman?*

Once again, he dropped off into the chaos of his own mind. Much later, somewhat revived, he tried to get more answers while figuring a way out of the chair that kept him firmly strapped in place. "The people on the *Burn List* are a threat to your new order, so they have to die. I get that. But, what's the rest of it? What comes next?"

"Patience, Agent Carter. Patience."

"I already told you I *have* the *Burn List*, and it's hidden somewhere no one will ever find it, so there will be no more assassinations, now. There's also no way you can stop the news from coming out, whether you kill me or not."

"*Kill you*? We're not going to *kill* you, Agent Carter. We're going to make you a subject in our little study!"

"What's left to study? You already know how the drug works. What are these electrodes for? What's this Nano-chip you mentioned?"

"Agent Carter, your infinite capacity for obtuseness continues to amaze me. Haven't you figured it out, yet? This is *all* a study! We instruct our subjects to kill, but we give them rules to follow. We watch them to see if they obey these rules. We study the deviants, and then we tabulate a trend which allows us to predict which personality-types will obey and which ones won't. That's it, Agent. That's all we want out of these experiments."

"O.K., I'll bite. *Why?*"

"Because there is a next step to take in the study before our plan is ready to be introduced into society. By then, no one will even notice the change; it will be absolutely seamless. You know, it isn't easy being *Pygmalion*, Agent Carter, but it's well worth the time and effort when the statue comes to life!"

The voice chuckled at his own metaphor as he injected Carter with another dose of the hallucinogen. "We have one more aspect of this drug to consider, Agent. We need to know what would happen in the event of an overdose. If you live, you will become another one of our assassins. If not…well, then, you died for humanity." The voice drifted off into the distance like the whistle of a train speeding past a station.

Down went Carter into the rabbit-hole. He squeezed his eyes shut hoping to fight it, but even with his eyes closed he felt the presence of a woman familiar to him. He assumed it was Jill. The woman wore a white lab coat. As in most dreams, he was both sure and *not quite sure* it was really Jill; she was wearing a mask that made her look like…

*That's not Jill. That's the Silver Man's assistant masquerading as my wife!*

*Galatea* spoke to him in Jill's familiar voice. "It's going to be a new America—a whole new world. You'll see…" She paused to fold her arms. "We'll be able to change, control and track *anyone* by implanting a simple microscopic chip in the brain at birth and with *one hundred percent accuracy.* No drugs! How do you like *that* for virtual reality? It's simple, really—just one technological step ahead of the chips already used to track our pets."

Carter tried to answer, but he couldn't move his mouth.

"Give in, Carter. It's so much easier. What good is an expanding universes if we don't grow with it? With this Nano-chip there will be no need for anyone to fear the future. It's the end of the ungenerous spirit and the closed mind. No hatred, no misers, no greed, no jealousy! Just think of it, Carter...we can finally create world peace without waiting for evolution to weed out undesirable D.N.A. and without pouring millions into altering it. This is the only way it will ever happen, and you know it. Why not just accept it?"

Carter was frantic, but his mouth refused to open.

*And the cost? Just a little thing called free will and human rights! All you're doing is trading out our current dictators and demagogues for a new one. All those Nano-chips will require updating, re-programming, and monitoring. Who's going to be the one to decide how and with what information? The Silver Man?*

She told him the rest of it. "Every newborn baby will be transformed at birth. It will be the new standard in hospital procedure. Parents will be told it's for tracking and medical monitoring, and there won't be any way of knowing otherwise. What parent wouldn't give *anything* to keep a child safe from getting lost, running away, or being kidnapped and *worse*? Why would anyone balk at knowing when to go to the doctor or call Emergency Services in plenty of time to treat an illness or prevent a heart attack?"

It was a rhetorical question, but Carter found he was finally able to move his mouth. "What about the ones who are too old to receive the implants when they're finally ready? What'll happen to them?"

"Within two generations, those born before the transformation will begin to die out without knowing a thing about the others around them."

"If the *Silver Man* really believes, as Omar Khayyam asserts, that we're the architects of heaven and hell, then each of us must be free to decide our own fate. To live among others in relative peace and harmony, every man, individually, *must* decide what he wants to be and how much control to exert upon himself. That's why there'll always be criminals and cops. *But we still don't lobotomize the criminals, and we don't need another so-called God.* The only possible outcome of his plan is the very thing he says he wants to end—war! If true enlightenment and evolution ever come, it will happen naturally if it was meant to. If not, then we had our day in the sun, just like the dinosaurs."

The *Silver Man* flew into a rage. "The world can't *wait* for enlightenment to make its way into the collective consciousness of people whose basest urges and decisions are controlled by their D.N.A. and the influence of family and friends! Science is the only way we can expect all people everywhere to obey the law and act with kindness, decency, responsibility, and respect. We can force the change now, Carter, and it's the right thing to do."

Carter's chest heaved with the effort it took to keep his heart pumping. "Why don't *you* learn a little something about those character traits before you presume to teach the rest of us a lesson?! I'll tell you one thing right now, you bastard, you can't *have* our children! I'll kill you and *Galatea* with my bare hands before I let either of you do a thing like that! Let me go! I'm going to send her back to the land of Nod on the broom she flew in on. *Tonight!*"

The old man observed Carter intently. Then, he smiled and scratched his head. "Not quite what I had in mind, but it'll do. All right, Agent Carter, go get her. She's home now, waiting for you..."

# Chapter Twenty Nine

The *Collective*, their meetings and the drug were everywhere, networking and crisscrossing the country. By now, the entire nation or even the globe could be as compromised as Carter was.

He drove home feeling an anger that no longer seemed foreign or shocking. He admitted to himself that the beast inside him was within us all. It was incredibly freeing to let go and express it. Carter had a sudden urge to take out two figures on the sidewalk just ahead. He laughed out loud at the old joke he heard inside his head.

*Ten points for the old lady and five more to back over her dog.*

A thought occurred to him out of nowhere; perhaps there *was* no reason for our existence and domination over all other species. Our rise to the top of the food chain could have been nothing more than one giant hell of a mistake. The model had obviously been defective from the get-go and should have been scrapped or weeded out. There is no other answer except to realize the traits we see as detractors, the ones we hate in ourselves, are also ones that helped us survive and thrive as a race.

Carter tried hard to convince himself of that.

*Murder is sanctioned by the church and government when it suits them and vilified when it doesn't, so they must know the impulse is innate, and therefore, natural, to all of us. If it is, then Eliza's right; any instinct, no matter what it is, can't be bad in itself if society can encourage, approve or turn a blind eye to it from time to time. Certainly, no one's ever been able to curb selected impulses or remove them from our D.N.A. All we really do is manage, deny or ignore them. If those idiots in Washington can wage wars in the name of humanity, and if the church says it's all right to kill in the name of righteousness and decency, then so can I. Galatea dies tonight.*

\*\*\*

Carter grew philosophical in a halfhearted attempt to justify what he was about to do.

*God and the Devil must be one entity that live inside of me, not outside, because I see no way they can be clearly or cleanly separated. The good, bad, profane – those urges are more like cake batter—all mixed up and raw. When there's a surplus or lack of one ingredient or another, we say the cake was ruined, but isn't it more accurate to say the cake is simply not to our liking?*

*Why must I prune myself like a Bonsai tree to prove myself worthy of both man and God's judgment? Why can't I just admit that, in the end, people always give in to their own particular nature, if not in outright action then in heart and mind?! Don't great people do bad things and think bad thoughts?*

But Carter was drugged and his thoughts led to a plan of action. He wanted to feel his hands wrapped around *Galatea's* chalk-white throat. It was payback for taking Jill away from him. He didn't want to think about it, and he didn't want to try to switch gears, either. He wanted only one thing—to be her end.

Carter parked his car in the underground garage and went upstairs to his apartment. He slid his key into the lock and quietly opened the door. His eyes moved to the kitchen chair where Jill usually threw her coat. There it was, draped over its back. She was finally home from work.

His skills in stealth and attack had been honed over many years, so this would be quick and easy, and yet, he wanted to prolong the rush of anticipation by playing a little game of cat and mouse, first; the hunt was half the fun, after all. But how to do it? That was the only question. Quietly, in her sleep? No. That would be efficient but very unsatisfying. He wanted this to be a vicious, bloody kill.

As soon as Carter stepped into the bedroom, the computer screen blipped on.

*The Silver Man is monitoring me. Studying me. He thinks I'm going to kill my wife, but it'll be his own creation that dies.*

Carter watched her as she lay sleeping in Jill's spot. Her vulnerability was incredibly enticing. He got rock hard just thinking about the power and intimacy of the act.

*You may look like my wife, but you aren't fooling anyone. I'm going to enjoy this. Oh, how I'm going to enjoy this.*

He couldn't wait another second. Reaching out with both hands, he pulled Seacrest, half-naked, to the floor. She woke up mad and confused.

"Carter! What the *hell*...?" Suddenly she was fighting him in earnest. He was hurting her.

"Where do you think you're going?" Carter was impressed by her will to survive, but she was as light as a feather. He picked her up and threw her down on the hard wood floor again.

"*Owwwww!* Carter! Stop! *Stop it right now!*" Seacrest knew now what was happening to him, but she still had to defend herself. Aiming for his crotch, she kicked him as hard as she could. She made a direct hit. He fell over in agony.

"Carter, listen to me! You were dosed with that drug! This is not real; none of it's real. You love me. You can't hurt me. *For Christ's sake, listen to me!*"

"This is real, all right, but you're not my *wife*! When I get off this floor, so help me, I'm going to bash your head in!"

He rolled to his left to pick up another chair. It would make a very nice club. Seacrest saw her chance and raced out of their bedroom to the front door with Carter on her heels. She stretched her arm out as far as she could to grab the doorknob just as the chair came crashing down on her head; she dropped onto the hard floor, unconscious and bleeding. He dragged her body back to the bedroom but decided against using the bed for what he had in mind. Too messy. He pulled her into the bathroom, instead, and while he waited for her to come around, Carter finalized his plan.

At last, she opened her lids, just enough to see what he was doing. When she was sure he was genuinely distracted and not just toying with her, she shrieked a command to *Alexa,* her electronic automated personal assistant. It began to play the same binaural isochronal beats Carter used on her when she was drugged. It was her only hope. She couldn't fight in this condition and from this vantage point.

Instantly electrified, he cocked his head and listened.

"Concentrate on the rhythm, feel the beats, and come back to me. You're not a killer, and you're nobody's puppet. There is *never* a good reason to hurt people. You *know* that."

Carter pounded his fist on the bathroom door. *"Shut up!* If destruction is what the old man wants, fine! But I'm starting with *you, Galatea.* He's going to know how it feels to lose you. The bastard's watching us right now, did you know that? We're going to give him a show he'll never forget."

"I am an agent of the law, Agent Carter. You will address me as Agent Seacrest."

The isochronal tones made Carter feel woozy. *"Alexa!* Stop that music!"

Something hit him on the head. In a daze, he watched his own blood drip onto a brass soap dish that fell on the floor. He picked it up, amazed. "You hit me."

"Carter! You've been drugged! Shake it off!!"

He just stood there, stupefied.

She tried again. "Listen to me, Carter; once you kill in cold blood, you're no different from any other criminal who ever crawled out from under a rock!"

He smiled, slyly. "Nice try, but the only person I'm going to kill in cold blood is *you,* and I'll be doing the world a favor."

Seacrest whispered a prayer. "God, help me! Help me to get up off this floor."

As if in response, an idea came to her. She grabbed his ankles and pulled his feet out from under him. Carter fell backwards head first out the bathroom door just far enough for her to slam it shut and lock it behind him.

"Do *you think a door is going to stop me, you bitch*?!"

She knew he could kick the door open in one try, but the maneuver bought her time to look around to see what she had to work with. When the door hit the wall, Carter found Jill mashed into the furthest corner of the room, white as a sheet and wide-eyed.

"You're making this much harder than it needs to be."

"That's what it means to be *alive,* Carter! I'm not going down without a fight. You want to hear me say it? *All right, you sonofabitch, I'll say it!* If I have to kill you to save myself, I will. But before you raise a hand to me, you better think it over very carefully, Carter, because whether I live or die, you'll be a murderer."

Carter felt his blood pulsing in his ears. "I am *not* a murderer; I am both Savior and Sentencer! I wield Heaven and hell. *Me!*"

273

Seacrest used the edge of the sink to pull herself to a standing position. She didn't know how much longer she could hold out against him. "I'm your wife! I love you! I *am* you! If you need a reason for living, there it is. If you kill me, you kill yourself!"

He lunged for her. At the last possible second, she slipped to the side, and Carter charged head first into the tiled wall. While he was still down, she ripped the cotton shower curtain off its hooks, threw it over his head and tied the two ends into a knot behind his head. Then she knocked him backwards into the tub and turned on the shower. Ice cold water poured down on him.

"*Ahhhhhhhhh!*" Clumsy and shaking, Carter tried to untie the cloth knot, but the more he struggled with it, the tighter and tighter the thoroughly soaked cotton fabric became.

Meanwhile, Seacrest half-hopped and half dragged herself to the bedroom door and freedom, swooping down to get her robe as she went. The floor had gotten wet during their fight, and as she made a grab for the robe, everything went sideways. She skated across the room and slammed into a mirror mounted on the back of the bedroom door.

It smashed into smithereens, turning the floor around Seacrest into a mine field. Carter recognized the sound of glass shattering and suddenly stopped bellowing. He knew she must be on the bedroom floor all cut up. He tore the fabric covering his head with his bare hands and pulled it down around his throat before reaching over to the shower knob to turn it off.

*Lucky thing she didn't turn on the hot water.*

Deadly calm, he dripped his way over to her, careful to avoid stepping on the fallen glass. This was it; she had nowhere to go. He bent to pick up a nice, big shard and then closed in on Seacrest, intent on disfiguring that beautiful face he'd once loved so much. "Now, you're going to get what's coming to you."

"And so are *you!*" Playing her very last card, Seacrest kicked him in the head with both feet.

Carter reeled across the room like a drunk who stayed too long at the party. He stumbled over a chair and fell across the bed still clutching the shard of glass in one bloody hand.

Seacrest wanted desperately to get up, but being surrounded by a hundred pieces of her own reflection meant cutting herself to ribbons if she moved. She was already too injured to attempt it, anyway.

He struggled to his feet unmindful of the glass slicing through his flesh and stood perfectly still for a long time, just staring at her. She stared back. Waiting…

Peaking up at him through half closed lids, Seacrest looked hard at his pupils and gasped. "*Thank God!*"

Carter was lapsing into the catatonia she experienced after the first twelve hours on the drug. In a whoosh, Seacrest let out the breath she'd been holding, and her whole body went limp with relief. She was safe now. They both were. It was going to be O.K.

He looked puzzled, as if he was trying to figure something out.

*I'm wet. Why does it look like a freight train came through here?*

The cobwebs blew away, and he saw his wife slumped on the floor, crying. Carter looked around and saw the weapon in his own hand. He dropped it to the floor and closed the distance between them in two giant steps despite the glass mine field. Gathering her up in his arms, he carried her to the bed.

"Oh God! I did that to you. I tried to kill my own wife." And he wept.

Jill raised a hand to his bowed head. "You did nothing of the kind, Carter. You were drugged, and whether you like it or not, you're human, just like everyone else. You could never have fought it. I know that."

He got up to get a basin of warm water and a pile of towels and bandages. As he washed her wounds, he remembered something she'd said earlier. "Do you really think love is the only real reason we're here?"

"I don't know, Carter, but it's as good a reason as any, and it works for me. Trust the universe. If you still believe we were put here for a reason, and if you have faith, you don't need an answer. The only thing I know for sure is that *how* you choose to live, particularly in terms of the amount of goodness you generate while you're here, is far more important than knowing *why* you live in the first place. If you focus on answering the 'how', you won't need a 'why' anymore."

"You're a pretty smart cookie, you know that? In all my years of prayer and meditation, I've never achieved one ounce of enlightenment, and yet you understand me better than I understand myself. I've learned nothing. I know nothing. Nothing at all."

"And that, my love, is the beginning of enlightenment. The more we learn, the more we realize we don't know. There's no finish line, Carter, and the journey's not linear. If you need to know you lived for a purpose, then you have to choose that purpose.

"I want you to know something, Carter; you've done your best to make every life you touch, better. Especially mine. You change the world every damn day—one person at a time—and you make it a better place because you choose to. It's that simple."

The mere sound of her voice was enough for him. He was comforted. He dropped off to sleep feeling the heavy burden he'd been carrying for so long melt away like snow on the first warm day of the year.

*I don't want to be an enforcer any longer, and I don't want to think like a criminal. What I want now is justice, and after that, a simple life with Jill.*

***

Carter and Seacrest had been through the worst night of their lives. She really should have called an ambulance, but she had everything she needed and was fairly confidant she could do a better job of it, anyway. Besides, she wasn't about to leave his side until this was all over.

Seacrest chained Carter to the bedposts until he was fully cognizant. She sat up with him for the rest of the night and well into the next morning, worrying and wiping away his sweat and tears. When there was nothing left to do, she sang to him.

***

Seacrest woke up cursing. Someone was rapping on their front door. She leaped out of bed, forgetting she could barely stand. "*Ow, ow, owwwww! Shit!* If it's a door-to-door salesman, call the police, because I'm going to kill him."

The voice outside was tired and fearful. "Jesus, *God!* Open the door, damn it! Am I too late?"

Seacrest slapped open the peephole and found a portly man in a charcoal gray overcoat staring back at her. "You better have a very good reason for being at this door."

276

"I do, Agent Seacrest."

"Who are you?"

He didn't answer.

"I said, who the hell *are* you?"

"Montgomery—Clayton Artemus Montgomery. Your husband knows who I am. We met at the *Cloisters. Please...let me in!* It's too dangerous to wait out here in the hall."

Seacrest got a heavy cast iron skillet from the kitchen before she opened the door. When she did, it was in the air, poised and ready to come crashing down on his head. "Carter, are you awake? This man says his last name is Montgomery and that you met him at the museum. Do you know him, or should I go ahead and swing?"

Carter perked up. "It's the curator who took over temporarily after Dalton Wells was murdered—you know, the man Deeprose recognized from the photo in that obituary. He's a former military sciences project manager with the Meese Corporation in Virginia."

"*This* is the man Fischetti wanted her to find? He thinks *this* is the prime suspect in all these murders and set-ups?"

Montgomery answered cautiously, as if he wasn't sure he could trust them. "That's what Agent Carter's been led to believe. Yes."

Carter couldn't believe his good fortune. "Come right in, Mr. Montgomery! Have a seat. We've been looking high and low for you. What we need is one good solid lead, and I think you're just what the doctor ordered."

Montgomery walked into the bedroom and looked around for a chair, but when he saw that it had been shattered into a million splinters, he gulped audibly and decided to stand. "Those maniacs chasing you murdered my wife as well as my closest colleague. I'll explain why, later. Look, time's up for me; there's nowhere to run and certainly nowhere to hide, anymore. The only thing I can do now is team up with you. I'm tired, Agent Carter, too tired to care about my own skin anymore. The only way I'll ever get any justice or payback before I die is through you, so I'm going to help you catch them."

Seacrest had had enough. "Run from *who*? Hide from *what*? Look, Mr. Montgomery, we've been through a lot the past few days. We've been watched, drugged and sent down nothing but blind alleys. One of our agents is in the hospital, so badly beaten during a kidnapping that we have no idea when she'll recover. Our own defense department is giving us the runaround, and we're not sure we can even trust our own boss. I am one small step away from committing a murder of my own, so I think you'd better tell us everything you know *right now* or I swear to God I'll take this frying pan and smack it out of you!"

# Chapter Thirty

"I'll tell you everything you want to know, Agent. Now kindly put *down* the cast iron maiden."

Jill limped back into the kitchen to put the frying pan back on the stove. Turning back to face Montgomery, she folded her arms to let him know that he was still on thin ice. "Tell me...how exactly does a man of science die, come back to life, find himself a job as a museum curator and end up involved in a murder fest?"

"Um, well, you see..." Montgomery's eyes darted in all directions as if he hoped to find an answer floating around in midair.

"I'm waiting."

He smiled, revealing laugh lines around his eyes and a dimple on his left cheek. "It's a long story. May I please sit down?"

Silently, she pointed to the chair she'd just dragged in from the kitchen.

"Agent Seacrest," he began, "You don't have the time to hear it. Once they find out your husband failed the test, you'll *both* be back on the hit list. We have to get out of here as soon as you can get him up and ready."

"Failed what test? And who are the hell are '*they*'?"

He exhaled audibly and looked at his watch. "You're going to make me tell you the whole story right now, aren't you?"

She stood, waiting.

"All right, if it'll light a fire under you. Just let me get through it quickly, and don't interrupt me. We don't have much time. First of all, my real name is Montgomery, not Moreland. Most people call me Monty.

"I've known who they are for years now—as an entity, I mean—because I worked with them at Meese. They began as a top-secret think tank created through a joint effort of the highest military, intelligence and private sectors of the country, to review and approve or deny funding—*unlimited funding*—of the most promising scientific research meant to push the entire world forward. This group was called the *JASONS*. They were so secret and had such tremendous amounts of money and power that their existence and individual identities were virtually unknown.

"Until now, their decisions were absolute and irrevocable—they had to be. We needed a group like theirs to quietly push civilization ahead without any constraints. They operated outside the law and outside of the democratic process. Without them, we could never have entered the space or information ages in the short time it's taken us to get there. Every significant discovery in science, medicine, technology, aerospace, agriculture, and energy, among many others over the past sixty-odd years, was possible only because they chose the projects that got the green light.

"As time went on, group members changed here and there, but their mission and resources never did. Without oversight, they had the power of God. They could shape the future any way they wanted without any responsibility to anyone or anything. Gradually their mission changed from helping the world to controlling it. The story is an old one.

"There was one government organization that had staying power, and it was the one that originally developed this think tank. They were the only ones who could arrange for the group's future funding and protection. Only the very highest officials knew about them. Eventually, when the *JASONS* were slated to be disbanded, the organization was blackmailed into providing continued support and protection. Exposure of collusion would have rocked the country right off its foundation. As part of the deal, all records containing the group's name and identities were destroyed."

Carter chimed in. "Are you talking about Meese?"

"No, it's not Meese. The group was planted there over time and assumed a new name and mission as a cover for their real activities. Essentially, they decided to hide in plain sight, and it worked like a charm. Meese has no idea it's a front for the *JASONS*. All they know is that this board of approvers has always been there.

"I found out who their protector organization was much later on.

My protégé was developing a drug that would have revolutionized the art of war. When the project was turned down, I began to smell a rat, but I never told her that. I guess I should have. Later, she killed herself, or so we were told. After that I began to butt heads with them. I invented nutty ideas that could never work in a million years and asked my scientists to present them for me." Monty stopped here, smiling at the memory.

Seacrest was hooked. "Then what, Monty?"

Warming to his topic, he cleared his throat and continued. "Up until the day my wife was murdered, a few years ago, I had absolutely no idea that they were the *JASONS*. After my wife's death, though, I received an anonymous letter telling me her death was a warning to me. It strongly suggested that I drop out of sight. Permanently.

"I had no idea what I had done to them, but I ran away, sent Meese a letter of resignation and then faked my own death. I've been running and hiding ever since."

Monty sighed and went on. "For years I tried to figure out what caused this shit storm. After Arleen passed away, I heard, through one or two trusted sources that the drug had disappeared from the Meese lab, but I was the only one who remembered what it was for and what it could do. No one in upper management seemed to care that the only sample was missing."

Carter wanted a clear statement from Monty. "Are you convinced the *JASONS* were responsible for the theft of the drug?"

"Yes. By coincidence, soon after the drug went missing, the group was disbanded so Meese could team up directly with the military to redefine their agreements and partnerships.

"When the old museum curator was murdered, I was offered his position, but I was afraid to accept anything other than a temporary assignment. You and Agent Deeprose were the local F.B.I. investigators on the scene, and that was how I heard about the *Collective*, as you call them, and about the murders being committed by their members. I still keep my ear to the ground. Then, when the video of one of their meetings went viral, I recognized Senator Pressman's face."

Seacrest wasn't a hundred percent convinced, yet. "Then why didn't you say anything about it to Carter when you had the chance?"

"He would have thought I was the killer, and I still had no way of proving I wasn't. I had knowledge, motive and opportunity. Open and shut case. You have to understand, Agent, that all I had were some pieces of a puzzle that didn't fit together.

"I racked my brains trying to remember anything I could about the *JASONS* and the drug we named *Hyzopran*. All I knew was that they turned down Kate's project, I pissed them off mightily after her death and the drug disappeared at the same time they did. When it resurfaced, I had no idea how to prove they were responsible. Who'd believe a crazy story like that?"

Seacrest tapped her foot. "Good question. Why are you convinced they're the ones who stole it?"

"They turned down Katherine's project for bullshit reasons, so there must have been a very good reason for hiding its existence, after all. Slowly, the pieces began to fit together. They assumed I knew of their plan to steal it and use it for another purpose. Or maybe I just had the misfortune of knowing the drug ever existed. Wrong job, wrong place, wrong time kind of thing, you know?"

Jill paced around the bedroom and then came to a short stop. "Wait a minute. Why weren't you eliminated at the time, then, instead of being merely threatened? Why haven't they ever been able to find you?"

"They probably planned on getting me later on when things cooled down a bit. My well-known enmity for the old geezers prevented any rash decisions. I think targeting my wife was the best way to punish me and scare me into silence at the same time. Sometimes I wonder if Katherine really committed suicide. We were all liabilities. The reason they haven't caught me yet is because I'm smarter than they are. Always one step ahead."

Carter put all the big questions to Monty now, no longer holding back. "Do you know who's protecting and helping them? Would you remember their individual faces if you saw them again, I mean, besides Senator Pressman? And how is he tied to them?"

"When I recognized Pressman's face, I realized he must have dropped out of sight and changed his name and career many years ago. Neither of us were supposed to live to be able to identify the rest of them. I knew a few names, but he knew them all, because he'd been one of them. The thing is, he was the genuine article. Pressman had no idea what their real agenda was. He wanted to approve funding for Dr. Blake's research because he'd been a P.O.W. in

Vietnam. He saw first-hand how a drug like that might have brought things to a quicker, more decisive end and prevent a ton of suicides, afterward.

"I'm pretty sure Pressman had no idea why the others wanted the project squashed, but as it turned out, he had a price. They offered him a career as a senator in his home state if he agreed to be the lone dissenter on Kate's project. The only reason the leader of the *Collective* appeared on a movie screen was to use Pressman's likeness and voice. It was an obvious setup. Pressman was a blind alley.

"The poor bastard almost had a heart attack when I walked into his office. He thought I was dead. We talked for a long time, that day. He told me just about everything he knows. He owes his career to them, and he wants to live to enjoy it. Pressman will never roll. That's definite. If he spills, he's dead."

Seacrest wanted more background Intel. "Monty, what else should we know about the *JASONS*?"

She threw her gaze over to Carter. He was falling back to sleep, so she lowered her voice. "You still haven't told us who's protecting them, Monty. Why are the *JASONS* using this drug on the members of the *Collective*? What exactly is *Hyzopran*? I also want to know why attendees are being programmed to kill. What's their real agenda, Monty, and who the hell is *Galatea*?"

"Agent Seacrest, I think I've told you enough to impress upon you the fact that we have to get the hell out of here. Can we finish this later?"

"Mr. Montgomery, the more I hear, the crazier the story sounds. We're not going anywhere until I know the rest of it. When you said Carter failed the test last night, what exactly did you mean?"

Montgomery closed his eyes and held up his hands in surrender. "All right. All right. Just promise me you'll get him dressed and ready to go as soon as I'm done talking. And if you don't want us all killed, for God's sake, take out your gun, and keep it aimed at the door."

When Seacrest returned with her gun, he continued. "Step one. His test began when the drug was forced on him. The rest of the test subjects were lured to those meetings and dosed without their knowledge. I suspect this *Silver Man* couldn't resist telling Carter his plan. He knew Carter wouldn't remember a word of it, later, anyway, and if he did, no one in his right mind would believe him. He'll have to be put down anyway, you know, as well as you and myself.

"Step two. When *Hyzopran* kicked in, he began to hallucinate. He became aggressive and paranoid. When they programmed his mind to kill, they repeated a mantra over and over again until he knew it by heart and believed it was the truth. He was given a name, address and a detailed plan to commit a murder so they could see how the drug worked on him."

"Go on. What about the others?"

"They were studied to see who would follow orders, who'd resist *Hyzopran* and who'd go rogue and kill someone of their own choosing while hallucinating. In your husband's case, they decided to use him as a test subject *and* get rid of him at the same time. They overdosed him and sent him here to kill you. Knowing you're a federal agent, they assumed you'd kill him in self-defense. If he succeeded, however, he would have killed himself afterward, most likely. With you dead, he'd most certainly be sentenced to life in a federal prison, if not executed. In the event he failed to kill either you or himself, well, you're just two more loose ends to get rid of. No big deal."

Seacrest was reaching the end of her rope, and her face was turning red. "Why would they try to kill us when Carter won't remember anything from last night? As far as they know now, we have no way of finding out who they are or who's protecting them."

"Because Carter has the *Burn List*, which leads straight back to David Florio's murder, Meese's computers, the development of *Hyzopran* and the *JASONS'* theft of it. Dalton Wells' name must also be on that list. The *Burn List* can put them in jail for a thousand years apiece and permanently screw up their plan."

Seacrest kicked a table leg to punctuate her frustration. "Carter has a…a what? A *Burn List*? Why was Florio killed for having it? Why is Wells' name on the list, and what the hell is their 'plan'?"

"Agent Carter found the *Burn List* on David Florio's hard drive, and I'm assuming Wells' name is there. Wells' killer was in possession of the drug when he was arrested, and your tests showed that he must have ingested it no longer than 48 hours prior to the murder and his arrest. He'd been at a meeting of the *Collective* during that time, Agent Seacrest, which you may or may not already know.

Agent Carter knows everything now, I'm sure of it—all except for who's protecting them. That's what forced their hand, Jill. They have to eliminate all three of you to make sure that secret never gets out."

"But we don't *know* who's protecting them! Do you? Is there a step three, Monty? I mean, why go through all this nonsense unless there's a larger purpose? Couldn't they just arrange professional hits? And who's *Galatea*?"

He shook his head. "I don't know. It would have made everything so much easier, if I did, wouldn't it?"

"Do you know who else is on the list?"

"No. I've never seen it. Pressman knows, though, and now your husband does. He's got it hidden away somewhere. If we could get our hands on a copy, it might tell us a lot more about why those particular names are on it."

Seacrest woke Carter to ask him if he remembered discovering something called a *Burn List* and where it might be, and whose names were on it. He told her there was a copy in the computer desk drawer but no longer remembered why those names were there. She rummaged through it until she found the list and then handed it to Monty.

"Take a look. Does it mean anything at all to you?"

He read the list slowly. Seacrest and Carter anxiously watched him puzzle it out. Those not already assassinated were now being protected, but there would be no end to this if they couldn't see the whole picture. All it would take was a new list to achieve the same goal. Both agents were afraid to compromise the operation by sharing information with anyone at the Bureau, including Fischetti.

It only took him five minutes to figure it out. Monty's head flew up; he looked like he'd seen a ghost. "I know what this is! It's a list of people in key positions of economics, government, industry, technology, the arts, and natural resources and so on and so on. They're all long-termers too—people who have a real impact in all those areas of work. Some seem trivial and low-level, but according to this list, they're all tied to a government, an event, or someone incredibly influential. The *Silver Man* will use them if he can and assassinate them if he can't. From the looks of some of these other names it seems there are those presenting viewpoints and laws and regulations that are in his way. My theory, right or wrong, is that once they're out of his way, he'll make sure that every last replacement is one of his own people. There'll be list after list of assassinations and replacements until they have control of everything, everywhere. But I'm with you; why use drugged amateurs to do it if it's a long-term plan?

"The people on this list are from all over the world, but the majority are from here. There's a Supreme Court justice, a civil service employee, titans of industry, a protest singer, philosopher, a ballet dancer, a scientist at area 51, etc., *and one museum curator in charge of priceless European art*, Agents."

Seacrest believed him now; there was no way not to. "So where do we go from here, Monty? Do you have a plan?"

"The plan right now is to get out of here! Every minute we waste is another nail in my coffin and yours."

Carter and Seacrest had been in tough spots before and weren't going to be rushed out the door without a little more information. Carter, as usual, boiled it all down to one simple question, and he wanted an answer before trusting Monty completely. "You could have told us all this without putting yourself or us in any danger, Monty. Why are you really here?"

"You know those kids aren't the real culprits, but you're being pressured to get their convictions without too much nosing around. Even I could see that much from what I read online and saw on T.V. Don't you see? You're being stonewalled. Sabotaged. The people responsible for that *must* be the ones protecting the *JASONS*. Now, you've got them after you, too. That's the reason I'm here. You need me because none of them would recognize me now. I can pick up where you left off last night."

Seacrest leaned forward, every nerve alive and humming. "Who do you think the protectors are, Monty?"

"I've been wondering about that for two weeks now. After hearing what happened last night to you both, and now after seeing this list, I have a pretty good idea. As I said, there was only one group of people who knew they ever existed, and they couldn't afford to be blackmailed and exposed. That's why the F.B.I. made a deal with them. You're fighting your own organization."

***

Carter saw Seacrest's face change color again. Knowing what was coming, he waited for her to blow. When she did, it was worse than Vesuvius.

Seacrest leaped off her chair, regardless of the pain it caused her, and slammed a fist on a table. She was no longer red. She was purple. "*F.B.I.? The F.B.I.?!*Are you telling me that every high official in the Goddamn F.B.I. knows about this and has always known about it? You think that the D.O.D. was ordered by our own office to confiscate the chemical evidence? I'm supposed to believe that we've been lied to and sabotaged right from Jump Street by our own *people*?!"

"That's about it. Yes."

"*Those fuckers! Those slimy, sneaking, black-suited, sunglass-wearing traitors!* Carter, we may not be able to stop them if this has been going on since the Roswell crash. Public knowledge of it could trigger riots, maybe even a civil war! This is so subversive that I'm not sure we should expose it to the public.

"There's just got to be international collusion going on. The F.B.I. and the *JASONS* have contacts all over the world! *Jesus!* They must be in bed with the C.I.A. If you're right, Monty, everything that's been happening over the last year is an attempt to destabilize this country and the world—defying the constitution, encouraging hate groups like the *Collective* to bring their activities right out onto Main Street, the illegal detention and deportation of Muslims and Mexicans, arresting reporters, tampering with the presidential election, the denial of climate change, intolerance, misogyny, bigotry and even the racism we thought would have ended by the 21st century—it's all been part of a larger agenda! Do you think the president knows anything about it?

"I think he ordered the confiscation of the drug, Agent."

Carter had a thought on that point. "I think he was elected because his agenda happened to fit the *Silver Man's*. The timing, his love of attention from rich, fawning internationals, his admiration of tyrants like Putin and his mountainous ego was just the combination the *JASONS* were waiting for all these years. The entire cabinet is gobbling up all the candy in the store. What they don't know is that the candy is poisoned with *Hyzopran*."

Seacrest dropped down onto the bed beside Carter, exhausted.

287

"Fischetti had to have known all along! I always wondered why he was so set on hiring us—a couple of nobodies from out of town. We were perfect for the job because we were above suspicion, beyond reproach and out of the loop. It was well known that Carter had taken down dirty cops in his own office which made it impossible for him to stay there. He was the perfect pawn, too glad to be offered a glitzy new gig to think beyond that. We were given big promotions, training, *carte blanche* in the lab and a more than generous budget. We even made the Goddamn papers! We were so busy trying to make good that it was easy to keep us in the dark. We weren't from inside the organization, so there was no way to know about the *JASONS* or make the connection between them and our cases. We were used just as much as the president was, Carter, and I'll be good and Goddamned if I'm gonna go out without getting every one of them before they get me."

Monty looked more scared of her than he was of the *JASONS*. Carter said benignly, "It's not that bad, Jill." He smiled, rested his head on the pillows propping him up and watched the show. This was the way he and Jill worked together.

Seacrest began rubbing her palms on her pants, ready for round two. "Fischetti could manipulate us without breaking a *sweat*! And *Deeprose! Ha!* A rookie on her first case thrown into an investigation of national importance, and we never thought *twice* about it! *Carter!* We walked right into the middle of the biggest, dirtiest double-dealing conspiracy in U.S. history with our eyes closed. We started asking questions, got too curious, broke some rules and had a few lucky breaks. *That's* why we have to be killed in the line of duty, isn't it, Monty?"

Monty didn't answer her; he didn't have to.

She stopped short and blinked a few times. "You're right, Monty, we've got to get the hell out of here."

"That probably would've been the wise thing to do the *first* time I said it."

"*Oh my God!* Agent Deeprose is a sitting duck in the hospital. We have to get her out of there. Carter, did you get all that?"

He answered her calmly. "I got it."

Seacrest directed her comment to the ceiling. "There's got to be someone who'll believe this story and help us blow the lid off this cover-up. Fischetti knows the identities of the *JASONS,* Carter, he has to. And he knows every person in the F.B.I. who's in on this."

"Who in the world is going to help us, Jill, without proof of any kind? How do you tell a wild story like that without sounding crazy, which is just what you thought of Monty a few minutes ago? All we have is the *Burn List*. And that means nothing without proof of who made it, proof that those experiments were carried out on members of the *Collective* and proof that the *JASONS* planned to eliminate and replace key members of world business and society for a reason we still don't know! Going after the F.B.I. is sheer suicide without hard evidence. We'll have to think of another way out of this. Monty, does the *Burn List* give us any leverage at all?"

Monty looked crestfallen. "It's our only insurance. To use it as supporting evidence we'd have to get a full confession out of the *JASONS* implicating your office as an accessory. Otherwise it's all circumstantial, and we don't stand a chance. Even if we did have hard evidence, who'd stick his neck out for us when it's a losing battle? No one can fight the F.B.I. and win."

Carter's brain was finally starting to percolate. "There's one thing I still don't understand; you think the assassinations have to continue until the *Silver Man* controls all those positions, but if he'd succeeded this time, wouldn't it become obvious that important people all over the world were being exterminated? Why would they make such a stupid plan?"

"Because they can, Agent Carter. Even if all these people dropped dead right now, none of them are even remotely connected to the others. Some are well known and some aren't known at all. It'd just be another day in world news. None of the investigations will lead anywhere; you know that. No one will ever suspect the F.B.I. is shielding a mythological group of mad scientists. After the experiments are concluded and the first batch of people on the *Burn List* are successfully taken out and replaced, who knows? I think there's another step in the plan, but for the life of me, I can't figure out what it is."

Carter had been told the plan in entirety the night before, but he had no recollection of it.

Meanwhile, Seacrest started making plans of their own. "I know we have to leave, but it's going to take some time to get Carter up and into clothes. We're going to need your help, Monty. We haven't eaten since yesterday morning, either, and I'm starving."

She limped into the kitchen, opened the fridge and made them all sandwiches. Monty helped Carter into a kitchen chair as she handed them ice cold beer in frosty glasses that she kept in the freezer for just such a moment.

Monty looked down at his sandwich but didn't move. Seacrest saw tears come to his eyes. "Thank you. This is very kind of you. You don't know how much I've missed the little things…how much I miss my wife every moment of every day."

Seacrest felt her heart melt.

*This is no crazy man sitting at my kitchen table eating a sandwich. He knew we stumbled into a trap, and he's here to help us.*

Seacrest sat opposite Montgomery in the kitchen, but addressed herself to both men. "Monty, Carter might recognize a face or two if he could arrange another meeting, but you might recognize them all."

She looked at Carter and decided to say what they were both thinking. "Carter, Fischetti would have to be brain dead not to know what's going on around him, but we need to be able to trust someone on the inside. He might not be guilty. Maybe his hands are tied. We could talk to him—give him a chance to cooperate."

"I thought of that too, Jill, but even assuming he's innocent, the heat is turned up so high that if he doesn't play along, he can kiss his own ass good-bye. He's obviously been told to make Mr. Montgomery the fall guy. We can't go to him. It would put him in an impossible situation."

Monty realized neither of them fully comprehended the significance of the old curator's name on the list. "Not necessarily! Agents, allow me to shed a little light on Dalton Wells' assassination. The old curator was executed for helping to arrange the return of a portion of the museum's priceless medieval art to its rightful owners—the European countries from which they came. The return of that art meant an economic loss beyond reckoning. He was involved in extremely high-level negotiations between the president and several ambassadors just before he died. The point is, his name is on the *Burn List*. Even circumstantially, it's pretty strong evidence— enough to capture the president's attention and launch a deeper investigation. He's the last man on earth who'd let the *JASONS* have the power he wants for himself, but he could be voted out of office by next year. The evidence has to reach him now or the *JASONS* will just go back into hibernation until another stooge comes along."

Monty finished his sandwich and took one last swig of his beer. "Gee, that was good. I feel like I haven't eaten in a year."

Carter leaned over his plate and grunted in pain. "Monty, there *is* a way you can help us, but it's dangerous, maybe more than dangerous."

"That's why I'm here, Agent Carter. What's your idea?"

"They might implicate themselves if you're willing to be the bait."

Seacrest perked up. "You want to send him in there wearing a wire?"

Carter nodded. "And a lapel video cam."

She looked over at Monty, so ready to be a hero. He really had no idea what he was getting into, so she spelled it out. "If you want justice for your colleague and your wife, Monty, this is the only way to get it. I won't lie to you; they'll beat you, probably drug you and most likely kill you in the end. You don't have to do this. You can walk away right now knowing why they died, even if we can't do anything about it. But Monty, if you could get footage and their voices recorded before you....well, we could carry on the fight. What do you want to do?"

"What Arleen would want, Agent. She'd want me to cut off their balls with a dull butter knife. Pardon the vernacular."

Carter rarely laughed, but he couldn't help himself. It came out as a wheeze followed by a groan.

Seacrest stole a quick look at her watch and drew in a sharp breath between clenched teeth. "Can you help Carter get cleaned up and dressed while I get some supplies together?"

Fifteen minutes later, all three met back in the kitchen. Monty wanted them to know he tried to help them once before. "I tried to point Agent Deeprose in the right direction by leaving a painting from my own collection at the *Cloisters* that clearly did not belong in theirs. It was a *Degas* of ballerinas at their rehearsal, his specialty.

"You see, by then, I'd already met with Senator Pressman. He'd found out why he was being framed and told me the *JASONS* were planning to eliminate people all over the world. He didn't know the whole story, unfortunately, and he obviously knew nothing about this list, but Pressman was scared enough to give me one name he was sure of - someone critically important to world relations. Her name was Clara, a prima ballerina with the *American Ballet Company*. The United Nations asked her to play a sort of peace Ambassador in the communist and third world countries."

Carter and Seacrest exchanged a significant glance. She answered for the both of them. "She's alive and well and in custody, Monty. Clara found out who her killer was and got to her, first."

"Poor girl." He got up to get his coat. "So how do we make this meeting happen, Agent Carter?"

"Hold on, Monty. If you can't get *all* the evidence we need in one shot, Meese will gladly offer you up as a sacrificial lamb to save their own hide. Everything we have still leads straight back to you. The list we have was found on their own computers, but you were the project manager who dealt with the *JASONS*. You knew all about Kate's research on *Hyzopran* and blamed them for deep-sixing her project and causing her death. Arleen was murdered, but you can't prove who was behind it. You could have written the anonymous letter of warning you received, yourself. You assumed it was from the *JASONS,* who, by the way, we still can't prove are the men you worked with or ever existed except in a legend. Senator Pressman can blow the whistle on them, but he's already told you he won't. You also assumed you were being threatened because you knew about *Hyzopran*, but you can't prove that, either.

"To a jury, Monty, you sound like a paranoid schizophrenic with delusions of grandeur. It wouldn't take a jury ten minutes to find you guilty of stealing *Hyzopran* and trying to frame Meese for everything that's happened since."

Monty looked ashen. He closed his eyes, said a prayer, and then said what he had to say. "I need to know exactly how we're going to get this information and exactly what I need to worm out of them for video and wire."

Seacrest rose. Taking out her laptop, she quickly typed up a list of her own. "Read this and memorize it. Get them to say what we have to hear and figure out a way to get the voice recording and video out of the meeting place and into the U.S. mail before they can kill you. We have to have a fool-proof plan before you go in."

### The *JASONS* Must:

- Admit they're the original *JASONS*. Names are preferable, because we have to assume their faces have been changed through surgery and by age and that their prints have been burned off.

- Say why they were originally created and by whom—and I mean ALL the people involved. That's the only way we can protect ourselves for the rest of our lives.
- Say where their current funding and sanctioning comes from, how much they receive and the extent of their power and authority.
- Say why and when their mission changed, what they're planning as their new mission, what they hope to gain by it, how they plan to carry it out and what exactly they did carry out so far.
- Admit they were placed at Meese without Meese's knowledge.
- Admit to torture, brainwashing, and murder, attempted murder, kidnapping and ordering the assassinations.
- Explain that they used Meese, Senator Pressman and the members of the *Collective* as test subjects, smoke screens and fall guys without their knowledge and against their will and turned them into murderers.
- Admit the *Burn List* found on Meese computers was written by them with the intent to assassinate and replace everyone named there. They have to say at least some of the names on the list to corroborate our own list. They need to explain why they were selected.
- Tell you what the next phase of their plan is, how and when it will happen and what their motive is.
- Admit to stealing *Hyzopran* from Meese before they were disbanded.
- Admit to ordering the murder of your wife as a warning to you, murdering your colleague and to drugging and brainwashing Carter into trying to kill me and himself.

When she looked up from the list, Seacrest tossed Monty a bone. "If you can get all of that, we can get reduced or even suspended sentences for the people paying for murders they have no memory of committing—with a few exceptions."

"Anything else you want to add to this list? I don't see the kitchen sink anywhere on it."

Seacrest and Carter looked at each other and then at him. His chances of making it out of that meeting were slim to none, and he looked like he knew it. Seacrest walked across the room and hugged him.

"What was that for?"

"For being on the team, Monty."

He cleared his throat and looked down at his hands. "We have something more on our side than the *Burn List*. I've been working with a techno whiz who was a favorite of theirs for a long time. He'll work for the highest bidder, but even that creep knows when to quit. He's been keeping them under surveillance for me for the past few weeks. I'll make arrangements for him to get me his own version of a lapel cam and wire. The feed will be encrypted and sent to him by V.P.N. simultaneously and in real time. He'll deliver it directly to the president's personal email inbox. This guy could infiltrate the Kremlin if he wanted to. Piece of cake."

# Chapter Thirty One

Carter told them he was going to stop at the office on the way to their safe house. "I've got to see Fischetti."

Seacrest grabbed her husband by the arm. "Carter, don't say anything about Montgomery to him. I know I wanted to give him the benefit of the doubt earlier, but not now, not anymore. I don't think we should put our faith in *anyone* working for the Bureau. He asked me to take that drug when he said the D.O.D. was going to confiscate it, and he knew it should have killed me. He's been pushing us all along to build a case for thrill kill convictions. If we give him Monty too, he'll throw him to the wolves. We can't afford to trust him, Carter. You can't go back there."

"We have to know whose side he's on, Jill. Don't worry; I'm just going to ruffle his feathers a little and see what happens. I'll tell him we found Montgomery but that I want to have a couple of days to build a stronger case before we make the arrest. When I walk out of that office, it'll be his move. He'll have to act either for us or against us. It's his turn to be tested, and it's pass or fail. I hope he's not dirty, but I'm not counting on it, honey. If I'm right, he's guilty."

Monty went ahead of them to bring his car around to the front of the building. Tentatively, Carter rested his hands on Seacrest's shoulders. He wasn't sure his touch would be welcome after what happened between them last night.

She looked up at him with a question in her eyes. He answered by lowering his head and risking a kiss.

"I knew you couldn't hurt me, Carter. I knew it."

***

Deputy Director Fischetti was nonplussed. "You mean you tracked down Moreland—I mean, Montgomery—without anyone else's help?"

Carter nodded and took a seat. "I can't say much right now. I think he has eavesdropping devices of his own. I'm asking you to trust my judgment on this."

Fischetti knitted his eyebrows. "Trust your judgment?" He fiddled around with the pen he was holding. "What do you mean? Why do you look all beaten up?"

"I fell down the stairs, sir. It's nothing. I'm going to tell Montgomery we're willing to cut a deal with him if he'll help us catch the people operating the *Collective* and their meetings. If I'm right, he'll lead me around in circles and then attack. If I'm wrong, he'll lead me straight to them, in which case I have every intention of sending him in there to get solid evidence for us. If he can get that evidence, I don't care if he comes out alive or in a body bag, but I need a few pieces of equipment to do it. Can you arrange it for me, sir?"

"Equipment? Right, sure, no problem. So, you agree he was one of the kingpins behind the murders? Do you trust him enough to set up a meeting with them and not double-cross us? It's a huge risk to take. The director is convinced he's the only one we want. No one's been able to find a thing on Meese or anyone else."

"I know that, sir, but I believe the evidence is there if we can get it."

Fischetti sighed. "I'm O.K. with the plan if you'll agree to have some back-up at your command. We'll need the time and place."

*He knows I suspect him. The back-up will come, but not to help us.*

"Agent Carter, are you sure you're up to it? No offense, but you look like shit."

Carter leaned back in the chair, practically green with nausea. "It's probably just something I ate last night. I'm fine."

*Hold it together just a few minutes more.*

"I'll start the paper work. What do you need?"

"Sir, I need to requisition a wire and the other usual surveillance equipment." Knowing the information would be leaked, Carter neglected to ask for a lapel cam.

The deputy director swept some documents into a drawer.

*Am I the one upsetting Fischetti, or is it those two men who stormed in here with no notice and no identification? Do they belong to the JASONS, the Bureau, the D.O.D. or the D.O.J.? At this point, it's anyone's guess.*

"Done. Is there anything else I can do for you?"

"Not right now. Well, yes, come to think of it. Sir, I think it would be better if we kept this just between ourselves. I don't want to spook anyone."

*Except for you. Go right ahead and tell 'em, Fischetti. Tell 'em all; that's just what I want. Shout it from the rooftops. I have no intentions of using your equipment, and your team won't hear a thing that happens tonight.*

Carter and Fischetti looked at each other head on. Carter saw fear and regret in his eyes. The higher officials at the Bureau had to know by now he was in possession of the *Burn List*, and if that was the case, Fischetti knew it too. He was anything but dumb.

*If he already knows we have the Burn List, he won't be able to resist the opportunity to take us all out for good and make a name for himself at the same time. Monty probably won't make it out of there alive. I just hope he gets what we need before this all goes down. If I were Fischetti, how would I make my final play? He can't afford to make any mistakes, and he can't afford to lose.*

\*\*\*

Since the Bureau expected them to be in hiding, Carter and Seacrest decided the safest place to be was in their own apartment. When Carter was sure they weren't being followed, Monty drove them back there.

Carter sat in front of his computer with Montgomery beside him. Jill sat on the bed just behind them, prepared to be amazed by Carter, who was online trying to set up a meeting with the *JASONS*. He assumed he could contact them the same way they reached him. He went onto *YouTube* and posted a message to his own wedding video and then prayed for an answer.

"I hope this works." Monty was in way over his head. He was thinking too much about the extreme danger and high probability of failure, and the anxiety was overpowering him.

Carter and Seacrest already discussed the possibility that he might shut down completely and blow their one chance of catching the *Silver Man* and whoever else might be there representing the *JASONS*. That was one risk they weren't willing to take. Quietly, Jill got up and rummaged around in the bathroom medicine cabinet. When she came back out, she touched Monty sympathetically on the shoulder. He turned and she handed him two small, white tablets. "Take these, Monty. They'll calm you down without knocking you out."

"Thanks." Monty didn't ask what they were, and he didn't need any coaxing. He took the pills from her and swallowed them without even a glass of water to wash them down.

Carter thought about the symbolism he experienced during his capture. The woman who injected him wore a mask, and the *Silver Man* said something about *Galatea*. Seacrest told him he thought she was *Galatea* last night and wanted to kill her for it. Essentially, though, most of it was a blur. If Monty failed to get the meeting videoed and wiretapped, the only way to bust them would be to raid them when they tried to kill him.

*Poor, Monty. He got a raw deal, lost everyone he loved and had to run away to survive. If I lost Jill and Agent Deeprose the way he lost Arleen and Dr. Blake, I'm not sure I'd want to survive, but I do know I'd kill the bastards myself if I got the chance. Monty's scared, but he wants this chance, and he should have it.*

Carter entered a comment to let the *Silver Man* know he and Jill both survived the night. Then he typed, "A man you know from the past is willing to meet with you to negotiate a deal tonight. Give me a time and place."

Before he could move the mouse again, the comment disappeared. Within seconds, he received a response. "We will text you the information. Have your man approach us alone. We're no longer interested in you."

They read as fast as possible, knowing the words would evaporate again.

"Not interested in me? Not much, they aren't. I have the *Burn List* on my hard drive, printed out, in the mail and right here in my brain!"

Montgomery spoke in a whisper to Carter. "You may have the list stored and sent ten different ways, Agent Carter, but unless they know it's been emailed directly to the president's personal account at the White House, we still don't have a leg to stand on. That's your only bit of life insurance."

"That won't work, Monty. If I tell them it's going to the White House, they'll only have to add the president to the *Burn List*. Look, maybe if *you* tell them, it'll derail them enough to cause an infight. While they're screaming at each other, you may just get us what we need on tape and still be able to slip out of the place. What do you think?"

Monty's face lit up. "That's brilliant!"

He looked thoughtful for a moment and then, with a genuine smile, added, "You know, now that those pills have kicked in, I'm actually starting to enjoy myself! Let's go catch ourselves some bad guys, Agents."

***

Carter and Seacrest parked three blocks from the meeting spot. It was to be held in a section of the Brooklyn Navy Yard at a location called *Admiral's Row*, which referred to a street lined with 19th century manor houses that were once used as quarters for naval officers. They were built in the architectural style known as *Second French Empire* and looked like mansions to Carter, except that they'd been abandoned so long ago that now they cast only the merest shadow of their former stateliness. Carter was sorry the march of time had not spared their beauty. He found himself thinking that it would have been kinder to knock them down so people could remember them as they once were rather than leave them standing on their last legs for everyone to see.

*It's like staring at a row of beautiful, naked rotting corpses.*

Carter fumbled around in a large paper bag for his coffee. He needed it badly. As he and Seacrest sat in an unmarked car, quiet and tense, Carter began to remember bits and pieces of the night before. He took a long, slow sip, intentionally scalding his mouth as punishment for what he'd done.

Jill nearly wore a hole in her jeans rubbing her hands back and forth on her lap. She was nervous and jumpy and twisted this way and that to see out of every window and cover every angle. "I hope you're right about this."

"Monty's wire is fitted with a G.P.S. tracking device. Fischetti will send back-up; I know he will. I'm still hoping he'll send them in to help us, crazy as it seems..."

Seacrest shook her head. "Don't count on it. He also has to protect the *Galatea Initiative* and keep it secret."

"The what? The *Galatea Initiative*? Where'd you get that from?"

"You talked your head off in your sleep last night. Since you thought I was *Galatea*, I decided to do a little digging online before we left the apartment, tonight. I found out who she is, or *was*, rather, and put two and two together."

"We have nothing to do until the fun begins, so enlighten me, darling. Who's *Galatea*, and what's the *Galatea Initiative*?"

Her nervousness evaporated as she wiggled around to face him, pulled an old blanket over her legs and prepared to tell him a very interesting story.

"She was the subject of a mythological tale written by Ovid, way back in ancient times. *Galatea* was a statue sculpted in the whitest, purest marble. She was more beautiful than any mortal woman. You see, her creator, *Pygmalion*, wanted the perfect bride, but no ordinary woman would do."

"Why?"

"Because they were *real*, Carter, with real faults, and real people aren't perfect. He scorned them all for being corrupt and false and began work on his own vision of purity and fidelity. *Pygmalion* became so obsessed with his own work that he fell in love with it. His need for the restoration of his faith in love and women brought her miraculously to life."

"What does that have to do with the *JASONS*?"

"Carter, they named their project after her for the same reasons; because they've fallen in love with their own idea of perfection, and because they consider their plan beautiful and noble and 100% *controllable*. The *Galatea Initiative* is the heart of the *JASONS'* new mission. They've set themselves up as the Creators of a new and perfect world, one without corruption or end."

"How do you know that?"

"When they drugged you last night, they must have given you enough information for your subconscious to dredge back up when you fell asleep. When Monty left, you dosed off and told me the rest.

"The woman who wears the mask and goes by that name is meant to be an intentional reference to the story and their motive. I guess they couldn't resist the opportunity to drop an obvious hint to prove to themselves how much more clever they are than the rest of us. Honestly, I don't know how we could have missed it, and we wouldn't have if we'd been up on our ancient literature.

"This must have been carefully thought out and planned down to the last detail for years. *Years!* And they must have a web of connections around the world waiting for them to make their move. With the kind of wealth and power the *JASONS* have, they can do it, Carter. They can bring the *Galatea Initiative* to life. We'll never find all of their connections, and even if we did, there'd be others to take their place. I've racked my brain, but I can't think of a way to get them to stand down, even with evidence and exposure."

Carter frowned. "Back up a little, honey. I have to get a handle on this. Did I happen to mention why they were using *Hyzopran* to study people and mind control to turn them into killers? And why make a *Burn List*? They can't keep killing off the opposition and replacing them forever."

"The *Burn List* is just a band aid. They won't need another one after this. By the time their operatives are ready to retire in twenty or thirty years from now, all newborn babies will have had Nano-chips implanted in their brain long ago. By then, anyone will be able to step in and take over those jobs and still be completely controlled—and with zero violence and none of the problems *Hyzopran* poses. The drug was never intended to be used past this first round of assassinations."

Carter rifled a hand through his hair. "Jill, I still don't understand why they're testing the drug out on people and ordering them to kill if they can use technology instead."

"The technology isn't developed yet."

"But *Hyzopran* doesn't work all the time."

"They don't care, Carter. It's just a workaround until the Nano-chip is developed. They can overdose people or program them to make mistakes so that they get caught and prosecuted individually. No authority I know of would believe a member of the *Collective* was being drugged and hypnotized into assassinating people all over the world. They want the killers eliminated or in prison for life after their part of the job is done. Then, when it's ready, they'll use the Nano-chip for the next stage of the initiative.

"They obviously got the idea from Dr. Blake's presentation. After they bought off Pressman and got him to be the one to turn down her project, they stole the drug from Meese and began using it on people. The *Silver Man* said they were testing it, but the test was not to discover *Hyzopran's* efficacy; it was make sure it would fail just enough for the killers to be caught and still not remember enough to implicate the *JASONS*. If anyone went rogue, so much the better! That would've made the case for thrill kills even stronger. They knew anyone who found out what they'd done would never tell a soul and that those that resisted the drug and the programming would just assume they'd had a bad nightmare. It's all very neat and clean, Carter, but all criminals make mistakes, and theirs was in not realizing that Eliza would resist it but remember it, realize where it must have happened to her, steal it, go rogue, and *then* get caught. It's her word against theirs, but more voices make a stronger case."

"I told you all this in my *sleep*?"

"Most of it. I figured out the rest after I did my research today. By the way, I'm the only one referring to it as the *Galatea Initiative*, but that's exactly what it is."

"Did I tell you when this Nano-chip would be ready to roll?"

"Nope, but you did know that they have a genius on their staff who's developing it for them. It could take years. All they have right now is a working prototype, but it still has to be tested before moving ahead with the implant. That's why they used you as a test subject. If you overdosed on *Hyzopran* or your brain got fried with their thingamabob, well, you and I had to be eliminated anyway."

"Jill, did I say what the prototype looked like?"

"Yes. You said they put electrodes on your head, and then you heard white noise that sounded like a buzzing or humming. Obviously, though, it's not ready for prime time. The use of *Hyzopran* to eliminate and replace all those people around the world was supposed to give them at least ten years to perfect the Nano-chip, but the scandals in Washington are forcing firings and resignations, and the threat of an impending impeachment left them with no time to test and produce it. Most of the assassinations were prevented because of our investigation, and the *JASONS* can't assume the F.B.I.

will continue to fund and protect them, either. That makes them desperate, Carter, and you know what that means…"

"Yes, unfortunately I do. They'll roll it out untested if they have to. It's all or nothing, now."

"Catching the whole network in time is impossible, Carter! We have no idea who they are, where they are, or if they're in untouchable positions. They'll find a way to regroup and refund. And we won't be here to stop it."

"We'll have more than enough to launch a full-scale worldwide investigation, but I have a more effective plan; if we put the whole thing on C.N.N. with the entire world tuned in, the *JASONS* and their accomplices will realize it's suicide to make the slightest move. That buys us a lot more time. No one will allow any such implant to be inserted into the brain of their child; I don't care what he thinks. Any death of importance will beg reinvestigation. Besides, if we can embarrass them on international cable news, the F.B.I. mucky-mucks won't cover for the *JASONS* anymore. They have way too much to lose. The whole damn thing will fall apart, no matter what they do."

"What if they can get money and protection from somewhere else? Do you really think we've got a chance, Carter?"

"Yes, I do, and after we expose them, there won't be an entity on earth powerful enough to support them. The *JASONS* may have taken poetic license to a whole new level, but what they're going to get back is poetic justice."

\*\*\*

They sat in silence for a while, thinking about everything that had happened since they moved to New York City. Carter suddenly put down his coffee cup. "By the way, there are live eyes on Agent Deeprose and Red 24/7. They'll be safe where they are, for now."

"That reminds me…there's something we need to…"

He interrupted her. "You're going to say that what happened last night was not my fault. I know that in my head, Jill, but I'll never feel it in my heart. Knowing I wanted to kill you—and that I almost did—is eating me up. I feel so guilty! I should have been able to control myself. I should have known that what I saw was you and not a witch wearing a mask! I feel like if I loved you enough, I couldn't have gotten to the point of no return. If the catatonia hadn't kicked in and saved you…" His voice trailed off, and he couldn't look at her anymore.

"You would've…"

"But, Jill, you have to believe me when I tell you that there is no way on this earth I could love you any more than I already do and always have. I'm so ashamed!"

"Carter, you can't…"

"There's something else eating at me, Jill, and I have to get it off my chest. I don't think I could've felt so heinously vicious and enjoyed it so much unless the capability for it had always been there, inside me, in the first place—buried maybe, but there."

"Carter, you don't…"

"I know now that it's in everyone, and all it takes is a little nudge to bring it out. No God could ever want that unless it was a necessary trait, and if there's no God, then it comes naturally. Even so, I can't ever make up for what I did, but I'll try—every day of my life, until I take my last breath."

"Carter, I…"

A voice on the car's surveillance speakers interrupted her.

# Chapter Thirty Two

Montgomery, outfitted with his recording devices, carefully approached the only three remaining manor houses on *Admiral's Row* in the Brooklyn Navy Yard. He couldn't help admiring their choice of location. The *JASONS* had chosen a building that was over one hundred and fifty years old. Even on the deadest, darkest night, it was breathtakingly majestic despite its crumbling and decaying walls.

*I wonder if they realize the irony of that.*

He stopped in front of a door that looked more like a gaping maw. Like a child without a nightlight, he feared being swallowed up by a monster he couldn't see. Looking up, Monty noticed a cloud lumbering slowly past the moon. He peered into a pair of inky eyes that had once passed for windows and said a silent prayer for just enough light to see by. The moon obliged him by gradually illuminating the entire ground floor.

*Will you look at that! No roof!*

He stepped inside the doorway and stood in silence, listening for voices that might give away the enemy's position and afford him a bit of time to plan his approach and spy out an escape route.

*I don't hear one blessed thing! I hope I'm in the right building.*

There were only a few left standing, so Monty explored a little further before moving on. A marble staircase, bowed from the weight of the countless officers who'd trudged up and down its pink spine, muffled his footsteps. At last, he reached the second floor landing. He stopped and squinted down the hallway to get his bearings.

"Welcome, Mr. Montgomery." A youngish man in a dark blue suit with a crooked nose and the thickest neck he'd ever seen stepped out from behind a corner and punched him in the face with the force of ten men.

Monty landed unceremoniously in a heap on the floor. Lying perfectly still, he played possum for a few minutes, searching for a window with half-closed eyes. A couple of teeth floated in the blood gushing from his mouth. The enforcer, curious to see if Monty was still alive, ambled over to the part of him that still resembled a head. When Monty finally opened his eyes, the enforcer looked down.

"You O.K.? It's a shame—you bleedin' all over your coat like that—but a job's a job, know what I mean?" He smiled like a good natured beast, shrugged apologetically, and pulled Monty to his feet.

"Look, where can I find the *Silver Man*? We have a few things to talk over."

In response, the no-necked enforcer shoved him into a room off the hallway. Inside were three people. One had silver hair, another, tall and slender, wore the mask Carter described to him, and the remaining man was obviously another strong-arm.

*There's a bay window in here, but it's made of lead-paned stained glass, and it's two stories up. That would not be my first choice for an escape route, but it may be my only option.*

The two strong-arms positioned themselves at the door; the other two stood to greet him. "Good evening, Mr. Montgomery. So nice of you to come. It's been a long time, hasn't it? I don't expect you to recognize me anymore, but we certainly remember you. How is your dear wife and Dr. Blake?"

"Dead, thank you. Look, let's cut the crap and get down to it, O.K.?"

The *Silver Man* nodded. "As you wish."

"I was sent here to get you to talk, but I really don't give a shit whether you do or not. I'm here for *one* reason—to kill you. I'm rigged with an explosive belt, so no one comes near me and no one moves. Before we all go to hell together, I want to know why you murdered my wife instead of myself; she didn't know a thing about your lousy group. And I want to know if Dr. Blake really committed suicide."

He took a few steps toward them, and the pair backed away. That little seed of doubt gave Monty the upper hand. He had every intention of getting that confession, but he was serious when he said he was there to kill them. As far as he was concerned, the confession was for Agent Carter and his team. He owed them that, but nothing more.

"Dr. Blake's research was turned down because we had an

altogether different use for her synthetic drug, one that in our estimation and according to her own preliminary research could only be used for short term and erratic results. It was never a reliable drug and would have been discarded in the end, anyway, but we agreed that it could be useful to us in the first stage of another project."

Monty hadn't been privy to Seacrest's explanation of what Carter heard the night before, so he wanted to hear a firsthand accounting from the *Silver Man*. "Would you mind explaining that to me, please? What project? Really. I want to know. The curiosity is killing me." Monty got a little closer to them.

The two strong-arms moved toward him from behind, but the *Silver Man* waved them away. "It's all right, boys, stay where you are. Unless Mr. Montgomery becomes unmanageable, I want the door covered at all times.

"All in due time, Mr. Montgomery. You asked why we turned down Blake's project, and I've told you. But, since we're putting our cards on the table, I'll tell you something else; after you went home, we asked her to come back to the board room and made her a very generous offer for the purchase of the rights to her formula. Had she accepted, she would have been a very wealthy woman, today. Unfortunately, she told us that the only way we'd ever get it was over her cold, dead body. We were happy to oblige. The one remaining lab sample was appropriated and reverse engineered." The *Silver Man* watched Monty very closely, waiting for the arrow to hit home.

Monty turned pale as death. He put his hand inside his coat, and took another step forward, forcing the pair back a little further toward the window. "You sick, demented, dirty, rotten slime bag! I ought to blow your head off right now!"

"Aren't you curious to know why we let you live, Mr. Montgomery, or doesn't that interest you?"

He didn't answer.

"It's very simple, really. We thought it might be far more entertaining to punish you first and kill you, later. We'll find the person who warned you off, too. It's only a matter of time."

"So my coming here tonight was a golden opportunity to finish the job. Is that it?"

"In a way, yes. We're going to kill two birds with one stone, Mr. Montgomery. We know Agents Carter and Seacrest are waiting and watching somewhere outside. His protégé is in the hospital, unable to move. That makes everything so tidy, don't you see?"

"No, I don't. Why don't you explain it all from the beginning?"

"You really haven't figured it out? I'm very disappointed; I took you for a much brighter fellow than Agent Carter. Please, Mr. Montgomery, have a seat in this chair by the window, and I'll let you in on the biggest and last top secret you'll ever hear."

"I'm listening, but before we start, I want you to know I never expected to leave here alive, so I have a few surprises up my sleeve."

The *Silver Man* gave Monty some details but was obviously holding back others. Monty had to get those details recorded or the case would never stand up in court.

"For instance?"

*Good! Keep him talking!*

"For instance, the *Burn List* is on its way to the president as we speak."

"Is it, now? That suits me just fine, Mr. Montgomery, because he'll be convinced that you were the one who wrote it."

"Why would he think that?"

"Because tonight, you're going to be overdosed with *Hyzopran*. These electrodes will be used to provide you with instructions to eliminate all three agents. By tomorrow, you'll be the most hunted man on the planet, and by nightfall you'll be dead. The official story will be that you became unhinged after your wife and colleague died and that you blamed the Meese Corporation for both deaths. Your motive was obviously revenge. Meese is completely in the dark, you know, so they will be cleared rather quickly. You stole the drug from their lab after they turned down your pet project, faked your own death and later turned up in New York under the alias of Arthur Moreland.

"Our friends at the F.B.I. will then be free to wrap up the few murder cases you've uncovered. The assassins we used will be found guilty based on the neuroscientific testimony of experts who will state that no drug or mental conditioning can take away free will. Once they are imprisoned, they will be forgotten. Mr. Montgomery, you're so naïve! We have eyes and ears even in the White House. Anyone who knows about the list will have to go—*including* the president!"

"You're forgetting there's a huge body of evidence that still points to *you*."

"Ah, but you forget the authorities are on our side. The F.B.I. will tell the entire world that *you* are the *Silver Man* who founded the *Collective*. You hatched up a crazy plan to take over the world by using *Hyzopran* on an unsuspecting public to assassinate key world figures. My two-faced technology whiz kid will take the fall for creating the programming and development of the Nano-chip, and the public will know that you planned to use it on newborns.

"You will be reviled as a Hitler and a Mengele all wrapped up in one, Mr. Montgomery, because had your plan succeeded, you would have effectively murdered every free mind in the world. When the dust settles, we will find someone else to make our Nano-chip, and the *Galatea Initiative* will continue."

"The *what*?"

"The *Galatea Initiative*, Mr. Montgomery. That is the name Agent Seacrest decided upon just this afternoon. I thought it was rather catchy. You know who *Galatea* is, I presume?"

"I don't make a point of studying Ovid in my spare time, but yes, I know the story. The *Silver Man*...hmmm. You know, I can't quite place your face, but I remember the voice very well. What was your real name back in the day? I want to know before I die. Just so you know, you're also being heard in real time by C.N.N. That's another ace I'm holding, *Silver Man*. The president and your techie are already warned and protected. *Jesus Holy Christ!* Your ego is so all-encompassing that you can't even conceive of making a mistake or underestimating the opposition. There are hundreds of tiny details you haven't taken into account, and every one of them points straight back to you. I'm holding one last ace, and it's a humdinger. The F.B.I. has turned on you. Even if you manage to make it out of here after I set off the bomb I'm wearing, they're in position out there, ready to rip you and your *Galatea* to shreds."

*God, I love to play poker with men who can't control themselves. CNN listening in real time—ha, haaaa! The bluff about the F.B.I. was truly inspired, even if it was wishful thinking. I hope he bought it.*

Although he was seated near the window, Monty's back faced the only exit in the room. His full attention was on their argument and not on the two enforcers who crept up on him from behind like two giant mice.

"Hold him for me, boys." The *Silver Man* nodded his thanks to them.

309

***

Carter and Seacrest were glued to the car speaker. She was shocked that Fischetti and the back-up team he promised were nowhere in sight. It was no use; they were on their own, outnumbered and outgunned. They'd taken care of warning the president and the I.T. prodigy already, thanks to Monty, but how would any of them escape the *Silver Man's* long arm?

Agent Seacrest spoke to Carter in a very grounded, even tone of voice. "We should go in, Carter. We can't just *sit* here. Fischetti's not going to help us; he made his choice. There won't be any back-up to help us *or* hurt us. All he has to do now is sit back and wait to see who comes out on top. If it's the *Silver Man*, he has no problem. If it's us, he'll make sure we never make it home, tonight."

"What is it you want to do, Jill?"

"I don't know, Carter, but we have to do something. No one else will."

Carter had prepared for this moment. Montgomery knew what to do if he got caught in a trap he couldn't get out of. Carter was counting on him to make the ultimate sacrifice. Monty had already given Carter a legitimate reason to go in shooting, and he was more than fine with that. Let the authorities believe it was a massacre. Let them think that everyone was dead, including himself and his entire team. He'd have to call in a few favors to get Deeprose to safety, but if they got away with this tonight, the four of them could lose themselves in some remote part of the world, beyond the reach of the F.B.I., the *JASONS* and anyone else in the western world.

"*We're* not doing anything, Jill. *I am.* You stay put. I need you to listen to what goes on inside the house and to watch for that back-up. They may still come, but if Fischetti's order really was countermanded, the director knew we were coming here before I told Fischetti about it this morning. He may be dead already."

"Carter, you can't go in alone! I'm coming with you; it's my *job!*"

He already had his gun out and was quickly inserting bullets. Carter had one foot on the pavement when he turned to give Seacrest last minute instructions. He fished a piece of paper out of his pants pocket. "There's no time to argue, Jill. Take this. If no one makes it out of the building, I want you to meet Agent Deeprose at Monty's

310

place. Call this number when you get there, and say your name is Seacrest. The man who answers will know what to do. After that, just sit tight and wait for help to come. Your first priority as my partner is to the mission. Now, I have to go."

After last night, he couldn't just leave without saying what was in his heart. "I love you, Jill. You're my life."

He kissed her and was gone.

***

Montgomery's voice brought her attention back to the car speakers. He was being beaten, savagely. She listened, helpless. Soon, though, the room became quiet again. Monty must have passed out.

The *Silver Man* had Monty put back in his chair, and asked one of his men to dump a bucket of cold water over his head. Seacrest knew the torture had resumed when she heard a sharp crack followed by a blood curdling scream.

"Don't break his other arm until I give you the order, boys."

The only sounds she heard after that were Monty's groans. He was completely untrained in combat, torture, and survival skills and far too old and out of shape to be in a situation like this.

*We were crazy for sending him in there!*

Now all she could do was wait. There was no one she could call for help.

*If Carter doesn't walk out of that building alive, I'm going in there to finish this mission for him.*

She picked up her service revolver and got out of the car.

***

The man known only as "Mr. X" knew Agent Carter must be close by, but there was no time to try to find him. He'd have to act alone and hope it would provide enough of a distraction to get into the building on *Admiral's Row*.

Quentin Borofsky had been invited to join a different think tank many years ago and learned too late that it was linked directly to the *JASONS*. *They all were.* Maybe he'd had a touch of the naiveté only youth and privilege could breed, but he really believed the power of

311

intelligent, peace-loving people was stronger than the power of the mob or any one corrupt individual.

He woke up every morning believing with his whole heart the words and ideology of his hero, John F. Kennedy. He would not ask what his country could do for *him*; he would *ask and do* what he could for his country. He knew Camelot, like perfection, was a place to which you traveled but never arrived; the closer you came to it, the farther away it seemed, and yet, the journey still had to be made. Getting there was far more important than arriving.

Quentin could no longer look in the mirror each morning knowing the *JASONS* had their own agenda and that no one was willing to step on their toes. One day, he dropped off the radar, changed his name and joined the military to fight in Syria. There, he learned the technical, mechanical and psychological tactics of espionage and warfare. By the time he came home, he was ready to do what he could to stop them or at least slow them down a little.

Now he stood staring at a proud ruin of *Admiral's Row*. Moss and wild flowers draped themselves across her floors. A large tree grew in the foyer. Nature was a woman without mercy, gradually and inexorably taking back for herself what man had once arrogantly assumed was his.

*This is what the entire planet will look like when all of humanity is dead. I'm going to fight him and go on fighting until there's nothing left of the JASONS. If I fail, there are others who will take up where I left off. I shall neither rest easily nor sleep peacefully until I've done everything I can to expose this man and his entire organization.*

Mr. X inventoried his coat pockets and went around to the rear of the building. In the left front pocket he carried C-4, a handy explosive the military often used to break down doors. In the other, he packed a bigger wallop.

*They won't go gently into **this** night.*

***

Carter trotted along quickly until he came to a bench just down the street from the building and stopped to get a better look at the layout. It was so cold that he could see his breath.

*I wonder if the soul really does escape through the mouth.*

He hadn't been able to connect with Mr. X tonight, but was certain he'd be there. Every time one of them hit a dead end or was backed into a corner, someone had been there to throw them a lead or save the day. He prayed Mr. X was preparing a diversion big enough to cover him.

Carter approached the open entrance of the old manor and hunkered down in its skirt of overgrown bushes to wait for the right moment to make his attack.

*\*\*\**

At headquarters, Deputy Director Fischetti barked orders to his S.W.A.T. team leader over the phone. "You will not fire unless I give the order. You will not shoot to kill without my order. Agents Carter and Seacrest are already there under cover, and I want them protected. Is that clear?"

His stomach was in knots. Agent Carter was making a mess out of his murder investigations.

*You couldn't have just accepted these as thrill kills, could you, Carter?*

Fischetti had been ordered tonight, in no uncertain terms, to wrap up these investigations by confirming that the motive was drug-related and thrill-related. The director explained to him in detail just how high up and far reaching the conspiracy reached. The F.B.I. had to play ball or be considered an acceptable loss. "I'm fairly sure Washington is on to us, Fischetti. There's no turning back now. You're going to have to figure out how to play both sides against the middle. It's imperative you appear to be backing up your team, but keep them on a tight leash."

"Yes, sir." And just like that, the deputy director became a co-conspirator. He left the office thinking about the ironies of the case.

*What were the odds that Carter would accidentally meet a bunch of barhopping college students who'd been to one of those nutball meetings? If I hadn't stepped in and sent Red's friends an email with the wrong address for the next meeting, he would have busted the thing wide open right then and there. Jesus, that was close!*

*And that rookie, Deeprose! Boy! Under any other circumstances, she'd be worth her weight in gold. If she wasn't the straw that's going to break my back, I'd pin a medal on her.*

313

*If it had all ended there, I might still have been able to save them and myself, too, but once Carter found the damn Burn List, he connected it to the JASONS as soon as he saw the curator's name on it. Now, I'm stuck.*

"Liz! Where's my bicarbonate of soda? *Liz!!!*"

*I did my best to shield them, but my orders were clear. Tonight, there's no turning back and no way out. How can I order their deaths and show up tomorrow like it's just another day at the office? Either I follow orders and let the JASONS go, arrange for Montgomery to take the fall, order the murder of Carter's team and prosecute a bunch of kids who had no idea what they were doing, or...or what?*

Fischetti buried his head in his hands and contemplated the biggest decision of his life.

# Chapter Thirty Three

The S.W.A.T. team arrived at *Admiral's Row* much later than Bill Fischetti would have liked. He did a little reconnaissance to see if he could locate Carter, Seacrest and Montgomery, but he couldn't wander too far from the scene. If he was going to keep his team in the dark about their real purpose for being here tonight, the only way to pull it off was to keep on top of things as they unfolded. They'd been told that Montgomery was their only target and to shoot to kill.

If the chairman of the *JASONS* and his executive assistant weren't able to escape undetected, the S.W.A.T. team would be ordered to stand down for them. They knew nothing of the *JASONS*, so Fischetti would simply explain them away as F.B.I. operatives who'd set a trap for Montgomery and his co-conspirators.

It was the third part of the plan he wasn't sure he could pull off. The S.W.A.T. team would be told that Montgomery could be holding Carter hostage. If anyone came out of that building using Carter as a human shield, it was to be considered an acceptable loss. Catching Montgomery, dead or alive, was their first priority. He hoped Carter had the sense to stay out of the way.

He briefed his men and headed out. Hidden in the brush across from the ruins of an officers' residence, Fischetti and the team had eyes on the openings where the front door, windows, and roof had once been. A few expert snipers were already in place at the four corners of the manor, ready to pick off Montgomery and Carter from close range no matter which way they came out. They arrived in silence and maintained a silence that coursed through them with nerve-racking electricity, begging for the moment of release.

\*\*\*

Monty regained consciousness to find the *Silver Man* sitting opposite him smoking a pipe filled with vanilla scented tobacco.

"Welcome back to the land of the living, Mr. Montgomery. We haven't finished our talk yet, and there's so much I want to discuss with you before we begin our experiment.

*"Galatea,* my lovely assistant, took the liberty of searching you. You have no explosives on you, Mr. Montgomery. I admire your courage and ingenuity, sir, but what you really need now is the courage to face what's coming. I believe the appropriate term for this moment is 'checkmate'."

Monty, more alert now, seized another opportunity to draw him out into conversation. He'd been searched and the wire had been taken, but they missed the lapel camera. The no-necks rested their backs against the drawing room door with both hands thrust in their suit pockets. They weren't very worried about Monty. They hadn't even strapped him into the chair because he seemed too battered and broken to move.

*This is my last chance to get the rest of the story documented and get the hell out of here before that masked freak injects me with Hyzopran.*

"Why are you really here, Mr. Montgomery? Any other law enforcement professional could have done a better job of infiltration and capture, and you still would have had your revenge in the end. Why were you chosen for the job? Or did you volunteer for it?"

"I have nothing to lose and nothing to live for; my wife is dead and you arranged it. If it'll help bring you down, I'm the only one with the right to volunteer for a suicide mission."

"Go on..."

"I think I...Yes. *Yes.* I remember you. Your name is Kenneth Anders Silverman. It's so simple that it's brilliant, except that Senator Pressman will remember the name right off, and he's no longer afraid to testify. Now I know it, too. It's a huge relief, really. You see, I don't have to worry about Arleen's real killer escaping justice anymore."

"That's enough, Mr. Montgomery."

"You think so? Because I'm just getting warmed up! Now, let's see...you were a brilliant but emotionally high strung child who came from big money. Your father died shortly after your birth. Your mother—well—let's just say she was over attentive in the *extreme*. When it became clear that her own mental illness was progressing, you were sent to school in Switzerland.

"You had all the advantages money could buy—all the right schools and upper crusty connections—except that you had not one single friend, isn't that right? You were hated and feared by all your schoolmates, even some of the teachers."

"*Enough!*"

"However, being in the top one percent does have its benefits. Your blinding brilliance protected you from retribution and punishment, alike. Your money bought their silence."

"Yes... it did. I suppose it did..."

"But power was the real drug you couldn't put down. Your work in bio-psychology and neuroscience won you a Nobel Prize at the age of twenty. You had one of the brightest minds the world had ever seen, and you came along at just the right moment in U.S. history. The space race was on. You were awarded the chairman's spot on a groundbreaking Washington think tank tasked with reverse engineering whatever the hell it was we found and stowed away in Area 51. By leapfrogging proper channels, you and your team were able to take us decades, if not centuries, into the future.

"I also remember you as an arrogant, unyielding *bastard*."

The *Silver Man* yawned politely. "I'm well aware of my own history, Mr. Montgomery. Is there anything else you'd care to get off your chest while you still have one?"

"Here it is, Silverman. Maybe you really do have an organization that spans the planet, bottomless pockets and endless power, but maybe—just *maybe*—you're nothing but a psychopath with a gift for story-telling. If the *JASONS* really made their home there, they'd have known right from the get-go you'd do something asinine like this fifty years down the line."

Silverman hissed, "How *dare* you! How *dare* you!!"

"You are responsible for murder, mayhem, assassination, kidnapping, dosing unsuspecting people with an unknown hallucinogen, mind control, and plotting to overthrow at least one government, Silverman, and I'm going to lead the looney brigade right to your door. *Personally.*"

*Oh boy! If that doesn't pull his tail, nothing will.*

317

Silverman was halfway out of his easy chair, the contents of his pipe scattered and forgotten, when he caught a glimpse of his own reflection in a mirror above the cold fireplace and stopped himself. He gripped the arms of the chair and slowly sat back down. There were more important things to do tonight.

"You require more proof that we're real even after what you've been through tonight? Even knowing what's to come? If you're working with Agent Carter, then you also know what he's been through the past two days, and you say you still need convincing? All right, Mr. Montgomery, you shall have it.

"You've seen the *Burn List,* I suppose? Then you must have seen Dalton Wells' name there. An I.T. consultant at Meese—David Florio—came across it accidentally and decided to save a copy. Why, I do not know.

"We've been operating at Meese for generations, you know. It was a comfortable place to work before they decided to put us out to pasture. As if they could! Perhaps we should have taken them into our confidence after all, but that's neither here nor there. The point is, Mr. Montgomery, that if you don't take the fall for us, they'll have to."

"They haven't broken any laws. What could possibly be pinned on them?"

"Why, only the planning and execution of the *Galatea Initiative*, Mr. Montgomery! They're entirely innocent, of course, but it's going to take years to figure out the truth, and by then it won't matter, anymore. By then, people will think what they're programmed to think."

"Why did you try to frame Senator Pressman?"

"It was always our intention to incriminate or eliminate him. He was easy enough to buy and will be just as easy to sell out." Silverman shrugged apologetically. "After all, somebody had to take the fall."

"But if you all agreed the drug was wildly unreliable, why did you steel it from Meese's lab and test it on humans? Why didn't you *all* turn down Dr. Blake's funding, drop the idea altogether and just move on to Phase Two?"

"The *List!* The *List!* How dense can you people possibly be? The implant wasn't going to be ready for another ten years, *at least*! But we must have our own people installed in key positions around the world now and keep them there until the first newborns who received an implant turn twenty-one. *Hyzopran* is perfect as a short-term solution *because* of its instability. Agent Carter did not overdose. Still, we couldn't have hoped for a better outcome of the test we performed on him."

*Time for a Hail Mary Pass, old boy. Just throw the old ball toward the end zone and hope to God there's a good receiver down there to catch it. Five more minutes. Just five more...*

"What is the *Galatea Initiative*?"

"*Galatea* was a code name we used for our project, but Agent Seacrest gave us a more fitting one just this afternoon."

"Is the Nano-chip the whole ballgame? I mean, programming the human brain goes way beyond the desire to line your pockets and govern the world. It makes us slaves and you our master. If all you want is wealth and power, the *JASONS* already have it. You already control every significant achievement of the 20th and 21st century, so what's your real goal?"

"It's not money, Mr. Montgomery, I assure you of that. The *Galatea Initiative* goes far beyond anything so banal. You're correct; we rule from behind the scenes and we profit from the advancements we approve. We always have. There's no need for outside funding, but the F.B.I. doesn't know that, and it keeps them very conveniently under our thumb. In ten years, the Nano-chip will negate the need to rely on any entity to keep our secret.

"What's the point, you ask? Agent Carter knows, but in the condition he was in at the time he heard it, he can't have remembered a thing. Well, it can't hurt to let you both in on it, now. The die was cast when the information on your wire was sent to Washington in real time. Anyone who knows about us now will take the secret to their grave.

"The human race is set to advance by several hundred years and very soon, Mr. Montgomery, without blowing ourselves up along the way. The Nano-chip can be programmed to suppress the neurotransmitter activity responsible for *any* undesirable urge and behavior—including the fight or flight impulse. The thalamus doesn't have to be tampered with in the least. It can continue to process and channel outside stimuli normally, but we will choose what gets past the neurons and into consciousness.

319

"*Think of it!* We can eradicate addiction, mental illness, war...the possibilities are endless! We can dispense with money altogether and work for the common good. As the *Creator*, I will make sure every man, woman and child have all they need and more. No more greed, jealousy or graft! It will be a world completely and perfectly controlled and maintained by myself for its own good. When the time comes, I will pass the baton to one of the others. It will go on that way for eternity, and I'll be revered as a God."

"So, this is about power and control. Surprise, surprise. You've decided you're uniquely qualified to rule the world, eh? Mr. Silverman, this is not a new story, but for the sake of argument, let's say you've put a new spin on it. I'll even go so far as to admit your reasons seem altruistic in nature. Fatherly. Benevolent. But consider this; life in Eden requires a complete reliance on God for everything. Having the power of life and death over people also requires fear, punishment and a commitment to keeping the populace ignorant. I know you prefer it that way, but every garden is full of snakes. One way or another, man will always find a way to regain what he's lost. We weren't meant to live in fear and ignorance.

"Sure we fight way too often, but we're still here, and we've earned the right to design our own future. Look, there's going to be snags and glitches in programming that allow some thought through. How will you keep humanity from forming a resistance and overthrowing you? You'll have to have an army, of course. Once you do, you'll be nothing but another petty dictator relying on thugs, violence and destruction to get what he wants. Surely you can see that?"

"You forget, Mr. Montgomery, my army consists of thousands upon thousands of dedicated followers ready and willing to go wherever I lead them. The meek will never inherit the earth, so I must."

***

Agent Carter was aware that back-up had finally arrived, but he had no way of knowing whose side they were on. Carter had a sixth sense for these things, though. His intuition told him that the total absence of natural noise in the surrounding woods meant that he was the one surrounded. He was near the front entrance when several spotlights glued him to the spot.

"Agent Carter! Halt and place your hands slowly over your head! Do not make any sudden moves or we will shoot to kill!"

*Here we go.*

Carter raised his hands but kept on walking until he was positioned directly in front of the missing front door. He faced the S.W.A.T. team, did not speak and waited for what was coming.

Fischetti was stunned. "What the *hell* are you doing? He's one of *us*! I told you to protect him unless it was the only way to shoot Montgomery! The ones we want are *inside* the house! Now, *stand down* or I'll bust every one of you morons down to a Grade One!" The veins on his neck and forehead bulged with his sudden rise of blood pressure.

Suddenly, he knew he'd been used. The director obviously wanted Carter and his team out of his hair. He must have briefed Fischetti's men privately, because they were no longer taking their orders from him.

***

Mr. X arrived at *Admiral's Row* just as Montgomery got the last of the story on his lapel cam. He crept around to the back of the building, knowing Agent Carter would have gone in through the front. His silencer took out the two men at both corners quickly and quietly. The one remaining back door may have been old, but it was bolted, deadlocked and carved entirely from one single slab of black oak. He couldn't even guess how thick it was, but hoped he could blow it open with what he had on him.

He held the C-4 explosive in a very shaky right hand. With infinite care, as if it were a Fabergé egg, Mr. X removed an M67 grenade from a small, steel box taken off a dead Syrian terrorist leader two decades earlier. That had been *his* personal contribution to a brighter, happier world. He looked up toward heaven and gave the stars a sharp, jaunty salute.

Stepping back behind a boulder as big as himself, he threw the C-4 at the massive door. It exploded on contact, projecting slabs, javelins and splinters in all directions. What was left of the black iron door fittings swung from side to side as if they'd been hanged.

The explosion shook the house. A mass of dense, coal-colored smoke flooded through the first floor and floated, unimpeded, up to the second. Mr. X raced through the hole and into the foyer. One of the enforcers was halfway down the staircase when Mr. X tossed his grenade. The thug caught the small, round object with one giant paw. "This looks like…"

There was no escaping the blast. Like a ruined soufflé, the walls fell in on themselves. When the smoke finally cleared, nothing was left of the enforcer. Most of the pink marble staircase was now just a pretty pile of rocks.

And Mr. X was gone.

\*\*\*

It sounded like the house got up on its hind legs and roared. The enforcer guarding Monty ran into the hallway, gun drawn. The distraction was a gift from heaven, and Monty didn't need to think twice; he shot out of the chair like a cannon ball and knocked over the *Silver Man's* easy chair with him still in it. Once he was out of the way, Monty backed up against the door of the drawing room, pulled his coat completely over his head and hands and ran straight into the stained glass picture window.

The three remaining survivors made their way through the wreckage to the stairs and carefully picked their way down them, a step here and a jump there, knowing full well the rest of the rock staircase was quickly coming down behind them. They stepped as one out onto what would have been the front porch.

\*\*\*

The impact of the blast threw Carter to the ground. He waited until the earth was still again and then patted down his entire body to make sure he still had all his working parts. When he was satisfied with the results of his survey, he got up and stood to one side of the missing front door, ready for whatever came next.

Fischetti shouted orders to one of his men. "Put the cuffs on him, Lieutenant Rafferty—that's all. Then start searching the grounds for Montgomery. Agent Carter is here on my orders."

Rafferty answered by spitting on the ground. He barked his own orders into the bullhorn. "Agent Carter, lace your hands behind your head and kneel. We will only say this one time! You have five seconds to comply."

Fischetti grabbed the bullhorn out of Rafferty's hands, aimed it at his entire team and shouted, "I am Deputy Director William H. Fischetti of the N.Y. F.B.I. and your *superior* officer! I order you to stand down! *Stand down NOW, Goddamn it!*"

Now that the voice and video recordings had been safely transmitted to the White House, all Carter cared about was finding Monty. He stood his ground.

*If they want to shoot me, I'm not kneeling for it.*

The lieutenant snatched back the bullhorn. "Cuff Fischetti, Agent Moreno, and keep him out of my way."

Rafferty resumed command. *"FIRE AT WILL!"*

Bill Fischetti could do nothing but stand there and stare as he witnessed the cold-blooded execution of Agent Carter by his own men.

\*\*\*

Aiming for the heart, a sniper fired three successive shots at Carter. All three bullets were direct hits. Seacrest knew the sound of F.B.I. sniper guns by their sound—*pew, pew, pew!* She started running and didn't stop until she saw Carter standing in front of a house without walls or a roof and sank gratefully onto the same bench where he'd rested earlier.

*He's O.K.! He's O.K.!!*

Carter remained standing tall and proud and never took his eyes off Fischetti. Then, like a rag doll, he crumpled up and collapsed.

Seacrest clamped a hand over her mouth. Time stopped. In a dream, she rose and ran, willing her legs to move faster and her heart not to burst.

\*\*\*

Even handcuffed, Fischetti could move and use his hands to a certain degree. He grabbed the gun out of the sniper's hand, took quick and careful aim and shattered the enforcer's knee cap. The behemoth screamed like a girl and fell to the ground beside Carter, begging for his life. When Fischetti looked up again, the *Silver Man* and *Galatea* were gone.

Rafferty bellowed, "We have orders to shoot you if you interfere in any way, Fischetti. Don't move!"

The deputy director marched toward Carter, refusing to acknowledge Rafferty's last warning or recognize his authority.

*Go ahead! Shoot me, you sorry piece of shit!*

Fischetti had already made his decision before they left H.Q. He had no choice concerning Montgomery's capture, but he would go on record as having taken responsibility for the protection of his agents, even if he died in the line of duty. Had Carter lived, the deputy director would have blown the whistle on the whole damn organization and gone willingly to prison to pay for his part in it, but all bets were off now, and Fischetti was ready to make his last stand.

***

From her vantage point, Seacrest had a clear shot at Rafferty's head. "Cease fire! Federal Officer!"

If she pulled the trigger, Rafferty, as well as every other man on the team, knew that she'd hit the bulls eye. She never missed. Bill Fischetti was risking his own life to guard Carter's body, and she would not leave him there undefended. Carter told her to save Monty any way she could if he didn't make it back to her, and that was exactly what she was going to do.

Rafferty started to sweat. He wasn't willing to die for a has-been deputy director and didn't doubt for a moment that she'd kill him before his team could take her out. He told his men to lower their weapons and waited to hear her terms.

Still aiming for the spot between Rafferty's eyes, Seacrest placed herself in front of the deputy director and the body of her husband. **"Anyone who takes *one step* towards my husband gets his *head* blown off!**

*"Now, you listen to me! All of you! You've done enough!* You *have* the ones you came here to protect. I have the ape on the ground and Bill Fischetti for insurance purposes. They belong to me now, and I'm taking them out of here. You can't have *them* or *anyone else*

324

on this property, so go home before I kill every last one of you, *myself!*"

The S.W.A.T. team had the two *JASONS* they came to rescue, so they had no real reason to stay. Agent Carter was no longer a factor. Several men had already combed the area searching for Montgomery, but he was nowhere to be found. They'd get him another day. The team dispersed slowly, sheep-faced and sullen, without waiting for confirmation from Rafferty. Seacrest never backed down, and they knew it. Not one man among them wanted to fight her, tonight.

\*\*\*

She dropped to the ground and cradled Carter's head in her lap.

Fischetti laid his hand softly on her head and said to the man lying perfectly still in her arms, "Thanks, Agent Carter, and good-bye. You were the conscience of the outfit. You never gave up, and you never gave in. Rest easy now, son. We'll get them all. I promise."

He knew Seacrest needed to be alone with her husband before help arrived, so he moved the sobbing giant to a nearby tree where they'd be sheltered from the bitter wind. Fischetti tore a long strip of cotton off the bottom of his own shirt to use as a tourniquet for the man's knee. The next order of business was to call 911 for an ambulance. He rode to the hospital with the enforcer, desperate to give him the comfort he couldn't give to Carter and stayed with him at the hospital all night.

\*\*\*

Seacrest bent down to Carter's face and stroked his hair. He was so handsome, even now. The catharsis came upon her in an overwhelming storm of tears. They cascaded over the sharp curves and smooth plains of her face and down onto his. There was so much to say that should have been said before.

In a voice strangled by grief she'd never prepared for, Seacrest sang to him. It was their song—*Stardust*—the one they'd danced to at their wedding reception, every New Year's Eve and again at the *Jazz Standard* just a few nights ago. From somewhere outside herself, she heard words that came from a place of such deep sadness and regret for things left undone that she knew the wound would never heal. She understood the lyrics now, because they were written in her heart.

She threw herself across his body, crying for all the years they'd never have together and all the days and nights she'd be alone with nothing but her broken heart as a reminder of how much his love had transformed her life.

"You were my heart, Carter! How can I live without my heart?!"

She remembered the promise she'd made to him long ago and kept her word. Looking up at the heavens, she said a prayer. "Please God, take care of him. He was a good man, and he loved me so, *so* much! He died the way he lived, protecting other...p-people. Every soul he touched was a little kinder and gentler for having touched his own. Bestow upon him your divine and everlasting grace, now and forever. Amen."

Searching the sky, she saw, or thought she saw, a group of stars in the shape of a tree with many branches. At the very top, one star glowed just a little brighter than the others. Seacrest smiled, knowing that wherever he'd gone, Carter was content.

# Chapter Thirty Four

Seacrest's mouth stretched itself into a sudden, hideous mask. Both hands flew to her face and stayed there. She rocked back and forth over him, screaming and crying, but after a long, long time, her cries quieted. She relaxed the vice-like grip on her face to brush away the tears on his. This would be her last chance to stare at him all she wanted without him asking her what she was doing.

*I'm just looking, Carter, that's all. Just looking.*

Finally, she sighed, and leaning over him once more, kissed him tenderly and hugged him tight. Her voice had to work its way past the lump in her throat. "I needed you, Carter, and you *left* me. You left me here all alone. If you had to go, why didn't you take me with you?"

She needed to tell Carter something she'd never known about herself until this moment. Lowering her head until her nose touched his, she whispered, "I'm not as strong as you thought I was, Carter. I can't make it alone."

Sniffling, she looked down and willed him to come back. "My tears are on your face, baby. I'll pat them dry again."

*My tears... on his face. Pat them dry again. Pat them dry...again?*

Electrified, her eyes flew wide open. "I already wiped my tears off him! They're not *mine*! *They're not my tears!!*" She grabbed him by the shoulders and shook him frantically. "Carter! *Carter!!!*"

With a sharp intake of breath, Carter shot up into a sitting position. Unable to speak and sucking in huge, gasping, gulps of air, he pointed to his chest.

Seacrest seized his collar and ripped his shirt wide open. A battalion of buttons fired themselves into outer space as well as the pavement with equal and unbelievable force. Carter had been wearing a Kevlar vest under his shirt, which lessened the impact of the shots. Tearing himself out of her arms, he flipped over onto his hands and knees and coughed like a chain smoker. She threw herself on him and knocked him flat.

Carter thought he might pass out again. "Hey, what are you trying to do, kill me or something?"

Laughing and crying, she kissed his whole face.

"Hey, hey, what's all this? This isn't the first time this vest has saved my bacon. Don't tell me you didn't know I'd have one on…"

"If you ever do that to me again, Carter, I'll, I'll…"

Carter smiled. "Yes, well, that's already been tried. Do you think you can ease up on the strangle hold? And why are you crying? Your face is all red and blotchy, and your eyes are practically swollen shut! Were you hurt?"

"*Yes*. By a husband who forgot to tell me he was wearing a bullet-proof vest."

He hugged her close and smiled gratefully.

*He still thinks I'm the strong one. That's what he wants, though, isn't it? Well, I am. And I'm not. He's always telling me that balancing Yin and Yang are important, but it's healthier to be who you really are than it is to put on an act. It takes too much energy to keep it up over time.*

*He never asked me to hide my weaker side from him. I'm the one who started this whole stupid game. I did! So it's my own fault if he doesn't know who I really am, deep down. And Carter's got to toe the line as well. He can't continue letting outside events decide the direction his life takes, and he can't keep ignoring everything that upsets him, either.*

"Carter, like you say, everyone is both Yin and Yang, but I don't think we were meant to keep up a constant internal battle of one over the other—no one can do that for long—but I do think we are meant to work on our issues. Listen to me, now; when we do things we're not proud of and that we know are wrong, those actions absolutely do not define us unless we allow them to. You were *drugged* when you tried to kill me; you're not the monster you think you are! But that lousy drug also freed every vile thought and emotion you've ever hidden from yourself. Face it; even the noblest of characters are

328

human. Join the club, Carter. Hate, anger and every other ugly feeling has always been there inside you, and it's normal. Just learn how to express and control them. But for God's sake, stop fighting it; you can't win."

"You've been holding back on me, too, you know. What is it that's been separating us for so long? What is it?'

"Neither of us has been much good at pretending we're something we're not, Carter. You're not as cool, calm, and collected as you'd like to be, and I'm much more sensitive than anyone knows. Sure, I put on a great show of it. I've had years of practice, and I'm used to wearing the armor, but I need your strength. I need *you*! I've been more afraid to say those words than I've ever been of a bullet!"

"But why?"

"I thought that was what you wanted, Carter. I'm your partner as well as your wife, so I buried the part of myself that needed to lean on you. I thought you wanted someone to keep the mood light—someone you didn't need to worry about. But I *want* to be worried about! Maybe that's why I do crazy things sometimes, I don't know. Look, Carter, if you'll try, so will I. I'll tell you and show you every single day of my life, without jokes or wisecracks, that I love you and need you and your strength every bit as much as you need mine. I promise to talk to you before I do anything that might seem rash to you. And Carter? I'll try to curb the sarcasm, but don't expect miracles right away. It's my only protection. I mean, it *was*. Now *you* are. Deal?"

"Deal." When she buried her face in his shoulder, he looked up and gave silent thanks to Buddha for bringing her into his life and keeping her there.

Desperate for a tissue, she used the bottom half of her sweater to wipe her nose. "Let's get back to the car. I'm freezing."

\*\*\*

Once they reached the safety of their car, he remembered a few urgent questions that were on his mind when he woke from the dead. "Jill, where's Fischetti?"

"He rode to the hospital in the ambulance with a thug he shot in the knee. The other one was killed in the blast. We thought you were

329

dead, Carter, but he still stood in front of us so I could take you home and bring that animal into custody for interrogation. The ones we really wanted—the other two—they got away. I'm sorry."

He clenched his jaw so tightly she could see the muscles twitch.

***

*Admiral's Row* was deserted. Carter gunned the motor and blasted the heater as high as it would go. He had loads of other questions for her, but first he wanted to look for the extra blanket they kept in the back seat. "Hey, I found the afghan... *and Monty*! *Hey, Monty*!!"

Curled up in a ball under the afghan like a comfy cat, Monty yawned and sat up slowly, groaning but beaming at the two of them like a teenager who'd jumped off the garage roof and lived to tell about it. "You want to know how I got away? Don't bother asking; I'll tell you. I took a running leap right through a plate of stained glass on the second floor! That's right! I jumped out a closed window. Who's the man?! *Who's the man?!*"

Carter answered for them both. "You're the man, Monty. Thanks. And congratulations! Boy, are we glad to see you!"

The two men pumped their arms up and down in a hearty handshake. Monty used his left hand because his right arm was broken and torn out of the socket. They grinned at each other like two idiots.

"I'm rather pleased to see you, too! I never thought I'd say this, but thank God I have plenty of padding in all the wrong places."

Monty was almost unrecognizable. Carter expected as much, and Seacrest had heard the whole ordeal over the car speaker. She got out to retrieve her medical bag from the trunk and then scooted into the back seat of the car. She began looking him over from head to foot starting with the cuts all over his hands and forearms. "The blood makes it look worse than it is. The lacerations are only in the places that were unprotected when you hit the glass." She cleaned and bandaged the deep cuts. "A few of these will need stitches. I'm more concerned about your broken arm. It needs to be set right away and put back into the socket, Monty, and it's going to hurt. On three, O.K.?"

He nodded.

"*One…*" She jerked his shoulder back into place.

Monty gasped in pain, but his protests were all formality. He wore the face of a boxer who'd gone thirteen rounds but won the decision.

"Monty! Your face is a bloody, black and blue stump and you sit there grinning! You had the time of your life, didn't you?"

Monty and Carter glanced at each other and then back at her. They shrugged in unison. He smiled sheepishly and nodded, revealing a mouthful of missing teeth.

Seacrest sighed and shook her head. "Oh, well, never mind. The most important thing now is to make sure you don't have a concussion or a cracked skull. Even so, we'll have to watch for signs of swelling of the brain and any cognitive damage caused by landing on the one part of you with no padding at all. Honestly!"

Monty looked splendiferous. He'd gone so terribly long without the care and attention of a loving woman that he relished the scolding she gave him. Seacrest was right; he *was* having the time of his life. He looked strong and proud, and somehow, a little younger. Arleen could rest in peace, now.

"Carter, put the pedal to the metal and head for *New York Presbyterian Hospital* on William Street. It's one of the best emergency facilities in the country, and it's only a few minutes from here. Take the Brooklyn Bridge."

*Some habits die hard, I guess. I'll try to be a little less commanding tomorrow.*

\*\*\*

*One day later…*

Carter went to the hospital to check on Monty and the enforcer. The man wouldn't be going anywhere soon, but he'd recover enough to face trial. Montgomery was in pretty bad shape. He'd been kept up all night and monitored for a concussion. His adrenaline level returned to normal a few hours after they got him there, so his body was finally registering the unimaginable pain of missing teeth torn out by the roots, broken bones and a head that felt like an anvil had been dropped on it.

"Do you want me to call a nurse for you, Monty? You look like you've been run over and dragged for ten blocks. Sorry, buddy. Maybe they can give you something more for the pain."

Montgomery tried to turn his head toward Carter, but the room began to spin, so he gave up. Swallowing down the nausea, he replied, "They have me on morphine. It's strong, but it doesn't last. I have to wait for the next dose and then wait for it to kick in; there's nothing I can do about it."

Carter sat down and frowned with worry before he plunged into the other reason for his visit. "Monty, I need to talk to you about something. Are you up to it?"

"The only thing I *can* do is talk. Sort of. What's on your mind?"

"I want to put you in the witness protection program as soon as you're ready for a wheelchair. Your testimony can be done by video conference. We want you to have a full-time aid and someone to watch your back from behind the scenes for the rest of your life. We owe you at least that much."

"Why would I need to go into the witness protection program, Agent Carter?"

"All we caught was one bodyguard. Even if we manage to break him or find the two that got away, there's still a network of conspirators all over the globe. We may never get them all."

"And that means…?"

"It means it's time to let us take it from here. My own organization is dirty from top to bottom. I can't be sure whether Fischetti stepped up to the plate to save me or himself. Someone upstairs ordered his men to disregard his orders and shoot us all before they left the scene. Agent Deeprose would have been next. They helped the *Silver Man* and *Galatea* to escape and would've hung the whole mess on your dead body if they'd been able to find you, Monty."

Monty sat quietly for a few minutes, digesting the update and gathering his thoughts. "Agent Carter, the game's not over. You just told me as much. I didn't come out of hiding just to go back in. What I'm trying to say is that I'm not afraid anymore, and I haven't finished what I came here to do. I thank you for the offer, but I'm going to have to turn it down. When the trial date finally comes up, I'll be there."

He picked up a hand-held mirror lying on his nightstand. "I can finally look at myself in the mirror again and respect what I see. Besides, operating in the shadows seems to work much better for our hero, the mysterious Mr. X. I don't know if he made it out of there alive, but if he lived through the blast, he's still on our side."

"I don't think he did, Monty. I had the area searched. If he's still there, he's buried under tons of marble. He was a tough old bird, wasn't he?" The two sat in silence for a while, sad to see the last of the man who gave his life to help capture Silverman.

"He gave me my one and only chance to escape, Agent. He's dead and Silverman's still alive and out there somewhere. I know we can't get them all—not right now, anyway—but I can help you make a deep crack in their foundation. The president knows all about the *Galatea Initiative* and has the *Burn List*. He has their full confession on voice and video, too. Others will take it from here, and they'll have an easier job of it once we start the ball rolling. No sir, I'm not going anywhere. I'm staying right here to see it through for you and Jill and Mr. X."

***

Carter left the hospital without interrogating the enforcer. He had the beginnings of a plan in mind, and he needed some time to think it through.

*If this guy saw or heard something I can use or knows where the JASONS and Silverman are hiding, we may still be able to capture them. The main thing is, though, I have to find a way to use him to my advantage so that all of it stops right now without us having to worry about who they are and where they are from one generation to the next. Justice is what I'm after. Screw the law.*

A never-ending swarm of people propelled Carter along the street. Soon, it became a sort of white noise, and his mind was free to wander.

*At least the director will be spending all his future Christmases in a federal penitentiary. General Breen has a little bomb waiting on his doorstep, too. He doesn't know it yet, but he's going to rat out the entire Department of Defense and still walk out of court one sorry, ruined piece of shit.*

333

His mind was a jumble of evidence and witnesses, but it was clear that forensics would play a key role in any convictions they hoped to get. He felt sure there was something he overlooked, but the harder he tried to remember what it was, the more elusive it became.

\*\*\*

Five minutes later, he burst through the lab doors just as Seacrest was walking past them holding test tubes of blood samples she hoped would prove he'd been drugged. She crashed to the floor yelling obscenities, just barely managing to prevent them from breaking. Seacrest stood up, red in the face and madder than a hornet. "What in the holy hell was *that*?!"

Carter winced and helped her up. "I'm sorry, I'm sorry, but I have to talk to you…"

"Slow the hell *down*, Carter! I'm right in the middle of running a toxicology test on your blood, which I'm fairly certain will match the drug given to the three women and Michael. Whatever it is can keep for a few minutes." She stole a sideways glance at her supervisor who looked furious for a change. She threw Carter a look of warning.

Carter tried again. "Agent Seacrest, this can't wait. You've got to process the skin underneath my nails and check Monty's, too."

"*What*?! You have Silverman's skin under your nails, and you're just remembering it *now*?"

"Yes! Assuming Monty also has Silverman's skin under his nails, we can place the same man who interrogated Monty last night at the location where I was ambushed the night before. Do you know what that means?"

Seacrest put down her test tubes and stood still. Her thoughts were moving faster than the speed of light; standing perfectly still helped her catch them. "*I …I…Yessss…YES! I DO!!* It means that if you test positive for the same drug that the other four had in them, if Monty and you can both give me viable D.N.A samples, if the drug is still in your system *and* if the D.N.A. in both samples match Silverman's…

"Carter! You can prove the same man who drugged you, drugged the other four. We know the *Silver Man's* real name now, so all we have to do is compare his D.N.A. to the results I get from testing you and Monty. If they all match, we've got him! And Monty knows his face! He saw him last night! We can all testify and back it up with hard evidence! *Forensic* evidence! We have Red's video to prove the meetings really occurred and the *Burn List* from Florio's computer! If we connect the *Silver Man* to *Hyzopran* and both your abductions, we can also connect him, circumstantially, to its theft from Meese's lab, the *Collective*, the *Burn List*, the killings, and the *Galatea Initiative*.

"That's everything, Carter, *everything!* And with the voice and video wire, it's not so circumstantial anymore. With testimony, we have an actual shot at this if we can find him. *Hooray!!!!*"

She got right down to work, carefully swabbing the underside of his nails to collect epithelial cells. She issued orders without looking up or stopping what she was doing.

"Contact *New York Presbyterian Hospital* and tell them we need a viable D.N.A. sample from underneath Mr. Montgomery's fingernails, *STAT!* It must be delivered to this lab for analysis as soon as humanly possible. I'm not going to lose that evidence because some overeager nurse went in there to clean him up!"

Her boss looked thunderstruck.

She knew she'd crossed the line, but the risk of losing vital evidence was greater than her interest in stroking his ego. Besides, Fischetti had always backed her up before, and she rather enjoyed the fact that her supervisor knew it. "I'm sorry, sir. I would do it myself if I wasn't already doing two things at once. There's no one else here to help."

He didn't budge.

*"I said **NOW**, sir!"*

He'd never heard Seacrest's *'don't fuck with me; JUST DO IT!'* tone of voice and jumped like he'd been jabbed in the rump with a long, sharp needle. He made that call so fast that Seacrest felt ashamed of herself. Well, *almost.*

"Carter, you haven't been home since the morning after you were attacked, so even with a day and a half lost, I should be able to find trace amounts of D.N.A. under your nails."

As soon as she was finished, Carter barreled out of the lab and ran straight back to the hospital to make certain Monty's swab was done and delivered directly into his own hands and then into hers.

335

*** 

Monty was relieved to see Carter. "Before you run back to the lab, there's one thing I forgot to tell you. The thing is, Silverman may still be untouchable, even with the mounting evidence against him."

"What? Why? I don't understand!"

"You see, the space race was on, and we had to beat the Russians to the moon. Not to be the first ones there, but because of what was *already* there—evidence of U.F.O's. Russia was never the threat they were made out to be. You see, because there was a common threat to all countries, there was no limit to what Silverman could ask for and get. No rules to follow. No red tape. Once they took him to Area 51, no law could touch him and no army could stop him.

"Out of everyone who ever tried to figure out what the hell the military ferreted away out there—before his time and even after—Silverman was the only one who could make sense of the flying machines, gadgets, technology, materials and even some of...*them*. All he had to do was walk in there, take a look around, and sleep on it for a few nights. He said he could see whole machines and processes in his mind in 3-D. The pieces and parts just floated around and around in his head, taking themselves apart and putting themselves back together again just the way they did in Tesla's head. And Einstein's. And Steven Jobs'. He didn't even have to reverse engineer most of it.

"Agent Carter, he was the one who took us from huge bulky televisions with vacuum tubes to transistors and from micro-chips to Nano-chips. We've lived like cavemen one day and extra-terrestrials the next. There are things going on in space that he's responsible for, and we still have no idea what they are. They need him, even if he is crazy."

It was now absolutely essential that Carter find a way to stop the *JASONS* without having to bring anyone to trial.

*** 

Later that afternoon, Carter went to see Fischetti. He wasn't interested in hearing anything the man had to say, but Carter had something to say to him. Keeping his voice low and hard and devoid of facial expression, he dove into deep water.

"Sir, there will be absolutely no negative spin from my team concerning this office as a result of our findings in the investigation. Internal Affairs can decide that for themselves. The media and the public will only be told that the thrill killers have been caught and prosecuted. I'm not going to pin a conspiracy on you or this agency. I only want the killings to stop, and I've got a way to do it."

Fischetti opened his mouth to speak.

Carter kept talking. "It won't be messy. No loose ends. I'm going to do this quietly...for the integrity of the Bureau."

Fischetti's mouth was still open when Carter slammed the door behind him.

# Chapter Thirty Five

Carter breezed into the interrogation room armed with the kind of ammunition that never failed to produce results. He told the truth. "I've got bad news for you, Goliath. Clayton Artemus Montgomery, also known as Arthur Moreland, is very much alive and ready to testify against you. With the evidence we already have, I figure you should be out in, oh..." Carter stared at the ceiling pretending to do a calculation. "...let's just round it out to about 150 years, or so. Give or take a few."

The no-neck had assumed Montgomery's flying leap through the thick, lead-paned glass of a second story window finished him off. It began to dawn on him that he might take the fall for something a lot more serious than assault and battery, so he tried to bluff his way out of it. "Ain't dat duh guy duh papers said was somekindova nut or somethin'? You know, duh one what stole a homemade drug, went crazy killin' people fuh nuttin', an' trieda kill duh old man we was protectin' at duh *Brooklyn Navy Yawd*? What's any uh dat gotta do wid me, huh? I donno nuttin'!"

"Yes, well, unfortunately that's neither here nor there. Look, let's try it again another way, just for me, O.K.? I would hate to leave here knowing we weren't able to come to some kind of an arrangement that was agreeable to both of us. It'd make me feel like..." Carter shrugged his shoulders. "Like we weren't friends."

He stopped the camcorder from filming the interrogation. "Look, I don't give a shit anymore about you, the rules or the limits of the justice system. I'm telling you *now* buddy—off the record—you're going to make the *Collective* and their meetings and murders go away, or you'll rot in here until they carry you out in a pine box."

"I awreddy tol' yooo, I donno nuttin'!"

The giant was starting to sweat, and that was just the way Carter wanted it. He paused, leaned over the table where the enforcer was shackled and dropped all pretenses.

"You were apprehended at the scene of a crime. You admitted you were hired to protect the old man. Mr. Montgomery and I have skin samples from the three of you under our nails. Do you know what D.N.A. testing is, Goliath? It means that no one in the world can help you now. No one except me."

He paused to let that sink in. Then he gave up. "You need it spelled out for you, don't you?"

Carter's question was met with stony silence.

"All right, here it is. We got the entire thing recorded on the lapel cam Mr. Montgomery was wearing. When you yanked the wire off him, we kept right on rolling. I'm afraid, *Goliath*, you're officially screwed." Carter gave him a nice, long look of helplessness and shrugged again.

He got up and paced. That was always a great way to make people nervous; it was how they knew the game was on. "Three women and a man were drugged and had their minds hijacked by the *Silver Man*—or the '*old man*', as you call him. They were programmed to commit murder for him. All four had the same drug in their system at the time the assassinations were to take place, and all four had been at one of his meetings the evening before. We know the drug only stays in the system for 48 hours, so we can pinpoint the time of ingestion easily. They were all dosed at the meetings hosted by the 'old man'.

"We can produce hundreds of people who will testify that they were drugged without their knowledge or permission at the meetings they attended. Our lab tests show, *definitively*, that these four individuals were high on the drug and were psychotic when they committed the murders. Know what that means? It means they're not guilty. They're off the hook." Carter snapped his fingers. "Just like that."

"But someone has to swing for it, so it might as well be you. I am going to testify, *under oath*, that I saw you stealing a black drawstring bag containing one hundred vials of *Hyzopran* from one of those meetings we raided. You were followed every minute of every day until you felt safe enough to sell it on the street. To kids. I am

339

also going to let it be known that when you were caught, literally holding the bag, you turned it over to us in exchange for a plea bargain. So you see, big guy, there's no way out for you. No one's going to stick their neck out for a strong-arm from Mulberry Street. There's a big, red, bulls-eye on your back, and all I plan to do about it is sit back and enjoy the show."

"I nevva stole drugs, and I ain't nevva sold drugs to no kids! I ain't stupid, mista. I know you gotta prove all o' dis. You can't getta conviction widdout proof. I got friends, mista. Big friends. Know whad I mean? I don' think you wanna screw around wid my friends."

Carter stopped pacing and sat down, perfectly calm and unconcerned. The more he waited, the angrier the Neanderthal got.

"Yeah. Yora big man right now. A *real big man* wid me sittin' hea in chains. But that ain't gonna last long, *stunad*. Montgomery's a dead man. He ain't *nevva* gonna tawk, an' I ain't got a worry in da woyld."

Having lived in Boston his whole life, Carter was very familiar with the word *"stunad"*. Goliath had just called him a moron, which amused him very much. "Oh, I know you think there are people who can make this go away, but they won't, Goliath. Not for you. I've got Montgomery protected, and he's our number one witness. I have mountains of evidence to use against you, *stronzo.*

"Maybe you don't quite understand me, so I'll make myself perfectly clear. If you don't cooperate with me, right now, this information and far more gets leaked to the media. That means T.V. News. The internet. The whole ball of wax. *Capeesch?* The public won't care that you're a 'nobody from nowhere' who doesn't know 'nuttin'. They'll rip you limb from limb the minute you step out these doors. You'll never make it to court."

"O.K., O.K! Let's play ball. Whaddya want?"

"You're going to ask your *own* organization for protection. It's worldwide, and much more powerful than the old man's. *La Cosa Nostra* owns the shadows, and that's the beauty of my plan. You're going to start a fight that'll keep the *JASONS* in check until we can find them all and crucify them. All you have to do is whisper the request in your Godfather's ear. Unless you prefer not to involve them. Your choice."

"Gimme a break! If I go da my own people an' ask for protection,

*I'll* be the one what gets wacked." He paused and looked down at the floor. "They ain't even gonna break a sweat ova me, mista."

"Ah, but that's where you're wrong! We know you have no knowledge of the old man's operation, but nobody else knows that. If your people think you know where he does business and with whom, you'll be a hero for helping them secure valuable territory and profits all over the world. Your people need to believe that their survival is in jeopardy and that you've come to warn them of it. That, they'll understand."

Carter was having a high old time, now. They'd buy the whole story—hook, line, and sinker—if one of their own went downtown to tell it. "The *JASONS* have to assume their enemies are everywhere. You're not going to get wacked, because I'm going to arm you with enough evidence to convince your *capo* that a war is brewing and that you've come to him like Christ, to save them all. As long as they can keep the *JASONS* looking over their own shoulders for the foreseeable future, we have a deal, and you go free. If, however, you refuse to do this little favor for us, or fail to make them understand the urgency of the coming crisis, you stay here and take your chances. You can hope for the best, of course, but you'd better expect the worst."

The enforcer opened his mouth, but Carter cut him off. "If you decide to sit tight and wait it out, we will arm you with no evidence at all. That means there'll be no reason for your organization to feel threatened in any serious way or feel especially inclined to protect you. In fact, I think you're right; here in jail, you're nothing but a liability to both organizations. The *JASONS* will have to assume you shared vital inside information, so they'll have to keep you quiet at any cost. If your organization thinks you were responsible for starting something they'll have to finish, you're toast. This fight will happen with or without you, Goliath, because if you don't help us, I'm going to make sure both sides think you talked. So what's it going to be, *stunad*? Yes or no?"

The gargantuan sat and thought. He wiped a hand across the sweat streaming down his face. Carter waited, cool as a cucumber. Finally he looked up. He was a simple man, after all, and all he wanted now was to go home.

"Yes".

\*\*\*

Carter walked past the first of three cells holding *The Unholy Three* and stopped there. "Up until now, every single decision you've made has led you here. You have one chance, and one chance only, to save yourself. You'll never walk out of here if you don't take it, and that's just exactly the way it stands."

He paused.

"Do you want to pay for crimes engineered by someone else? Don't you know you wouldn't be here today if the *Silver Man* had been caught before you went to a *Collective* meeting? He didn't give a damn about your economic plight. He didn't care about you. Everything he said during his speeches was nonsense meant to attract pockets of scared, angry people to his events. And why? It's the same old story, ladies. He wanted the people in his way to be moved out of his way, and he wanted to tear everything down so he could be the one to build it all back up the way *he* wanted it for himself and his friends.

"He lied to you, used you and threw you on the dung heap. If he's not stopped, he'll grab everything he can while you rot in here for the rest of your lives, victims of your own ignorance and jealousy. You were had. Right from the beginning. He's as mad as a hatter, and you were mad to believe in him."

Carter strolled to the second cell, stopped, and went on. "When did you decide to build walls instead of bridges? You told us you went there because the one percenters put you in an untenable position. You wanted things to be fair to everyone. So when did you decide to look out for number one and screw everyone else? You walked into those hate rallies with your eyes open and your mind closed. You're *worse* than he is; you listened to him and *applauded*!"

Carter made his way to the third cell, stopped again, and made his final point. "You don't cheat or rob people, because you know it's wrong! You don't hurt or kill people who have it better than you do, because it's wrong! And you don't fight wars to make the world a better place because wars never end and they never lead to permanent peace.

"What do you do, instead? You try to understand the other guy's point of view. You tolerate and respect all the puzzling, quirky, great and wonderful things that make us *different. And the same.* You help your neighbor if you can, and if you can't, you offer him a shoulder to cry on. When you die, God won't care if you were a king or a beggar. He will not ask you how successful you were in business; he will only ask if you tried to make your corner of the map a little better, any way you could. You see, all that really matters is that you share an open and generous heart with the world. If we could all do that, I wouldn't have to put people in cages."

Carter walked back to the middle cell so that all three girls could see him. "If you receive any mercy at all, it'll only be because you helped us catch a killer and a traitor to all mankind. You want a better America? A better world? Start with yourselves! Give us anything you can on the *Silver Man.*"

Carter looked at his watch. He had an appointment with Fischetti, and it was time to go. He strode out without another word.

*** 

Carter left thinking about Alison, the only one of *The Unholy Three* worth any consideration at all.

*Alison's different. All she ever knew was abuse, punishment, self-recrimination, and self-sacrifice. No wonder she doesn't know up from down. Of the three of them, she's the only one who killed, and yet her nature is not that of a killer. In every one of these scenarios, she's the one trying to protect, defend and save people. If it hadn't been for her, Agent Deeprose wouldn't be here today. The others would be here, but not her.*

*I'm going to see what I can do to get her moved into a psychiatric hospital. She needs help and compassion, not jail time. The other two can go straight to blazes for all I care.*

# Chapter Thirty Six
*One Month Later*

Carter faced a great failing in himself when he told the three imprisoned women that the only thing that mattered in the end was if and how you were remembered by the people whose lives you touched. The fact is, he never understood or connected with anyone other than Seacrest. He wasn't sure he ever even had the ability. Refusing to face that truth, he steeped himself in a quest to find answers through the study of Buddhism.

*Then I went around pontificating to everyone else like a pompous ass. I was the man with all the answers. The man who had it all together and never broke under pressure.*

He learned, from the *Silver Man,* that he had no right to impose his philosophy or his answers on anyone. He'd turned to Eastern religion and philosophy because Christianity didn't give him the answers he wanted to hear. He used Zen to maintain his cool instead of using it to find a way of controlling or changing his own mind and behavior. He never tried to understand himself or his needs and desires, and so he had no framework with which to construct his own philosophy, meaning or purpose for living.

Carter took a cold, hard look at his life and didn't like what he saw. He'd used his job as an excuse to avoid emotion, commitment, and the difficult choices that could have defined his true desires. The things that disturbed him, the things he didn't understand, he ignored.

*I could have dragged out those boxes and examined the contents any time I wanted to, but I didn't.*

Carter knew he'd never given back half the emotional support he took from Seacrest. She never asked him to share more of himself than the little he could manage.

*The worst of it was that I knew it all along, but I didn't want to do the work it would've taken to be a better person and a better friend and husband. That ends right now. Today. She's all the meaning I need and all the purpose I want.*

\*\*\*

Carter was knee-deep in paper work, but he took the time to visit Agent Deeprose at the hospital every day. "We've started to cast a net wide enough to catch all our mystery men, and it's mainly because of the big pieces you put together right after the old curator's death."

"How're y'all gonna do that, sir? That strong-arm won't do us any good, and the *JASONS* have been operatin' globally for generations. Do you know somethin' Ah don't, sir?"

"Washington feels we have enough circumstantial evidence to warrant a full scale investigation. The F.B.I. has been compromised, so they're out of it. We can't afford to trust the C.I.A., D.O.D., D.O.J., or the military. Independent investigations will focus on evidence of treason and collusion. It'll be a long road, but we'll get there."

"But sir, by that time, the *JASONS* will have gone underground and traded our current suspects for new faces. We'll never get them if we have to wait so long just to get the process going."

"Well, that's just it, Agent Deeprose. I was able to obtain a helping hand from the enforcer's home organization. They made me an offer I couldn't refuse."

"Home *what*? *Whose* help? Ah don't understand, sir."

"I just pointed out that if the mob had a little tangible proof of who killed one of their own and framed the other, they'd have a real reason to protect their interests and territory while they still could, and they agreed. The enforcer goes free as long as we have their help ferreting out the *JASONS* and as long as they can keep them too scared to move forward in any way. As long as the killings stop, I'm satisfied."

"What about a trial, sir? If the bodyguard goes free, who's going to stand trial in his place so our evidence can be presented?"

"There won't be a trial for him, Agent. The deal is that the mob helps catch or kill the *JASONS* and for that they get back their new man of the hour. They'll have their revenge and protect their own interests at the same time. What could be better than that? We still have the F.B.I, *The Unholy Three* and Michael to stand trial, though. I'm trying to work out a deal for Alison that would take her out of prison and put her into a place that can help her get well and back into society so she has a chance to lead a full and happy life. She saved your life, you know."

"Ah understand that, sir, but…"

"Agent, no one's going to get away with anything. I promise you that. Michael, Eliza, Clara and Alison will all be tried and sentenced. It absolutely must go down the way I've arranged it or the *JASONS* will never be stopped. The heads of the families of organized crime all over the world are the only ones with the kind of reach and money it'll take to end it."

"All right, Agent Carter, but Ah'm not gonna soft soap anythin' those three devils did to me. Even Alison. She may've tried to call 'em off at the last minute, but that's all. If that motorcycle man came around the bend one second later or had hesitated before stoppin', he would've been too late."

Carter broke out in a sweat.

*You idiot! She was almost beaten to death!*

"I'm…" Carter cleared his throat. "I apologize. I was tactless and hurtful. Sometimes I forget that what I have to say is not as important as how it'll make you feel when I say it. If there was any other way to do this, we would."

Deeprose looked out the window next to her bed and took time to think before she answered. "Is that all of it, sir?"

"That's all of it, except that Mr. X is gone. I don't know if he died at *Admiral's Row* or just wants to retain his anonymity, but he won't be around to help us wrap this up. The director of the F.B.I. is in custody, and he's talking his head off. I heard Fischetti turned state's evidence. I'm glad; it was his only hope."

"Where do we go from here, sir?"

"Agent Deeprose, you did a hell of a job under circumstances that I consider exceptional for any seasoned pro. No one can call you a rookie, anymore. The *Galatea Initiative* is dead, or will be. For us, the case is closed. I'm sorry you had to pay such a high price for it, and I'm even sorrier that I left you alone with nowhere to turn for support.

"Do we still have our jobs?"

"If you still want this job, you'll always have a place here. As for myself and Agent Seacrest, well, even if they ask us to stay, I'm not sure we can. For now, we're focusing on wrapping up loose ends and Christmas gifts, and we don't want to think any further out than that."

"Agent Carter, Ah wonder if Ah could trouble you to sit down for a few minutes. There's something Ah'd like to tell you while it's fresh in my mind."

\*\*\*

"Agent Carter, Ah didn't see my daddy's face when Ah thought Ah was goin' to die. Ah always thought he'd be the last thing on m'mind when Ah died, but it wasn't. Ah regretted not bein' around to finish the job with you and Agent Seacrest. Y'all accepted me right away, gave me room to breathe, and regardless of what you think you might or might not have done durin' this investigation, you were *always* there when Ah needed a soundin' board. Ah can't say my education this year's had anythin' to do with learnin' procedure or even the rules..." She smiled. "...but Ah still want to thank y'all for givin' me the opportunity to shine. And Ah *did* shine, sir, didn't Ah?"

"You sure did, Agent Deeprose."

"Ah'm stayin', sir."

\*\*\*

Carter stepped into Fischetti's office and fell heavily into a seat, bracing himself for what he had to tell him. It was time they came to an understanding. He looked around quickly and saw half packed boxes, everywhere.

"Sir, I cut a deal with the bodyguard. It was the best we could do in a no-win scenario. He goes free and his organization agrees to help us hunt the *JASONS* and keep a friendly eye on anyone we think might be the target of an assassination."

He handed the deputy director a file containing psychiatric evaluations of the four perpetrators in custody. "We both know you manipulated this investigation, sir. I don't know what the Bureau means to do about it, and frankly, I don't care. But I'm here to make a deal with you. I'll keep *La Cosa Nostra* working for us and back you up with the Feds as a lone hero hung out to dry if you'll get Alison out of jail and into a psychiatric hospital."

"I don't make deals, Agent Carter, but I'm prepared to do anything I can to make restitution."

"Three out of the four deserve anything they get. I have no issue with that. But I want special consideration for Alison. Read the file, sir. I'm asking you to do the right thing by her. Alison needs to be placed in a facility—a *good* one—where she can get the intensive help she needs over a period of perhaps several years. I don't know if she'll ever be able to make it on her own, but she's the only one of the bunch with a heart and a conscience. She was tricked into everything she did. She's not planning to defend herself in court, sir, but prison will kill her. She deserves a break for once in her life. Let's be the ones to give it to her."

Fischetti sat back in his chair and closed his eyes. He squeezed them shut and pinched the bridge of his nose. After a moment, he opened them and sighed. "O.K., Carter, I promise you, I'll do everything in my power to get Alison's sentence commuted to an indefinite amount of time served in a sanitarium with a first-rate reputation. I will present the evidence in this folder after I read it, of course, and meet with the prison psychiatrist to hear her diagnosis, prognosis, and professional recommendations. If she agrees with you, we'll talk to Alison about it. That's the best I can do."

Carter nodded and rose to leave. He'd said all that he had to say and had reached the only agreement he cared to make with the deputy director. Now he had to go home and decide what he wanted to do next.

"Agent Carter, wait. Please. Sit down for one more moment. There is something I'd like you to know before you leave my office. I may never get the chance to say it to you again."

*Damn! I was almost out the door.*

However, he sat.

"I know you think I'm about to feed you a load of bullshit. Relax, I'll spare you that nonsense. It's far too late, and it's over now anyway, but I'm not a bastard, and I do feel the need to explain myself to you. I'm far from innocent but not quite guilty, either.

"Here it is in a nutshell. Whether you believe it or not, I have upheld my duties to the highest degree for three decades. I did *not* know the Bureau was rotten until these murders began. As it turns out, for the past sixty years, *at the very least*, Bureau superiors have *all* been working for the *JASONS*. That is why the Feds view me in a slightly different light than they do the director and the rest of them.

"I won't try to say I didn't know what I was asked to do. I did. As I saw it, the only way to save you was to sacrifice Montgomery. That's not an excuse. It's just the facts.

"I had two choices: obey or disappear. But the world's not a big enough place to hide in, anymore. I've already admitted to the boys upstairs that I intentionally steered your team in the wrong direction time after time during this investigation. That's all of it, Agent."

"Sir, that's *not* quite all of it. When push came to shove, you had to decide whether to save me and risk your neck or commit yourself to the other side. You knew the net was closing in on them, so it's just possible you tried to make yourself *look* like a hero. Why should I or anyone else have any faith or confidence in you now? How can anyone ever trust you again? I really didn't expect you to be here today; I thought I might be speaking to a temporary replacement. Aren't you more ashamed to be talking to me right now than you might have been if you tucked your tail and just quietly slipped away into retirement?"

"No, Agent Carter, I'm not, because I made the decision to face the music and to give you and everyone else the chance to tell me what they thought of me. You just had yours. I won't try to change your mind, but I will always feel deep shame and sorrow that I lost your respect and trust."

He sighed and swung his chair around to the window behind him. "Whether I'm prosecuted or not, I know I'm a traitor, because I feel like one." Fischetti turned back to Carter. "That's all I wanted to say, Agent Carter. If you want to go, you're excused."

Carter got halfway out of his seat before Fischetti spoke again. "However, there are a few new developments I'd like to share with you, if you're interested."

Carter raised an eyebrow and sat back down.

*Damn it!*

"Well, sir?"

"There are going to be some changes. I'm being promoted to director of the New York office."

"Excuse me?"

"Yes, I know it's a shock, Agent. It's time for me to get out of the game, and I told them so upstairs, but they think it took balls to go against the director and stand up in front of that firing squad to protect your body and take custody of the bodyguard. I can't believe no one searched you to make sure you were dead, but I think they were more afraid of Agent Seacrest than they were of facing the director."

They exchanged their first brief smile of understanding since Carter had come to work for him.

"They hardly even bothered to look for Montgomery. They had what they came for. Everyone figured, I guess, that I'd get it in the back on the way home, and that would be the end of that—killed in the line of duty. I rode to the hospital with the prisoner, though, and somehow I'm still alive."

*How can they consider him for anything else but the glue factory? And he's getting promoted to the big office?! There absolutely can't be any such thing as divine justice or this man would be shitting bricks in a federal prison right now.*

"There's no one who can fill in for the director from any state bureau because of, well, you know, they don't know who's clean and who's dirty. Until they sweep the house and vet new agents, the top brass decided they'd rather keep an eye on me than someone else.

"They're giving me a chance to show them I am what I say I've always been, and I'm taking it. Then, as you suggested, one of these days, I'll slip quietly away into retirement. I'm a very lucky man, Carter. I should have been shot. That was the plan."

*Damn straight, sir.*

Carter knew he was expected to say something to the contrary, but he didn't say a word. He just sat there, waiting.

Fischetti turned scarlet but forged ahead. "Yes. Well. I'm moving into the new office this afternoon, and I'm bringing Liz with me."

"Who's your replacement, sir?"

"The top brass has hand-picked Natalie Rodgers for deputy director despite the public relations mess she's been dealing with since Agent Dawkins almost killed the prime suspect in Arleen

Montgomery's murder. She bleeds Bureau blue. It'll be at least a month or so before she can transition and be brought up to speed on our cases.

"In the meantime, I want you to step in as the acting deputy director. I'd give you time to think it over, but I need to know now if you plan to stay on here. There's no one else I can trust, and I do trust you, even if you don't trust me. Will you take it? It would be a great opportunity to make your mark in the executive office. With experience as acting deputy director from time to time, especially in New York City, you could eventually write your own ticket."

Carter looked more than a little dubious.

*There are three possibilities here: he's doing this for me because he believes in keeping his friends close and his enemies even closer; the brass wants me to keep tabs on him to see where he leads us; or he really is a straight arrow career man who got in way over his head and the Bureau is giving him the chance to prove it. Maybe he really does want me watching his back.*

"Look, Carter, I'm asking you to do what you've always done unhesitatingly and without fail. The right thing. So?"

"An office chair actually looks pretty good to me, *temporarily*. If I accept your offer to be acting deputy director now and again, I want the power to give Agent Deeprose a special commendation and a promotion for bravery above and beyond the call of duty. Agent Seacrest risked her life to test a drug that might have killed her. I want her to be named Lab Director. I don't care what you do with that jerk down there, but I want him gone. Additionally, Jill should have the authority she deserves. She'll take it anyway, you know."

They both broke out in broad smiles and shook their heads.

Fischetti described the entire scene at *Admiral's Row* as it unfolded. Carter couldn't believe his ears. "She really is something else, isn't she, Agent Carter? Her anger is worse than the wrath of God. I wouldn't want to be on the wrong end of it. She scared the living hell out of those men. I wouldn't be surprised if they wet their shorts on the way home."

Liz came in and offered the men coffee.

*Is she actually smiling at me? The only time I ever saw her smile was to show her fangs to some poor intern. I guess miracles really do happen.*

351

The two men sipped their coffee as they pondered the choices they'd made over the course of their careers.

Director Fischetti raised his eyebrows as a stray thought raced back to him. "Agent Carter, if you don't mind telling me one small detail, just who the hell blew the back door off *Admiral's Row*? And how'd you manage to get your hands on C-4?"

"I didn't, but I was very glad to discover that Mr. X *did*. Now *there's* someone I wouldn't want to meet in a dark alley."

"Neither would I, Agent. Just think, I could have had him on my side the whole time, and I thought he was just an old crackpot." He shook his head and chuckled. "I won't make *that* mistake again."

"You won't be able to, sir. I'm fairly certain he never made it out of the building."

# Chapter Thirty Seven
*Christmas Eve*

Carter plodded into the apartment with disheveled hair and his tie askew.

"Long day at the office, Carter?" Seacrest tossed a magazine onto the coffee table and yawned. "At least you're on active duty again. I can't wait to be cleared. House cleaning is not therapeutic, just in case you were wondering."

Her usual brand of sarcasm seemed so dear to him now that he started to laugh, and once he did, he couldn't stop. He laughed so hard he had to sit down and hold his stomach with both hands to stop it from hurting. Seacrest knew she hadn't said anything particularly funny, but being a woman, she recognized the final release of the burdens he'd been carrying around since well before they moved to New York.

"Jill, I can't even remember the last time I laughed. Oh God, my stomach!"

"Carter, I've waited a long time for this."

He stood and held his hand out to her. Taking his hand, she stood and melted into his broad chest, inhaling his scent. He always smelled so damn good! Then she looked up at him.

"What're you looking at?"

"Nothing, Carter. Just looking." She smiled into his chest knowing his heart was hers.

Carter snapped his fingers over his head and commanded his voice-activated assistant. "Alexa, play *Stardust*, by Hoagy Carmichael. Dim the lights to the lowest setting, and show us some real stars while you're at it."

A million diamond-white stars emerged from the ceiling and winked at them as soft music seeped into the room out of nowhere and everywhere. They began to move to the melody that had always meant so much to them.

"This is spectacular, Carter! How are you doing it?"

"That's a trade secret, my girl."

They dipped and swayed and twirled their way to a new intimacy. She nibbled on his lower lip, the song forgotten. Carter felt it travel from his mouth all the way down to the pit of his stomach. He grabbed her upper arms, jerked her away from himself roughly and looked at her in a way he never had before. He looked savage and ferocious.

Seacrest felt electricity and masculinity all around her. She looked shocked but waited for whatever came next.

He jerked her back to him and planted a long, hard kiss on her mouth. A hundred years of pent up emotion fell away in that moment. Their hands traveled everywhere, learning each other all over again. They made love on the cushy carpet, smashing and obliterating the silence and sadness that had grown between them. They were one again, each an extension of the other, neither knowing nor caring where one began and the other ended.

\*\*\*

Time drifted as they lay on the floor watching the stars. At some point, Seacrest returned to earth and turned to Carter, who had temporarily lost all capacity for speech and thought.

"I do, too, Carter."

"Do too, what, honey?"

"Love you. Play *Stardust* again a little later so we can actually dance to the end of the song this time, hmmm?"

\*\*\*

They sat together like two teenagers in their little kitchen, spreading thick slabs of brie on French bread and sipping sweet, red wine. The atmosphere tonight was cozy and romantic, as if they were the only two people left in the world and were glad of it.

"Carter, I saw something strange at *Admiral's Row*."

Happily chewing away on his bread and cheese, Carter lifted an eyebrow and waited for her to continue.

Seacrest blushed. "Don't you dare laugh at me, but as much as I hate to admit it, I saw a sign in the sky. Right over your head."

"Really?" He did a lousy job of hiding a smirk. "And what exactly was this sign you think you saw, my love?"

"It was…well, it was a big tree with a lot of branches."

He looked like he didn't understand what she meant. "A tree?"

"Yes, a *tree*, Carter, a *tree*. The stars made a crazy pattern in the sky right over your head, and it looked just like a big *tree*."

"And this was a sign because…"

"Carter! Stop laughing at me! You *know* what tree!"

He did become serious, though, because she was. "It was the tree of life. What do you think it meant?"

"There was one star at the very tip of the highest branch that was brighter than all the others. I thought it meant that wherever you were, and even though you were gone from me, you were happy.

"Carter, I changed my mind. You don't have to change for me. I don't need you to go on some great expedition of self-discovery, and I don't care if you ever clear out your stupid mind boxes. You're perfect. If you can live with my bossiness and dark humor and still love me as much as you do, I wouldn't ask you to dial back the Buddha in you for all the tea in China. All I want is to be with you every day of every season of my life."

"I've always known that, honey, but I want to take this journey; I need to do it because I'm not satisfied with myself anymore. In a nutty sort of way, this whole experience with the *Silver Man* gave me the answers I've been looking for my whole life. Wanna here what I've learned?"

"Fire away."

"I've been lost and didn't know how to get home. Then the *Silver Man* showed me what life was like for a man who refuses to accept the world for what it is, who's incapable of recognizing his own weaknesses, and who tries desperately to force people to live by his rules and philosophy rather than try to understand and accept theirs. I don't have to change the world to feel fulfilled, Jill, I just need to change myself."

"You learned all that in a few days after ignoring it your whole life? I don't believe it. Who are you, sir, and what have you done with my husband?"

Carter got up and took a sheet of paper out of the junk drawer. "I've been keeping this here because it seemed like the right place to leave all my crap. I left the women's detention center last month with a lot on my mind, so I went back to the office and wrote down the things that I think are true, but don't feel comfortable with, yet. I made an appointment with the cognitive behavioral therapist I saw the night we went to the *Jazz Standard*. I don't care *why* we live, anymore; I'm going to learn *how* to live. Take a look at this."

## Carter's "Keep the Home Fires Burning" List

1. Knowing how to live is more important than knowing why I live and what may or may not come after death.

2. To know and understand myself is the road to understanding and helping the people around me.

3. Opening up my heart and speaking my mind is accepting that I'm as vulnerable as anyone else and that talking things over with someone I trust can help me make sense of things in a more objective manner.

4. Learning is not always linear in nature, and it's a journey with no end.

5. To move forward, I might sometimes have to take a few steps back.

6. I can't change the whole world, but I can change myself.

7. I can't protect myself from things that bother or confuse me by ignoring them.

8. To move past those things I can't seem to get over, I need to look at them, chew them and swallow them without forgetting their bitter taste.

9. Having wisdom means that people other than myself value my experiences and insights.

10. It's O.K. to change my mind.

11. Celebrate everything you can whenever you can.

12. Being a little silly sometimes is a good idea. Letting my guard down won't destroy the respect people have for me.

"*Wow!* This is a very ambitious list, darling, but tell me why you decided these changes are ones you want to make. I hope they're not here because I said they were important. Your list should reflect changes based on *your* needs, not mine."

"It does, honey, and the list will grow as I do."

"Have you decided, then, that Yin and Yang are no longer the cornerstone of your philosophy of personhood?"

"Actually, no. All I did was adjust my understanding of it as a result of everything that happened to us before and since we moved here. I decided that it's not my job to worry about the destination when it's all about the journey. If I had to describe Yin and Yang now, I'd say they're what we are when the journey begins as well as what we experience and learn from it along the way. I'd say the opposing forces within us are not good vs. bad; I'd say they're more like needing and being needed, giving and being given, understanding and being understood. I guess even extremes are normal in extreme situations. The point is, we change as our circumstances change. If sometimes one desire overpowers the other it's because it has to for our own good or even our own survival."

"Are you saying that the girls' extreme behavior was natural and acceptable based on the situation they were in?"

"No, honey. It's one thing to defend yourself when you're forced to, and that's what Alison did at the micro-brewery, but it's another to have options and choices and still choose the wrong ones, like the others did.

"Alison wanted friends so much that she developed an extreme sense of altruism to get them, but all it led to was extreme self-sacrifice. She couldn't find a happy medium, and that left her with nothing.

"On the other hand, Eliza's brutality and Clara's machinations, unchecked, would've left everyone *else* with nothing. Eliza was born to see life as a win or lose/eat or be eaten proposition. She was wired up for instinct only. Did you notice that when she was finally caught, she accepted it as fair and square?

"But, it's clear—to me, at least—that Clara *always* knew right from wrong, but her uncle taught her that people were inconsequential if her own desires were at stake. She learned that smart, successful people don't believe in win-win scenarios, so she got the things she wanted by lying and manipulating the people who stood in her way, and that extended even to himself. I think it's what killed him in the end.

"She'll still be denying her guilt and blaming the others when she's sentenced. Clara knows what shame and remorse are, but she's only ashamed of getting caught and remorseful of her exposure and punishment. She'll never accept responsibility for her actions, and she'll never walk out of those prison doors."

"And Michael?"

"Michael is scum. Instead of going directly to the police after the first *Collective* meeting, he planned to steal the vials of *Hyzopran* and proceeded to coerce the three girls into helping him do it. He's a three-time loser, Jill, and he's going down for this."

Seacrest handed him a glass of wine. "O.K. I get that, Carter, but I want to know one more thing; if the *Good Witch of the North* floated in here and asked you to sum up what you've learned from Silverman before you could click your heels three times and go home, what would you tell her?"

"That we can't all be saints or sinners with no in between. I think *Dr. Jekyll* would agree that you can't sustain an 'all or nothing' attitude without being consumed by it."

Seacrest's eyes grew wide. "So you learned the secrets of the universe from the *Silver Man,* three female convicts, and a fictional character straight out of a cautionary tale about playing God?"

"Well, yes. And Monty. And Agent Deeprose. Even Bill Fischetti and young Red."

"What about me, Carter?"

"Especially you, Jill. You were right; denying what I thought were undesirable emotions didn't mean I didn't have them. Not talking to you or anyone else about things put an insurmountable wall up between us. You should have been able to talk to me about yourself, but I made that impossible, and I'm sorry, baby. I'm so, *so* sorry."

"It wasn't all your fault, Carter; you had a little help from me. Promise me one thing, O.K.?"

"Anything."

"Practice expressing yourself here before unleashing your new self on the general public, will you please?"

\*\*\*

It was late Christmas evening when they heard three sharp knocks on their front door. "Oh, who can that be at this time of night, when lovers want to be left alone to stargaze?"

"I'll get it, Jill. I forgot to tell you I asked Agent Deeprose to stop by for a celebratory drink tonight. Director Fischetti contacted her at home today. She's cleared for duty. I'm giving her a commendation and a promotion."

"Well, open the door! After all, it's Christmas, and I want to hear all about hers with *Wilson*." Carter blushed and grimaced simultaneously.

The two women locked themselves in hugs. They talked and laughed at the same time and then did the same thing all over again and still understood each other perfectly. Carter was lost.

*Here, we go again...*

Before Deeprose left, Carter raced to the closet and shoved a box into her arms. "It's a Christmas present from us—a full length, hunter green winter coat. You're not down South anymore, Agent Deeprose, and the winters here are brutal. That little red thing you've been wearing falls woefully short of the mark. Jill and I want you to have it and to know that you're part of our family now. I promise you'll never be out on a limb again."

Deeprose had never been given anything so beautiful in her life. "Ah, don't know what to say! Oh my God, Ah just don't know what to say!"

Carter smiled. "That would be a first, Agent Deeprose. Merry Christmas from us to you."

"Thank you both so much. Ah feel the same way about y'all."

"Well," Carter said as the door closed, "that's another reason we need to stay at the Bureau, Jill. Agent Deeprose needs us."

"Not quite, Carter." She hugged him close and whispered in his ear, "We need *her*."

\*\*\*

In a small, quaint countryside with an unpronounceable name, *Galatea's* exquisite form reawakened in the hands of an ancient

359

sculptor named *Pygmalion*. His timeworn face looked like a sheet of thin parchment paper that had been crumpled up and smoothed out again, but his voice still contained the sharp edges of the corruption and vanities of his bygone youth.

"We must wait a little while longer, my dear, but when the time comes, I will make the world just as lovely and perfect as I made you."

He was no longer encumbered or impeded by the *JASONS* whose help he'd needed until technology caught up to the plans he'd devised more than two thousand years before. The vast resources he amassed over the past twenty centuries ensured that the very latest and top-secret advances could be applied to the perfection of his Nano-chip. Following the execution of Carter's team and everyone named on a new *Burn List*, it would be offered to and installed for excited new parents everywhere immediately following the birth of a child.

"I will still pull the strings to which all humanity dances. Ha, haaaaaaa! They won't be able to get enough of them! They'll have to order them *years* in advance!"

He raised his glass of schnapps and drank it down. The artist's fingers shook as he stroked her, so afraid was he of hurting the symbol of all his desires. "They think because they have forgotten us, we no longer exist. But when people forget, my dear, and they always do, we will return…as we always have and always will. And then we will make the world great again, according to my design and your image."

**To contact us or be added to the mailing list, send you email to:**

ven123star@yahoo.com

Place **The Killing Collective** in the subject line

**Turn the page for extras…**

# The Killing Collective—NYC Tour Guide

## Cloisters
www.metmuseum.org/visit/met-cloisters
99 Margaret Corbin Drive
New York, NY 10040
Tel: (212) 923-3700

Architectural styles: Romanesque and Medieval

The Cloisters is a museum in Upper Manhattan, New York City specializing in European medieval architecture, sculpture and decorative arts, and is part of the Metropolitan Museum of Art.

## Metropolitan Museum of Art
www.metmuseum.org/visit/met-fifth-avenue
1000 Fifth Avenue
New York, NY 10028
Tel: (212) 535-7710

The Met Fifth Avenue presents over 5,000 years of art spanning all cultures and time periods. Since the Museum opened its doors to the public in its current location in Central Park in 1880, its footprint has expanded to cover more than two million square feet. Today, art comes alive in the Museum's galleries and through its exhibitions and events, revealing both new ideas and unexpected connections across time and cultures.

**McGee's Pub**
http://mcgeespubny.com/
40 W 55th St
New York, NY 10019
Between Broadway & 8th Ave
Tel: (212) 957-3536

A friendly Irish neighborhood pub located in the heart of Hell's Kitchen and only 3 short blocks from the world famous Central Park, the Theater District and Times Square.

This triple decor of fun boasts 22 HDTV's, internet jukebox and top of the line sound system for customers' enjoyment located throughout the first and second floor bar and restaurants. We feature all the local, national and international sporting events here.

Located on our third floor is our Symphony Room, a great place for parties, special events and social get together. Serving lunch and dinner daily, we've got something to suit all our customers' needs.

**On Location Tours to McGee's Home of "How I Met Your Mother":**

McGee's is working with On Location Tours on their NYC TV & Movie Tour. Tours begin at 10 a.m. and arrive at 12:30 p.m. at McGee's Pub, the final stop on the tour.
For those of you who don't know, McGee's is the inspiration for McLaren's Pub on the hit TV series How I Met Your Mother. McGee's is offering a special 15% discount for customers on the tour.

**Mahayana Buddhist Temple**
http://mahayana.us/en/
City Campus Mahayana Temple
133 Canal Street, New York, NY 10002
Tel: (212) 925-8787

The Mahayana Buddhist Temple is one of the newest places on this list; nonetheless, with its colorful exterior and two golden lions guarding the door, it is one of the neighborhood's most alluring places to visit. The temple, which is situated at 133 Canal Street, is the largest Buddhist temple in New York City. If you make your way deep into the back, you'll find a 16-foot golden statue of the Buddha, also the largest in the city.

The temple was erected in 1996 by the Eastern States Buddhist Temple of America, Inc. (ESBT). After building several other smaller temples around the city, one of ESBT's co-founders, Annie Ying, saw that the many storefront temples in the city weren't large enough to host functions for a substantial amount of people. Mrs. Ying had the temple completed just in time for the 83rd birthday of James Ying, her husband and ESBT's other co-founder.

**Florence Gould Hall**
**http://www.fiaf.org/rental/index.html**
55 East 59th Street
New York, NY 10022
Tel: (646) 388-6669

Centrally located on the Upper East Side in an elegant Beaux-Arts building reminiscent of Paris, FIAF is steps from Central Park, the bustling energy of 5th Avenue, and Grand Central Station. Florence Gould Hall Theater

Florence Gould Hall, FIAF's premier venue, seats 361 guests and features a proscenium stage with state-of-the-art sound and projection equipment. With excellent acoustics and superb sight lines, the stage is perfect for corporate meetings, concerts, film screenings, and theater and dance performances. Opening in 1988, Florence Gould Hall is distinguished in NYC by its intimate atmosphere and classic jewel-box theater décor.

Available individually or with Tinker Auditorium or Le Skyroom, the venue can be customized according to request. FIAF also offers an on-site Box Office, full service catering packages, and professional meeting and event planners for the production of all types of special events.

## Zabar's

www.zabars.com/ZABARS_STORY.html
2245 Broadway at 80th Street
New York, NY 10024
(212) 787-2000

Founded by Louis Zabar, this gourmet emporium is one of the best known commercial landmarks of the neighborhood, and is known for its selection of bagels, smoked fish, caviar, coffee, olives, and cheeses. Zabar's is frequently referenced in popular culture. It is mentioned in the 1998 film *You've Got Mail, the 2009 TV series V,* and *episodes of Northern Exposure, Will & Grace, Dream On, The Green Inferno, How I Met Your Mother, Mad About You, Friends, Sex and the City, Broad City, The Nanny, Seinfeld, The Simpsons, The West Wing, Studio 60 on the Sunset Strip, 30 Rock, The Daily Show, The Colbert Report, Hart of Dixie, Castle, Pardon the Interruption, Law & Order,* and *Gossip Girl.* (Wikipedia)

## Bustan

bustannyc.com
487 Amsterdam Avenue, New York, NY 10024
Tel: (212) 595-5050

Bustan is a contemporary pan-Mediterranean restaurant that brings the shores of Southern Europe, Western Asia and North Africa to Manhattan's Upper West Side. Showcasing the region's culinary diversity, Bustan stands out in New York City's sea of Mediterranean restaurants with their distinctive palate-enticing multicultural approach to food.

## Jazz Standard

www.jazzstandard.com
116 E 27th St, New York, NY 10016
Tel: (212) 576-2232

One of NYC's largest jazz clubs, featuring new & established musicians. For over a decade, Jazz Standard has been setting the standard—world-class jazz, warm hospitality, pitch-perfect sound, and award-winning Southern cuisine and barbecue in an intimate and comfortable environment. As one of the world's top jazz venues, Jazz Standard hosts both legendary artists of today and bright stars of tomorrow.

## Blue Smoke

www.bluesmoke.com
info@bluesmoke.com
16 East 27th Street (between Park & Lexington)
Tel: (212) 447-7733

Southern food and BBQ

### The Story

Founded in 2002 by Danny Meyer's Union Square Hospitality Group, and named after the curl of blue smoke that rises out of perfectly smoked meat, Blue Smoke celebrates the diverse culinary traditions of the American South with a range of soulful barbecue classics alongside revived family recipes and new favorites from Executive Chef Jean-Paul Bourgeois. An all-American beverage menu complements the Southern cooking with a wide range of whiskeys, wines, cocktails, and craft beers from coast to coast.

The flagship Blue Smoke, with the club Jazz Standard, is located on East 27th Street in New York City, and a second location opened in 2012 in NYC's Battery Park City. Blue Smoke also has two Blue Smoke on the Road baseball concessions at Citi Field, home of the New York Mets, and the Washington Nationals ballpark. In 2013, Blue Smoke on the Road opened at Delta Terminal 4 in John F. Kennedy International Airport.

## Ben's Pizzeria

123 MacDougal Street
New York, NY 10012
Open until 5 a.m.
Tel: (212) 677-0976

Hot slices & people-watching at a counter with late-night hours near Washington Square Park.

**Ess-a-Bagel**
www.Ess-a-bagel.com
831 Third Avenue
New York, NY 10022
Tel: (212) 980-1010

"Essen or Esse" is German and Yiddish for "eat" or "Eating".

"Delicatessen" is a German loanword which first appeared in English in 1889 and is the plural of Delikatesse. In German it was originally a French loanword, délicatesse, meaning "delicious things (to eat)". Its root word is the Latin adjective delicatus, meaning "giving pleasure, delightful, pleasing". (Wikipedia)

**About Ess-a-Bagel**

Ess-a-Bagel, Inc., was established in 1976 on 21stStreet and 1st Avenue by Gene and Florence Wilpon and her brother Aaron Wenzelberg. By popular demand we have now come to midtown Manhattan. Coming from an Austrian baking family, it is not surprising that within two years our hand-rolled bagels were voted the best in the Tri-state area. We have continued to win national acclaim, not only for our bagels, but also for out luscious, appetizing salads, varieties of cream cheese, choice meats, and individualized catering orders. Ess-a-Bagel, Inc. has the finest assortment of cakes, pastries, rugelach, muffins and cookies. Espresso, cappuccinos, and multi-flavored cappuccinos are brewed to your individual taste. We have also added gourmet, flavored coffees brewed fresh every morning. Ask about our daily flavors. Ess-a-Bagel, Inc. has been known for our catering. All of our bagels, cake, fish, packaged salads and soups are certified kosher.

**Millenium Hotel**
www3.hilton.com/en/hotels/new-york/millenium-hilton-NYCMLHH/index.html
55 Church Street
New York, NY 10007
Tel: (212) 693-2001

## Hotel Highlights

- Across from the World Trade Center, 9/11 Memorial and Museum, and One World Observatory
- Breath-taking city views from this high rise lower Manhattan hotel
- Steps to the Oculus, home to Westfield WTC Shopping and Transit Center
- Within walking distance of Wall Street and adjacent to the Freedom Tower, Ground Zero and World Trade Center Memorial. Spectacular skyline views and a glass-enclosed pool
- 10 Subway lines within 1 block of the hotel
- Located only 6 stops to Times Square via express subway
- 5 Blocks to the Brooklyn Bridge or 10 minutes walking to Statue of Liberty Ferry

## Morton's

www.mortons.com
www.mortons.com/experience/culture
551 5th Ave
New York, NY 10017
Tel: (212) 972-3315

Upscale chain for aged prime beef, seafood & other traditional steakhouse fare in a clubby space. Their first restaurant opened in Chicago in 1978. Morton's stands for "Quality. Consistency. Genuine Hospitality."

## How it all began...

Morton's actually exists today because of... hamburgers! Years ago, before co-founders Arnie Morton and Klaus Fritsch really knew one another, they both worked at the Playboy Club in Montreal. The club was changing the menu, and Klaus cooked a hamburger that was sent out for Arnie to try. Arnie burst into the kitchen, demanding to know "Who cooked that hamburger?" When Klaus stepped forward, he wasn't sure if Arnie was going to be pleased or not but was relieved to hear him say that it was the best he'd ever tasted. From that day forward, they called it the "Million-Dollar Hamburger"!

**More than 3 decades later...**

Morton's has grown to over 74 restaurants, but the vision is the same today as it was when we opened our first restaurant in Chicago in 1978. **Quality. Consistency. Genuine Hospitality.** Driven by the desire to provide genuine hospitality—for our guests and our employees—we offer a setting where people truly care about one another, and show it in everything they do. The high level of respect and enthusiasm that runs through our entire organization is evident in many ways, including the longevity of our staff and managers, some of whom have been with us for decades. Morton's achievements are not limited to its four walls of the restaurants. Our culture is one that's also committed to community service, both locally and nationally.

**Radisson Martinique Hotel**
www.radisson.com/new-york-hotel-ny-10001/NY, New York
53 West 32nd Street (also known as 1260-1266 Broadway)
New York, NY 10001
Tel: (212) 736-3800

A member of the prestigious Historic Hotels of America, the Radisson is a testament to French Renaissance elegance, rising 19 stories above the "Great White Way. The Radisson Martinique on Broadway, formerly the New York Radisson Martinique Hotel, is a historic hotel in New York City built by William R. H. Martin in a French Renaissance style. It was the setting for Jonathan Kozol's study, *Rachel and Her Children: Homeless Families in America (1988).*

**The Ginger Man**
www.gingerman-ny.com
11 E 36th St, New York, NY 10016
Tel: (212) 532-3740

Spacious pub whose ever-changing beer selection includes 70 drafts & more than 150 bottles. Bona fide beer geeks come to this Herald Square bar for the dozens of drafts and the bar's serious approach to beer. Retro posters cover the walls.

**Pig 'n' Whistle on Third**
http://www.pignwhistleon3.com
922 Third Avenue (near 55th Street)
New York, NY 10022
Tel: 212-688-4646

Here we are, the Irish in New York. Stop in a stay a while!
NYC's best Irish Pub since 1969

The name Pig 'n' Whistle derives from "Piggin" and "Wassail," a medieval lead cup and the spiced wine that went in it, but it's beef and beer that predominate at these midtown pubs. The bar opened in 1969. Try the signature Bloody Mary—it's spicy! Or the pulled pork sandwich, slow roasted for 5 hours. The Shepard's Pie is timeless. Try it with a 20-ounce glass of Guinness– perfection in a pint! Fine selection of single malts and craft beers...some local classics. Entertainment 7 nights per week. Every Saturday and Sunday brunch 10:30—4 p.m. Sports? Count the TVs!

**Whiskey Trader**
http://whiskeytradernyc.com
71 W 55th Street
New York, NY 10019
Tel: (212) 582-2223

NYC's trendiest multilevel sports bar for club-goers and Lounge-lovers. Dimly lit with drink specials & free popcorn, it also offers a large wooden bar, candlelit seating areas, a fireplace, plush sofas, a video game nook, internet jukebox, and plasma TVs in every room.

## Dead Horse Bay
Belt Parkway, New York, NY

Just off Aviation Road near the entrance to Floyd Bennett Park.

The bay was given its name sometime in the 1850s, when horse-rendering plants still surrounded the beach. From the New York Times: "Dead Horse Bay sits at the western edge of a marshland once dotted by more than two dozen horse-rendering plants, fish oil factories and garbage incinerators. From the 1850s until the 1930s, the carcasses of dead horses and other animals from New York City streets were used to manufacture glue, fertilizer and other products at the site. The chopped-up, boiled bones were later dumped into the water. The squalid bay, then accessible only by boat, was reviled for the putrid fumes that hung overhead." As the car industry grew, horses and buggies—thus horse carcasses—became scarce, and by the 1920s there was only one rendering plant left.

It was during this era, around the turn of the century, that the marsh of Dead Horse Bay began to be used as a landfill. Filled with trash by the 1930s, the trash heap was capped, only to have the cap burst in the 1950s and the trash spew forth onto the beach. Since then garbage has been leaking continually onto the beach and into the ocean from Dead Horse Bay.

Thousands upon thousands of bottles, broken and intact, many over 100 years old, litter the shore. Other hardy bits of trash pepper this beach of glass: leather shoe soles, rusty telephones, and scores of unidentifiable pieces of metal and plastic. The beach is usually empty, conjuring a quiet, eerie post-doomsday kind of scene. The horses aren't quite gone either; found throughout the bay are one-inch chunks of horse bone, a somewhat unpleasant reminder of Dead Horse Bay's pungent past.

—Take the #2 Train to the last stop, Flatbush Avenue/Brooklyn College. Come upstairs and transfer to the Q35 Bus, which stops right in front of the Payless Shoe Store. (Note that other buses also stop there!) Tell the driver that you will be getting off at "the last stop before the bridge."

—Drive there using the Belt Parkway or another route to Flatbush Avenue, heading out towards Rockaway. Just before the toll plaza for the Gil Hodges Memorial Bridge, make a left onto Aviation Road and you will come to the parking area.

*There are no signs pointing toward the area and it is not on the map to the Park Entrance area across the street from the Floyd Bennett Parking lot. If you go to Fishing beach there is a fence and it is on the other side. You can park at Floyd Bennett/Rest Stop but you have to cross the highway to the other side and walk where it says Park Entrance all the way to the end to reach Glass Bottle Beach. You can walk straight or turn all the paths lead to Glass Bottle Beach which is located in Dead Horse Bay. Tours stop here for those interested. (Atlas Obscura, 2017)

## Abandoned Police Station under the Brooklyn Bridge

Fictional structure based on the real Sunset Park, Brooklyn abandoned police station, built in 1886. It is a former stationhouse at the southwest corner of Fourth Avenue and 43rd Street and served as the headquarters of Sunset Park's police for 84 years. Designated a city landmark for its castle-like architecture, it has fallen into such disrepair that it has become a magnet for crime. It attracts unsavory characters who frequent the building. Cars parked outside have also been broken into.

## Admiral's Row at the Brooklyn Navy Yard
ny.curbed.com/2015/6/11/9951238/revisiting-brooklyns-abandoned-admirals-row-before-its-gone
16 Flushing Ave
Brooklyn, NY 11201

Admiral's Row was a street lined with 19th century manor houses built in the architectural style known as "Second French Empire" at the Brooklyn Navy Yard. It was used as naval officers' housing for over a century before being abandoned in the 1970s. Once enticingly visible from the street, they were demolished to build a supermarket and parking lot in early 21st century America. Nature was increasingly unkind to those 19th century buildings. Prior to their demise, however, they remained in the same splendorous state of utter dishevelment that previously transfixed the neighborhood and lured in curious visitors. During an exploration in 2008, the houses were found to be wide open to the elements, but with interior details intact, including chandeliers, wallpaper, plasterwork, bathrooms, and kitchens. The relentless pressures of winter snow and falling trees crushed many of these features into rubble, and in 2009, heavy summer rains caused the collapse of Quarters C, the second oldest building on the row. The encircling forest rose far above the buildings, all of which had lost roofs, floors, walls, and windows. The 11 residential buildings on the Admiral's Row campus became completely overgrown by ivy and trees. The front steps of Quarters K and L were almost unrecognizable. Peeling paint, floors with holes, and crooked doorways were some of the lesser problems found inside the houses. Feral cats, birds, and other wildlife made them their home. On the buildings' upper levels, entire rooms went missing over the years, though the exteriors of the buildings remained intact. Snow, rain, and falling tree limbs caused walls and windows to cave in. Vines and soil entered the premises, blurring the boundary between interior and exterior, nature and fabrication. (Revisiting Brooklyn's Abandoned Admiral's Row Before It's Gone, Curbed New York, by Nathan Kensinger, June 11, 2015).

**New York Presbyterian Hospital**
www.nyp.org/lower Manhattan
170 William Street
New York, NY 10038
Tel: (212) 312-5000

New York-Presbyterian/Lower Manhattan Hospital is a not-for-profit, acute care, teaching hospital in New York City and is one of the few hospitals in Lower Manhattan south of Greenwich Village. It is ranked steadily among America's best hospitals by U.S. News & World Report. (Wikipedia)

# THE KILLING COLLECTIVE—BOOK CLUB QUESTIONS

1. New York City is a major character in the novel. How does its many sights, sounds, food, and culture affect the feelings, choices and actions made by the other character(s)?
2. Do you think Carter is the Zen master he thinks he is? Why or why not? Does prayer, meditation and the Tao of Zen help him to better understand himself and the world around him? Why/why not?
3. Seacrest is a forensic scientist but she's also a risk taker. Do you think one person could have two such opposite character traits? Do you think Seacrest does the right thing when she takes an awful personal risk? What's the difference between Seacrest taking that kind of a risk and Deeprose doing something equally reckless?
4. Why is Seacrest so flippant with Carter? Why does she throw acerbic witticisms and sarcasm at people? Is it possible to be weak and strong and the same time? How so?
5. What is it about Deeprose's personality that might allow her to deal with adversity better than the other characters? Is it naïveté, impulsiveness, or inexperience that causes her to take huge risks with her own life? Deeprose was in the military, so she's no stranger to the importance of protocol. Why would a disciplined soldier ignore authority and make decisions that could affect not only her own life but the lives of others? Do you think the pros of her job outweigh the cons, in her own opinion? Why?
6. Do you think Deputy Director Fischetti was a victim as well as a collaborator? Was he playing both sides against the

middle? Did he ask Seacrest to test *Hyzopran* on herself because he needed to know what the drug would do prior to his investigation against strict rules of the D.O.D. or because he wanted her dead?

7. If you were Bill Fischetti, which of these would you have done and why:

a. Obey your superior no matter what he did and protect him.

b. Refuse to carry out his orders and risk being terminated.

c. Pretend to follow his orders but blow the whistle on him.

8. Should one person or any group or organization be allowed limitless money and authority to change society for the better? Do you think that having money and power tends to encourage disregard for other people's values? Do you think wealthy people have the right to decide what's best for the rest of us? Do they also have the right to become the guardians of society? Would a more fair distribution of wealth create a stimulus for the economy or destroy it?

9. What was the *Silver Man's* idea of a perfect society? Is there any merit in his ideas? Why or why not? What's your idea of a perfect society? How would you go about achieving it and enforcing it?

10. Do you think that in order to get along with each other, certain drives and emotions have to be suppressed and controlled? Which ones? Do you agree or disagree that we'd all be better off without certain character traits?

11. Are killers born or made? Is it nature, nurture, or both? Do you think our D.N.A. is solely responsible for how we think, act, and react? Could any of the killers make a possible return to society and live happy, productive lives despite their genes or home life? Why?/Why not?

12. We never find out what becomes of Eliza and Clara. What do you think their future will bring?

13. What are the various ways you try to control or manipulate people at home or at work? Why do you do it? Does it work? Do you feel the end justify the means, and if so, why?

14. If it's considered our duty to fight for our country to protect our land and way of life, is it OK to protect yourself, family, friends, and community by any means possible, up to and

including committing manslaughter? Do you own a gun? If you had to use it, would you shoot to kill or to incapacitate? Do you think all of us have the capacity and the will to kill if we have to? Is that a good thing or not? Why?

15. Many countries, including our own, have had civil wars. Consider the current social and political climate. If it was widely understood that the loss of your rights, freedoms, and the democratic process were imminent, would you join a resistance group or take part in revolution? Our country is very young and always vulnerable. Do you think that revolution or anarchy could ever happen again? What would it take for it to happen and how do you think it would come about? Do you see any signs of it happening even now?

16. Carter, Seacrest, and Deeprose represent a trinity of mind, heart, and courage. Which traits represent which characters or are they each a combination of all three? Give examples. What are the other major characteristics of these three? How do those character traits help or hinder them? What happens to each of the three that causes sudden clarity and subsequent insight into their own drives, thoughts, choices, and actions? Do any of them grow and change as a result of coming to understand themselves?

17. Why do you think Seacrest ultimately decides it's not necessary for Carter to change for her? Has she really decided she can accept him the way he is?

18. Are relationships a constant work in progress that both partners should commit to, or do you think relationships last longer and happier when you turn a blind eye to certain things and don't rock the boat? Which way would you rather have it? Do you think men are capable of verbalizing and discussing their feelings, thoughts, wants, and needs? If your partner is not a great communicator, hates to talks about feelings, and is clearly troubled at times, should you let him or her alone or try to find a way to make him open up to you?

19. Do you think all people are a mixture of normal and abnormal impulses? Are we all a conglomerate of good and evil, generous and stingy, etc.? Give examples. Do you know people who either try to or succeed in hiding aspects of their

personality from the rest of the world so they can survive and thrive? Do they succeed? With whom? How? Why?

20. Alison was willing to do anything to be part of a community of like-minded individuals. Do you think her personality was a result of her own D.N.A. or of an emotionally and physically abusive home-life, or both? Whether Alison was born that way or not, why was she able to rise above her habitual reactions in the end? Why does she grow? How does she accomplish it?

21. Why was it so easy to turn the *Silver Man's* audience into a mob out for blood? What was it he told them that fueled an already burning fire in their hearts and minds?

22. Some people seem to get all the breaks in life and some never seem to get any. If you could change that aspect of society, would you? If so, what system would you use to make things fair? Should things be fairer in a capitalist society than they are in a socialist or communist society? Why or why not?

23. Are we locked in an eternal struggle with ourselves to find a balance between our Yin and Yang? Should we be? Does Yin and Yang exist separately or is it all mixed up inside ourselves? Is there such thing as balance? Is it possible, and is it objective or subjective? What does a balance between Yin and Yang mean to you? Should we even concern ourselves with balance or embrace all our character traits? In what circumstances is it OK to express anger, fear, hate, jealousy, self-protection, extreme aggressiveness, etc.?

24. Is the *Silver Man* mad or is he a genius with the ability to change humanity for the better? If he has that ability, is there any reason he shouldn't use it to realize his dream of a better world?

25. What are the differences between isolationism, nationalism and protectionism? Is it ever desirable for an individual or society and government as a whole to adopt those points of view?

26. What is the contagion theory? What is the convergence theory? Do you believe they exist? Give an example of a current social or political mass movement, protest, riot, etc.,

for each and discuss why you think one of these theories applies to that event.

27. How does the legend of *Pygmalion* and *Galatea* parallel the *Silver Man's* dream of creating a better world? Are his motives purely personal or are they born of a desire to bring humanity into a new era of peace and prosperity?

28. Would you rather have one world leader who had the power of life and death at his fingertips and who kept the peace by weeding out undesirable human characteristics and controlling your thoughts or would you rather live in a democracy, take your chances, and hope humanity wouldn't wipe itself off the face of the earth?

29. Do you think it's true that no drug or other method of mind control can work on us if we don't want it to? Is Alison guilty because she didn't resist the drug or is she an innocent victim no matter what she did? Why does Carter's team want to help her, the only one of the "unholy three" that killed more than once?

30. If you had to choose, would you rather know the secrets of the universe and why we're here to live, suffer and die and what happens to us after we pass on? Or would you be satisfied not knowing as long as you had the chance to live, laugh, and love? What matters more—why we live or how we live? If you knew the former, what would you do with that information? How would knowing change anything for you? If you chose the latter, what does a full and happy life look like to you?

31. Carter struggles between spiritualism and formalized religion. Explain the difference between the two and why you think Carter is so torn between the two?

32. Carter also struggles with traditional fundamental Judeo-Christian beliefs because Buddhism seems so much more joyful in the present and hopeful for the afterlife. Why does he think this? Do you agree with him? If there is a permanent heaven somewhere up in the clouds? If so, what rules would you change in order to make sure you got in when the time came?

33. Do you believe in karmic reward and debt? Do you think we

might really come back as some other form of life if we don't learn our lessons in this one? Is that fair? What does Nirvana look like to you, and what should we have achieved to go there?

34. Why does Seacrest think that she and Carter need Agent Deeprose far more than she needs them? What does Deeprose symbolize and/or represent to them?

35. Is there a difference between the law and justice? Has Carter done the right or wrong thing by allowing the enforcer to go free? Why?/Why not? Why do you think Deeprose has an issue with how Carter decides to close the case? Would you feel the same way in her place? Why?/Why not?

36. Does evil revisit us over and over again through time when we forget the evil that's already been done? Must we stay vigilant to prevent evil and people of bad intent from taking over?

## TO OBTAIN DISCOUNTED PRINT COPIES FOR BOOK CLUB DISCUSSIONS, CONTACT:

Gary Starta at: ven123star@yahoo.com

## SIGN UP FOR THE MAILING LIST TO RECEIVE THE LATEST UPDATES ON NEW BOOKS:

https://www.facebook.com/GaryStartaSciFiFanPage/app/1002658966 90345/

Made in the USA
Lexington, KY
23 May 2018